THE INNOCENTS

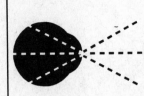

This Large Print Book carries the
Seal of Approval of N.A.V.H.

THE INNOCENTS

ACE ATKINS

THORNDIKE PRESS

A part of Gale, Cengage Learning

GALE
CENGAGE Learning·

Farmington Hills, Mich • San Francisco • New York • Waterville, Maine
Meriden, Conn • Mason, Ohio • Chicago

GALE
CENGAGE Learning®

LIBRARY OF CONGRESS CATALOGING-IN-PUBLICATION DATA

Names: Atkins, Ace, author.
Title: The innocents / by Ace Atkins.
Description: Large print edition. | Waterville, Maine : Thorndike Press, 2016. |
  Series: A Quinn Colson novel | Series: Thorndike Press large print basic
Identifiers: LCCN 2016025682 | ISBN 9781410491503 (hardcover) | ISBN 1410491501
  (hardcover)
Subjects: LCSH: United States. Army—Commando troops—Fiction. |
  Mississippi—Fiction. | Large type books. | GSAFD: Mystery fiction.
Classification: LCC PS3551.T49 I56 2016b | DDC 813/.54—dc23
LC record available at https://lccn.loc.gov/2016025682

Published in 2016 by arrangement with G.P. Putnam's Sons, an imprint of Penguin Publishing Group, a division of Penguin Random House LLC

Printed in the United States of America
1 2 3 4 5 6 7 20 19 18 17 16

*For Billy and Jess
Just some good ol'boys
Never meanin' no harm.*

It was too late. Maybe yesterday, while I was still a child, but not now. I knew too much, had seen too much, I was a child no longer now; innocence and childhood were forever lost, forever gone from me.

— **WILLIAM FAULKNER,** *The Reivers*

No matter whether we travel in big parties or little ones, each party has to keep a scout twenty yards ahead, twenty yards on each flank, and twenty yards on the rear so the main body can't be surprised and wiped out.

— **ROGERS' RANGERS STANDING ORDER NO. 12**

1

Lillie Virgil stood high on a north Mississippi hill at daybreak listening to old Ruthie Holder talk about the man who'd run off with her grandson's Kawasaki four-wheeler and her brand-new twelve-gauge Browning. Ruthie said she'd just gotten home from the Piggly Wiggly with a week's worth of groceries when this skinny, buck-toothed varmint jumped out of the bushes and started in with a lot of crazy talk.

"What exactly did he say, Miss Holder?"

"He told me that the g.d. Mexican cartel was in my kitchen making chorizo and eggs and if I walked inside they'd have their way with me," she said. "I told him it was a lot of foolish talk, but he insisted on going in without me. Next thing I knew, he was running out with my Browning and headed to the shed."

Lillie reached down and lowered the volume on the police radio. She was tall, with an athlete's lean muscles and lots of crazy light brown hair she kept neat in a bun and under a ball cap. That day, she wore gold aviator glasses, a Glock 19 on her hip, and chewed gum, as she asked, "Have you ever seen this asshole before?"

"This man wasn't wearing a shirt or shoes, just a pair of ragged old Levi's," Ruthie Holder said. "He had a tattoo of Hank Williams Junior on his back. Do you think I'd ever consort with trash like that?"

"No, ma'am," Lillie said. Ruthie ran the Citizens Bank for years, served as president of the local chapter of the Daughters of the American Revolution, and still offered her harp-playing skills to local weddings and funerals. Lillie didn't think she even knew "All My Rowdy Friends" or "Whiskey Bent and Hell Bound."

"I sure love that gun," Ruthie said. "I won it in a raffle. And since my husband died, it gave me a lot of comfort."

"Understand that," Lillie said. "I feel the same way about the Winchester I had at Ole Miss. I won a lot of tournaments with her."

"Her?" Ruthie said. "Didn't know a gun could be a woman."

Lillie smiled and shrugged. Standing tall, feeling good after running five miles that morning, finishing it off with a hundred push-ups and a hundred sit-ups. If she was going to watch over Tibbehah County in the years to come, better be in shape. "Makes complete sense to me," she said. "What'd this man look like and which way did he head?"

"He was ugly."

"Yes, ma'am," Lillie said. "But can you be more specific, Mrs. Holder?"

"Skinny and rangy. Black hair, but shaved down," she said. "Wore an earring. And had thin little hairs sprouting on his chin. Like some kind of animal. What does all that matter? How many folks do you know riding four-wheelers without shirts and sporting a tattoo of Hank Junior?"

Lillie grinned at her. "In this county?" she asked. "About every other son of a bitch."

Lillie told her they'd find him, already knowing they were looking for an authentic piece of crap named David John Norwood. She'd arrested Norwood for aggravated assault and drug possession a few weeks after becoming acting sheriff, back when the newly elected sheriff Rusty Wise got himself killed. Norwood only got probation and was left to raise hell and stir shit across the county as he pleased.

Lillie climbed into her Jeep Cherokee with its big gold star on the door, grabbed the

11

mic, and called in to Mary Alice at dispatch. "Can you get me D. J. Norwood's parole officer?" she said.

"Oh, Lord," Mary Alice said. "What's that boy done now?"

"Same old shit," Lillie said. "Lost his fucking mind. Also get me Jimmy Deets over at Wildlife. I think Norwood's headed way, way off road and into the Big Woods."

"Which direction?"

"Headed north," Lillie said. "I say he's going into the National Forest, looking for the Trace."

"Why?"

"Probably because he wants to be with the rest of the animals," she said. "Let Deets know he is armed, dangerous, and crazy as hell."

Lillie Virgil knocked her Cherokee in gear, following the muddy ATV tracks until they hit a dirt road into the hills. The back wheels of the Jeep spun out dirt and gravel before finding solid footing. She lowered the window and listened, chewing gum, rifle in the passenger seat at her side.

"So you were a cheerleader?" Fannie Hathcock asked the young girl sitting in a chair in front of her.

"Yes, ma'am."

12

"Don't 'Yes, ma'am' me or I won't ever give you a job," Fannie said. "Just how old do you think I am?"

"I don't know," the girl said. She shuffled in her seat and glanced away. "Hate to say."

"But old," Fannie said. "You think I'm over-the-hill? Too old to show my goodies to fat old truckers?"

"I didn't mean nothing by it," the girl said. "I just was trying to be respectful, is all. You dress real nice. Smell good. And you own your own place."

Fannie smoothed down the lace on her white Valentino skirt, black shirt open wide at the throat. She wore a bright ruby in the shape of a heart on a chain around her neck. "You like it better than the old place?"

"I never saw the old place," the girl said. "My dad used to go there. When he'd go on a drunk with his uncle and them. My mom said it was against God. But she's always saying things like that."

Fannie, a true and authentic redhead cap to cat, rested her butt — nice and tight, for a woman in her forties — on the edge of her desk. Her office door was open, and from where she looked over the girl's shoulder she could get a good bird's-eye view of the floor of Vienna's. Vienna's Place is what she'd rechristened the renovated space of a

13

true Mississippi shithole called the Booby Trap. Vienna was Fannie's grandmother, the woman who taught her the Golden Rule — *Men will do anything for pussy.* Vienna sure had made her rich.

Fannie tapped at a Dunhill box and lifted a small brown cigarillo into her mouth and looked down at the girl. Bleached blonde hair, a dull, freckled face, and one piercing in her nose and one in the tongue. She also had a streak of black in the blonde. Girl said she was eighteen, but Fannie would need to see some ID. That's the last thing she needed — trouble with the law over damn Southern jailbait.

"You know some tricks?" Fannie said.

"Excuse me?"

"I don't mean your twat, baby," she said. "I mean with all the cheerleading. Flips, tumbling. A damn naked handstand."

"I was a flyer."

"What the hell's a flyer?"

"I was on top," the girl said. "Bigger girls would lift me up and toss me into the air."

"Nobody will toss you around here," Fannie said. "We look out for our girls. Nobody gets hurt. I'm not Johnny Fucking Stagg."

"I hear the money is real good."

"It is," Fannie said, spewing smoke from

14

the side of her mouth. "But the house gets forty percent. And you need to tip your bouncer and the DJ every damn night. You need to get straight with that right off."

The girl's freckled face dropped. She looked down at her stubby little fingers, with black nail polish, probably thinking that she could keep all that trucker cash as long as she showed off those perky young boobies and shook that smooth, shaved tail.

"OK," the girl said. "When can I start?"

"When can you show me some ID?"

The young girl opened up her purse. She had on a short pink T-shirt, cutoff jeans, and cheap brown boots inlaid with cactuses and cowboys. She showed her ID. Looked to be she was telling the truth.

"Ever get nekkid?" Fannie said.

"Sure."

"For money?"

The girl shrugged.

"All of it flashing and jiggling on a hot white stage," Fannie said. "With nasty old truckers and gray-headed perverts wanting to lick you like a damn ice cream cone."

"I can do it."

"Lap dance is forty bucks," Fannie said. "I never minded the grind. But I sure minded the smell."

"What if they mess with you?" the girl

15

said, looking Fannie full on in the eye now. "What if they're wanting to touch you and all?"

"They can touch up top all they want, but never below," Fannie said. "One of them wants to start dialing home with his digits, you just make sure Lyle knows."

The girl looked confused. "Who's Lyle?"

"Runs a group of Bad News Bears around here called the Born Losers," she said. "They ride bikes and raise hell out of the motel across the street. The Golden Cherry. When they're not too drunk or stoned, they offer us some protection. That's the other rule — Don't mess with the bikers. They're hired help."

"Yes, ma'am."

"God damn it."

"Sorry."

Fannie smiled while the smoke scattered from the office and out into the big open space of Vienna's. Ceiling fans broke it apart. She'd taken down old Johnny's place to the studs and built it back up, with a new tin roof, heart pine floors, and a long old bar she'd had shipped piece by piece from Kansas City, Missouri. Fannie "Belle" Hathcock had just upped the class in this north Mississippi town by a hundred and fifty percent.

16

"Whatta you say, girl?" Fannie said.

"Forty percent?"

"Let me know if you find better job opportunities in Jericho," Fannie said. "I heard they're hiring a fry cook down at the Sonic."

In his previous life as the go-to Hollywood stuntman, Quinn Colson's dad, Jason, must've landed on his head a few times. Ever since he'd come back to Jericho, he'd been filled with all kinds of crazy ideas, schemes, and various delusions. There was a kids' go-cart track he wanted to open in the parking lot of the old Kentucky Fried Chicken, or bring a Hooters to the people of Tibbehah County — he knew some people in Memphis who'd back him — and, lately, he'd been talking about turning Quinn's farm into a dude ranch.

Quinn didn't have time for any of it. He'd been going on little sleep since returning from Afghanistan seven days earlier, where he'd been training a local police force on behalf of the U.S. government. He was in his mid-thirties now, tall and lean, with a sharp-chiseled face, the high cheekbones from some Choctaw blood mixed in the ornery Scotch-Irish. Overseas, he'd let his hair grow out a bit, and now he sported a neat dark beard. He had on an old white tee and a pair of Levi's, as he watched the sun rise across his land, smoking a Liga Privada, with his cattle dog, Hondo, laying at his feet.

Jason rode up soon after, lashing his quarter horse to Quinn's truck's tailgate. "Hadn't you shaved yet?" Jason said.

"Barbershop's been closed since Mr. Jim died."

"Might oughtta keep it," Jason said. "Women sure do love outlaws."

"That what you were?" Quinn said. "Out in L.A.?"

Jason grinned. "If that's what they wanted," he said. "Then, sure. Beach bunnies could call me Jesse James. Come on and walk with me, I got something to talk about."

"We can talk right here on the porch."

"Be better if we get up, see some things, get the old imaginations working."

"Hell, Dad," Quinn said. "I know exactly what you're wanting to show me and the answer is no thank you. Can't you just let a man rest a bit? Sit back and fire up a stick with his dog he hasn't seen in a long while?"

"Plenty of time for Hondo," Jason said. "But opportunity? Opportunity doesn't come around that often. Can't you hear that sound?"

"That's just the cicadas," he said. "Screwing in the trees. They sure love all this heat."

Quinn stood up, stretched, and walked back into the old tin-roofed farmhouse that had stood on his family's land since 1895 and grabbed a pair of beaten cowboy boots. He slid them on, broken-in and comfortable, and returned, the screen door thwacking behind him. The house had a natural shotgun cooling effect between front door and back that helped as the summer wound down.

He reached for his cigar, burning on top of a coffee mug, and followed.

Jason was in his mid-sixties, wiry and fit, with a weathered face from years of drinking, fighting, and professionally racking up the odometer on his body. He kept a mustache and goatee, now snow-white like his longish hair. His T-shirt read STUNTS UNLIMITED, an organization he'd helped found in the 1970s with a crazy man from Arkansas named Hal Needham. As Jason walked, Quinn noted the limp in his right leg was growing worse. The ball socket in his dad's hip and some of his femur had been telescoped when a landing platform busted on the set of *The Fall Guy*.

It was hard for Quinn to pass judgment on someone who punished his body.

Quinn's ten years as a U.S. Army Ranger, most of it as a sergeant in some godforsaken country, had left him with a lot of mileage and scars. The years he'd spent as Tibbehah County sheriff had earned him a couple of gunshot wounds, which the people repaid by voting him out of office a year ago.

He followed his father through a ragged, twisting trail into some second-growth woods of pine, oak, and cedar, fringes of the land being eaten up by kudzu. It had rained the night before and the air smelled of damp earth and leaves, the canopy above him a bright green, lichen on the big trunks of oaks almost glowing. Water continued to drip on pine needles.

"I know you've just gotten home," Jason said, "but you need to think on the future. You need to think about what's going to be here after I'm gone and you're gone. Don't you want to leave something for Little Jason? Or if you and Anna Lee start having kids of your own?"

"Nothing's going to happen to this land," Quinn said. "And I don't think I'm having kids anytime soon."

"Y'all talking?"

Quinn didn't answer.

"I started late," Jason said. "Missed out on a lot of things."

"You missed out on a lot of things because you lived thousands of miles away."

"For a damn good reason."

Quinn just nodded, not sure if his dad had seen him or not, the older man intent on getting up the trail with that bad leg, cresting the hill over to the land that he wanted to discuss with Quinn. When the trail ended, so did the trees. And most living things. That rotten son of a bitch Johnny Stagg had strip-cleared one hundred acres of property that had once belonged to Quinn's uncle. When Uncle Hamp had fallen behind on some gambling debt, Stagg had swooped in, taken over the land, cut down every single tree, and bulldozed what was left. Johnny Stagg was like that. *Conservation* and *the environment* were four-letter words to his kind. And the reason every morning was a little brighter now with Stagg in federal prison.

Jason walked out on the ridge as Quinn lit his cigar. Hondo trotted up behind them, sniffing the smoke on the windless summer morning. His body a patchwork of grays and black. He had one brown eye and one blue.

"I don't want it," Quinn said.

"Not now," Jason said. "Not now. But in five years, nature will have taken back over out here. All this scarred-over shit will be

21

gone. Now is when we get the property, double your holdings, and we can make some money. What's the use of having land if you don't use it?"

"To have some personal space?"

Jason laughed like a man who wasn't squatting on Quinn's back half acre in an old broken-down trailer. His only assets seemed to be a collection of belt buckles and saddles given to him by Burt Reynolds and a rusted-out 1978 cherry-red Firebird that Jason claimed had been the star of the film *Hooper.*

"This is something for both of us," Jason said. "We can do this together. You got the land and I know horses. There's nothing like this anymore. You know how many folks want their kids to learn how to ride? Down there, I thought we'd dig out a pond. It would be the center of all the cabins we'd build."

Quinn ashed his cigar and toed the burning end in the dirt.

"Stagg will sell," Jason said. "Look how quick he unloaded his damn truck stop and snatch palace."

"I know he had some serious pressure on him." Quinn blew out a long bit of smoke. The cigar was too good to put out and risk getting stale on the porch. It had been a gift from his commander in AFG when he'd gone back to work as a civilian to train the locals.

"Only one question."

Jason looked his son in the eye and smiled big.

"Just where is all this money coming from?"

"Don't worry," Jason said. "Don't worry about nothing. Leave all that piddly shit up to me."

Quinn shook his head. In the distance, he heard the high whine of a small motor. He turned to see a shirtless man on an ATV cut through Stagg's property and dip into his woods.

"Who the hell's that?"

2

Lillie drove for about six miles, deep into the northwest county, almost to the National Forest, until she found Deputy Reggie Caruthers stopped at the fork. She rolled down her window as Reggie walked up, letting her know that Jimmy Deets and a couple more folks with Wildlife & Fisheries were headed their way. Reggie was new, only six weeks with the sheriff's office, and grinned as he relayed the news. Excitement at last.

"Anybody seen his ugly ass?" Lillie said.

"Not yet," Reggie said. "But he'll screw up. Norwood's good at that."

"You know him?"

"Had some trouble with him last week," Reggie said. "He's back on the meth. Wanted to know what the world was coming to. Me, a black man, harassing a God-fearing white man."

It was hot as it got in Tibbehah County,

nearly a hundred, and sticky humid, with the thirteen-year cicadas out in full force, escaped from the ground to copulate and make a ton of racket in the trees. Lillie had to wait until the boiling-up of their chatter died down to speak again.

"I don't think Norwood fears anyone," she said. "Or feels anything."

"If we don't snatch his ass up, he's going to kill someone. I don't like the idea of a paranoid meth addict zipping around Tibbehah County with a loaded twelve-gauge."

"Miss Holder said Norwood was convinced a Mexican cartel was after him," Lillie said. "Said they were going to kill a bunch of folks just as soon as they finished up their chorizo and eggs."

"Sure," Caruthers said. "Can't shoot no one on an empty stomach."

Lillie had known Reggie Caruthers since fifth grade. His mother had been Lillie's teacher and she used to bring Reggie, then four, to class with her. He was twenty-nine now, but he still seemed like Little Reggie to her, with his dimples and bright smile. When he applied for the job, she had to reconcile that he was now a four-year Army vet and had done two tours in Afghanistan with the 10th Mountain Division. About every other day, she had to stop from calling him Little Reggie and pinching his cheek.

"You think he's got a plan?" Reggie asked.

"No, sir."

"Just keep on running until he runs out of gas or turns that thing over?"

"He'll probably just pass out somewhere," Lillie said. "Maybe the buzzards will start to circle. We can follow 'em to his bones."

"You know his daddy rents some land up in the hills," Caruthers said. "He's got a single-wide for a hunt club. Or a drinking club. Black people don't go up there for a reason. Those hill folks are crazy as hell. They hangin' out the Stars and Bars just to make sure we know."

"Can you show me?"

Caruthers walked back to his cruiser and returned with a Tibbehah County map. He ran his finger over Highway 9W, running west of where they were now. He kept on moving his finger closer to the Fate community and the Natchez Trace.

"Shit," Lillie said. "He'd have to cut right across —"

Her cell phone rang and she reached into the console for it, recognizing the number. Reggie tilted his head at her and flashed a big smile. "Quinn?" he said.

"Yep."

Caruthers smiled. "Maybe we better change over from a chase to a rescue mission."

"Would've been nice of you to stop by the SO and say hey," Lillie said. "Maybe bring me some trinkets from Kabul. Like a fucking scarf."

"I've been catching up on my sleep," Quinn said. His father walking along with him back to the farmhouse. Ole Hondo trotting close by, tongue lolling from his mouth.

"Sure," Lillie said. "Yeah, I bet you've been catching up on a few things."

Quinn ignored her. Lillie never liked Anna Lee or thought much of her unresolved marriage to Luke Stevens. Anna Lee and Quinn not so much living in sin as occasionally delving into it. Lillie knew. His family knew. Hell, everyone knew, including Luke.

"Listen," Quinn said.

"You got some crazy son of a bitch on a four-wheeler raising hell out on your property?"

"Damn, you're good, Lil."

"It's D. J. Norwood."

"I thought we busted his ass two years ago," Quinn said. "He sent me a homemade Christmas card from Parchman. Told me he

27

found Christ at Unit 27."

"He's served that time and gone back for more," Lillie said. "And now he's back to pick up where he left off."

"Remind me."

"Being this county's A-1 fuckup," Lillie said. "Shoplifting, drug dealing, breaking into houses and trailers when the mood strikes him."

"What'd he do?"

"Stole that ATV from Ruthie Holder's shed."

"That all?"

"And a loaded twelve-gauge Browning she won in a raffle at the Baptist church."

"Well," Quinn said, turning back to his house. "Guess we better get 'em back."

"How about you just sit this one out until the law arrives?" she said. "He's got no truck with you. He's just flying high on eleven different herbs and spices."

"Glad to show him some hospitality."

"I really wish you'd rethink that plan."

"I won't shoot him," he said. "I'm too damn tired."

"Son of a bitch," she said. "Quinn, would you fucking listen to me?"

Quinn turned off the phone, walked down the gulley and up onto the Indian Mound and into his house. He reached for the crossbow he'd hung over the stone hearth as a decoration until deer season. He carried the bow, along with a quiver of arrows, moving outside toward the woods.

His dad stood outside by his painted horse, named Hooper. Jason held a Winchester lever-action, like John Wayne preferred. "Like some company?"

"Just why did Quinn come back?" Reggie Caruthers said, following Lillie down a winding deer trail. "Heard he was gone again for good."

"Probably to change his Jockey shorts and get laid."

"Long way to come home and get laid."

"Quinn's got special motivation back here," Lillie said. "It's what always brings him back. He's tough. But, in that department, the man can't help himself. He's got a woman who'll destroy him someday."

"Anna Lee Stevens?"

"Yep," Lillie said. "Can't anyone have a personal life around here?"

"Nope," Reggie said. "Speaking of friends, aren't you worried Quinn might want to run against you for sheriff?"

"He got treated pretty bad," Lillie said. "Some real Will Kane shit. They believed all kinds of lies about both of us and voted that insurance man into office. He was a nice man. But —"

"That didn't work out."

"No, sir," Lillie said. "Never saw what hit him."

They hadn't heard the stolen ATV's motor since setting foot in the woods. The cicadas were louder than ever, buzzing up to a boiling point and then calming down a bit. Lillie rested the rifle against her shoulder as she walked along the worn deer trail, dead leaves and fallen twigs at her feet. It grew cooler as they walked deep into Quinn's land. Fresh springs bubbled up out of the ground and ran in zigzagging patterns down the hill. Moss grew along fattened oaks and the warm air smelled of cedar trees.

It was almost pleasant.

D. J. Norwood was naked save for a pair of work boots, wet as a rat, on top of the ATV, rubbing down the twelve-gauge with an old T-shirt. He seemed to have gone swimming in Sarter Creek and then found a patch of bare earth to dry out in the sun. So intent on cleaning the gun and whistling to himself, he didn't hear Quinn walk up a dozen meters from him. But as Quinn raised the crossbow, Jason called out, wanting to know if Quinn saw anything.

Norwood was surprisingly fast with the shotgun, up onto his shoulder, teeth chattering and telling Quinn to back the fuck up. His eyes zipped and darted over the rolling land around him.

"I think jail made you dumber than ever, Norwood."

"Who the hell are you?" Norwood said. "I don't know you."

"Quinn Colson," he said. "You're trespassing. And polluting my creek."

"I can wash my ass where I please. And you ain't Colson. Colson don't have no beard."

"Damn, you are observant," Quinn said. "Now, how about you lower that Browning you took off Miss Holder."

Quinn's father stepped up into the clearing, Winchester pointed direct at Norwood's skinny white body. Norwood's hair had been shaved as short as the stubble on his face. He had small, mean black eyes and a caved-in, hairless chest. A tattoo of a dream catcher decorated his sternum, providing a perfect target. Below the tattoo was the word PEACE.

"I didn't steal nothing from Miss Holder," he said. "She told me I could borrow this here gun. Shit."

31

"And the four-wheeler, too?"

"Shoot, yeah," he said. "She wanted me to kill a turkey for her."

"Turkey season's not until spring," Quinn said.

"Yeah," Jason Colson said, moving up shoulder to shoulder with Quinn. He spit on the ground. "But it looks like shitbird season started today."

"Y'all better put down those weapons," Norwood said. "Hurt me and I'll hire goddang Morgan & Morgan up in Memphis to sue your ass for every penny you got. Them folks don't mess around. You hear me?"

Norwood stood up fast off the ATV in anger, naked, limp, and moving sloppy in boots with loose laces. A leaf had stuck to the side of his head as he walked. Quinn rested his index finger light on the trigger and breathed slow and easy.

"Boy," Jason said. "You move again and I'll shoot that little pecker from here to Hot Coffee."

"Why y'all putting a boot on the throat of a white man?" Norwood said. "I didn't do nothin'. That old woman's the one who's gone crazy. She's can't remember jack shit. I cut her damn grass. She thinks of me like her own son."

"OK," Quinn said. "Wait till the sheriff

gets here and you can explain everything."

"Y'all called the sheriff?"

Quinn just nodded, a close eye on Norwood's every move.

"God damn. Son of a bitch."

"Get off the four-wheeler, Norwood," Quinn said. "And put down that shotgun."

"Hell with you."

Quinn didn't answer.

"Either pull that trigger, Robin Hood, or get the fuck outta the way." Norwood held the shotgun in his right hand and mashed the starter with his left.

Norwood raced forward on the ATV, kicking up rock and dirt, scooting away with a rebel yell. Naked as hell and firing off the shotgun into the air. Quinn got a quick glimpse of skinny white ass, bucking up and down, and the broad tattoo on the man's back as he drove off. Hank Williams Junior grinning at him behind enormous mirrored sunglasses, cigarette dangling from his mouth.

"Family tradition," Jason said.

"His tats?" Quinn said, lowering the crossbow.

"No," Jason said. "His daddy and two uncles were true pieces of shit, too."

"You hear that?" Reggie Caruthers said.

"Shotgun," Lillie said.

"Yep."

"You don't seem worried."

"Quinn promised not to shoot."

"Y'all have that kind of trust?"

Lillie didn't answer as she walked. The woods filled with the high whine of a four-wheeler motor, growing closer as Lillie and Reggie followed the narrow path downhill. Lillie knew the trail, linking up to the dirt road to the south and Quinn's pond farther up to the west. The path had been smooth and well worn from Hondo, but now also from Jason Colson's three horses.

"Norwood's coming."

"How do you know?" Reggie said.

" 'Cause this is the only way out of the woods," she said. "Quinn must've shaken him loose."

"Can we shoot him?"

"I'd rather not," Lillie said. Walking and searching, trying to find a little cover in the woods, seeing a tangle of wild privet and thinking it was a fine spot. "Too much paperwork. Unless the bastard asks for it."

"If it wasn't Quinn shooting," Reggie said.

"You stand by that fallen tree," Lillie said. "He comes up this path with that shotgun and you do what needs to be done."

"Where are you going?"

"Advanced police tactic," she said, reaching down and finding a fallen oak limb. She lifted it up, not rotten, with plenty of heft. She knocked the bark off the limb and found a narrow spot to grip.

"You're going to knock his ass off that four-wheeler," Reggie said, "aren't you?"

"He'll cut up this hill and be looking straight at you."

Reggie nodded, unlatching his Glock and aiming it toward the buzzing sound. Lillie moved behind the privet with the heavy limb in both hands, chocked up high for good measure. As he hit the tree line from the open pasture, zipping up the hill, Lillie noticed D. J. Norwood was grinning and yelling, the twelve-gauge laying prone across the handlebars.

"Here we go," Lillie said.

Reggie stepped out onto the path and yelled for him to stop. Norwood gave another rebel yell and gunned it as Lillie stepped free and swung hard.

3

"You think he's come to yet?" Anna Lee asked Quinn. Both of them in his farmhouse kitchen, grilling two venison steaks in peppers and onions in a black skillet. He added a little more salt and pepper, charring them in a stick of fresh butter.

"He was awake when Reggie Caruthers hauled him off," Quinn said. "He was making all kinds of threats to Lillie, saying that she'd broken his jaw. Calling her a crazy-ass dyke bitch."

"Did she break it?"

"I sure hope so," Quinn said.

"You don't mean that."

Quinn didn't answer, turning the steak, checking it with a fork. Still a little too bloody for his taste.

"Something a-matter?"

"Thought you were going to bring Shelby with you?"

"Shelby's five and easily confused," she

said. "Besides, she's with Luke this weekend."

"Does Luke know where you are?"

"We're separated," Anna Lee said. "I don't need to check in with him. We've been through all this crap before. Until things are done, I don't want her thinking that she's got two daddies."

"I'm not backing up," Quinn said. He turned the steaks, getting a nice sear on both, the smell of burning meat, onions, and butter filling his kitchen. He reached for a cold Budweiser and took a sip.

Anna Lee, in cutoff jeans and an ole miss baseball T-shirt, leaned against the kitchen counter. She'd grown her strawberry blonde hair out long that summer and her skin had a burnished red-brown glow, making the freckles even more pronounced. As she moved and stretched, the gray T-shirt rode up a bit on her flat stomach.

"I know," she said.

"I know what I want."

"So do I."

"But what?"

"Luke knew you were coming back home," she said. "He was worried you'd want me and Shelby to leave with you."

"That's crazy," Quinn said. "Luke might realize I have two aging parents and a crazy sister to look after. Not to mention a wandering cattle dog."

"He believes the only reason you came back to Jericho was for me. And, now that you have me, you'll keep on moving."

"Do I have you?"

"Slow steps," she said with a grin. "Isn't that what we agreed?"

"I don't like you being with Luke."

"He's still my husband."

"Not for much longer."

"I have to see him," she said. "I'll always have to see him."

"But you're with me," Quinn said. "Right?"

Anna Lee gave a weak-as-hell smile, walking toward him. Quinn took the steaks from the skillet and set them on an old china plate to cool. He reached out and pulled her close, his hand touching the warmth of her low back, and kissed her. She kissed him back, but barely, a stiffness in her lips and back. He told her he loved her and she told him she loved him back.

They ate outside. Anna Lee cut up some heirloom tomatoes for a salad and served them with a couple baked sweet potatoes. Quinn drank his second beer and Anne Lee had a Pepsi, still too much Baptist in her. You can't commit adultery and drink alcohol at the same damn time.

"My dad wants me to invest in some more land," Quinn said. "Said I need to be thinking of the future. Planning a family."

Anna Lee nearly spit out her Pepsi but caught herself and wiped off her chin. "Are you kidding me?" she said. "Jason Colson giving you advice on how to plan ahead. I really don't think he knows what he's going to do from day to day. All he does is play old Creedence tapes and work on that piece-of-shit Pontiac."

"It's something," Quinn said. "He's pretty much just getting to know us."

"You know what I think of him and his excuses," she said. "Your momma feels the same way. She doesn't care a damn bit about how he's trying to show off his horses to Little Jason. Acting like he's goddamn Grandfather of the Year."

"He's trying," Quinn said. "And he thinks I need to buy up that logged-out land Johnny Stagg owns."

"Why?"

"He wants to open up a dude ranch," Quinn said. "Well, he's not calling it that. Basically, he wants us to double our cattle and add some horses. He thinks we can dig a big lake and maybe rent out some cabins. He believes folks would pay for lessons or to board their horses."

"That's crazy."

"You know, he was the wrangler on both *Pale Rider* and *Silverado*."

"Have you actually seen his name in the credits?" Anna Lee said, finally getting down to slicing into the steak. Bloody and nearly raw, just as she liked it. "I mean, to make sure?"

"I have."

"Be careful, Quinn Colson," she said. "I just don't want that man to go and break everyone's heart again."

"Aren't I always?"

"Why do you keep those animals around?" Mingo asked.

The boy stood with Fannie Hathcock in the parking lot of the Rebel, watching the Born Losers race each other up and down the strip between the truck stop and the Golden Cherry Motel, where they sometimes lived. The Golden Cherry was a classic old fifties hotel, with a twenty-unit brick building surrounding a swimming pool. The green-and-bright-red neon sign flashed WELCOME to all the weary travelers coming off Highway 45.

"I don't know," Fannie said. "Maybe because they have character."

"They scare the crap out of me," he said. "I don't like them in the bar."

Mingo was a good kid. Dark, handsome, and smart as a whip. Fannie had brought him along down at the place on Choctaw land when he was thirteen. He was in his early twenties now, skinny, with long black hair and a handsome native face. More than anything, Mingo was loyal. In this business, Fannie appreciated that above all else.

"The Born Losers," Fannie said, watching them gather by the motel pool. One of them stripped off his nasty leathers and jumped on in, to a bunch of hoots. "We do for them and they do for us."

"Don't like them," Mingo said. "Don't trust them. I don't get it, Miss Fannie."

She and Mingo were taking a smoke break after hanging some new light fixtures in Vienna's. The noontime sun was harsh and the late summer was hot as hell, heat waving up off the asphalt. Across the road, the Losers were gunning their bikes and playing loud music, the doors of the units they rented wide-open. They were dirty, stinky, and mean, but they were the key to making Highway 45, from the Gulf Coast to Memphis, really work. Without them, the Mexicans would think they were weak.

"We get a lot of good stuff running

through the Rebel," Fannie said, spewing smoke from the side of her mouth. "I do a little window-shopping and sometimes they get that stuff for me."

"That chop shop in Olive Branch?" Mingo said. "With that old trucker who busts up what you send him?"

"Yes, sir."

"I don't like him, either," Mingo said. "He's a damn crook."

"We all are, baby," Fannie said. "Me, the Born Losers, that old red-neck in Olive Branch. We all do for each other."

"But a motorcycle gang?" Mingo said. "Couldn't you get someone else to do their part?"

"Crooks work in wild and mysterious ways," Fannie said. "Nobody wants to testify that those boys hijacked your truck."

"Guess not," Mingo said, strands of black hair flying in front of his flat face. "But they're really messing up the motel. Two of the doors are broken. All the TVs are gone. If I were you, I'd burn the sheets when they take off for Biloxi."

"Good idea," Fannie said, tossing the nub of her brown cigarillo to the ground. "Will you see to that?"

"Yes, ma'am."

"I wouldn't worry too much about TVs,"

Fannie said. "Those boys just liberated a whole truck from Best Buy. You got a laptop?"

"Yes, ma'am."

"Need another?"

Mingo smiled, his dark Indian hair nearly blue in the hot August light. He'd been full of so much potential down at the Rez. He'd been living with a crackhead sister and her mean-ass boyfriend when Fannie took him. When they came for Mingo or some money, Fannie handed over enough cash to get them high for the rest of the month.

"They piss in the pool."

"I know."

"Dirty bastards."

"But they're our dirty bastards," Fannie said. "We just can't let them ever forget who's boss."

Back when Milly Jones was a cheerleader, she'd been a Big Fucking Deal, all eyes on her as the girls would toss her high in the air, twirling and spinning, being blinded by the stadium lights and bright green of the field. The lightest on the team, a damn two-time state champion, who'd learned how quick your life could turn to shit. Not a year out of school, working two goddamn jobs, the Dollar Store in Jericho and the Build-

43

A-Bear Workshop in Tupelo, and now thinking about scrounging for dollar bills at a titty club.

The team tossed up the new flyer that Friday night, a little girl named Tiffany, building a damn human pyramid, and Milly grinned down from the bleachers and clapped and cheered louder than anyone. She was happy for them. Really, she was happy as hell. The band from Lafayette County blared out "Party in the U.S.A." and for exactly three seconds she forgot that she wasn't a part of this anymore. It was a hot August night and the grass was green and cool. The lights, the players, the students and families all packed in tight. Everything so familiar.

"I hadn't heard from you in two weeks," Nikki said.

"I told you what I'm doing."

"Oh," Nikki said. "That big secret thing."

"You remember that writer I told you about?" Milly asked. "The one that writes romance novels, but about Christians. So they talk about the Bible and Jesus more than just doing it?"

"Sure."

"Well, she's signing books over in Tupelo tomorrow," Milly said. "If she can't help me tell my story, ain't no one can."

"Can your car make it over to Tupelo?"

"I'll see that it does."

"So you'll tell her, but you won't tell me," Nikki said. "Son of a bitch. I've known you most of my life, Milly. And I've never known you to act stranger."

It was true Milly had known Nikki since second grade, best friends since they were in eighth grade and went on that mission trip to Belize. In between smoking dope and fooling around with the pastor's son and his best friend, they'd both finally realized the world looked a hell of a lot brighter away from Tibbehah County. And they'd never be like their mommas, not knowing which way to cross the road. Nikki reached down and held her six-month-old son, Jon-Jon, tighter in her lap.

"I don't want you hurt," Milly said. "This thing — this secret — will turn Jericho inside out."

"Shit," Nikki said. "I don't think there's a lot that would shock this place."

Milly looked down at the field, the sidelines crowded with players and coaches. Everyone waiting for the coin toss in the center of the field, seeing which way things would go. A hot wind blew in from the west, smelling of burning leaves and fresh-cut grass. The summer was about over.

"This will."

"What is it?"

"Damn you," Milly said. "Don't you listen?"

"Oh, come the fuck on," Nikki said.

"It's not my secret," Milly said. "It's about Brandon."

And that stopped Nikki cold from opening up her mouth. Ever since Milly's brother had blown his goddamn head off while supposedly cleaning his .308 in the woods, there hadn't been a lot of interest in discussion. For a long while, people would walk the other way when they'd see her. What the hell do you say to the girl who had a defect for a brother? Killing yourself is a cold, hard sin to these Baptists.

"Can you at least tell me where you're living now since your momma tossed you out?"

"Momma didn't toss me out," Milly said. "I left because I was tired of all her shit. All she does is watch *The View* and sell her essential oils to her dumb friends. I moved in with Daddy."

"I thought you hated your daddy."

"When I was dating Joshua, me and Daddy butted heads," Milly said. "He couldn't wrap his thick redneck head around the fact that his little blonde angel

46

was going with a black boy. You know what he called him?"

"I do."

"But now that me and Joshua aren't together no more, he's not so damn pissed-off," she said. "He takes out his shit on his new girlfriend."

"Did you tell him what you're doing?" Nikki said. "This top secret writing project, filling up those little journals with your book."

"It's not my story."

"I know."

"And I don't want to talk about it," she said. "Not until things come together."

"And you blow the fucking roof off Jericho, Mississippi?"

"That's right."

"Why do you need this woman to help you?"

"This isn't the kind of thing to whisper," Milly said. "This is something that's gotta be told right. She'll know what to do. She knows people. How to tell the story in the right way. I mean, do you start at the end or go back before it all happened?"

"He was cleaning his gun," Nikki said. "Right? That part is true."

"We all tell ourselves lies," Milly said,

reaching down and touching little Jon-Jon's face. "It's what gets us through the night."

4

There were times when Lillie Virgil wasn't so sure she wanted to be sheriff. She'd spent Saturday morning hosing down the cell where D. J. Norwood had pissed himself, that turd not flushing quickly enough through the justice system and out of her jail. After, she hadn't even had a chance to return a few calls and grab some breakfast when the local high school coach wanted to have a sit-down. Last night, Reggie Caruthers pulled over one of his former players hotboxing around the Square with a baggie full of pills, enough weed to choke Matthew McConaughey, and a loaded pistol on the dashboard.

"He's just a fine boy who made a mistake," Coach Bud Mills said, smiling, wanting the woman to know the ways of the world. "He's a hard worker, tough-minded, and a good Christian. His momma is a pastor out in Blackjack."

"Besides the weed and pills," Lillie said, "you do know we got a loaded Smith & Wesson .357. We traced the gun back to Clarksdale, where it was stolen last year. We also have good reason to believe he's running with a crew here called the North Side Boys. Heard of them?"

"What's that, some kind of rap group?"

"It's a gang," Lillie said. "They've been known to work with some pretty rough folks up in Memphis."

"It's hard for my boys," Mills said. "They come out of high school with everyone patting their back. But when they don't get recruited or can't get a scholarship, they're nothing. They get chewed up and spit out. If Ordeen gets put in the system, he can't get out. I prayed with him this morning. He's learned his lesson. Y'all scared the hell out of him. Keep the gun. Let him move on."

"We intend to keep the gun," Lillie said. "It's stolen property."

"It wasn't his."

"Then where'd he get it?"

Mills shook his head. He reached for a Styrofoam cup at the edge of her desk and spit out a little Skoal. He leaned back and folded his arms over his hard, round stomach.

"It's not easy in that culture," he said. "You know? Most of them don't have no good role models, with Daddy knocking up Momma and then shagging ass. Ordeen is different. His momma is a preacher. Good family, knows right from wrong. He's just restless, is all. Can't find his way. Can't find any work . . . Thanks again for that cup of coffee. It's real early for me."

"Nice of you to bail him out."

"Ordeen is special," Mills said. "If he'd had better grades or could run just a little faster, he'd be up at Ole Miss right now instead of cleaning out toilets at the Rebel Truck Stop."

"Is that what he's doing?"

"That was the job I got him," Mills said. "Before all that business happened to Johnny Stagg."

Lillie nodded. She never thought of Johnny Stagg as anyone's victim. Hard to feel bad for a man who'd been sucking off the county's tit for more than two decades without anyone questioning him.

"All I ask is for you to consider the situation."

"You want me to drop the charges?"

"Now, Lillie," Mills said. "How long have you known me? You forget how close I was to your momma. We all miss her. She was the best damn secretary the school ever had. Every Christmas, she baked me a tin of sugar cookies."

"We all miss her."

"I know, Lillie," he said. "How's that daughter? She's named Rose, too, isn't she?"

"Yes, sir."

Mills spit some more in the cup. He had on a mesh ball cap with the Wildcats logo on it, red coach's shorts, and a gray T-shirt. Didn't look like he'd had time to change from the season opener last night. Even if you'd never met Bud Mills in your life, you'd peg him for a coach. Ruddy cheeks, weak chin, and small, clear blue eyes. He was bald on top and graying on the sides. The way she remembered it, her mother always thought he was an asshole.

"Yeah," Lillie said. "Y'all were friends."

"I'm so sorry, Lil."

"It's been six years."

"Your momma had a big heart," Mills said. "Especially when it came to kids from poor homes. She knew some children just weren't loved. They didn't serve no purpose in their homes and got treated worse than dogs."

Mary Alice walked up to her glass door, held up her hand holding a callback slip, and Lillie waved her away. She leaned into the desk that had once been her mentor's, Hamp Beckett, and then had been her friend Quinn's for a few years. The top of the desk was battered, still scarred with cigar burns from Quinn. It needed a good resurfacing.

"You keep up with most of your former players?"

"Those who want to."

"What about Nito Reece?"

"Ole Ranito?" Mills said, laughing. "Hadn't seen him in a long while."

"Hard to find Ordeen without Nito nearby," Lillie said. "When we arrested Ordeen, Nito was in the backseat. It was Ordeen's car. He had the weapon on him."

"Nito is another story," Mills said, grinning. "I'm not coming here and vouching for Nito. I kicked that boy to the curb last season. He embarrassed everyone. Smokin' dope and putting it out there for the world to see on the Internets."

Lillie looked across the desk at old Bud Mills, hero to Tibbehah County, the name on the sign when you hit the county line. Two-time State Champs. He smiled back at her as she stared, reaching for his spit cup again, taking a big breath, waiting to hear the game plan.

"You can talk to the prosecutor, Coach,"

Lillie said. "But Ordeen and Nito scare the hell out of me. They got a hell of a bad thing going. And either you're gonna have to start mailing 'em cheese and crackers to Parchman or visiting them at the cemetery. But they're long down a fucked-up patch of road."

"You sure talk straight for a woman."

"A woman should talk around the point?"

"I sure loved your momma."

"That's what you said."

"And I like to believe in the good side of people, Lil," he said. "It's served me well in the last twenty years. People in this county look out for one another. Maybe a time when you might need to reach out to me for a favor."

"The gun was loaded," Lillie said. "He never told my deputy until he took it off him."

"Weren't you young once?" Mills said. "Running wild and free. Making bone-headed mistakes?"

"Maybe," Lillie said. "But I was too damn busy shooting in tournaments to be fooling around with stolen guns."

"He didn't know it was stolen," Mills said. "And you just might think about how people still love that boy around here. We wouldn't have ever made the play-offs without him. I'd think on those things, Lillie."

"Because of the election."

"Because of the election, and because of the way people might view a woman running for office," he said. "Has there ever been a woman sheriff in Mississippi?"

"Mississippi is a state that needs a lot of firsts, Coach."

Coach Bud Mills stood, stretched, and tossed his Styrofoam cup loaded with brown spit in her trash. "Well," he said. "Can't blame me for trying to do some good around this town."

"How long?" Caddy Colson said.

"Six weeks," Quinn said. "Maybe eight. Depends on the next job. How many trainers they need."

"You like being a contractor?"

"I'm not a contractor," Quinn said. "I work for the U.S. government and NATO. It's an organization put together by General Petraeus. Men come to train and return as part of the Afghan local police. Officially, they don't have arrest powers. But they protect small villages where we're pulling out and the national police can't reach. We teach 'em how to shoot, look for IEDs, that kind of thing."

Quinn stood out in a barren field with his sister, after spending the last two hours running his uncle's old International Harvester tractor over the dead corn stalks and a big patch where there'd been rows of tomatoes that had burned up in the heat. Caddy had cut her hair boy-short again, bright blonde, almost the color of straw. She had on a Merle Haggard T-shirt saying MAMA TRIED, blue jean shorts, and muddy work boots. The MAMA TRIED would've been funny if it hadn't been so damn true.

"You feel like you're doing some good?"

"Contrary to some folks who never left Mississippi, all Muslims aren't terrorists," Quinn said. "We help locals look out for their own. There are so many different dialects over there that some Afghanis can't even talk to each other."

"Kind of like sending someone down to Tibbehah from New York."

"Something like that."

"Shit, I can't understand some of the people in my own backyard," she said. "It ain't the Mexicans. It's folks who've been here their whole life who have English as a second language."

Quinn smiled.

"Thanks for tilling up the garden," she said. "Time to plant the fall greens. What do you think? Turnips or collards?"

"I say live on the edge and plant both."

Caddy handed him a bottle of water and a clean towel to wipe his face. He pulled off his ball cap, plain green with an American flag patch, and wiped his wet brow. Since he'd been gone, Caddy had a new wooden barn built where the old one had burned. She'd added a smaller metal building out back to collect secondhand clothes and supplies and frozen and fresh food for the needy. The River — church and community outreach — started a few years back by a former convict-turned-preacher named Jamey Dixon. Caddy had run the show ever since he'd been killed, except for last year's trip to rehab.

"Does it ever get you that you have to go to the other side of the planet to help people out?"

"Maybe."

"We need roads, food, medical aid right here," Caddy said.

"I tried."

"And it bit you in the ass."

"People over there are more grateful," Quinn said. "Their word means everything."

"I thought that was true of a Southern man."

"When he's not speaking out of the side

of his mouth."

Caddy laughed and Quinn hopped back on the tractor, circling the garden and riding up to the trailer hooked up to his Army-green F-250. The truck still bore the mark of the sheriff's star where he'd peeled off the decal with a straight razor. It was a big truck, jacked up tall, with KC lights, and heavy winch under the grille. His buddy Boom nicknamed it the Big Green Machine.

Caddy's son, Jason, stood up on the truck's tailgate watching his uncle chain the old tractor to the platform. Now eight, he waited, in a pair of brown overalls, carrying a .22 rifle. He'd been target-practicing with the .22 on some Coca-Cola cans while Quinn worked, waiting for him to trade out the tractor for a johnboat and take him out on Choctaw Lake to hunt for bass and brim.

"Ready?" Little Jason asked.

"Gotta head back to the farm first."

"Can Hondo come with us?"

"Yes, sir," Quinn said. "He'd be disappointed if we didn't. We also need to stop by Varner's for some crickets."

"Can we cook what we catch?"

"You bet."

"I mean, tonight," Jason said. "You know, tonight is *WWE Raw*. John Cena is going back for the belt. You know he lost it to that son of a bitch Seth Rollins?"

Quinn looked over to his sister. Caddy shrugged and leaned against his truck. She spent most days out here at The River when not working part-time as a receptionist for a dentist in Tupelo. Caddy was sunburned, towheaded, and determined as he'd ever seen her to make her mission work. It had been a long road and some rehab, but his sister was finally back.

"He's right," Caddy said. "That Seth Rollins is a son of a bitch. I'm a Cena fan, too. Although he's not my all-time favorite."

"The Undertaker," Quinn said. "I remember. You always liked that guy."

"You know he's still wrestling?" Caddy said. "Jason has his action figure. Cena, too. But The Undertaker is taller. And meaner. He's all-time. Like The Rock."

"How about you come fishing with us?" Quinn said.

"I promised to help Momma shell peas tonight," Caddy said. "There's an Elvis Double Feature on TCM. *Paradise, Hawaiian Style* and *Blue Hawaii*. She's cooking a ham with pineapple, making poi. Wanted to know if you want come over."

"I'd rather fry up some fish and watch wrestling with Jason, if it's all the same."

"She didn't mean it."

59

Quinn nodded. He stared at Caddy, smiling, knowing there was more to come.

"You know how she gets after a few glasses from the wine box," Caddy said. "I don't think she gives a damn about you and Anna Lee. She's just upset about what she heard Daddy is doing out on the farm."

Quinn continued to watch. He took a long, deep breath.

"Dude ranch?"

"That's Jason Colson talking," Quinn said. "Not me."

"Can't blame Momma. It's her family's land and it's the house where she grew up," Caddy said. "How'd you feel if the man who left you came back to town and wanted to squat on your family memories?"

Quinn wiped his face and neck again with the towel. An old car wound down the dirt road toward The River and stopped outside the wooden barn used as a church. On Sundays, they'd have guest preachers and local bluegrass music. A hand-painted sign on a piece of charred wood from the old place read LEAVE YOUR PAST AT THE DOOR.

"What the hell is poi anyway?" Quinn said.

"A taro root cooked and beat to shit," Caddy said. "Kind of like a tropical mashed potato."

The car door opened and a short black

woman and two children crawled out. While Caddy waited, the woman fired up a cigarette and leaned against the car. The woman looked tired and beat, worn-out physically and mentally. She reminded him of faces he'd seen in those northern Afghan villages when their world had been turned upside down.

"You know her?"

"Never met her, but I know her." Caddy smiled. "It's not if you get knocked on your ass. It's if you get back up."

As Quinn and Jason drove off, the tractor on the trailer rocking back and forth, he watched Caddy from his rearview. She wrapped an arm around the woman and led her and the children toward the metal shed for whatever it was they needed.

5

"I'm taking his ass out for what he done," Nito said.

"What he done?" Ordeen said.

"Man called the cops," Nito said. "Shit. You know I'm right."

"Hell no, I don't know you right. All I know is, I spent the goddamn night in jail and don't want to go back."

"We gotta get straight on this shit," Nito said. "Blackjack is our world. We the North Side Boys. We own this place."

" 'Cause no one else want it," Ordeen said.

"Got damn."

"Come on, man. Sammi's our friend. He wouldn't call the cops. He fuck us, he fuck himself. You know how much money he making 'cause of us? We do business and he do business. Why else folks come to Black-jack 'cept to die?"

Nito Reece sat behind the wheel of a '72

Chevy Nova, electric blue, with chrome rims and an airbrushed license tag reading HERE KITTY KITTY. Ordeen Davis leaned back in the passenger seat, bare feet up on the dash, with the stereo pumping out Rick Ross. Down on Elvis Presley Boulevard. *Got the dogfood, the soft, nigga, and the hard / You can tell them crackers they can go and get the dogs.* They passed a big fat blunt between them. Ordeen had rolled it just right.

"Well, someone knew we had that gun, pills, weed, and shit," Nito said. "Police got us not ten minutes after leaving the Gas & Go. What the hell's that about? Come on. Use your fucking head, Ordeen."

"You say he snitchin'?"

"Now you thinking, boy," Nito said. "Got damn. I think football done scrambled your brains."

"OK. OK."

"OK?" Nito said. "OK? OK what?"

They sat parked at a crazy angle about twenty yards from the front of the Gas & Go. Windows all smoked-up, whole body of that Chevy shaking like hell. "We doin' it?" Ordeen said. "Then let's do this shit."

"Gotta leave the motor running. Don't want to wake up Little Ray. You seen him in the game last night? Ooh, shit. That boy need his rest. He goin' D-1."

"Boy can hit, but that motherfucker better grow a foot."

"Fuck you, man."

"Look at your brother," Ordeen said. "Big ears. Big feet. Small body. Look like a damn gremlin."

Ordeen crawled out of the Nova, radio still cranked up high, as Nito followed, cupping his hand to the hot wind to light a cigarette. The fluorescent lights over the pump shone on Nito's lean body and hard swagger. He had short hair, light gray eyes, and a mouthful of gold teeth. Both of them wore dark jeans, loose at the waist, big ole Chicago White Sox jerseys, and thick gold chains that weren't real gold. Ordeen wore his hair in long braids with a gray ball cap worn sideways.

The Gas & Go windows were filled with ads for cold beer, cigarettes, fried chicken, and pizza. When he pushed open the door, a little bell rang and Sammi looked up from the counter, where he'd been messing with his phone. The damn place smelled like old grease and cigarette smoke. "Surprise, motherfucker," Nito said. "Can't keep them North Side Boys down."

Sammi was a little older than them, his daddy owning the store, and two more over in Pontotoc. He was Iraqi, Pakistani, Muslim, or some shit, but tried like hell to fit in with the niggas in Tibbehah. He'd shaved his black beard in razor-thin strips along his jaw and over his lips. He wore a ball cap just like Ordeen's and a blue T-shirt about four sizes too big that said GRIT AND GRIND. His black hair was long and curly, shining with some Mideast oils or Jheri Curl.

Nito walked up to the cash register and leaned his forearms against the counter. Sammi looked back down at the phone, like he was trying to figure out something, and paid them no damn mind.

"You talkin' to the cops again," Nito said. "Ain't you? Tellin' them to come on back to Blackjack and take ole Ordeen and Nito's black asses to jail."

Sammi lifted his big brown eyes from the phone and just stared directly at Nito like he was bored as hell. *Oh, hell no.*

"You messin' with us," Nito said. "You seen us in here with that gun we sportin'. You knew we were rolling last night. Don't know who else could have done it."

"You want something?" Sammi said. "Fried chicken's old. I'll give it to you for half price."

"Don't want no old-ass chicken," Nito said. "I want you to be straight. You call the police and tell her we got a pistol, rolling up into Jericho, smoking a blunt."

Sammi put down the phone and shook his head. "You're crazy, Nito."

Ordeen shook his head. He took a deep breath and tried to look away, look at all that damn snack food. He could stand the talk. But, man, he sure hated to see the blood.

Nito kind of smiled and shook his head, offering his hand to Sammi. Sammi glanced up to Ordeen, who shrugged and reached out to meet Nito's hand. The hand shot back and bitch-slapped that Middle Eastern boy right across his face. "Don't you fuck me."

"I'm not fucking you."

"I say you called the sheriff. You tell me why."

"I didn't call anyone."

"Come on, man," Nito said. He slapped Sammi again, this time harder, and the crack of it filled the Gas & Go. Ordeen pretended to look at some chips, seeing that the BBQ Lay's now had half the fat of other chips. He reached for some pork cracklins and walked back to the cooler for a six-pack of Keystone.

"If you don't leave, I will call the cops."

"Last thing you do."

"Hit me again."

Nito slapped Sammi again. Ordeen reached for some hot sauce to go with the cracklins. His momma wasn't cooking tonight, staying at church until late. Either it was them cracklins or a cheeseburger at the Sonic. Tonight he'd be sleeping on the couch, watching that ESPN, trying not to hear what was going on in the back room with his sister and the men she brought home from Club Disco. Sunday she'd be hungover as hell and praising Jesus for four hours. Hell of a thing being kids of a preacher.

"Come on, man," Ordeen said. "Man says he didn't do it. Y'all keep cool. I don't want no more trouble."

Sammi wiped the blood off his lip. His head shook a little bit, black eyes darting around the store, staring out to see if anyone was coming to help. He looked to the glass wall and saw a truck pull up, an old black man, Mr. Bobo, get out, lifting a pint bottle to his mouth and wiping it with the back of his hands. Nito didn't care one damn bit and pulled that pistol out from his deep jean pocket, pointing it right in Sammi's face.

"Do it again, nigga."

"I didn't do nothing," Sammi said.

"Shoot you right in the fucking snout."

Sammi just stared at him with his big black eyes. Didn't raise his hands up or nothing. He stayed cool as shit and reached down for a little brown cigar burning in a metal tray and lifted it to his lips. "We done, man?"

"You call the cops and I tell the cops about all that Chinese shit you selling in the back room," Nito Reece said. "Don't you be telling me that it fell off some damn truck."

Mr. Bobo saw Nito with Sammi and turned back the way he'd come, headlights clicking on, backing out that old brown truck. Man didn't get to be that old from being dumb.

"I thought you were my friend," Sammi said.

"Shit," Nito said, flipping the gun around butt first. "Who the hell tole you that?" As he swung for Sammi, Ordeen turned his head the other way, blood flecking on the hot glass protecting all that chicken and pizza.

"They're real," said the old stripper. "You can touch them if you want."

"That's OK," Milly said. She had a book in her lap, *The Christmas Promise,* with an inscribed note from the author: *Dream Big.*

68

Share your stories with the world!

"You can tell real titties from the droop," the woman said. "All these fake titties flying around this place are easy to spot. No jiggle. Hard as damn bricks. I had mine since I was fifteen. You don't have to take my advice. But don't ever get implants. You'll cut your tips in half. Men like to look at 'em but don't care for the touch."

Milly wished the woman would be quiet. It had already been a long as hell day, trucking up to Tupelo to meet that famous author and then the author not having time to hear her story. All the woman wanted was Milly's last thirty dollars, her gas money, for a "Christian Romance Just in Time for Christmas!" How could Milly have been so dumb, bringing those little journals, trying to pass along her true stories.

Milly and the old stripper sat together on a long bench in the locker room at Vienna's Place. After Milly had signed the paperwork, Miss Fannie showed her to a locker and gave her the combination, saying it was up to her to keep up with her own shit. She said some of these bitches would steal her ass blind. The older woman pulled up a garter high on her leg and snapped it against her thigh.

"This is my first night," Milly said.

"I could tell," the woman said. "Make sure you take a shot of Jaeger before you hit the stage. Your legs will be shaking like a newborn fawn. But it gets better each time. By the end of the night, you won't even care if you're nekkid. It's a job and that's your uniform. Hell, you're young. These boys are going to love you. Men know that new-car smell."

"Excuse me?"

"You're fresh, is all," she said. "Truckers will know it. Play it. Tell 'em you're nervous. They'll tip out the damn ass for that."

The woman had long blonde hair, probably extensions, and bright blue eyes. Her white skin had been stained the color of mahogany and her teeth bleached the highest white. She had on lacy white panties, white bra over her double D's, and long white stockings. A white ribbon wrapped the sagging skin of her throat. Milly looked down at the cover of *The Christmas Promise* — a clean-looking guy in a shirt and tie and suspenders standing before a church. A dove had been photoshopped in behind him, flying high.

"Where you from?" the woman asked.

"Here."

"Here?" the woman said. "Damn. That's a new one on me."

Milly was in her street clothes — T-shirt, jeans, and Keds. She'd brought a sexy little red bra-and-panty set she'd bought at the Victoria's Secret in Tupelo. Only person to ever see her in it was Joshua and Joshua had been so thrilled about it he'd said she'd wear it on their wedding night. Which didn't make a lot of sense to her since they'd been doing it all that summer. Like she could go back to being a virgin. Joshua was smooth, slow, and gentle. If he found out where she was working, it would damn near kill him.

"I just need to make a little money."

"Yeah?" the woman said. "I told that to myself about twenty years ago."

"Is it hard?"

"Sometimes," the woman said. "You just have to set personal boundaries. Make rules for yourself and don't break them. Like, can a man touch your titties? The law says no touching above or below the waist. But if you got a man you feel OK about, think he's a good tipper, then it doesn't matter much to me. Other thing is that men are always trying to kiss you. You can touch my titties all you want, but don't you kiss me on the mouth. I don't know where that nasty trucker mouth has been."

"Anything else?"

"Don't worry too much about your time

on the pole," she said. "You ain't up there for no art project. Just shake it and twirl. It's just a chance for the men to see what you got to offer. Trust me, honey, they're gonna like you good. You don't need to sell it. Just show it. You could bounce a half-dollar off that little ass."

"I used to be a cheerleader," Milly said, smiling but not really feeling it.

A black girl not much older than Milly walked into the locker room buck-ass naked and smoking a long, thin cigarette. "Y'all can have it," she said. "Crazy out there tonight. Man tried to stick a beer bottle up my ass. Like I'm into that shit."

"We got a first-timer here tonight, Damika," the woman said. "Trying to pass down a little knowledge."

"You tell her about the sell?"

Milly looked at the black girl and stood up, taking off her T-shirt and jeans, folding them carefully and packing them in the locker with a pack of cigarettes, a pint of Jim Beam, and a small overnight bag filled with makeup. She dropped the romance novel on the floor with a thud.

"It's all about the sell, baby," Damika said. "That's where you make your money. Ain't about nickels and dimes tossed to you on the stage. You got to get their fat, sweaty, nasty asses into the VIP Room. Or whatever Miss Fannie call it."

"Champagne Room," the woman said.

"Yeah, well, what the fuck," Damika said. "Be cool about it. But don't waste time on no deadbeat. You see a man ain't interested or don't want to pay, you move right on down the line."

"And be yourself," the woman said. "Don't be superficial. Men are dumb as shit. They can't tell if you're into them or not. You act like it and they believe it. Show directness. Confidence. Look 'em in the eye when you grind their lap."

"And don't be asking them if they like this?" Damika said. "Or would like that? You're not asking them. You tell them. Don't say, 'Would you like to kick back with me in the Champagne Room?' Flirt with them, get them all horny, and just say, 'Let's go' or 'It's time.'"

"And after their first lap dance, drag your fingernails across the back of their neck, lean into their ear, and whisper you don't want to stop," the woman said.

"Oh, hell," Damika said, giggling. "Oh, hell."

"I just need money."

"We all need money," the woman said. "You think this shit does it for me? Just

73

don't think you can start it and drop it. Money is too good."

Milly changed out of her threadbare panties and washed-out bra into the red silk satin. She pulled out a compact and mirror from her bag and started in on her eyes. She'd add some lashes, draw them up big and bold. It made her look older and fierce. She could use all the confidence she could get even if it was painted on.

"Just whatever you do, don't forget to tip out," the black girl said. "You cheat the house and that eye in the sky will know."

"She have cameras?"

The older woman looked at her, fluffing up her hair in a mirror, then looked over her shoulder. "Fannie doesn't need cameras," she said. "Sees it all."

"You pick a stage name yet?" Damika said.

"No."

"Don't ever tell anyone your real name," the woman said. "Don't ever let anyone know the real you."

"Mmm-hmm," Damika said.

"How about a song?"

" 'Wrecking Ball,' " Milly Jones said. "Miley Cyrus."

It was nearly seven, but Quinn found Boom Kimbrough still at the County Barn, working on one of the patrol cars, the one that had been Ike McCaslin's before his long-awaited retirement. He had the hood up, bent at the waist, reaching deep into the guts of the old Crown Vic, turning something with a ratchet attached on his prosthetic arm. The arm having been a casualty of his time in Iraq with the Guard.

Lillie Virgil sat on a discarded car backseat now used as a sofa. She was drinking some of Boom's burnt coffee in a paper cup. She smiled and gave Quinn a silent salute with two fingers.

"You payin' overtime, Lil?" Quinn asked.

Boom didn't budge, grunting, working on tightening something up. "It's my pleasure to stay late," Boom said. "Sheriff lets me work on some real classics."

"Classic pieces of shit," Lillie said.

"Supervisors won't get y'all new vehicles yet?" Quinn said.

"What do you think?" Lillie said. "They blow what they don't skim on kickbacks on conferences in Biloxi or Tunica. If we didn't have Boom, we'd be riding around Tibbehah on bicycles."

Boom pulled himself from under the hood. He reached for a rag, wiping the grease from the ratchet and turning it free of the artificial arm. A tall and substantial black man, he grinned at Quinn and shook his head. "Damn good to see you, Quinn."

Quinn wrapped his right arm around Boom's hulking body and patted his back. He handed him a box of Cubans he bought in duty-free on the way back home. Boom said he couldn't tell a Cuban from a Puerto Rican, but he sure loved the way those sticks smelled. Quinn reached into his back pocket and pulled out a handmade silk scarf that he offered to Lillie.

"Ha," Lillie said. "You can take a hint."

"Bought it in a bazaar in Herat," Quinn said. "It's your favorite color?"

"Nope," Lillie said, taking the scarf from his hand and wrapping it around her neck. "But it'll do."

" 'Bout time you stopped by," Boom said.

"Had to deal with a few things."

Lillie grinned but didn't comment, left leg crossed over the right, kicking her foot up and down, as she sat on the old backseat. She was examining the end of the scarf, probably making sure Quinn didn't buy it at the local Walmart.

"You get those things straight?" Boom asked.

"Nope."

Boom nodded. He used a pocketknife to slit open the cedar box, smelling the twenty-four neatly aligned cigars. He grinned and widened his eyes. "Go ahead," Quinn said.

"I can wait."

"Wait for what?"

"Special occasion."

"Seems like one right now." Quinn cut a cigar for Boom and offered another to Lillie. Lillie declined but said she just might take a puff off Quinn's.

"Since you made good and actually remembered me," she said.

"I always think of you, Lil."

"Bull-fucking-shit," Lillie said.

The inside of the County Barn was pin neat, with its clean concrete floors, aligned tools on pegboards, and four large Husky toolboxes on wheels. Quinn noted Boom had gotten a new *Playboy* lingerie calendar since the last time he'd stopped by. A woman looked coyly over her shoulder, a blue sweater slipping down over her shapely back. Just the kind of woman who'd be hanging out in a Jericho, Mississippi, garage.

Quinn clicked open the old stainless Zippo he'd had for years. Busted and dented, the lighter had made it through four tours of Vietnam before being handed over to Quinn for thirteen in Iraq and Afghanistan. He lit Boom's cigar and then his own, filling the space with the rich tobacco smell.

77

All the movements and sounds in the garage amplified with a deep echo.

"Heard about that thing at your farm," Boom said, puffing on the cigar, the end starting to glow bright orange. "D. J. Norwood is one crazy son of a bitch. Almost as bad as his entire worthless family."

"I think Lillie might've knocked some sense into him."

"She'd have to hit him pretty damn hard."

"No idea what y'all are talking about," Lillie said, reaching for Quinn's cigar and taking a puff. "I practiced restraint with that shitbag. If I hadn't, they'd have found his head in Eupora."

"Shit," Boom said. "Let's get the hell out of here and go get a beer."

Quinn nodded, looking to Lillie, a little surprised Boom was drinking again. The last time Quinn and Lillie caught him drinking, he'd nearly leveled an entire juke joint down in Sugar Ditch.

"Don't worry," Boom said. "One beer. All a sheriff can be seen drinking. And all I can handle."

"Fine by me," Quinn said. "Southern Star?"

"Like we got somewhere else to go?" Lillie said.

"Always the Booby Trap," Quinn said, smiling.

"Ain't no more," Boom said. "Hadn't you heard? Woman bought it has gone high-class. It's called Vienna's or some shit."

"Fannie Hathcock spells class with a capital K," Lillie said. "That's one evil bitch, if you ask me."

"Come on," Boom said. "We'll get you up to speed on all this shit. I'll shut down and meet y'all in town."

Lillie stood, still in green uniform, red scarf wrapping her neck. Some chatter heated up her police radio before she walked out the open mouth of the barn and into the lot. Quinn followed into the fading gold light, Lillie now talking on her cell phone, and then turning to him. "Sorry," she said. "But I have to go."

Quinn looked to her and waited.

"Some moron is robbing the Gas & Go up in Blackjack," Lillie said. "We got Reggie Caruthers and Kenny headed up there now. I better head on."

"I'll catch Boom later," Quinn said. "Been a long while since we rode together."

"Sure," Lillie said. "What could go wrong?"

6

Quinn had never met Sammi Khouraki but knew and liked his father, a tough old Syrian who used to work at Luther Varner's Quick Mart. His dad was a surly little guy who chain-smoked and kept the local sports book before taking over a string of convenience stores. The old man had a thick accent, but Sammi talked like someone who'd grown up in Mississippi, country twang by way of the folks in Sugar Ditch. He wore a flat-brimmed baseball cap and a blue Memphis Grizzlies T-shirt. His face was a mess, bloodied lip and swollen-shut right eye. To hear Sammi tell it, he'd just been careless and walked into a wall.

"Pretty fucking mean wall," Lillie said.

They all stood outside the Gas & Go, sun finally going down in Tibbehah County. Dust from the county road had kicked up, leaving a soft yellow haze in the fading gold light. Quinn leaned against Lillie's Cherokee as she interviewed Sammi, Reggie and Kenny already back on patrol. No money taken. A victim who wouldn't press charges or even admit anything happened.

"How about the security tapes?" Lillie asked.

"Busted," Sammi said.

"That a fact . . ." Lillie said.

"It is." Sammi nodded. "We need to get that camera fixed."

"You wouldn't have happened to have a run-in with any of the North Side Boys?" Lillie said.

Sammi, fat lip and swollen eye, shook his head. "Never heard of 'em."

Quinn hadn't said a word since they'd found Sammi outside, sitting next to the gas pumps with a bloody towel on his face. It was good to see Lillie again and always a pleasure to watch her work.

"Never heard of the North Side Boys?" Lillie said. "Now, that does amaze me, Sammi. There isn't shit to do up in Blackjack but join a gang or watch the Illinois Central pass. I seen plenty of those boys hanging out at your store, doing a little business outside."

"Nope." Sammi said.

"Nito Reece?" Lillie said. "Everyone around here knows Nito. He's a real mean motherfucker."

"You sure don't talk like a sheriff," Sammi said.

"Really?" Lillie said. "A good sheriff should talk in a way to elicit an answer to a question. So far, you haven't told me jack shit about who messed up your face. If I were you, I'd relay a little information so it didn't happen again. You don't want to get in thick with any of the North Side Boys. Especially Nito Reece."

Sammi looked to Quinn and nodded. Quinn nodded back. Sammi knew him but didn't know his name. Could recognize he was somebody from Jericho, maybe even remembered him as the sheriff. Sammi looked away.

"We get a call that a young black male is in your store waving around a gun," Lillie said. "But you didn't see it because you were too busy walking into walls."

"Yeah," Sammi said. "That's right."

"Sammi," Lillie said. "Son of a bitch. Don't lay down for these boys. I had one of them in last night. Once you make excuses for them, they'll eat your ass up."

Sammi looked over Lillie's shoulder, again to Quinn, and said, "Don't I know you?"

Quinn nodded. "Maybe," he said. "I knew your dad. Back when he worked for Mr. Varner at the Quick Mart. How's he doing?"

"He owns three gas stations now," Sammi said. "And a tobacco super-outlet and cell phone store over in Tupelo. He doesn't like Tibbehah County. He says people cheated him here."

"He's right," Quinn said.

Sammi looked confused. Easy to look confused with a big flat-brimmed ball cap and lots of blood on your face.

"Johnny Stagg used to put the squeeze on him," Quinn said. "He made him pay protection for his store until I became sheriff."

Sammi looked doubtful, wiping the blood from his lip. "Which one of you is in charge?" Sammi said. "Because I'm confused who I'm supposed to be talking to."

"Come again?" Lillie said.

"Which one of you is the sheriff?"

"She's the sheriff," Quinn said. "I'm just the impartial observer."

"But you were the sheriff."

"Yep."

"I heard you were just like all the rest," Sammi said. "Isn't that why you didn't get reelected?"

"No, sir," Quinn said. "Not at all."

"I heard you shot some men," Sammi said. "And that you got state people to cover it up."

Quinn grinned, just a bit, and shook his head. He looked to Lillie and her face had turned a bright shade of red. She took a long, deep breath and Quinn lightly touched her arm. Wasn't worth it. "We want to help you," Lillie said.

"I don't want help."

"Don't take their shit," Lillie said.

"I walked into a wall."

"Keep on doing that and it's gonna tumble down on your thick fucking head, kid."

Sammi stood up from the gas pump island, looked at the blood soaked through the rag, and tossed it in the trash. He shook his head and walked back into the Gas & Go.

"Still miss being the law?" she said.

"Hearts and minds, Lillie."

"And sometimes a swift kick to the nuts doesn't hurt."

"Ma'am, it sure is good to finally meet you," said the young man across from Fannie. "I've heard a lot of good things about you from some important folks."

"Is that a fact?"

"Yes, ma'am," the boy said. He was probably in his late twenties but looked nineteen. Unkempt shaggy hair, wrinkled khakis, blue button-down with an Ole Miss tie. "You have a top name in the hospitality industry. We just wanted to make sure you had gotten our messages of welcome."

Fannie nodded. She reached for her pack of cigarettes and pulled out a skinny brown cigarillo. She lit it with her Dunhill lighter and waved away the smoke that clouded the space between her and Junior.

"We just never heard back, is all," said the boy. "And some folks thought I might just stop by and say hello. You know, see if there was anything at all you needed."

"What's your name?" Fannie said.

"Bentley Vandeven."

"Of course it is," Fannie said, leaning back in her office chair. The office had been scraped clean of every inch of Johnny Stagg, painted a smooth beige, nothing hung on the walls. New light fixtures and a glass-topped desk. "And you came all the way to Jericho just to say hello?"

"Well, ma'am," Bentley said. "Some folks have just gotten a little worried. They're wondering if you don't want our company."

"Speak English, Bentley."

"Folks wanted me to make sure you wanted to continue the same arrangement as Mr. Stagg's," he said. "People look to this county as an important little sliver of Mississippi, being so close to Memphis and all. They think on it as true Mississippi hospitality."

"Because of the free pussy?" Fannie said.

"Ma'am?"

"Because of the free pussy afforded to all those assholes from the capitol."

Bentley's young, smooth face colored a bit. She blew out some more smoke from the side of her mouth and adjusted the cuffs on her red silk top. She cocked her head and studied Bentley a bit more, waiting for him to shift a little in his chair. If those important men had any sense at all, they would have sent someone more substantial.

"I don't know," he said.

"You don't know if your folks in Jackson want more pussy?"

"They just wanted to make sure you were our friend," he said. "You know who has a big spread of land here?"

"I do."

"And you know what a good friend he's been to Mr. Stagg."

"Couldn't keep him out of the federal pen in Montgomery, Alabama."

"That was Mr. Stagg's own doings," Bentley said, grinning. "But for a long while he was given a lot of friendship, lots of protection."

Fannie nodded. "Well, I don't need any of

that shit."

"Excuse me?"

"I said, I don't need any more friends, Bentley," she said. "I don't need protection and I'm not interested in kickbacks from chicken shit road-and-bridge projects if it means sucking up to a bunch of big fat assholes from Jackson. You may have not noticed, but I am not Johnny Stagg in any shape or form. And if your people down there want to do business with me, they need to come themselves, not send some jack-off kid from Jackson Prep."

"How'd you know I went to Jackson Prep?"

"Bentley," Fannie said. "Go back into the Rebel and have a meal on me. The chicken-fried steak is very good, but our barbecue is better. Enjoy yourself up here and then go back to Jackson and tell the boys to leave me the hell alone."

Bentley shook his head. His face dropped. And, from where she sat, Fannie noticed his khakis were wrinkled and his loafers scuffed like a kid who'd always had money and didn't give a damn to appreciate it. Fannie ashed her cigarette in a little gold tray set neatly on the side of the desk.

"I'll pass on the message," Bentley said, trying to look cocky as he stood and shook his head. He brushed the longish hair from his eyes. "But they're not going to like it. And they'll probably send someone not as nice as me to tell you how things are going to work."

Fannie smashed out the last bit of her cigarette and reached down for her Prada bag, reaching deep inside and finding the familiar handle. She smiled and waited, taking a long, slow breath.

"You're a beautiful woman, Miss Hathcock," he said. "I bet you were a real knockout when you were young. But you can't set up the kind of business you're doing without some friends. I'd be real careful if I were you."

Fannie stood up quick and pulled a twenty-ounce claw hammer from her purse. She raised it high as she stepped around her desk and told Bentley he better get going.

"I heard you were one crazy bitch," he said.

"You heard right," Fannie said. "Now get the hell out of here."

"You don't get it, ma'am," he said. "You don't know what kind of folks you're messin' with."

Fannie smiled. "Son," she said. "I think you have it the other way around."

■ ■ ■ ■

Milly's father, Washburn L. Jones, who most folks just called Wash, hadn't said two words to her since she got off her shift and brought him home his damn Subway sandwich. Extra ham with extra mayo. He grunted as he ate, watching a rerun of *Dancing with the Stars* with his live-in girlfriend, Charlotte, a woman who weighed about three hundred pounds on her lightest day. Charlotte snatched up the pickles he'd tossed aside, munching on them as she tried to tell Milly who had talent on the show and who had flat feet. Charlotte knew she was an expert on the matter since she taught dance and tumbling at a strip mall out by the highway.

"Wadn't that girl's daddy killed by a sea snake?" Charlotte said.

Wash grunted and shook his head. "Got barbed by a fucking stingray right in the chest," he said, wiping the lettuce off his T-shirt. "Where the hell you been, Milly? You said you'd bring me a sandwich."

"What's that in your hand?"

"Damn about starved to death," her daddy said, still chewing. "I said, where were you?"

"Work."

"They change your shift?"

"I got a second job."

"Good for you," Charlotte said. "Baby, you gonna eat those chips?"

"Yeah, but you can have a couple," Wash said. "Don't eat 'em all. Shit. Second job? Where?"

"Walmart," she said. "Pet section."

"Hmm," Wash said, turning his eyes on her. "Pets? Ain't what I heard."

Milly didn't say anything, waiting until he swallowed that big wad of sandwich in his cheek. Wash just took another bite, more fixings landing on his white T-shirt, as he watched Bindi Irwin launch into a slow routine with some boy with wild blond hair. She dedicated the dance to her late father, who she called a ray of sunshine.

"I know that boy with her is queer as a three-dollar bill," Charlotte said. "But to look at 'em, you'd think they was in love. He's got a lot of grace about him."

"Sick," Wash said. "This goddamn country is headed into the toilet. Damn, don't eat all the chips. I said, just eat a couple. Son of a bitch."

"Good night," Milly said. "I'm beat."

"You gonna tell us the truth or just lie to our faces?" Wash said, tapping at his chest with his knuckles to stop a burp. "Charlotte got a call that you was out dancing at the titty bar tonight."

Milly shook her head.

"Right or wrong?" Wash said.

Charlotte looked to Milly and gave a weak smile before shifting her eyes down to the carpet, unsure what to say or do. Charlotte never knew what to say or do unless Wash Jones told her the way. She had on a pair of XXL pink sweatpants and a huge sweatshirt that said DANCE LIKE NO ONE'S WATCHING. Milly didn't think there was much trouble with that.

"You don't know what you're talking about," Milly said.

"You just like your momma," Wash said. "Let you loose and you're a wild-ass whore."

"Wash," Charlotte. "What's the matter with you? Don't talk that trash."

"Her momma tosses her out and I open my gosh-dang home," Wash said. "But I ain't giving no shelter if she's gonna whore it out. You know how embarrassing that is? You don't think people gonna be talking about it?"

"Like when you got busted for running drugs?"

"Shit," Wash said, shaking his head. He turned away from staring at her and concentrated on the television. The couple had

91

dressed up like they were in *Dirty Dancing* in that finale where Patrick Swayze picked up Jennifer Grey up over his head. Milly liked the movie, but she preferred Swayze much better in *Road House.* They didn't make men like that anymore.

"You sure that boy is queer?" Wash said.

"I read it in *Us Weekly,*" Charlotte said. "Or was it *People*?"

"Damn," Wash said, chewing on the sandwich.

Milly turned to head back to the small room behind the kitchen. She had her overnight bag and a Dell computer and a pink puppy stuffed animal she'd had most of her life. That was pretty much it.

"Hold up," Wash Jones said.

Milly stopped and looked behind her, eyeing her father, who wadded up the sandwich paper and fingered the ham caught in his teeth. Her daddy looked her over, lingering on the makeup on her face, and shook his head like he'd just seen the sorriest sight of his life. He reached for the level on his La-Z-Boy chair and hoisted his bad back up to straight and got to his feet. He was a short, round little man. His chin quivered with anger before he spoke. "Get your things and get gone."

"What?"

"This is the last time, Milly," he said. "It's for your own good."

"Wash," Charlotte said.

"You shut the hell up," he said. "Ain't your daughter out there shaking her titties for a couple bucks. I never thought I'd ever live to see such a thing."

"You won't do nothing about it like you didn't do nothing about Brandon."

"Shut your mouth."

"You didn't do nothing to help him."

"That's a lie."

"You only cared what folks thought of you."

"Get the hell out of here."

"Don't you worry," Milly said. "I'm gone. I'd sure rather be a whore than a fucking coward."

On the way out, she found his goddamn stash under his bed — Ziploc baggies full of pills and weed — and stuffed them into her pockets. She didn't get a half mile before she tossed the pills out on the roadside but kept the weed for herself.

7

Quinn didn't get back to the farm until late, after drinking a few beers with Lillie and Boom at the Southern Star and catching up on the local gossip and bullshit. As he hit the farmhouse, he spotted the colored Christmas lights glowing from his dad's trailer and heard music and talking as he walked through the back fields. He moved past his dead cornfields and down a well-worn path to find his dad and a young man he'd never seen before drinking clear liquid from Mason jars.

"This is Bentley," Jason Colson said. "His daddy and I go way back."

Quinn shook the young guy's hand. He had a limp, soft handshake and careless hair. He told Quinn it was a real honor to meet him and appreciated all he'd done for the country. The kid looked to be drunk on Colson moonshine.

Quinn nodded but didn't sit down.

"I taught this boy to ride at the spread in Pocahontas," Jason said. "Bentley knows horses. We've been talking about the family plans we have here for the ranch. I told him it didn't seem like much now, but after some backhoe work, this place could really be something."

"It's something now."

"I know, I know," Jason said. "But you know what I mean. Say, you want a little nip?"

Quinn shook his head. "Getting late," he said. "Just wanted to say hello and good night."

"C'mon, son," Jason said. "One drink isn't gonna kill you. I was just telling Bentley here about how many Dodge Chargers were ripped up on the *Dukes*. Damn, I wish I could've saved just one of those cars. I'd be rich, wouldn't need any help on this deal. I heard John Schneider had gotten into refurbishing. I think he sells them for nearly a hundred grand each."

"You better finish that '78 Firebird first," Quinn said.

"You bet," Jason said. "Yeah, we did most of the work at the back lot in Burbank. They shot the first five or six episodes in Georgia, but that was before I came along. The producer was impressed I came from the

South but didn't believe me when I told him I'd run shine myself. He thought I was pulling his leg. Quinn's grandfather made some of the finest stuff in north Mississippi. Damn, we gave the local sheriff hell."

"Who later became my uncle."

"Damn," Bentley said, taking another pull. "Whew. This is some good shit."

"So what do you, Bentley?" Quinn said.

"Sales," Bentley said. "I was coming up this way and my daddy told me to stop by. I hadn't seen Mr. Colson in a long while. We just been catching up and talking a little business."

Jason winked at Bentley and Bentley closed his big mouth, filling it with some more warm moonshine. Jason motioned Quinn to an empty metal chair that had been on the porch at the farmhouse the last time he'd seen it. Jason passed him the shine and Quinn smelled it before handing it back. He preferred a good aged bourbon.

"You were the sheriff here?" Bentley said.

"For a bit."

"You ever have to deal with that Hathcock woman who bought the Rebel Truck Stop?"

"After my time," Quinn said. "I've been gone most of this year. She came into the picture after Johnny Stagg went to jail."

Bentley shook his head. "Sounds like Mr.

Stagg was taking the fall for some other folks," he said. "You can't trust half of what you see in the media."

"He was convicted in a federal court," Quinn said. "He was a crook who'd grown sloppy in his company. Trust me. He was long overdue."

Bentley nodded, looking like he didn't believe a word of it. "I just heard some bad things about that Hathcock woman," he said.

"Like what?" Quinn said, finding the rest of the Cuban in his T-shirt pocket and snapping open his Zippo. The cigar cracked and burned back to life. Quinn readjusted in the seat and crossed his legs.

"Like she's running whores at the truck stop and at that old motel across the street."

Quinn gave a hard look to his father and then settled his gaze on Bentley. Quinn let some smoke out of the side of his mouth, nodding. "And how's that different from Johnny Stagg, kid?"

Jason Colson held up a hand and grinned, knowing Quinn wasn't one to back down over the subject of Stagg. The older man got to his feet and poured out what looked to be the rest of the moonshine from a plastic jug into Bentley's glass. He talked about how doing business in Hollywood was

97

a damn cakewalk compared to the folks he had to deal with back in Tibbehah County.

"I heard Hathcock used to be a whore herself," Bentley said. "Made her money on the flat of her back until gravity took her titties and closed down that cooch."

"Is that a fact?" Quinn had met a lot of boys like Bentley from Jackson and none of them had been worth a shit, either. Jason Colson just had a true and authentic knack of being drawn to money and influence and didn't give a good goddamn what kind of company he kept. Quinn figured Hollywood, California, could do that for a man.

"Whether he's a crook or not, we're going to have to reach out to Stagg," Jason said, smoothing his long gray goatee. "We're going to have to make him an offer on that old property."

"We have a lot to discuss," Quinn said to Jason Colson.

"And we need to come up with a couple more investors," Jason said. "Bentley and his daddy can help with that. And I got some other people in mind."

"Like I said, we need to talk," Quinn said.

"We got one hell of a piece of property here," Jason said, craning his neck around, looking but seeing nothing in the damn dark. "It was even better years ago, before your stupid uncle pieced it off bit by bit."

"He may have been a crook," Quinn said, "but Uncle Hamp wasn't stupid."

"Man, this shine sure is good, Mr. Colson," Bentley said, not paying attention or even listening. "You make it yourself?"

"I know this black fella down in Sugar Ditch," Jason said. "He used to work for my daddy and knows how to work the magic on the still. He has some real sweet stuff he makes for special occasions called birthday cake shine. I'll get some for you, if you like. I know your daddy appreciates a good scotch, but he ain't above his raising."

"I know he'd like that, Mr. Colson," Bentley said, getting to his feet and having to hold the rail of the chair for a little balance. "Good to see y'all. I'll talk to some folks and see what kind of interest we can get down here. Always appreciate the hospitality."

Bentley nodded at Quinn and Quinn knocked off his cigar ash with the heel of his cowboy boot. His dad took a sip of moonshine and stood to give Bentley a hug and a solid old pat on the back.

After he was gone, Quinn turned to his father.

"You taught that boy to ride?"

"Sure did," Jason said. "Got real good at it, too."

Quinn just nodded and walked back to his house, the glowing lights of the front porch welcoming him back.

"I got nowhere to go," Milly said.

"You got me," Nikki said. "You can sleep on my couch tonight. I got an entire shithole trailer I rent from my folks. We could be roomies."

"You're about busting that trailer, as it is," Milly said. "You and Jon-Jon don't need me and my crazy-ass problems busting into that single-wide."

Nikki nodded and passed the joint back to Milly, who took a long, deep drag and held it. They sat on a big pile of concrete blocks near the Gas & Go dumpsters, the Gas & Go being the only real action in Blackjack. It had closed up an hour earlier, but if you wanted to find friends and meet up, open or closed, this is where you came. On a good night, if you were lucky, the train might rush through town at two a.m.

"Wasn't that woman any help?" Nikki said. "That author in Tupelo?"

"Hell, no," Milly said. "I had to pay $29.95 for her book, too. I told her I had a story to tell and she asked me how I wanted

100

my book signed. I wanted to tell her I couldn't afford a damn book, but it was too late. There was a line behind me as we talked and it was like she wasn't even listening. Just scribbling in her shitty book. All she wanted to know is if I had made a pact with God about not having sex until I was married. You know, that's her thing. She writes something called *The Sacred Promise* series and she's up to a book now called *The Christmas Promise.* Basically, every book is about how a man keeps on trying to get his girlfriend to take off her panties, but she knows how this might really piss off Jesus. She's gotta decide between Jesus or getting laid. You got to read the whole three hundred pages until they get married and she can get nekkid. That's what keeps you flipping pages."

"Damn, Milly," Nikki said. "I'm real sorry."

"I spent the whole summer long writing in journals about things that's happened in my life," she said. "About my folks getting divorced, Daddy going to jail 'cause of the meth and shit, and what happened with Brandon. There are things that happened around here that people should know. Everybody just smiling and grinning like life is grand. The reason Daddy threw me out of his house is because I called him a coward."

"I thought he was pissed because you were dancing down at Vienna's?"

"That started it," she said. "But I don't think he would've followed through if I hadn't called his ass out. That's why he couldn't handle Momma and why he shacked up with Big Charlotte. Charlotte won't call him on nothing. You should have seen her there tonight, asking him for permission to eat potato chips. I bet he even tells that woman when and where she can take a crap."

Nikki was wearing yellow silk pj's with green flowers and plastic flip-flops. Her hair was in a short ponytail and she had on her glasses because it was late and she had already been in bed when Milly called. Milly had brought the weed and they'd smoked it up right there in the space behind the Gas & Go and the path back to Nikki's house. This had been their meeting spot since they were girls, sneaking out to drink flavored vodka, talk about boys, escape from their parents. Nikki used to escape out back regular when her parents got in fights. Milly recalling hearing the screaming and beating inside the house while Nikki pretended all was right in the world. If you don't point out the shit, then it doesn't happen. The Southern way.

"You think I'm doing right?" Milly said.

"What's that?"

"I want to get things straight before I get the hell out of here," Milly said. "Today was the most humiliating day of my life. I tried to open up to some crazy woman who thought a woman's goodies were a lockbox and then I had to give a lap dance to a sixty-year-old trucker from Meridian. He showed me pictures of his grandkids while I grinded in his lap. How fucked-up is that?"

"Pretty fucked-up," Nikki said, laughing. "Say. Pass that joint back to me. Where will you go?"

"I don't know."

"What will you do?"

"I don't know."

"But you can't stay here?"

"Why would anyone want to stay here?"

"Roots," Nikki said. "You don't want to grow 'em, but, damn, how they spread."

"You could come with me."

Nikki tried to let out the smoke cool and easy but started to giggle and it spewed from her nose. "I got a baby, a shit job, and two worthless parents to support," she said. "Tell me how to get around that?"

Just then, an old car painted a fresh metallic blue rolled up by the gas pumps. The windows were tinted, bass shaking the frame as it sat there, headlights lighting up the space where Milly and Nikki sat smoking the joint. The front license tag read HERE KITTY KITTY.

"Nito," Milly said.

"Yep," Nikki said. "Come on."

The passenger door opened and Ordeen Davis got out, smiling and pointing right at the girls. "What y'all doing, out here smoking it up in your nighties?"

It was well past one and Vienna's was closed. Fannie had done the countdown herself and stood tall on the catwalk, house lights on, staring down at the two stages around the golden poles, groupings of easy chairs, and the long wooden bar where two of the Born Losers sat drinking beer. Fannie was dog tired, sipping on a hot cup of coffee and knowing she had plenty more to do until she'd walk across the street and crash at the Golden Cherry.

Mingo walked up the stairs and Fannie kicked a fattened canvas bag toward him. The skinny Indian nodded, hefted the cash under his arm, and walked back down to the main floor. The Born Losers saw it was coming and looked up to the catwalk to give a nod and a thumbs-up to Fannie. They'd ride the cash down to the coast together and be there before dawn.

As she walked back to her office, her phone rang.

"How'd it go?" a man's voice said.

Fannie read out the totals down to the last nickel.

"Slow."

"Not the best," Fannie said. "Not the worst."

"How were the girls?"

"New girls did fine," Fannie said, sitting at her desk and grinding the heel of her hand into her eye socket. "Picked up some local talent, too."

"Had any trouble with the law?" the man said.

"Nope." Fannie said. "Are you going to call like this every night? Because it doesn't make the countdown go any faster."

"It's what you agreed."

"Are you going to tell me your name?" Fannie said. "Maybe I can talk a little dirty to you."

"Would it matter?"

"I guess not."

"You're doing fine," the man said. "We're happy with the arrangement."

"I'm so fucking glad," Fannie said. "But I

still want a meet with Mr. White."

"I don't know that name."

"Sure you do," Fannie said. "He's your goddamn boss. And he's who set me up in this shithole of the year. You tell him I need a little face time. He can meet me on tribal land or we can meet down at the coast. Doesn't matter a good goddamn to me."

"What's your trouble?"

"Tell him I just got a visit from the fucking junior Rotary Club of Jackson," she said. "Someone down there is under the impression that Johnny Stagg still runs the show and I should step right in line."

"We don't work with Stagg."

"No shit."

"I'll see what I can do."

"Good," Fannie said. "Because I got a feeling they won't be sending a kid to do a man's work next time. You tell Mr. White that?"

"Who's Mr. White?" the man said, a little coy this time.

"Son of a bitch," Fannie said. She clicked off on the phone and tossed it facedown on her desk.

"Will you open up a fucking window?" Milly said.

"Can't take it?"

"I'm so damn high, I think I'm gonna puke."

"Don't you puke," Nito said. "Not in my car."

"Slow down," she said. "Open a window. Please."

"God damn," Nito said.

Ordeen sat in the front seat, giggling, finally cracking that window a bit. It had been Ordeen's idea to hotbox after they rode the Square for an hour and then headed on back to Blackjack. He had in a Ying Yang Twins CD and then switched it out with Yo Gotti while they followed that long white highway line.

"You at your momma's?" Ordeen asked.

"Nope."

"Daddy's?" Nito asked.

"Y'all just take me back to my car at the Gas & Go. I got to work tomorrow."

"I drop Ordeen, then I drop you," Nito said. "Cool?"

Nito's eyes shifted up in the rearview to connect with Milly. Milly didn't like Nito or his staring, but she wanted to get back to her own piece of shit, find some place to park for the night, and then figure it all out in the morning. She had things needed to be done, some money to get, and then she could get free of Tibbehah County.

Ordeen lived off ReElection Road with his family, about fifty of them crowded in a dozen trailers on his granddaddy's old land. The Davis family had the nicest stretch of road in the county, as their supervisors had paved it in exchange for the whole bunch of them casting their vote on Election Day. Nito slowed the old car to a stop, turning down the music to a soft bass bump. Ordeen popped open his door, spilling smoke out into the warm night. Crickets and frogs making a racket.

"Y'all OK?"

"Cool," Nito said.

Ordeen looked to Milly and Milly nodded. He slammed the door and Nito Reece asked Milly why didn't she crawl up front with him, riding on the way back to the Gas & Go.

"I'm good."

"Come on."

"No," she said. " 'Cause you're going to try and mess with me."

"Ain't like that," Nito said. "Shit. You don't want to be seen with a black boy?"

"You know that's not true," she said. "And I just got seen with two black boys circling the Jericho Square. Who the hell's gonna see us up in Blackjack?"

"Your daddy."

"Fuck my daddy."

"Whew," Nito said. "Come on up, girl. Ain't much longer to go. We about to run out of road."

"I don't need no shit," Milly said.

"I ain't gonna give you no shit."

They rode up the curving county road, on the way to Blackjack, Yo Gotti pumping from the speakers. *I done been through it all / I done been through it all.* Milly had the window down, hot wind blowing in and washing out all that weed, air rushing against her bare arm, feeling good to breathe again, and get free of all that pressure in the club and at her daddy's house. Old ranch houses and busted trailers whizzed by, old wooden barns and brand-new metal sheds. Dogs barking in the middle of the night and deer waiting, glowing yellowed-eyed, to cross the big road.

She closed her eyes, nearly falling asleep, until the car stopped cold back at the lone Gas & Go and Nito killed the engine. He didn't wait two seconds before he'd pressed himself on her and slid his hand down into her shorts.

"Here we go, baby" he said. "Here we go. Shh."

"Get the hell off me, you son of a bitch."

"What you got?" he said. "You ain't got

nothing else, Milly Jones."

She twisted his hand away from her and reached for the door handle. As she jumped out, trying to catch her breath, Nito nearly toppled out onto the asphalt but caught himself with the flat of his hands. He smiled up at her, drunk and high, with his gold-tooth smile. "So it's like that, Cheerleader," he said.

"I never liked you, Nito," she said. "Your head is broken."

"Yeah?" Nito looked her up and down. "But you know where to find me. Won't be long."

8

Lillie drank coffee early that Wednesday morning at the Fillin' Station diner, saying hello, doing the standard meet and greet, before Boom Kimbrough showed up. He had on his blue coveralls, right arm folded and pinned to the shoulder, taking a seat across from her. "You easy to find," Boom said.

"I think I do more business here from six to eight a.m. than all day at the sheriff's department," she said. "I get tips, find out where fugitives are hiding, know about who's gotten into it with who. It's really one-stop shopping."

"You eat breakfast?"

"Not yet," she said. "Want to join me?"

"Why I'm here."

"No," Lillie said. "You're here because something's on your mind. You get a sausage biscuit every day of the world from the Sonic, along with a tall Mountain Dew. Tell me I'm lying, Boom Kimbrough."

"Hard being friends with the law."

"Hard being around folks who've known you too long," Lillie said. "What? You worried about Quinn getting in deep with his two-bit old man? I saw that shit a mile away. I never bought the notion of Jason Colson showing up here and now because he wanted to connect with his kids. You know that's bullshit, right?"

"Don't know," Boom said. "Not sure. I wanted to talk to you about something else. I had a call last night from Coach Mills."

"Hmm."

Boom nodded, but before they could continue, Miss Mary, a frizzy-headed old woman who used to shack up with old Sheriff Beckett, showed up to take their orders. Lillie wanted a fried egg, over easy, with some toast. Boom wanted a sausage biscuit and a tall Mountain Dew. He looked to Lillie as he ordered, cracking a smile.

"Can't beat a man of routine," Lillie said.

"Coach thought maybe you and I could talk through things," he said. "He said he didn't feel comfortable asking too much of you."

"But since you used to coach his linebackers, you could translate?" Lillie said. "Not to mention, you have a penis."

"Come on, Lil," Boom said. "Let's not go down that road. He just wanted to save us some trouble. He thinks if Ordeen Davis gets put into the system, he won't ever get out. I know you ain't like Hamp Beckett, thinking that every black boy running loose has trouble in mind."

"He loved you like a son."

"I was good at football," Boom said. "And I spoke his language."

"Hunting and fishing?"

"That's right."

"Ordeen is good at football," she said. "Doesn't make him a good person. He had a gun in his car. A shit ton of weed and pills."

Boom nodded. Miss Mary poured some more coffee for Lillie and set down Boom's tall glass of Mountain Dew. Lillie had set her scanner on the table. Cleotha was giving directions to a fender bender down off County Road 380 involving a truck and some loose goats. According to Cleotha, the goats were still loose and causing trouble.

"I'll let Kenny handle that one."

"Man hates goats," Boom said. "Thinks they the nastiest thing on earth."

"I know," Lillie said.

Boom leaned back into the booth, tapping his left index finger at a framed photo on the wall of *Daredevil Jason Colson* jumping a dozen Ford Pintos back in 1977. She shook her head at the sun-faded image, Colson in helmet and black jumpsuit flying high and wild back in those days. Somewhere near the cash register was another story about Quinn, only ten years old, being lost in the National Forest while Jason experienced some halcyon days out in L.A. Quinn made it through — just barely. The headline out of Memphis was COUNTRY BOY CAN SURVIVE.

"I'm not asking you to give the boy any breaks," Boom said. "I just want you to consider that Ordeen Davis is a hell of a lot like I used to be."

"How do you know that?"

"His momma's my pastor," Boom said. "I known that kid since he was born. Coach said he nearly made it to D-1 but got fucked on account of his grades. He ain't stupid, he just hadn't had the chance. Almost good enough to make it out."

"Isn't that what we're all trying to do?" Lillie said, taking a sip of hot coffee and putting it back down. "Be just damn good enough that we can all escape this purgatory."

"Gate's open," Boom said.

"Who says?"

114

"You consider going easy on Ordeen," Boom said. "Coach believes in him."

"And you believe in Coach?"

"Damn right," Boom said. "I don't know where half the boys in this county would be without him. He's a good man."

Lillie nodded as Mary set down the platters of breakfast.

"So what do y'all do out here?" Milly asked.

"Well," Caddy said. "We started out as just a church. My boyfriend wanted to build a place different than traditional churches we'd both grown up in."

The girl had just shown up that morning, wanting to know if Caddy had a place to take a shower and do some wash. She said she'd heard good things about the kind of work Caddy did and could use a little help. They stood together in the middle of the barn, where Caddy had opened up the doors to let out all the stale heated air and let some light come inside. Hay bales had been spaced out evenly on the dirt floor in place of pews.

"How's that?" Milly asked.

"He wanted it all stripped-down," Caddy said. "Back to the basics. Ole-time religion and all that. That's why we started to hold services in an old barn."

Milly looked up at the rafters and clean, unfinished walls. "Doesn't look that old to me."

"That one got burned down," Caddy said. "This is the new one, but it serves the same purpose. We have services on Wednesday night and Sunday. A lot of our members make up the band. We play everything from 'The Old Rugged Cross' to 'Ring of Fire.'"

"Cool," Milly said. "First Baptist is all into the contemporary stuff. Praise music, wanting you to raise your hands and all that. I remember one song said it was supposed to be sweet incense to your heart and that bugged me. How can your heart smell something?"

"Whatever works," Caddy said. "But that sugary stuff wasn't helping me a bit. Jamey just wanted folks to have a place that got back to the roots of things without all the bullshit. He liked good food and good music. More than anything, he wanted a place where people didn't judge each other. He didn't care what you'd done. He believed every person had the right to start over and walk in His path."

"Sounds like a good man," Milly said. "I'd like to meet him sometime."

Caddy nodded. "He died," she said. "A few years back. We're just trying to keep things going in the way he would have wanted. We got another trailer to help folks who need a place to stay. Just this summer, we added three little cabins, mostly for battered women with nowhere else to go. That big shed out back is filled with fresh and frozen food we grow here or that is donated. The Piggly Wiggly gives us some scratch-and-dent cans and such to help people supplement. It's been hard. Especially hard after the tornado."

"I don't need much," Milly said. "Just a place to shower. Get some clothes clean."

"When's the last time you ate?"

The girl shook her head. She had blonde hair, bangs cut blunt above her black eyebrows, and a mess of freckles across her pug nose. The nose was pierced with a blue stone and the back of her hair tipped with black dye. She wore a tight black T-shirt and cutoff shorts with cowboy boots. "I got your name from a girl I work with."

"Where do you work?"

"If you don't mind, I'd rather not say."

"That's fine," Caddy said. "You don't have to tell me anything."

"She said you'd helped her a few years ago," Milly said. "Said not to say her name because you might be ashamed she'd gone back into the life."

"You work at the Booby Trap?"

"They call it Vienna's now," Milly said. "Miss Fannie is trying to make the place more respectable. She's got an antique bar she bought in Kansas City and everything."

"You got a place to sleep?"

"I'm not staying here much longer," Milly said. "I'm only dancing to make enough tips to leave town."

"You know where you're going or what you'll do?" Caddy said.

Milly shook her head. She looked down at her hands, short fingers with short nails painted black. Milly chewed at a cuticle, looking out a little square window at her white Kia loaded down with probably everything she owned.

"I left here a long time ago thinking I would start over," Caddy said.

"What happened?"

Caddy smiled. "Got as far as Memphis."

"And then what?"

"And then the bottom really fell out," Caddy said. "I was up there a while. I never thought I'd live to see thirty."

"I don't know if I'll make twenty," Milly said, sort of laughing. "I used to be someone. And now I've gotten about as low as I can get. My daddy thinks I'm nothing but a whore."

"What do you think?"

"I think my daddy is a coward," she said. "I think he's just like everyone else in this rancid county, wanting to be all smiles and pats on the back and not facing the bad stuff that goes on. People around here hate when you tell the truth."

"Don't I know it."

"Your brother was the sheriff," Milly said. "Wasn't he?"

Caddy nodded, walking toward the mouth of the barn, where a little wind had kicked up. She pulled the wet T-shirt away from her body, nearly sweating through the thin white cotton that morning in the garden.

"My daddy said he was a troublemaker," Milly said. "He said that Sheriff Colson got kicked out of office because he didn't understand the law."

"That's bullshit," Caddy said. "My brother is the bravest person I've ever known."

"My daddy is good with bullshit," Milly said. "I wish I still had a brother. I got a sister and, to be honest, she's about the furthest thing from brave there is. All she does is play on her phone all day and eat Klondike Bars."

"Let's get you fed."

"Are you going to preach to me?"

"No."

"Good," Milly said. "Because I don't think Jesus can help with my troubles."

"You'd be surprised," Caddy said. "There was a time after Jamey died that I felt I had to handle everything myself. I think it was mostly about pride. I believed I was the only person who could make things right. You put too much weight on your back and it's going to break you."

"I don't want any more on my back," Milly said. "I want to take some off. And I want someone to listen to what I have to say."

"OK," Caddy said. "But how do you get that done?"

"Folks got to stand up," Milly said. "I can't carry all this mess on my own."

"I understand."

"How can you?" Milly said. "I've done some rotten things in the last year. Mainly, just for the money. Or drugs."

"Come on," Caddy said. "Let me tell you a little about myself and where I've been."

Quinn could tell his mother had been crying the moment she opened the door of his childhood home over on Ithaca Street. She wiped away the tears and told him to come on inside, she was just making a pimento cheese sandwich for Little Jason and would be glad to make some more. Quinn told her he'd appreciate that and she snapped open a bottle of Coke and sat it on top of the kitchen table.

"What's the matter?"

"It's just so sad," Jean Colson said. "So damn sad."

Quinn knew. He'd heard it a hundred times. But he knew all he could do is agree with her.

"You see it in Charley Hodge's face when he brings out his guitar," Jean said. "He knows how much Elvis is hurting. He stands there by his side, not knowing if he'll be able to get through 'Are You Lonesome Tonight?' They knew it was the end. They always did."

"I thought you weren't going to watch those last concerts anymore," Quinn said. "Elvis looks terrible. He sounds terrible."

Jean turned around from the sink counter where she was cutting his sandwich and pointed the end of the knife at her son. "Hush," she said. "He was putting his soul into those last few performances. The last concert, the one that was on that CBS Special, shows him hitting those high notes on 'Unchained Melody.' That's a very difficult song."

"Momma?" Quinn said.

Jean looked to him. He pointed to the knife in her hand. And she looked down at the blade, glinting in the light. "Oh," she said. She set the sandwich in front of him and called to Little Jason, who was in the family room on the same couch Quinn had played on growing up. He bounded into the room and gave Quinn a hug, wanting to know if he wanted to play some video games. "Maybe we can get that Call of Duty?"

Quinn looked over his shoulder to Jean and smiled. She smiled back. "Not until you're twelve," she said. "Besides, your uncle's played that game plenty."

Quinn ate some of the sandwich, Jean Colson never short on talent in the kitchen. She added something to the pimento cheese making it smokier and richer than anything he'd ever tasted. She'd won two local awards for it but refused to share the recipe. Jean was good at keeping secrets. Served with a side of Golden Flake chips and bread-and-butter pickles.

"Good?"

"Yes, ma'am."

"Good to have some real cooking?"

"Food's not bad in Afghanistan," Quinn said. "I kind of miss it. My favorite was this *qabuli pulao.*"

"What's that?"

"Qabuli pulao," Quinn said. "It's made with lamb, rice, raisins, and carrots. It's their national dish. Good stuff."

"Better than my meat loaf?"

Quinn looked to Little Jason, Little Jason stifling a giggle, as neither of the Colson boys were fans of her meat loaf. But Quinn just smiled and said, "No, ma'am. Just can't compete."

Jean finished washing off the utensils and the cutting board and came up to the table, taking a seat, still drying her hands. Jean, like Quinn, had a face of sharp angles and prominent cheekbones, but with much lighter coloring than her son. Her eyes were a bright blue that matched her pale skin, and her red hair that once was natural was now colored. She had on faded mom jeans and a flowered shirt open at the collar, a gold cross on a chain around her neck. "Everything all right on the farm?"

"Yes, ma'am."

"Your father still not paying you any rent?"

"I didn't ask him."

"Well," Jean said. "He should. If he had any pride 'bout himself."

Quinn finished the last bite of sandwich and pushed the plate away. He'd known by

123

coming over to his mom's house, he'd soon
be talking about the original Jason Colson.
He just didn't think it would've happened
so fast.

"I hear he's thinking of opening up some
kind of dude ranch," Jean said. "You two
being partners."

Little Jason was drinking a big glass of
milk and his big light eyes looked up to
Quinn over the glass. Quinn asked his mom
if they might discuss farm business a little
later.

"Jason, baby," Jean said. "Why don't you
run into the living room and find Grandmomma's cigarettes?"

Jason bounded out, always happy to ditch
his lunch and have a challenge.

"Your cigarettes are on the counter,"
Quinn said.

Jean smiled. She folded her hands in front
of her.

"What you're hearing is just talk," Quinn
said. "I haven't agreed to do anything."

"Well," Jean said. "I certainly hope not.
Your father is playing around with something that isn't his."

Quinn knew this part was coming, had
expected it after talking with Caddy. Beckett
land, now being in the family for a hundred
and twenty years, was some serious busi-

ness. Jean had grown up on the farm, her father — the old farmer — had, too, and so on. They'd worked that land since they'd cleared it in 1895.

"I don't like it."

"The only consideration is what will happen to the farm while I'm gone," Quinn said. "It would be nice to have a caretaker. That place can grow wild quick."

"Then set something up with Boom," Jean said. "I'm sure he'd be happy to stay out at the farm and look after Hondo and the cattle while you're gone."

"He doesn't mean anything by it," Quinn said. "It's just Daddy's way, you know?"

"Better than you," Jean said. Little Jason bounded into the room and said he couldn't find her cigarettes or her lighter anywhere. "That's OK, baby. Go watch a little TV. *Andy Griffith Show* is about to come on."

"What about Uncle Quinn?" Little Jason said. "Are we gonna play?"

"Just a second, sir," Quinn said. He waited until the boy had left and then turned back to his mother. "I have other things on my mind right now. I can let him dream all he wants. He can't get the money anyway."

"What's he need money for?" she said. "You own it outright."

"He wants to buy the parcels Uncle Hamp

sold off to Johnny Stagg."

"Why?"

"For more pasture," Quinn said. "Riding trails. But it doesn't matter. You and I both know Stagg's got nothing better to do than hold that land hostage."

"So if you're not worried about your daddy," Jean said, "then what?"

"The future."

"What of it?"

Quinn stood up, walked to the old coffeepot plugged into the wall, and poured out a cup. There was always hot coffee at his mother's house. He sat back down and looked at his boots for a moment and then lifted his eyes back to his mom. He nodded, sure now he should tell someone. "I want to ask Anna Lee to marry me," he said. "I take this next job and I'll be back in the spring. We could think on how to move forward then."

Jean nodded, reached for the gold cross on her neck, and played with it back and forth on the chain. She took in a long, deep breath and Quinn waited. A warm breeze blew through the room, knocking a vase of flowers off the sill, glass breaking and water pouring to the floor.

"Let me get that," Jean said.

9

Milly made it to the Wednesday night service just in time to hear Pastor Zeke Traylor let everyone know, who hadn't heard it already, that man doesn't live by bread alone. "God's word is alive and sharper than a two-edged sword," Traylor said. "The Psalms of David tells us that thy word is a lamp upon my feet and a light unto my path to see where I'm going clearly."

Traylor spoke more laid-back on a weeknight, the old man wearing a blue golf shirt and khaki pants, casual for a man who seemed to be born wearing a suit. His hair was white as Christmas snow and he had on the same bright, round gold glasses she'd seen him wear her whole life. When he really wanted to make a point, he softened his words, making you strain to hear the whisper. "You hear what I'm saying?" And when folks nodded along because what the hell else could you do, he'd say, "Amen." And things would continue on and on like that. On and on.

It had been a while since Milly had shown her face at the Jericho First Baptist. A couple folks craned their head around to make sure it was really her. *That girl.* She'd taken a seat in the back row, a place she'd always preferred since her parents insisted on sharing the same church after the divorce. Her daddy and Charlotte's fat ass sat on the right side of the sanctuary at First Baptist and her momma and sister on the left. As the song wound down to the last note, Traylor said, "Lift him up. Lift him up. Slam the devil!"

Traylor dropped to one knee, battered old Bible in his right hand, and began to pray that the church would be a light on Jericho's Main Street, the congregation a light to all those lost, and each member a light to family and friends who'd lost their way. Words filled up the big screen again and the dozen folks who made the service sang: *Lord, I sing your praises. I'm so glad you're in my life.* The written words scrolled over a video of a car driving down a long, twisty road. Nothing but blue skies and green mountains. A couple folks raised their palms high. Pastor Traylor sang off-key about how Jesus came

128

from heaven to earth to show us the way. Milly bowed her head and hoped they'd be wrapping things up real soon because Reverend Traylor was her last damn hope. She prayed that the old man would come through.

Come on, Milly said silently. *Jesus H. Christ.* Come on.

Despite their differences, several interventions that didn't go so well, and a failed attempt to get her to date a pimply-faced grandson from Pontotoc, she believed Traylor was on the side of right. After the sermon, a few more big-screen gospel tunes, and a call to the leaders of this God-less country to seek His wisdom, Traylor stepped down from the sacred red carpet of the pulpit with old dog-eared Bible in hand.

He invited everyone to join him in the events room for chocolate chip cookies and homemade punch before spotting Milly. "I don't believe it," Pastor Traylor said. "Our own little lost sheep."

Milly wanted to quote the Bible about how the shepherd should've been out looking for that goddamn sheep. But she kept her mouth shut and smiled. She'd even worn a simple summer dress to church that night. She hadn't worn a dress in two years.

"I need to talk, Pastor."

"Yes, ma'am," Pastor Traylor said. "But how about some cookies first?

"You mind if we skip the damn cookies and punch?" she said. "I ain't in the mood."

Milly turned to watch the last of the parishioners head out the front doors. With a lot of effort, Pastor Traylor sat down on the carpeted steps and motioned for Milly to join him down on the floor. It was just like the kids' sermon he delivered every Sunday, spoken seated from the steps in words even the simplest child could understand. *Jesus was the shepherd. The kids were the sheep. Stay on the path and don't get lost.* Milly straightened her short skirt over her tan legs and wondered if Pastor Traylor ever spoke about young sheep working that pole.

"Yes, ma'am?"

"I don't even know where to begin," she said. "Things are real messed-up."

"I know some of it," Traylor said. "Your daddy and I have been praying for you."

"Is that a fact?"

"Drugs can warp a young mind," he said. "Boys, too. Lead you to do things you never imagined. But you never get too low for Jesus. Jesus will lift you up."

"This ain't about me, Pastor," she said. "It's about what happened with Brandon."

Pastor Traylor took off his golden glasses, blew a hot breath on the lenses, and cleaned them with a white hankie from his shirt pocket. His old skin was real white and sagged at the neck. His eyes were the clearest blue, and he smelled of old hymnals, musty old coloring books, and something sugary sweet. He'd always had that smell about him — peppermint candy and the Word of God.

"Your family's been to hell and back," he said. "When someone makes a decision to end their own life, it can be the most selfish thing they've ever done. They don't think about everyone they're leaving behind."

"You think Brandon had a choice?"

"God gives us free will," he said. "We all have choices."

"I don't blame him," Milly said. "We all know he was exposed to things that no young boy should ever know. He got saddled with all that sickness and he didn't have nowhere to run."

"He was a very confused young man."

"You didn't believe him?"

Pastor Traylor swallowed hard and put the glasses back on, lenses still smudged with a fat thumbprint at the edge. He smiled real wide, showing off those thick yellowed veneers. "He did a lot of finger-pointing in this town," he said. "But he never looked on himself and saw things he might've made different."

Milly looked at the pastor's old grandfatherly face and saw it as a hollowed-out, saggy mask. She stared into his unblinking clear blue eyes and said, more to herself than him, "You're the same as the rest, aren't you? You know but don't care."

"Come on, Miss Milly," he said. "Leave your burden with Him. Let's pray on it. But I want you to leave that burden your brother left right here and now."

"It ain't no burden," she said. "It's more of what I call a responsibility."

The pastor reached for her small hands, held one close, and closed his eyes. "Lord, Lord, Lord."

"You know," she said. "Don't you? That man is real sick?"

"Good Lord," Pastor Traylor said. "Let's pray for Milly and her family. Let's pray for forgiveness and healing."

Milly stood up on the steps where she'd heard all the good stories about Jacob and his coat of many colors, Moses lost in the bulrushes, and Jesus walking on water. Every kids' sermon had a purpose, a moral lesson, to be learned. She'd never heard a story about shutting your mouth in the face of true evil.

"I'm letting it all out."

"Milly," Pastor Traylor said, still seated. "I'd be careful. A bunch of tall tales could hurt a lot of folks in this town."

"You think I really give a shit, Pastor?"

Pastor Traylor licked his old dry lips and shook his head. "And coming from you," he said, "after the places you been, they won't be heard any more than a dry summer wind."

Milly watched the old man use two hands to get back on his busted-up old knees and stand, clutching his old Bible under a frail arm. A fat woman in a pink jumpsuit came to the door and called out, wondering if everything was OK. "Can I bring y'all some cookies and punch?"

The fat woman grinned brightly as Milly brushed past her, halfway down the aisle, and then turned back. The preacher watched and waited. The fat woman kept on grinning.

Milly lifted her middle finger to Pastor Zeke Traylor and slammed the church doors behind her. Somewhere inside the sanctuary, the fat woman gasped.

"I think we just broke that chair," Quinn

said, searching for his blue jeans and cowboy boots.

"Good," Anna Lee said. "It belonged to Luke's grandmother. I always hated those damn things."

"You don't feel guilty?"

"About what?" she said. "Serving a purpose other than just collecting dust in this big old drafty house."

"I thought you loved this old house."

Anna Lee walked into the foyer, where Quinn was getting back into his clothes. She still had on a short black T-shirt but had lost pretty much the rest of it in the rush. They didn't have long until her mother would be bringing her daughter Shelby home for the night. Anna Lee shook her head, finding one of Quinn's stray boots and tossing it over to him. "Not anymore," she said. "It's so damn big and empty. I hate the sounds it makes when I walk."

Quinn watched her as she got her cutoffs. "Lillie offered me a temporary job," Quinn said. "Says I can get on the payroll until I make a decision on heading back overseas."

"Take it," she said. "And then look for something else. With your Army training, people will be lining up to hire you."

"You think?"

"I do," Anna Lee said. "I know some folks

in Memphis and Oxford you should meet."

"No thanks."

"You'd rather go back to the other side of this earth and have people shoot at you?"

"I guess it wouldn't be bad to make a little extra," he said. "Especially if you hate living so much in this big old drafty house so much."

"After being sheriff," she said, "how would that feel?"

"Like a paycheck," Quinn said.

"You don't mind working for Lillie?"

"Why?" he said. "She's more suited for the job than me. Always has been."

"Lillie has a temper," Anna Lee said. "She blows up quick. That's what scares folks. There is being direct. And then there is Lillie Virgil's way."

"I'm well aware," Quinn said. "She say something to you?"

"I saw her the other day at the Piggly Wiggly," Anna Lee said. "She told me to either quit fucking with your head and get married or go ahead and let you go free."

"We need to talk."

"Can you do something for me?"

"Whatever you want," Quinn said.

"I want you to be part of my life," she said. "My world. I want you to know my friends. Drive up to Oxford with me this

135

fall before you leave. I want to show you off."

Anna Lee disappeared for a moment and rejoined Quinn, fully dressed, on the front porch of the Victorian, which sat up on a low rolling hill looking down on Jericho. It was late evening and that big orange sun going down lit up the storefront windows, the water tower casting a long shadow through the green town Square.

"OK," Anna Lee said. "Talk. But just promise me you won't say anything you don't mean or that you really don't want to do. I've made too many mistakes in this life already. I don't think either of us wants to go down a wrong road."

"I don't know who called you," Fannie Hathcock said, "but I promise you, Miss Virgil, that we're conducting business as we always do. We adhere to all county ordinances."

"*Sheriff* Virgil," Lillie said. "And there aren't any Tibbehah County ordinances on nude dancing. We just have the unspoken rule that y'all do business in this fucking barn, but don't let it spill out into the parking lot. But now I'm hearing things might've changed and your girls are dishing it out in the open."

Fannie Hathcock tipped a long brown cigarette, checking out Lillie from head to toe. Lillie didn't care for the appraisal or being called up to Fannie's office instead of Fannie coming down to meet Lillie at the bar, where she'd been invited. She also didn't like not being addressed as "Sheriff" — she got enough of that bullshit in town. Lillie looked over at Deputy Reggie Caruthers, who'd rode along with her, and nodded at him.

"Nice place," he said.

"You're welcome anytime, deputy," Fannie said. "But as far as the law, I don't know anything about my girls 'dishing it out.'"

"Come on," Lillie said. "Y'all show the goods up on the great lit stage and then blow it or throw it out in the cabs. I don't mind you arguing about the finer points of the law, but let's not spew bullshit on what kind of business this is."

"Did you have these kind of arguments with Mr. Stagg?"

"Johnny T. Stagg?" Lillie said. "Bet your ass, Miss Hathcock. He was an A-1 shit-bag."

Lillie could tell the Hathcock woman wasn't used to being addressed so directly. She looked like a true madam of means, in a red silk top, black flared trousers, and patent leather slingbacks. Her makeup job looked expert and expensive, seeming to Lillie like something out of a high-fashion magazine. The woman was well into her forties but well preserved, with possibly a little work on the face and definitely a lot on her titties.

"Why'd you tear down the Booby Trap sign?" Lillie said. "Nothing like truth in advertising."

"I thought it sounded rough and vulgar."

"Why'd you call it Vienna's?" Lillie said. " 'Cause of the sausages?"

"My grandmother," Fannie said, exhaling a little smoke. "She was a fine old Southern lady."

"You mind me asking you a direct question, Miss Hathcock?" Lillie said.

"No, ma'am," she said. "Go ahead and shoot, Sheriff."

"Just how did you get this place free of Johnny Stagg?" Lillie said. "I always figured we'd have to drag him out of here feetfirst."

Fannie let out a little smoke from the corner of her mouth. She tilted her head in thought and said, "I don't think Mr. Stagg had many financial options, from where he was sitting. And I was looking to get out from where I was."

"Indian land?"

"I managed a few things for the Nation."

"Bless your heart," Lillie said.

Reggie Caruthers looked to his boss and swallowed hard. He looked like he'd very much like to get the hell out of there. Downstairs, girls were working the pole at the lunchtime shift, sweaty, naked bodies hopped up on barstools, and big boobies flopping wild. Reggie was a good man, but all the sweaty summer flesh was a bit too much for him to handle.

"Appreciate you dropping by."

"Keep your business inside this barn," Lillie said. "I don't want to be riding your ass every day."

"We operate a nice clean joint with nice clean girls."

"I really don't give a shit how you view things," Lillie said. "I just don't want a bunch of whores advertising on my streets. You got me?"

"Damn, you are a straight shooter, aren't you?"

"Good night, Miss Hathcock," Lillie said. "Don't make me come out here again."

10

"Y'all close that door and come on in," Coach Bud Mills said. *"Come on. Come on. I ain't gonna bite."*

Ordeen waited for Nito to walk on ahead and then closed The Cage door shut behind them. The Cage was where the coach kept all the football equipment, helmets, shoulder pads, and shit, and the managers did the wash. Coach always had a mess of young boys running around picking up dirty jerseys and pants, turning it around for the next day. The back room always smelled like sweat and piss, funky as hell.

"You boys doing all right?" Coach asked Ordeen.

Ordeen nodded. Coach had a brand-new helmet he was tinkering with, adding on a short face mask and the growling Wildcats sticker on the sides. Tomorrow night's home jerseys sat in a big pile on a center table, washed and folded and ready for the locker room. Socks, compression shorts, elbow pads. The Wildcats' colors of yellow and black, same as Southern Miss.

"Yes, sir."

"Don't you worry about that bond," Coach said. "That's on me. We'll get this crap taken care of. The sheriff is fighting me some. But the DA will drop all that shit. He's a supporter."

"Yes, sir."

"How about you, Nito?" Coach said. "You gonna speak or you just gonna let Ordeen here hold your flaming pile of dog shit?"

"What?" Nito said, snapping his head around.

"I said, I know who owned that peashooter and I know who's running drugs in this county," he said. "Since all those arrests, looks like you've turned into a real business-man."

Nito looked at Coach and rubbed his goatee. "Naw, man," he said. "You ain't hearing right."

"I ain't your man," Coach said, poking Nito straight and hard in the breastbone with a long finger. "I may not be your coach no more. But you sure as shit call me Coach. You understand, son? You want to get smart and me, you, and Ordeen can talk about fairness and the way the world works.

No man needs to be holding on to your fuckup, Nito Reece."

"Yes, sir," Nito said, smirking some. "Coach, sir."

Coach nodded his old grayed head, belly sagging over his tight black shorts. He had on old-school white socks rolled up to his fat knees and a pair of Nikes so out-of-date, they looked older than Ordeen's momma. He hadn't shaved that morning and white stubble grew on his saggy cheeks. "OK," Coach said. "I did for you two knuckleheads. So what are y'all gonna do for me?"

"What you mean?" Ordeen said.

"I already got something for you, Ordeen," he said. "Don't you worry about that. I want you to meet me at six a.m. this Saturday. We'll have a lot of work to do on the field after the game. I'll feed you breakfast and lunch. And I'll want you to do the same for me again in two weeks. And a week after that. You got me?"

"Yes, Coach."

Nito crossed his arms over his chest, standing sure-footed in wide-legged jeans shorts and a V-neck white Walmart tee. Overhead caged lights glinted off his gold teeth. He was smiling big as shit, waiting for what crazy-ass stuff Coach was going to be asking of him. Nito wouldn't have any of it. He still blamed the coach for kicking him off the team just for posting some crazy shit up on YouTube. It was just for fun, about smoking a blunt and waving around that pistol. All a big joke.

"Ordeen?" Coach said. "How 'bout you give me a minute with Mr. Nito Reece? Me and him got to have a little heart-to-heart."

Milly and Damika hit center stage at Vienna's to Damika's anthem, "Bottom of the Map" by Young Jeezy. Damika explaining to Milly that the song was spot-on when you worked that pole down in Jericho, Mississippi. Milly did a handstand and then slid right into bending over, her tight little ass facing three men who'd just walked into the bar. Damika was shaking that rump like nobody's business, bouncing that big ole black girl booty like Milly could never imagine. Milly had on a Rebel Truck Stop tee, pulled up tight and tied high, with red bikini bottoms, while Damika was buck-ass nekkid. Girl just didn't care.

It was the first time she noticed the scrolled tattoos on the girl's rib cage. It looked to be the drawn cartoon heads of two babies. *I'm on fire, kid's outta control. Competition wants me to stop, drop, and roll.*

Milly shimmied up close to the pole and

jumped up as high as she could go, grabbing hold and then flipping her heels up over her head and clamping tight with her legs, letting her hands and arms go and slowly twirling down to earth. A couple bucks flew up onstage. A fat man in overalls and a trucker's hat whistled and hooted. She jumped up again, grabbed the pole tight with only one hand this time, and twirled and twirled, feeling the greased metal beneath her fingers. And something she hadn't felt in a long time: her own damn strength. She could spin herself around and around, holding right with that one arm. She inverted herself, locking on with both hands, kicking her legs out to the side and looking up, spotting Fannie on the catwalk staring down as she worked, the music pumping from the speakers, the other truckers coming up to the island and showering that lit stage with money.

Milly moved a bit, stroked the pole up and down, and collected the money. When the new song hit, she shimmied all the way up, scissoring her legs straight out, inverting, and then grabbing hold with the crook of her legs, sprawling her chest and arms out, stretched all the hell out, staring up at the bright lights of the club. Power and strength never felt so good.

When the song was over, she got down to her knees for all the loose cash and tried sharing it with Damika. Damika took a handful but told her that the cash belonged to her. "I ain't never seen no white girl spin like that."

"I knew I could do this," she said. "It's just gymnastics. The pole just running sideways. I really like it."

"Don't get fucked-up when you do it," Damika said. "You spin too much and you puke on the customers. That way, ain't no one gets paid."

After five, Vienna's really filled up. A crew of frat boys had come over from Ole Miss in a busted-ass church van and some cowboys from Kosciusko had gathered at the old bar. The cowboys from Kosciusko wore work boots and Carhartt pants caked with mud. But they carried big fat pockets full of money and knew how to tip. One of them, back in the Champagne Room, whispered to Milly that they'd just dropped off fifty head of cattle at the meat processing plant in Tupelo. The man was drunk and wanted to know if anyone ever told her she looked just like Britney Spears's little sister, Jamie Lynn?

"I used to get that," she said.

Not two hours into her shift and she'd

pulled in nearly a thousand dollars. Milly Jones had never seen that much money in her life, keeping wads of it in her two garters and the rest in the little pink purse. For the second time that night, she flattened out about two hundred dollars on the old bar, the bartender bringing her bottled water, while she caught her breath. When she got called back to the stage, she looked up high on the catwalk and saw Miss Fannie staring down and watching.

The song kicked on and she got back to work. If she got a little more, maybe she could get gone for good.

"She's gone," Wash Jones said. "Left here two nights ago and ain't seen her since."

"Did y'all have a falling-out?" Lillie asked.

"Of a sort."

"You mind if I ask you to expand upon that, Mr. Jones?"

"Well," Wash said. "That's a bit of a personal nature. I don't think we need to get into all that mess."

"You're the one who called me and wanted to meet because you were so worried about your daughter," Lillie said. "You told dispatch that you were concerned some physical harm might come to her soon if she can't be found."

"Oh, well," Wash said. "Damn."

Lillie stood outside the ranch house in Blackjack, where Wash had waited in pajama pants and no shirt next to his brand-new blue Chevy Silverado. He knew she was coming and hadn't seen fit to put on proper clothes. His belly was so big, he looked like he might explode any minute. Man couldn't put on pants but wore a .44 Magnum belt around his waist.

"I think she done lost her mind," Wash said.

"Come again?"

"Milly," he said. "She's on the drugs. I seen pills in her things. And she's been dancing at the Booby Trap, showing off her cooch, spinning on that pole."

"OK," Lillie said. "But do you think she's missing?"

"Yes, ma'am," he said. "I sure do. Hell, I can't find her."

"And you think it's because she's been living a risky lifestyle?"

"Damn straight," he said. "Just last year, she started dating a black boy. I guess it's true what they say."

"What's that."

"Well," he said. "You know. About dating them blacks and not wanting to go back."

"I'm sorry, I don't," Lillie said, even

147

though she did. She just took a moment to look at the fat man in the pajama bottoms scratching his nuts in the gravel driveway. Worried, but not that worried. Wash Jones just seemed pissed-off and wanting to make some trouble. Lillie followed along, took some notes. She'd write up a report later. Maybe send out a patrol to Vienna's.

"Why do you think your daughter is missing?" Lillie said.

"Listen, Miss Virgil," Wash Jones said. "I knew Sheriff Beckett real good. I got a lot of years draining the shit tanks of our so-called respectable citizens. I think I'm afforded some goddamn respect when my wild hare daughter done took off."

"All I'm asking," Lillie said, taking a deep breath and thinking on control, "is why do you think something's gone wrong? I can't imagine why a young lady would want to leave the care of such a fine man as yourself."

"You trying to get smart with me?"

"How about you show me both your hands," Lillie said. "That's right. Quit scratching your goddamn nuts and look me in the eye and tell me why you're worried. Give me something to go on."

"I don't like the sound of that."

"I really don't give a good goddamn, Wash

148

Jones," she said. "But let's look to your daughter. I'll find her, I'll let you know."

"She's a good girl," he said. "Or she was. Until she became a whore."

Lillie stared at the shirtless fat man, too damn lazy to change out of pajamas at one in the afternoon. She shook her head over the shame of it.

"She ain't even eighteen," he said. "Wild as a March hare."

"Nice."

"Sex," he said. "She's popping pills and laying with all kind of men."

"You think she's working out back of the Rebel?"

"She's got a little white Kia," he said.

"OK."

"She left two nights back," he said. "She ain't got no money. She told me to go and fuck myself and then destroyed some of my personal property. Things she ain't got no business messing with."

"What were they?"

"Me and her got into it," he said. "You hear me? We done got into it because of her shaking those titties."

"At Vienna's."

"What's that?"

"What used to be the Booby Trap."

"OK," he said. "Yeah. All right then. Girl

don't got no sense."

"Come again?"

"I said, girl got no sense," Wash said. "Shit. She's gonna go and get herself kilt. Why don't you just go do your gosh-dang job and bring her ass back home."

"Hard to imagine why she ever left," Lillie said.

"What'd Coach want?" Ordeen said.

"Oh, man," Nito said. "Just talking shit. You know, 'Yes, sir / No, sir' shit. Wants me to do something for him."

Ordeen and Nito were back in the electric-blue Nova, circling the Jericho town Square, waving to a couple cute girls in halter tops sitting under an old oak tree, gunning the motor at a couple city boys who needed to show respect. Nito circled three times and then hit Main Street north, heading on back to ole Blackjack.

"What's he want you to do?"

"I don't know," Nito said. "Just some dumb shit. He's been getting some trouble from some folks. He thinks I might be able to straighten it out. He knew all about what we been up to around Tibbehah. He also said he doesn't want me hanging with you. Ain't that something?"

"What'd you tell Coach?"

"I told Coach that's your decision, not mine," Nito said. "I told him I'd help him with his troubles, for not fucking me on that gun charge. He was about to call up the law and make sure they knew that pistol was mine. He said he'd make sure he got you a lawyer and pinned all that on my ass."

"I wouldn't do that."

"I know that," Nito said. "But ole Coach thinks you still his boy. He think he blow that whistle and you come running like a dog. Trained, obedient, come to him with you tongue hanging out. Ready to lick that ass."

"Fuck you, man," Ordeen said.

"Ha, ha," Nito said. "Damn. Maybe I come out on Saturday and watch you lay down them white lines. I'll sit up in the stands and cheer you on. I'll be smoking a blunt and eating a big-ass Super Sonic and some tots. Crack open some Aristocrat vodka and pour it into cherry limeade."

"Coach Mills is all right," Ordeen said. "Don't make no trouble. You make trouble for him and he can't help me. He done a lot for kids who don't have nobody. Including your sorry ass."

"Sorry, man," Nito said, punching the gas on the old blue Nova, crooked back highway flying by as they left city limits. "You right.

Coach is a damn winner." He fired up the rest of a blunt and let down the window. Nothing but warm breezes and the last of summer days, an endless white line of road.

"We cool?" Ordeen said.

"We cool."

Milly sat in the toilet stall and counted out the final tips from a half-dozen lap dances. She had close to sixteen hundred, give or take a few bucks. Damn. This would do it. Fill up the Kia, get far from this town, and get a clean start. She'd leave everything she had with the police — the old phone, those notes — and let them figure it all out. She couldn't live like this, with no one wanting to listen and no one wanting to help. Out of respect for Brandon, she'd try one more time.

"Whew," Milly said, packing the money tight as hell into the purse. She left out a hundred to make sure it looked like she was giving her tip-out. Most in small bills. If it pissed anyone off, what the hell were they gonna do? She was done with this fucking town.

Milly opened the stall door and walked back to her locker. The old white stripper and Damika were changing into their street clothes. They looked at each other and then over at Milly. But neither of them opened their mouths. Both of them staring like they knew what Milly was about to do.

"You did real good," Damika said. "Damn, you shoulda seen that girl work that pole. Girl's got talent."

"I saw it," the woman said. "Where'd you learn all that? You said you'd never danced before."

"Gymnastics," Milly said. "I did some cheerleading in high school."

"No shit," Damika said, popping some chewing gum. "Huh."

"Well, good night."

"Girl?" the white woman said.

Milly turned at the changing room door and looked back.

"Don't you forget to tip out," the old stripper said, eyeing her.

Milly nodded, clutching that little pink purse even tighter than ever, and headed through the big barn of a building and to the front door and that last light outside. As she passed the main stage and the long old-fashioned bar, she looked up to see the glowing orange tip of Miss Fannie's little cigar in a big cloud of smoke.

It burned bright and then went dark. Milly rushed outside.

"Did you see that?" Fannie said, arms resting on the high railing.

"Yes, ma'am," Mingo said. He had his slick black hair in a ponytail, doing the whole Geronimo thing.

"One of 'em starts this shit and it never ends."

"You want me to get Lyle?"

"You know where he is?" Fannie said.

"Sleeping it off at the Golden Cherry," Mingo said. "I saw him fixing that old Shovelhead this morning."

"Follow that little bitch and see what she's driving," Fannie said. "Then go get Lyle and a couple boys to track her down and bring me my goddamn money back. Did you see all that shit she was doing on the pole?"

"That little girl got some talent."

"Too bad this is her last damn night," Fannie said. "Go on and bring her ass back here."

11

"Good night for a football game," Lillie said. "Want some popcorn?"

Quinn took a handful as he sat right next to Lillie. Lillie would stand up every so often and greet someone in the stands. She'd gained a much easier way with people since he'd been gone, knowing she'd have to lose a little roughness if she wanted to stay sheriff. A few people wanted to shake Quinn's hands, while others looked away. Those had been the ones who'd voted him out of office, believing all the lies being spread by Johnny T. Stagg.

"You remember Wash Jones?" Lillie said.

"Sure," Quinn said. "He used to be the right-hand man of Brother Davis, emptying septic tanks, before Davis got hung on the cross by our old friend Gowrie."

"You know, he about killed his first wife," Lillie said. "I believe Hamp made some adjustments to the original reports."

155

"Sounds like something he'd do," Quinn said. "Since Brother Davis was in tight with Stagg."

"While you were gone and I'd just come back from Memphis, we caught Wash cooking a little meth," Lillie said. "Wasn't much. But he should've gone to jail."

"And, instead, my uncle made some adjustments."

Lillie nodded. "Yep."

The marching band took the field for the National Anthem. Quinn and Lillie stood up together, both placing a ball cap over the heart. After the final off-note of the kid playing trumpet, the crowd cheered, the band left the field, and the boys gathered around Coach Mills for the final pep talk.

"What exactly is ole Bud Mills saying?"

" 'Remember your assignments,' " Quinn said. " 'Take it to them hard and fast.' 'Everything full-speed.' 'No half-assed.' All that kind of stuff."

"Same as with you and Boom."

"Football hasn't changed," Quinn said. "Or Coach Mills."

"I never liked him," Lillie said, offering the popcorn bag to Quinn. "He hates women."

"C'mon, Lil," Quinn said. "The man's been married forty years."

"Probably hates her, too," Lillie said. "Jesus Christ, would you please look behind you? Son of a bitch. I do think Kenny would fuck up his own funeral."

Quinn looked over the edge of the bleachers to see traffic backed up a quarter mile from the grassy area by the stadium used as the parking lot. The bleachers were half-filled, most of Jericho still sitting in traffic.

"You put Kenny on traffic detail?"

"It's Friday night," Lillie said. "Not a lot of folks volunteering for the job."

"Kenny's a good man," he said. "But, damn, he does get flustered."

"I got Reggie Caruthers working down there, too," she said. "But he's new. He's just following Kenny's lead. I'm still running two deputies low. I have interviews all next week and I need to fill 'em fast."

Quinn followed Lillie down the bleacher steps and back down the ramp to the front gate and the ticket takers. She was saying a few choice words to Kenny over the police radio about him backing up traffic all the way to Memphis. Quinn heard her use the term *clusterfuck* about four times. He followed her out into the weedy parking lot, where she'd parked her Jeep. The lights bloomed bright in fading August light as the crowd cheered and yelled and clapped at the kickoff.

"Son of a bitch," Lillie said. "You know who's gonna take the blame? Hard to live in a town where you only have one goddamn show. Someone messes up that show and shit will roll right back on me."

"Lillie?" Quinn said.

She looked to him, hand resting on the open door, straining her ear to hear Kenny's reply on radio about how everyone in the whole gosh-dang world started coming to the game at the same time and something about an accident back on 201.

"I want to come back."

"Come back?"

"To work," Quinn said. "I don't want to leave before the first of the year. I have some personal matters to clear up. Caddy and my dad could use some help getting settled and I need to start looking at some long-term work in Mississippi."

Lillie grinned and nodded. "The hours are lousy," she said. "But the pay's not worth shit."

"Don't sweet-talk me."

"I'd be proud to have you back, Quinn," Lillie said. "I need help. But as your friend, I don't want to see you screwing up the rest of your life."

"I'd only want some part-time work,"

Quinn said. "You can keep the personal advice to yourself."

"Don't let her domesticate you, Quinn," Lillie said. "A dog ain't worth a shit once you take its balls."

Quinn just shook his head and walked away. He saw his mother up by the ticket takers with Little Jason. The band started to play, more cars and trucks drifting in with Kenny winding his arms like a clock and motioning toward the lot with a light stick. Headlights bumping up and down as they hit the uneven patch of ground.

"Monday morning," Lillie said, calling out to his back.

Over his shoulder, Quinn raised an index finger and pointed forward.

Lyle was tough and loyal, but sure wasn't much to look at. Fannie wasn't fond of his smell, either, but with the motel door open, a cigarillo burning in the ashtray, she could endure it. He had on nut-hugging blue jeans and a black leather vest without a shirt. He'd walked in the door carrying a pair of sloppy biker boots, his feet wet from dipping them in the pool. A black beard hung down to mid-chest, held in a tight wad by a bunch of rubber bands.

"She lives with her daddy and some fat

woman up in Blackjack," Lyle said. "I talked with one of the girls. She's just a kid. I'd take it easy on her."

"It's not your fucking money, Lyle," Fannie said. "What if one of the Southern Cross boys rode on over here to the Golden Cherry and swiped all that weed you keep in your saddlebags."

"I'd beat the dog shit out of them."

Fannie gave a modest shrug, reached for the cigarillo, and took a puff.

"How much'd she get?"

"I think she's cheated me out of a few thousand since she started working here," Fannie said. "I promise you, that girl knows what she's done. And sure as hell doesn't plan on coming back here anytime soon. Or until her money runs out."

"What do you want me to do?"

"I want you to find her ass and bring her to me," Fannie said. "If she puts up a fight, make it hurt real good."

"I don't like it," Lyle said. "We don't beat up little girls. This ain't part of our deal."

"Bullshit," Fannie said, standing up. "You think I'm keeping you sonsabitches around with free room and board on account of your celebrity endorsement?"

"We're bouncers," Lyle said. "You know? And shit."

"And this is the 'And shit' part," Fannie said. "Now, get your fucking boots on and y'all bring me that cheating little bitch."

"Tonight?"

"Tonight."

Lyle stood up, grabbed hold of his pecker for a readjustment, and stared at Fannie. A bunch of his boys lounging about, drinking cheap beer and doing cannonballs off the diving board. "Can I ask you something?"

Fannie just stared at him, seeing all the scars on his face, the ink down his arms and hands, across his neck. Man used his body like a damn Etch A Sketch.

"What makes you so goddamn mean?" Lyle said, smiling.

Fannie reached the little round table and smashed out the smoke. "I ain't your momma, Lyle," she said. "You remember that and we'll be just fine."

"Where will you go?" Nikki said. "What will you do?"

"I'll call you when I'm safe," Milly said. "Right now, it's best you don't know. Especially since you have Jon-Jon and have to take care of your whole damn family."

"Do you have money?"

Milly nodded just as the Wildcats ran in their first touchdown of the second half, tying things up. The running back was Nito Reece's little brother, a short and tough little shit who some thought might get a scholarship. The crowd screamed and yelled, hammering their feet on the old aluminum stands, shaking the whole damn thing like they were having an earthquake. A little boy ran in and kicked the extra point and the Tibbehah fans yelled and screamed even more. Up by a point. An old woman behind where Milly and Nikki sat wanted the Wildcats to kill them bastards from Pontotoc. Everyone shook their black-and-yellow pompoms, Milly lifting up an arm to join them, smiling a bit at Nikki.

"Well, do you?"

"I got enough," Milly said.

"I can give you some," Nikki said. "I got about sixty dollars saved up for Christmas. I don't need it until then. It's no big deal or nothing."

"I appreciate that," Milly said. "I don't need money. I need you to do me a favor."

"Anything."

Milly reached into her purse and handed her over an old beaten cell phone with a cracked screen and a plastic baggie filled with three spiral notebooks. "I want you to keep these for me until I get back," she said. "Don't try and mess with the phone. It's

162

not activated and it needs a charge."

"Where's your phone?"

"That was Brandon's phone," Milly said. "It's important to me. Just tell me you'll put it somewhere safe and wait until I get settled somewhere, OK?"

"What are you worried about?"

"Nothin'."

"Come on, Milly," she said. "What the hell's going on? Is it something with your daddy? Your daddy isn't a nice man."

"No," Milly said. "He's not."

"He almost killed you once."

"That was my own damn fault," she said. "But that old man don't scare me none."

Milly sat with Nikki all the way to the fourth quarter. When the clock ran down and the buzzer sounded, she took her friend's hand and squeezed it. Milly winked at her, said she better be getting on, and joined the crowd snaking their way down to the concession stands. Milly caught a big lump in her throat, knowing she had no damn intention of ever coming back to this place.

Caddy heard the growling motorcycle engines from nearly a mile away. The guttural sound brought her walking from the barn and out into the warm summer night. She'd been playing Charlie Rich's *Greatest Hits* on her phone while hosing out the public bathrooms that had become a downright disgrace. She looked a mess, in cutoffs and a man's white undershirt and tall rubber boots. She had dirt and grease up under her nails and streaked across her arms. She'd spent the whole day trying to get an old push tiller working again, changing the oil and cleaning the carburetor, without luck. Her ancient Ford truck parked outside in the gravel lot.

She walked to it, seeing a dozen or more headlights jostle up and down on a road that only led to The River.

She watched the single lights as she reached into her cab and grabbed a bottle of water. She drank the water, still feeling hollowed and dehydrated from the day's work, as the motorcycles rolled closer. Dumb bastards probably thought The River was some kind of bar, not a church. The sun had set, the sky growing a light purple and blue to the west, the riders coming into focus, dark figures kicking up a trail of dust behind them.

Charlie Rich sang "Behind Closed Doors" as the bikes rode up to the barn, slowed, and killed their engines. A tall, gangly man with a black beard slid off an old Harley and asked, "Are you in charge of Jesus Land out here?"

"I'm Caddy Colson," she said. "I run The River."

"No need to get excited because of a couple of scooters," he said. "I came out to see a friend of ours. Girl named Milly Jones."

"Don't know her."

"I heard she was tossed out of her daddy's house and is staying out back in one of your shacks."

"If she was, it's nobody's business," she said. "People come here for shelter, not to be hassled."

"Do I look like someone who'd hassle a young lady?"

"Mister, you look like that's your main occupation."

"Colson, Colson," the biker said. "You any kin to that soldier who was the sheriff?"

"You bet," Caddy said. "And I got the new sheriff on speed dial. So unless you want to start explaining trespassing, y'all better ride off into the sunset."

"Sun has already set."

"So it has," Caddy said, arms resting on the bed of her truck. Charlie Rich sang "The Most Beautiful Girl" from her phone as she glanced into the cab and spotted her old Sears & Roebuck twelve-gauge Quinn had given her. It had belonged to their Uncle Hamp. "Good night."

"I guess you wouldn't mind if we checked them shacks out back, then," the biker said.

"What's your name?"

"Lyle," he said. "But folks call me Wrong Way."

"Fitting."

Some of his boys crawled off their scooters, making themselves at home. Lyle nodded back through the gaping mouths of the barn — open front to back. "Through here."

"We have women who've gone through hell and back trying to get some rest back there," she said. "All they need is some greasy peckerwoods to come knocking on their door and sending their hearts up into their throats. So, no. It's not that way. The only way is back down the road you came."

"Oh, baby," Lyle said. "No need to be like that."

And if you did. Was she crying, crying?

Caddy opened the door to the truck and pulled out the twelve-gauge. "Get gone."

"Come on, Pastor," he said. "Don't be that way."

"Do I look like I went to divinity school?" Caddy said. "I've been hosing shit and piss down after a three-day revival. And now I sure as shit don't mind firing off a few rounds into those beautiful scooters of yours."

The bikers started to make cat noises, hissing and meowing, laughing like hell. The whole scene just a damn joke to them. Some skinny little girl in rubber boots threatening to shoot their asses.

"All right," Lyle said, showing his palms. "All right. But you see that Milly Jones, tell her we were asking about her."

Tell her I'm sorry. Tell her, I need my baby.

The stock felt heavy and solid up under Caddy's arm, a steady sweat pealing down from her short hair and into her eyes. "Back down the road, fellas," she said. "Unless you've come to worship. Door's always wide-open for that."

Lyle walked back to his bike and threw his leg over his Harley. "Just might take you up on that sometime, ma'am."

They started their bikes together and inelegantly turned right back around and rode into the oncoming black night, leaving dust and exhaust hanging over the tilled garden patch.

Milly had said good-bye to her momma and her sister before the game. Now, she needed to find a place away from Jericho where she could just live for a while. When she got on her feet, she could make things right. She could send back the money to Miss Fannie, talk to her daddy about those stupid threats. The only thing she wanted was to get some breathing room and figure out a way for folks to hear her. The last few years had felt like screaming underwater with no one hearing or seeing what she was saying.

Milly drove away from all the cars and trucks bunched together behind the stadium and past the fat little deputy standing at the edge of the road. She figured she'd ride through Jericho, 'round about the Square, to see who was about. Maybe she'd see her sister or run into Joshua — maybe wanting to see Joshua more than anybody. He was the only one who believed her, believed in her, until things became such a goddamn mess.

The Square looked good that Friday night, calm and empty, with most everyone at the game. A few boys had cut out early, parking their jacked-up trucks and custom muscle cars up by the gazebo and veterans' memorial. A couple boys from high school added to the monument now. One of them had gotten in her pants once, then he'd gone off to Afghanistan and got blown to bits. She was glad she gave herself to him before he left. He wasn't a handsome boy — pimply face, big Adam's apple — but he'd been kind and sweet. About the most you could ask for.

Even though it was August, the old oaks twinkled with white Christmas lights, and at least two of the storefronts shone with light. Pizza Inn and the Panda Buffet. The others were either closed up for the night or closed up forever. The old movie house that had been one church or another Milly's whole life had been bought up last year and redone. They had a cheap marquee on it now, a special double feature of WHITE LIGHTNING AND GATOR. SPECIAL APPEARANCE BY STUNTMAN JASON COLSON!

She headed north out of town, past the old post office, taking the new bridge over the Big Black River, a gentle curve of concrete lifting her way up above the dark waters and sending her on toward Yellow Leaf and then beyond toward Highway 45 North. Her old Kia sputtered and coughed, the incline of the bridge being maybe more than it could take. She checked her gas, knew she had enough to at least get to Tupelo, but as soon as she heard the pop and saw all that steam, she knew she was screwed. That burned antifreeze smell filled the car, the engine shut down, and only through damn gravity was she able to roll down from the bridge and turn onto the landing where folks set their boats into the river in the spring and summer. As the Kia rolled to a stop, she rested her forehead on the steering wheel. Steam hissing through the cracks of the hood.

Milly made two phone calls and then walked to the water's edge, where she smoked a cigarette and paced up and down the muddy bank.

Twenty minutes later, she saw a car turn off the end of the bridge and wind down toward her. Milly waved to the car, the headlights lighting up high and bright in her face. She had to use a forearm over her eyes so she could see who'd given a shit enough to come help.

The door opened. Milly saw the face and stepped backward, tripping over her own legs. "Get the hell away from me."

"Finally rolling," Indiana Jack said, calling in to dispatch in Memphis. "Shipper was having equipment problems."

"Make sure you stop by the office," dispatch said. "You need to get your permit books updated and those IFTA stickers."

"Ten-four," Indiana Jack said. "I'll be headed backwoods on the way to Wally World. May shut down for an hour if I'm having shutter trouble."

"Drive safe," dispatch said. "See you back at the mother ship."

Indiana Jack hung up the CB and thought about a warm bed, hot breakfast at the Flying J, a T-bone and two eggs sunny side up, side of grits, and a pot of hot coffee. He'd be sleeping in until Monday, get a couple days with his wife and their two grandkids. Maybe go to the zoo or the Bass Pro Shop. He'd been living down South now for the last four years, having met Sheri online on that farmersonly.com, not that he was a farmer, but he wanted a woman who was looking to meet a regular joe. Sheri was a good woman, a stout widow with four kids and eight grandchildren. She ran her own business, a knitting supply company in Cordova. Indiana Jack and her had been cohabitating now for the last two years and things couldn't be better.

Jack knocked it down a gear as he slipped down the snake of the new Big Black River Bridge, headlights lighting up a fine early evening. He reached for some coffee from the Thermos cap and took a big sip. He'd been running and gunning since Mobile at four a.m. He didn't mind being a company man. He'd been working for Walmart since he moved to Memphis. It wasn't a bad thing knowing you had steady work, not having to hustle a load.

Jack kept on the radio to listen, never being the kind of driver to get ratchet jaw. He drank some coffee. Set the AC on high to dry the sweat off his face and keep him awake. He punched up the next stop, computer calculating the mileage and his fuel load. The back road to the highway had plenty of rolling green hills and lots of cattle. He could see himself settling down in a little place like this county. Maybe getting some acreage, building a shop to tinker around with once Sheri got tired of minding store.

Indiana Jack shifted down and hit a steady fifty, the night shining bright under a full moon, signs leading him back to 45. He rolled past a couple of rural churches, two convenience stores, and a cinder-block beauty shop called Nanette's.

"Breaker, breaker," he said. "This is Indiana Jack slow-rolling to Memphis. On channel one-nine. High Plains Drifter, you got your ears on?"

High Plains Drifter, a coffin hauler out of Batesville, answered right back, calling him a sorry so-and-so, just as a bright patch of light caught Jack's eye. He shifted down, the bluish light nearly stepping in front of him, and he saw the bright light was a human form, someone walking, and he hit the brakes, nearly losing the whole rig as it slid for another forty yards to a hard, skidding stop. Burnt rubber hung heavy in the air. Indiana Jack hopped out of the cab with the shipping blanket he kept on the jump seat and ran toward whatever it was, thinking something was maybe playing with his mind. But he knew when he saw a bluish orange flame walking down the centerline.

"Sweet Jesus."

Indiana Jake ran toward the thing, covering up the smoldering fire with the old gray blanket, trying to smother the flame that just wouldn't die. The body was small and frail, with bright red skin beyond belief. Never a praying man, Jack began to pray over and over, call out to Jesus on the main line, or whoever was listening, to help this screaming, crying little mass. It had no hair and not much of a mouth. Words, or something like it, were coming out between the screams. There were eyes in all the burned flesh staring right at him, trying to say something.

He ran back to the truck and grabbed his cell phone and called 911. "Help. We got a dying woman out on 421, a half mile or so from 45."

"What's the medical emergency?"

"It's a girl," Indiana Jack said. "She's been set on fire, god damn it. Y'all come on right now. She ain't gonna make it."

13

"Will she make it?" Lillie said.

"No way," Ophelia Bundren said. Lillie had called Ophelia, the county coroner, right after the Burn Unit in Memphis. The helicopter blades on the medevac started to spin, kicking up dirt, grit, and plastic bottles from the bridge where it had landed moments ago. Ophelia turned away, black hair covering her face, as she closed her eyes.

"Jesus, God," Lillie said. "I've never seen anything like that. And I hope to never again."

"EMTs pumped her full of morphine," Ophelia said. "There's that."

Ophelia was two years younger than Lillie, two inches shorter, but prettier, dark hair and eyes and a tight red mouth. She didn't talk a lot, but when she did, it was often explosive. She'd once thrown a steak knife at Quinn Colson when she found out about him and Anna Lee.

"How could she be alive?" Lillie said. "After all that? Christ, the girl was walking while on fire."

Ophelia shook her head. The helicopter lifted up high and big over the Big Black River, red light pulsing on the tail, and dipped its nose toward Memphis, flying fast and away. Ophelia walked to the edge of the bridge and held on to the wall, taking deep breaths. She just kept on shaking her head, looking like she might toss her cookies.

"Her mouth was the worst of it," Lillie said. "Someone had poured something into her before they lit her up. She kept on trying to talk, tell me something, but nothing made sense. I didn't know who or what I was looking at until we ran the tag on her car. Now I see her eyes. Her eyes were bloodshot but focused. She wanted us to know who did this."

"Someone wanted that little girl shut up fast."

"You OK?" Lillie said.

"You bet," Ophelia said. "I've seen some things half as bad."

"Good." Lillie put her hand to her own mouth and walked down the road to where the flares had been set, burning down to their final sparks. She stepped off a good two or three paces before she ran toward the edge of the bridge and lost her lunch.

"It's OK," Ophelia said. "It happens."

"Fuck it all," Lillie said. "I don't want anyone seeing me be sick. I've worked a lot of homicides. It's, just, the smell. God damn, it's all over me. It's her. Burning. It's all on me."

"Lemon juice and bleach mixed with water," Ophelia said. "If that doesn't work, I have strong soap at the funeral home. You can take some."

"I don't know how you do it," she said. "Every damn day."

"Old people die," she said. "What gets to me are the kids. Or bad accidents. People with parts missing. Or their faces real fucked-up. But I promise you, I have never seen anything like this. Ever. Did you say she was walking?"

"Some old trucker from Indiana stopped her," Lillie said, wiping her mouth, looking around to see who may have seen her throw up. God damn it. Everyone looked intent on watching that helicopter, a bunch of folks stopped on the side of the road to pray. "Someone needs to buy that old boy a drink. He's a goddamn mess. He said she was all lit up like a candle, seeing fire in her mouth and over her back. He knew it was a girl from her screams. He kept on talking about those screams, how it was so high-pitched, he couldn't get it out of his head. And that man had been in fucking Vietnam."

"Christ Almighty," Ophelia said. "I sure as hell hope no one wants an open casket."

"Don't worry," Lillie said. "I'm no expert. But I don't think that'll happen."

"Who is she, Lil?"

"Teenager named Milly Jones," Lillie said. "Her father filed a missing persons report on her two days ago. Said she'd been messing around with drugs. He told us he'd heard she'd been stripping, maybe turning a trick or two."

"Boyfriend?"

"You can bet your ass we'll find out," Lillie said. "This kind of hate, meanness, doesn't have a place in this world. Only a goddamn animal would do something like this."

"In my experience," Ophelia said, "animals are more kind."

"Did you get photos?" Lillie asked. "For after."

"Yes, ma'am."

Lillie nodded and shook her head. Her mouth tasted metallic and she spit on the bridge. She wanted very badly to take a shower in lemon juice and bleach, maybe burn her whole uniform. A hot wind shook the trees off the Big Black. In between the passing cars and occasional whoop-whooping siren, you could still hear the old river turning and churning. That was a strange comfort.

"Oh, shit," Ophelia said. Her black hair blew across her face and dark eyes, catching in her mouth. Ophelia still was wearing the black uniform of the Bundren Funeral Home. *Serving Jericho's Families Since 1962.*

Lillie looked toward the end of the bridge and in the darkness she saw Quinn Colson talking with Kenny and Kenny, pointing their way. Ophelia had done her best to stay clear of Quinn since things had gone Deep South. That knife being thrown had been the punctuation in their relationship.

"Will they release the body back to the county?" Ophelia said.

Lillie nodded. "Might have some state people take a look, too," she said. "No offense."

"None taken," Ophelia said. "I'm pretty good. But I'm better at putting together than taking apart. I'm just damn glad you're the sheriff right now."

"Hadn't you heard?"

Ophelia swallowed and shook her head. There was a great deal of noise and light at the foot of the bridge. An empty ambulance bucked up onto the asphalt from the landing. Lillie had taped off pretty much the whole area. Kenny, Reggie, and the rest were out with flashlights. It was going to be a long night. News crews coming in from Jackson, Tupelo, and Memphis.

"I offered Quinn a part-time job," Lillie said. "Until he heads back to Afghanistan."

"Why the hell does he just keep coming back?" Ophelia said. "He should've gathered up that trophy and left a long time back."

Ordeen forgot to get his momma some whole milk. She'd asked him three damn times already and then he came home without the milk and she'd sent his ass back to the Gas & Go. You back-talk her and you're in a world of hurt. Sammi was there, as always, his face all fucked-up, cut and bruised. He should've known Ordeen didn't have shit to do with it. That was between him and Nito. Nito was fucking crazy, Ordeen thought, walking down the aisle with the freezer buzzing on high at midnight.

"Five ninety-five," Sammi said, when Ordeen set down the jug.

"For a gallon of fucking milk?"

"Five ninety-five."

"That's bullshit, man," Ordeen said. "You

180

fuck people 'cause you can. 'Cause if we don't pay that much, you send us down to Jericho. Cost that much in gas."

"Cost me that much in gas," Sammi said. "Five ninety-five."

"Shit," Ordeen said, reaching into his pockets. "Bullshit, man."

"Bullshit?" Sammi said, handing back his change. "Bullshit? OK. Bullshit."

"C'mon."

Sammi put his fingers over his bruises and cuts, swollen lip and half-closed eye. "Yeah, I know that real bullshit. You and Nito. You all bullshit, man."

"Wadn't me."

"You don't ride with him?" Sammi said. "In the *Here Kitty Kitty* car? You his boy. I know it. You ride with him all over the place, doin' whatever y'all doin'. Schemin' some shit. I know that."

"Thanks for the milk, Sammi."

"Y'all really think you can win?" he said. "Just the two of you?"

"What kinda shit you talkin' now?"

Sammi sat back down on a stool behind the cash register. He ran his hand over his face like an old man, not a kid who hadn't turned twenty-one. "Come on," he said. "You don't know? Nobody gets out of that Miss-i-ssippi, right? This is a place to live

181

till you die. And then they just scrape you off the highway like a fucking animal."

"You high?"

Sammi jumped up so fast, Ordeen thought he had a gun and was about to shoot his ass. But then he just reached over and turned an old-fashioned little TV around so that Ordeen could see the screen. Late-night news from Memphis — only they say they down in Mississippi. A white woman standing in front of a bunch of flashing ambulance and cop car lights. Down below, Ordeen read on the screen: BURNING GIRL FOUND WALKING JERICHO, MISSISSIPPI, HIGHWAY.

"What the fuck?" Ordeen said.

"Don't forget your milk."

"Who burned up?" Ordeen said. "Who burned up?"

"Milly," Sammi said. "Little Milly Jones. God damn this place."

Sammi ran his hand over his sweating young face again. He reached for a half-finished Coke and took a big ole swig. "She was nice to me," he said. "Real nice. She looked at me and smiled at school. Nobody did that. Not you two fuckers."

"Milly's dead?"

Sammi pushed the gallon of milk across the counter. He slumped down into his

182

crossed arms, laying his head over his elbows. He didn't turn as Ordeen snatched up that milk jug and walked out into the hot night. Damn, his head was fucked-up. Milly Jones was dead? That didn't make no goddamn sense. The milk felt cool in the palm of his hand, the cracked asphalt at the Gas & Go still giving off heat.

Nito was parked by the do-it-yourself car wash behind the convenience store. He had the water wand in his hand, hosing down the tires, big rims, and the soap off the windshield and hood. He flashed a bright gold smile at Ordeen, car shaking for the bass inside, but Ordeen couldn't really hear the music above the spray.

Ordeen shuffled out a cigarette, sweating deep through his T-shirt, and sat on some concrete blocks, waiting for him to finish up. *Milly Jones burned up. Maybe dead.* That was some fucked-up shit. Nito started the car, the engine growling from the twin exhausts, windows dark as hell, and rode up to where Ordeen waited with his momma's milk.

Nito Reece didn't say nothing, just tapped that gas, and made that electric-blue machine purr.

Quinn saw Wash Jones arguing with a

highway patrolman and pointing down the hill to where the techs, EMTs, and sheriff's deputies had gathered by the boat dock and the shell of the Kia. The helicopter had taken what was left of his daughter to Memphis and it looked as if Wash was about to punch someone in the jaw if he didn't get answers. Quinn remembered Wash from when he used to drain his uncle's septic tank, leaning against that stinking truck and telling racist jokes about Mexicans and blacks, wishing they'd go back to their own goddamn countries. Quinn headed up the hill to meet him. About halfway there, he pointed to Quinn and called out his name. He called Quinn "Sheriff" in the confusion.

Quinn nodded to the highway patrolman and the man let Wash duck under the yellow tape. He looked a mess, wearing plaid pajama bottoms and a *Duck Dynasty* T-shirt. He was unshaven and red-eyed and out of breath by the time he met Quinn. His camo ball cap read MAKE AMERICA GREAT AGAIN.

"What the hell's going on, Quinn?" Wash said. "Nobody is telling me nothing. Kenny called me at the house and said that Milly had been in some kind of accident. I get down here and folks are talking about her being set on fire. Lord Almighty. Set on fire."

Wash breathed hard and shook his head. He wiped his sweating face with the back of his hand and swallowed hard.

"She's in rough shape," Quinn said. "She's been burned pretty bad."

"Did she get in a wreck?"

"We don't know what's going on," Quinn said. "A trucker found her walking a little ways from here. She couldn't tell us what happened. We found her car down by the landing, nearly gone."

"Milly," Wash said. "Lord. I need to get to Memphis. I need to be there."

"Yes, sir," Quinn said. "We can get highway patrol to get you up there fast."

"She's gonna be all right?" he asked. "They said she was walking. If she was walking, it means she's alive. Strong."

Quinn put his hand on Wash's shoulder. He smelled like Jack Daniel's and cigarettes. He looked Wash straight in the eye and shook his head. Wash Jones began to cry, dropped to his knees, and wrapped himself with his meaty arms. He sucked in a lot of air and started to wail. Some EMT ran up the hill toward him, worried the old man was having a heart attack.

"It's the girl's father," Quinn said. Quinn got down to a knee and patted Wash on the back just as Lillie appeared from down by that burned-up Kia.

"He needs to get to Memphis," Quinn said. "Faster the better."

Quinn took one arm and Lillie the other and hoisted him back to his feet. He coughed and sputtered, wiping his face, composing himself and then spotting Boom Kimbrough hooking up what was left of the white compact. The entire vehicle had been burned up quick and hot, windows busted out and tires melted away. Wash swallowed again and shook his head. "My little girl," he said. "My little girl. My sweet little baby."

"Mr. Jones, did you hear from Milly after she went missing?"

Wash didn't answer.

"Mr. Jones?" Lillie said with a little more force than the man needed right now. "I need to know if you've seen or heard from Milly in the last forty-eight hours."

"No," he said. "No. I ain't seen her. Who done this? Who the hell done this to my daughter? Christ Almighty. I'm going to kill them. I'm going to fucking kill them all."

"Who?" Lillie said. "Mr. Jones? Who do you want to kill?"

Wash Jones wasn't listening, back turned, while he lumbered back up the hill. He spoke to the highway patrolman and the patrolman opened the rear of his cruiser. A second later, the flashers were going and the siren sounding to get the crowd who'd gathered on the closed bridge out of the way.

"He called his daughter a whore."

"He didn't do this," Quinn said. "He's a lousy drunk. But he's not a killer."

"He said she'd shamed her family by dating blacks and working the gold pole."

"She worked at the Rebel?"

"That's what he said," Lillie said. "Said she'd lost all respect for herself and her family."

"Does her mother know yet?"

"Reggie Caruthers is driving her and Milly's sister to Memphis right now."

"What's this I hear about the new owner of the Rebel?"

"She's a piece of work," Lillie said. "Come on. Good a time as any to meet her."

14

"So I see y'all got ZZ Top, Merle Haggard, and Jerry Lee all in the same month," Fannie Hathcock said. "Hot damn, that's impressive, son. A fucking all-star geriatric lineup."

"I wish you'd called ahead," said the serious little black man, name tag on his lapel saying LAMAR. He had on a stylish black suit with crisp white shirt and blue power tie. "No one was expecting you, ma'am. We could have made special arrangements."

"I didn't know I needed an invite," Fannie said. "Maybe I just came down to play a little poker and have a Japanese fusion dinner. As hard as it might be to believe, nights grow long up in Jericho, Mississippi."

"You should have called," Lamar said. "Especially if you wanted to talk with the partners. The partners are very busy men."

"Don't I know it." Fannie blew out a long stream of smoke and tilted her head. She

188

sat outside on a wide, ornate balcony that looked like it should front the Mediterranean, not the damn Gulf of Mexico filled with rusty oil tankers and crappy shrimp boats. It was early, not even nine a.m., and already the pool below was crowded with little fat families and long, skinny housewife bitches with saggy jugs. It would've been depressing if the resort didn't generate so much cash. No matter what you peddled, common folk were your goddamn bread and butter.

"Lamar?" Fannie said. "May I call you Lamar?"

"Yes, ma'am," Lamar said. "You may. I'm the general manager of this resort."

"Yeah," Fannie said, spewing a little more smoke from the side of her mouth. "No shit. That's why I asked for your skinny ass. By the way, I appreciate the vouchers for a free breakfast buffet. All the eggs Benedict and mimosas I could put away."

Lamar gave her a long, cold stare. He continued to stand, sweating a bit in the black suit and tie right off the Gulf, no sunglasses, probably not expecting a meet and greet to take so long. "Can I get you anything else?" he said. "Your room has been comped."

"I want to see Mr. White."

189

"I don't know who you're talking about."

"Sure you do," she said. "By the way, what happened to George?"

"George is no longer with the resort."

"Hand in the cookie jar?"

"Excuse me?"

"He fuck up again?" Fannie said. "Never should've hired a GM who'd spent a five-year stretch in federal prison. Did you know George was a damn TV preacher before he got busted? He had a real shit show out of Tampa where he got old people to put their hands on the television and get themselves healed. He was good. Real good. I don't think he called himself George back then. I think it was Bill. Reverend Bill. Or some shit."

"No, ma'am," Lamar said, smiling over clenched teeth. "I didn't. Please enjoy your stay."

"Lamar?"

"Yes, ma'am."

"I have no intention in leaving this phony shithole until I get to talk to one of the boys," she said. "I remember this town when it was nothing but hot pillow joints and jerk shacks from one end of Beach Boulevard to the other. I had the pleasure of riding out Katrina in a boarded-up Waffle House when God put a fist through your

190

pleasure palace down here, before the big boys arrived and found out a way to dress up sleaze with high-end Southern bullshit and titties-in-your-grits hospitality. Where were you during the storm, cuddled up to your momma?"

Lamar dropped his eyes on Fannie Hathcock, sitting there in a wide-brimmed straw hat and a sparkly red two-piece. Her boobies on high display, as they should be at fifty grand a pair. The trick of doing it right was working the sack into the nipple. Almost no scars. Lamar bit the side of his lip. "New Jersey," he said. "I worked as a GM in two hotels in Atlantic City."

"Hot damn."

"None of the partners are on the grounds," he said. "But I can send a message you've made a surprise visit."

"You do know who I am?"

"Yes," he said. "You're well known around here, Miss Hathcock."

"Where I made my first buck," Fannie said. "Those Keesler AFB boys sure were generous to a lady."

"We discourage bringing in Air Force personnel," he said. "Unless they're officers."

"Little fat families, bored housewives," she said. "Horny middle-aged men on expense

191

accounts. Everyone's got his dick out."

"I'll let the partners know."

"You do that," she said, adjusting the top of her swimsuit. Fifty grand weighed a lot in that flimsy, stretchy polyester. "Tell them Fannie says we're all about to get down to Fist City."

"Of course."

"And Lamar?"

Lamar turned to her, though clearly not happy about it, and widened his eyes.

"Bring me another mimosa, while you're at it," she said. "Looks like it's going to be a gorgeous day out by the pool."

"I don't know why we got to drive to Memphis for hot wings," Ordeen said. "Shit. They got two good places over in Tupelo. A true Wing Stop in Oxford."

"We ain't going to Memphis for the fucking chicken wings," Nito said. "We got to talk to the Twins."

"You joking?" Ordeen said, countryside whizzing by the Nova's open windows. "I ain't fucking with those boys. They straight-up crazy. You know they the ones who took out Craig Houston, right? I heard when they found the body, the man didn't have no head."

"Wasn't the Twins," he said. "The Twins

192

worked for Houston. It was some mean-ass Mexes took him out. They were his boys."

"Ain't what I heard."

"Well, don't be talking that kind of shit while we at the wing shop," Nito said, one hand on the wheel, the other tapping out a beat on his thigh. "Just hang back and be cool. Anybody got any sense know you got to talk that business face-to-face."

"Man, I'm so goddamn tired," he said. "Couldn't sleep. Couldn't eat. That's some fucked-up shit about Milly Jones."

"Mmm-hmm."

"That don't get to you?" Ordeen said. "That don't bother you, someone lit her ass up? I thought you liked that girl."

"Naw, man," Nito said. "Milly Jones wadn't nothing to me but a punch. I hit that shit a few times. She wanting it a whole lot more. I ain't got time for all that."

"Someone killed her."

"Too bad," Nito said. "So sad."

"Man," Ordeen said. "You one sick bitch."

"I got my own problems," he said. "Whatever that white girl got into was her own fault."

"She say anything to you?"

"When?"

"What you mean, when?" Ordeen said. "When you driving her home the other night. She scared of anybody?"

"Naw," he said. "We too busy fucking 'round."

"Bullshit," Ordeen said. "She wouldn't touch your gold-mouth ass."

"Want to bet?"

"Come on."

"Go ahead," Nito said. "Open that glove box. I got some little red panties inside there. Lacy thong. Tell me they don't smell just like Milly Jones."

Ordeen didn't touch the glove box. He damn well didn't want to know.

The kid looked straight off the Rez, with long black hair, serious, chiseled face, and a red T-shirt advertising a stickball tournament from 2012. He said his name was Mingo and that he worked for Miss Hathcock. Twice he swore to Lillie that Fannie Hathcock wasn't up in her office.

"When do you think she'll be back?" Lillie said. "If you hadn't noticed, I'm not with the chamber of commerce."

"Yeah, yeah," Mingo said. "I know. You're that woman sheriff."

Quinn stood with Lillie. He hadn't changed out of a green tee, jeans, and boots. There hadn't been time since he'd heard about the burning girl on the river bridge.

He'd get home when he could, get cleaned up and back in uniform.

"She's here every day," Lillie said. "Why not now?"

"She had business," he said. "That's all I know."

"Where?" Lillie said.

"Don't know," he said. "Don't care. Hey, can I get back to work? We open up at noon. I got to vacuum out the Champagne Room."

"Hate for any of those truckers to be disappointed," Lillie said. "They sure love that fine champagne. Caviar, too."

The kid shrugged. He didn't look old enough to be tending bar, let alone the biggest titty bar in north Mississippi. He looked to Quinn and stared for a moment as if Quinn could help him out. *Get this woman off my ass.*

"I can leave her a message," the kid said. "What do you want me to say?"

"Tell her we need her fancy ass back in Tibbehah ASAP," Lillie said. "One of her girls just got burnt to a crisp. Or don't y'all watch the damn news?"

Quinn headed back to the farm at dawn to shower and change into uniform. The crime scene by the bridge had been sealed off,

195

techs from Jackson going over the Jones girl's car, and deputies and volunteers walking a three-mile radius for anything that might help. In the shower, he used a wet/dry shaver to take off the beard and added a spacer to run over his head and get back to regulation length. He shaved his face again with a disposable over the sink and changed into a crisp TIBBEHAH SHERIFF'S OFFICE shirt, blue jeans, and boots.

He knelt on the floor of his bedroom, opening up several floorboards, and keying open a lockbox where he kept his guns. He found his old Beretta 9, a constant companion since Ranger school, extra ammo, and the holster he wore on his belt. In the kitchen, he made a pot of coffee and watched the morning news, Lillie having to stand in front of the cameras and tell the Mid-South she didn't know a damn thing about an eighteen-year-old cheerleader walking one of her roads all in flame.

"She's good at her job," Caddy said. "But terrible on TV."

"When'd you sneak in?" Quinn said.

"I heard the water running, sat on the porch with Hondo until you were done."

Quinn made Caddy a cup of coffee with a lot of milk and a lot of sugar. She lifted out a cigarette to smoke, knowing Quinn didn't care who smoked in his kitchen. The front and back doors were wide-open, morning breeze shooting through the house.

"I need to talk to you."

"I can't talk about Dad right now," Quinn said. "I got to get back and help out."

"Nice haircut," Caddy said. "I knew you couldn't handle that hippie look. You feel better?"

"Like a hundred dollars."

"Dad can wait," Caddy said, finding a chair. She hoisted her legs off the floor and tucked her knees close to her chest, arms hugging them close. "But just for the record, Momma won't stand for his shit. She's prepared to go to court if she has to."

Quinn drank some black coffee. Hondo wandered in from the front porch and Quinn poured him out some special dog food made from wild-caught salmon and then replenished his water.

"I knew that girl," Caddy said, pointing with her cigarette. "She came out to The River three days ago. She needed a place to stay, get some wash done. She said her father had tossed her out of the house."

Quinn walked over to the kitchen table and sat near his sister. Both of them a strange version of each other, one dark-headed and one blonde. But both with the same high cheekbones, pointy nose, and long, gangly limbs. Caddy was a good deal smaller, but now that they'd both cut their hair short again, it was damn-near two sides of a coin.

"Was she in trouble?"

Caddy reached for the ashtray set by the sugar dish. She tapped off the ash and took a drag, shaking her head at the same time. "No," she said. "No more than the rest. She said she wanted to get out of town and would do anything she could to make that happen. She said she'd been dancing a bit at Vienna's Place. You know that's the new name of the Booby Trap, right?"

"I keep up on things like that."

"But she didn't say anything about a boyfriend or a customer wanting to hurt her," Caddy said. "She seemed more sad than afraid. Kept on talking nonsense about wanting to write her life story but getting spurned by some Christian romance writer over in Tupelo. That make any sense to you?"

"You know who her daddy is, don't you?"

Caddy shook her head. Quinn was wrong, her hair might be even shorter than his, her face brown and sunburned, whiter spaces around the eyes where she wore sunglasses in the field.

"Wash Jones."

"The fat guy who drove the shit truck?" she said. "Every time I saw him, he was drunk as hell, empting septic tanks with a smile."

"Yes, ma'am."

"He's a mess," Caddy said. "No wonder. The girl was sweet, kind. Real naïve about things. Thought she could figure things out with nothing to go on. She believed she could get into that life and walk in and out as she pleased. She told me getting naked was no big thing, she said it was more a game than anything."

"What'd you tell her?"

Caddy shrugged, tipped off the cigarette. "I told her all about who I was and what I'd done," she said. "I told her it was a hell of a long walk back. I tried to keep on the here and now and kept that afterlife talk to a minimum. Maybe I was wrong."

"Did she leave anything at The River?"

"No," Caddy said. "Packed up at one of the shacks yesterday morning. I hadn't seen her since."

Quinn drank some coffee. His cell phone started to buzz on the table. It was Lillie. "I was worse than a deer in headlights," Lillie said, talking before Quinn could even say hello. "I was like a deer caught up in the fucking truck grille. What a mess. We have about twenty reporters down here now hanging out in the meeting room. I got both Cleotha and Mary Alice working. Mary Alice brought in boxes of Krispy Kreme for the jackals. I need you back here."

"Headed that way," Quinn said, mashing the off button.

"The girl had visitors," Caddy said. "She wasn't there. But I talked to them."

"Who?"

"You got to promise me you'll be real careful on this."

"Aren't I always?" Quinn said. "Anything you know can help."

"A whole crew of those boys Daddy used to ride with," Caddy said. "The Born Losers. The head one wore a patch that said 'Wrong Way.' "

"When was this?"

"Last night, around sunset."

"Shit," Quinn said.

"Yes, sir," she said. "We've stepped right in it."

15

"You weren't kidding," Quinn said, peeking through the blinds of Lillie's office.

"Yep," Lillie said. "It's an outright cluster-fuck."

The whole time he'd been sheriff, Quinn had never seen the parking lot behind the jail half full. Now it was packed with TV news trucks, topped with antennas, and all the damn newspaper reporters from all over the Mid-South. Lillie had just gotten off the phone with a reporter in Birmingham and said it's only going to get bigger, spread out into a national story.

"She was pretty," Lillie said. "And white. Her momma put up some pictures on Facebook of Milly in her cheerleading uniform. She looked the very ideal of cute little Southern girl."

"You gonna tell them different?" Quinn said.

"Not my job," Lillie said. "I only care

about what that girl was up to if it helps find the motherfucker."

"What do we know?"

"Not much," Lillie said. "Say, you cut off your beard and hair. Why'd you do that?"

"Felt like the right time," he said. "Appreciate the clean shirt."

"Wasn't clean as much as it just didn't say 'Sheriff' on the patch."

"I get a badge?"

Lillie nodded, chewing on a nail, looking out the plate-glass window to more cars and TV trucks rolling into Tibbehah County. The only time the town had this many visitors was during the Sweet Potato Festival and then it was only for two days. Sometimes, they got a lot of folks from Louisiana and Alabama during the regional rodeo. Lillie reached into the right-hand drawer of a desk and tossed a gold star toward him. He snatched it right up.

"Caddy tells me that motorcycle gang stopped off at The River yesterday."

"That a fact?" Lillie said.

"Looking for Milly Jones," Quinn said. "She had to pull out Hamp's old shotgun before they'd leave."

"Fannie Hathcock's looking better and better."

"How's that?"

"Fannie runs those boys," Lillie said. "Everybody knows it. They mooch off her bar, the diner at the Rebel. Shit, most of them live out at the Golden Cherry. You can smell them when you pass by if you don't roll up your windows. Worse than a paper mill."

"Who was Milly with last?"

"Working on it," Lillie said. "State folks are tracking her phone."

"You find the phone?"

"Burnt to a crisp in the car."

"But the cell company can track her movements."

"That's the idea," Lillie said. "Just like we did those shitbag thieves last year out at Larry Cobb's place."

"You ready to round up some of those current shitbags?"

"I don't want to shut them down," Lillie said. "I want to make them skittery and nervous. If they were making noise to Caddy, they were doing it other places, too."

"No reason we can't stop by the Golden Cherry."

"When's the last time you stopped by the Golden Cherry?"

"Prom."

"And how'd that work out for you and Anna Lee?"

"She puked all in the bed after drinking some Boone's Farm strawberry wine," Quinn said. "And I had to sober her up by dawn before her folks found out."

"Good times."

"What about the reporters?"

"I promised to talk to them all at five," Lillie said. "So let's go out and do some actual police work and then I can get back here and do my makeup."

"You don't wear any makeup."

Lillie picked up a Remington 870 Express and held it in her right hand. Quinn nodded to it. "Oh," Lillie said. "That's right."

Fannie Hathcock waited for a long while in the resort bar, looking up to the flat-screen, before she pressed her hand to her mouth. The TV had no sound, but there was no mistaking the girl in the cheerleading outfit for young Milly, the cheerleader who twerked to Miley Cyrus before she robbed Vienna's blind. The words under her picture said SMALL MISSISSIPPI TOWN SEEKS AN-SWERS.

"Fuck me to hell," Fannie said.

"Ma'am?" the bartender said.

"Yes," Fannie said. "I'll have some more champagne."

The bartender poured the rest of the

bottle, Fannie not even a little bit drunk. She'd been drinking on the house since nine that morning and now it was nearly three. Still no sign of White or his boys and, as it got this late, she wasn't sure they'd ever show. The bartender was a bone-thin, older woman wearing a crisp tuxedo shirt and a bolo tie.

"Springs rolls and jalapeño poppers are two-for-one," she said.

"Goody."

"Would you like an app?"

"No thank you," Fannie said, trying to get the woman to go away. "Can you turn up the news?"

Acting sheriff Lillie Virgil says the girl was found shortly before midnight. She had been walking a county road near Highway 45 while completely engulfed in flames. The girl was identified this morning as Milly Jones of the nearby Blackjack community. She had attended Tibbehah High School, where friends remember her as popular, bubbly, and outgoing. She died earlier today at the Burn Unit at the MED. A spokesperson for the hospital . . .

"All right," Fannie said, lifting a hand. "You can turn it down."

"Ain't that horrible," the woman said. "Can you imagine being lit on fire like that?"

"No," Fannie said. "I really can't."

"I can turn it to the ESPN," the woman said. "Can you believe it's football season already? You for State or Ole Miss?"

Fannie didn't answer, taking a sip of champagne, thinking that son of a bitch, that moron Lyle, had really done it this time. She'd asked for a simple thing like find the girl and haul her ass back to the club. But he couldn't handle it. He'd been too damn thickheaded and mean just to get the cash back she'd taken. The girl must've smart-talked him or one of the boys. Or one of the boys just couldn't control himself, touched the girl, and then needed to cover up the mess. This was bad. Real bad. Little bubbles lifted to the surface of the glass. The champagne was dull as hell, probably cost them eight bucks and marked up to fifty.

"You mind if I take a seat?" a man said.

Fannie looked up to a familiar craggy face. "Jesus, Ray," Fannie said. "You scared the crap out of me."

"Fannie," Ray said. "Damn, you're looking good."

"If I didn't know you were full of shit, I'd blush."

"Wish you'd called ahead."

"That's what your lawn jockey told me."

"Fannie, how long do we go back?"

"The fucking Stone Age."

"And so we have a good deal of trust built up between us?"

"Sure, Ray," Fannie said. "If you say so."

Since the last time she'd seen Ray, his salt-and-pepper hair had gone completely salt. But he'd been part of the New Orleans crew, working with some of the real old-timers who got run out of Corinth years ago. He knew the names and the crimes and had weathered and endured it all. He wore a nice seersucker suit with a yellow-and-purple-striped tie. A nice show hankie in his pocket. If she had to deal with anyone, at least Ray had some class.

"I want to see White," Fannie said.

Ray looked to Fannie, pursed lips, and shook his head. "Not a good time."

"Tell me a good one."

"He's getting lots of attention lately," Ray said. "Kinda makes him nervous."

"I don't like anyone thumbing their nose at me," Fannie said. "Thinking I owe them a favor for cleaning up some shit they started."

"That tribal chief wanted you tied to the stake and burned."

"Not my fault," Fannie said. "Not my problem. That chief was about as much Choctaw as my Irish grandfather's lily-white ass."

"Well," Ray said, turning to her with those sad hound dog eyes. "It was a real mess. You're lucky you landed on your feet."

Fannie shrugged, finished off the champagne, and used a fork to tap the glass and bring the bartender back around. Great thing about champagne was that she could down a couple bottles and barely feel a damn thing.

"How about you head on back to Tibbehah County," he said, "and we'll be in touch real soon. I promise I'll set something up. At the right time and place. You know?"

"You're sweet, Ray," Fannie said. "And you were a hell of a lay. Did your wife ever find out?"

"Yeah," he said. "Said she didn't blame me a bit. Said you had great tits and a hell of an ass." He continued to grin and played a bit with the cuffs of his seersucker jacket.

"Listen to me," Fannie said, leaning in and whispering in Ray's ear. "Don't fault me if the fucking highway patrol shuts us down and hauls my ass to jail."

Ray leaned in more to the bar, cutting his eyes over to Fannie. She now had his fucking attention. "Who?" he said, more mouthing it than talking.

"Some high-dollar rednecks from Jackson who think they own that county," she said. "Someone needs to let them know different."

Ray nodded, rubbing his hand together as he did when thinking, almost like he was about to conjure up some kind of ceremony or sacrifice a virgin. "OK," he said. "Let me see what I can do."

Fannie reached over and grabbed her purse, not even thinking about paying the tab, as much as she made for those assholes. "Good seeing you, Ray."

"Did you see the news?" Ray said, eye lifting to the television set. "Some teenage girl was lit on fire up there. They found her still alive walking a back road."

Fannie tossed back the last of the champagne and laid down a fifty for the tip to let Ray know she was nobody's punch. "You don't say."

"Those are some fugly motherfuckers," Lillie said.

"How do you want to go about this?"

"Find Wrong Way," Lillie said. "Since he

was the one asking about Milly. His real name is Lyle Masters, a two-time loser from Macon, Georgia. I don't know much about him because, to be honest, they never caused much trouble. In a way, they did my job for me."

"How's that?"

"I never had a customer complaint at the Rebel."

"I bet," Quinn said. "If anyone complained, they'd take him out back and stomp the ever-living shit out of him."

"Come on," Lillie said, grabbing the Jeep door handle. "Let's quit jawing and get some answers."

"You know they want to help," he said. "We won't be able to shut them up."

A dozen or so bikers lounged about the Golden Cherry's pool. Most had beards and potbellies. Some wore shorts, others had just stripped down to their underwear, denim and leather scattered about. Lillie had on her shades, tailored uniform, and boots, with a ball cap over her eyes and the Remington twelve-gauge in her hand. None of the bikers paid her any mind when she walked up to the lounge chairs.

"Hey," she said.

One of the bikers turned up the music louder. A bunch of the boys laughed. Someone cannonballed into the pool and scattered water across Quinn's cowboy boots. Considering they were shit kickers, he wasn't offended. Lillie kicked at the feet of a snoozing biker wearing shades, tighty-whities, and combat boots. "Hey, fuckhead."

The man stirred and lifted his shades off his face. "Yeah?"

"Where's Lyle?"

"Wrong Way?"

"Lyle Masters," Lillie said.

"Who's asking?"

"Sheriff Virgil and Assistant Sheriff Quinn Colson."

"He's sleeping," the man said. "I'll tell him y'all stopped by."

"Which unit?"

"Don't know."

Quinn eyed the guy, lifted his chin, and said, "Don't I know you?"

"Mister, I ain't never seen you before in my life."

"Jacob," Quinn said. "Jacob Lee. You beat up a woman who said you stole money in her purse. You got charged, but I don't believe you ever showed for court. Give me a second and we can check."

The man slid glasses back down on his eyes and reclined back in the chair. "One thirty-seven."

"What's that?" Lillie said, grinning.

"Wrong Way's in 137."

Lillie tipped her ball cap, walking along the lounge chairs filled with the all-star lineup of north Mississippi shitheads. Someone cat-called Lillie, but she kept on walking, shotgun in hand, eyes on the far side of the Golden Cherry Motel. Quinn moved alongside her, watching everyone they passed, listening for a hint of a quick move or someone trying to surprise them. But it looked like Coors Light, some reefer, and the hot sun had done most of the work. Everyone drunk, sleepy, and stoned as hell. More than twenty bikes sat parked side by side, bright chrome and mirrors gleaming in the sun. Music came from a far open door. Guns N' Roses. "Sweet Child o' Mine."

In the half-light, two bikers sat around a small round table. A woman in a Confederate flag bikini danced on top of a bed while they showered her with dollar bills. The room looked like it needed more of a Hazmat team than a maid. Dozens of crushed beer cans on the ground, ashtrays overflowing, and crumpled-up hamburger wrappers.

"First a naughty nurse and now a cop," a man with a black beard and no shirt said.

"Get on up there, doll."

Quinn let out a long breath and shook his head. Lillie stepped into the light and yanked the CD player cord from the wall. The girl had her eyes closed, a smile on her lips, and kept on dancing.

"Wrong Way?" Lillie said.

The man with the long black beard and long black hair smiled. Quinn thought a lot of these guys looked like figures in old biblical comic books he'd read as a kid. All they needed was to trade out the biker gear for some robes and sandals and they'd be set. Wrong Way swigged some more beer and told the girl dancing on the bed to come on down.

"What's the matter?" the girl said, nearly tripping as she got down to the floor. Glassy-eyed and happy as hell.

"Ain't no music," Wrong Way said. "Shit."

Lillie stepped forward, gun loose in her right hand. "You rode out to The River last night looking for Milly Jones," she said. "Why?"

"What's The River?"

"Jesus camp for adults," Lillie said. "Why were you looking for Milly last night?"

"I don't know," Wrong Way said. "Who said I was?"

Quinn looked down at him: "You threatened to rip apart the place until you found her."

"That's bullshit, man," Wrong Way said. "Who told you that? That woman looks like a little boy out there?"

"That's my sister, Wrong Way," Quinn said. "Think before you speak."

"I don't care if she's your brother or your sister or your momma," Wrong Way said. "What's the crime in asking a girl to come out to play?"

"That's what you were doing?" Lillie said.

"Yes, ma'am," Wrong Way said. "She ain't no angel. Works across the street at Vienna's. She knows a few of the boys. Said she wanted to come out and ride with us sometime. I guess the other night was 'sometime.'"

"Why'd you threaten to trespass into shacks out back?"

"We didn't," Wrong Way said. "Your sister said the girl wasn't there and we rode off down to Ackerman to get some fried catfish and hushpuppies. Are y'all going to arrest us for looking for some fun? Last I heard, we still had American rights in Mississippi."

"Did you find her?" Lillie said.

"Who?"

"The girl, dipshit," Lillie said. "When's the last time you saw Milly Jones?"

Wrong Way let out a long burp and reached down beside him. Lillie brought up the weapon, snicking in a round. "Hold up, baby," Wrong Way said. "Don't scramble my brains just on account of a cold Silver Bullet."

Wrong Way slugged back his beer, crushed the can, and belched. "Other night, she was riding one of my boys' laps, talking about how much she'd love to get on the back of his bike for a cool summer drive. OK? We done here?"

"I don't like you, Lyle," Lillie Virgil said.

"That's OK," he said. "Neither did my momma."

"Did you find the girl last night?"

Lyle leaned back, trying and failing to look cool and relaxed, studying the ceiling for answers. "Yeah," he said. "We found her up at that Gas & Go in Blackjack."

"She come with you?"

"No," Lyle said. "We saw her, asked her to come out and play. She said no. And then we rode off. Scout's fucking honor."

"I guess no one saw all this?"

"Don't believe me," Lyle said, "then go and talk to that towelhead who runs the store."

Lillie looked to Quinn and Quinn nodded back. "If we find out you came within a mile

215

of that girl after that, you better start greasin' your A-hole for Parchman."

"Christ, woman," Wrong Way said. "Damn, you got a mouth, for a public official."

"The girl's dead," Quinn said.

"And you aren't in the clear," Lillie said.

Lillie's stare stayed on Lyle for a long while before she lowered her gun and followed Quinn back out into the light.

16

Sitting there in the MED's waiting room, Linda Carlton's mind started to wander off through the grief, the downright horror of it all, trying to remember just what had she seen in Wash Jones. Wash was there with his new wife, or girlfriend, or whatever the hell she was, with his arms folded across his fat stomach, breathing through his mouth and leaning over every few seconds to whisper in her ear. Linda believed the woman's name was Charlotte — apparently, some kind of head case if she'd moved in with Wash. The only kind of consolation Linda had in their marriage was being young and stupid and that the union had produced their son and two daughters. Milly was beautiful. *Had been beautiful.* It was tough as hell to think about it like that. But she'd been through it all before, losing a child.

She cried for a bit more. The pills they'd given her gave the whole damn world a fuzzy glow. It wasn't unlike that sleep pill commercial where that green butterfly floats through the window and lands on your chest. She wouldn't think twice if a big green cartoon butterfly shot down the hospital hall, landed on her knee, and said hello.

She could hear Wash's breathing from across the room. Every few minutes, the fat woman leaned into his ear and he'd say, "Huh?" He'd been a drunk, a pill popper, and a horny goat. She'd once caught him in the Baptist church rec room with meek little Janet Taylor, her panties around her ankles and her lipstick all over Wash's face. What the hell was wrong with those women? What the hell had been wrong with her?

"Are you OK?" her other daughter, the living one, asked.

"No," Linda said. "I'm not."

"Should I get the doctor?"

"I just want to get Milly and get home."

"Milly's not coming home, Momma."

"I know that," she said. "Nothing's wrong with my head. I just want what's left of her. What that son of a bitch didn't take from us."

"Who, Momma?"

"Who the hell do you think?" Linda Carlton said. "Lord, I need a cigarette. Can we smoke here?"

"No, Momma," her other daughter said. "It's a hospital. They got rules."

Linda reached into her purse and pulled out a little bottle of essential oils: ylang-ylang, orange, tangerine, patchouli, and blue tansy. She added a dab to a Kleenex and inhaled the blend. She'd been huffing the stuff as if it had been gasoline since they left Milly's room. That charred smell did something real bad for your brain.

Fat Charlotte leaned in and said something to Wash. And Wash gave a stupid little grin and chuckled. Here they were, waiting to learn what to do next when there wasn't a thing left to be done, and that son of a bitch was laughing. She thought back on that call from him two years ago, calling her out and calling Milly everything in this world but a white woman. She knew that kind of rage too well. When Wash would get to his third beer, he'd look to pick a fight. She'd say one cross word back and, Lord, he'd backhand her and make her fly across the room. He gave her black eyes and busted ribs, Linda spending most of their married life telling folks she'd fallen off a horse. Linda had never owned a horse in her life.

"What is it, Wash?" she asked, giving him

a look from across the room.

The grin hadn't left his face, still dripping off his lips like an egg yolk.

"Huh?"

"I said, what's so funny that y'all are giggling about?" Linda repeated, hand shaking a bit, reaching into her purse for her cigarettes and lighter. Let 'em haul her out of this godforsaken place. "Y'all have a little joke going between you. Let's hear it. I sure do need a laugh."

"We were thinking on Milly, is all," he said. "Charlotte reminded me of that time when she was in that competition up in Southaven. Them girls tossed her up in the air, caught her, and then her shoes snagged on that Tate girl's hand. Remember? Looked like a bunch of bowling pins scattered across the field."

"Wasn't funny to Milly," Linda said, trying the lighter with shaking hands. Damn thing couldn't catch. She kept on flicking it and flicking it. "That cost them the competition. That was for state champs. She blamed herself."

"It was funny to watch, is all," Wash said. "Made me smile a bit. That's the only things gonna get us through now. Got to smile as Milly is with Brandon and the Lord."

"With the Lord?" Linda said, flicking and

flicking that Bic. God damn it. "I think she was with the devil first."

Wash looked to Charlotte and Charlotte's face went even doughier and blanker than usual. She pulled the straw from her big Sonic cup to her mouth and started to suck. Wash stood up, using his right hand against the chair on account of the bad knee that supposedly caused his filing for disability. Not because of his damn beer and pill habit or that he'd tried to take the hand of his boss's secretary and put it on his peter.

"What you getting at?" Wash said.

"You remember calling me the other night?"

"Hell, yes, I do."

"You stand behind what you said about Milly?"

"I was dang pissed-off," he said. "I was concerned for my daughter's welfare."

"You called her a dirty whore and a nigger lover," Linda said, pointing the unlit cigarette at him like a stick. "You said you wish you could strangle the holy shit out of her. Is that love, the worry you gave my girl?"

"Shut your mouth."

"You said she had a sickness about her," Linda said. "You said she had that jungle fever that turned her to popping pills and riding the gold pole. You said you wished she was dead."

"That's a lie," he said. "Liar. You're a filthy liar."

"Always wondered why you didn't raise that big voice for Brandon?" she said. "You let him stick a damn gun in his mouth rather than listen to him tell the truth. Our children died in shame."

Wash Jones charged across the waiting room, the little TV in the corner playing FOX news, a blonde woman yukking it up about the president being delusional for wanting to take all of America's guns. He stood over Linda Carlton, just like he had in their kitchen and their bedroom, red-faced and breathing crazy. He gritted his teeth and raised back his hand.

"Do it, Wash," Linda said, saying it calm in her head but not hearing much besides a whoosh in her ears. "Hit me. Let everyone know just what a loving father is capable of."

He narrowed his eyes at her, his little fat friend at his side, tugging at his arm, telling him they could go get a Coke and some fries downstairs. Linda reached into her purse for that Kleenex.

Damn, Linda had her baby's smell all over her.

■ ■ ■ ■

Sammi Khouraki didn't seem happy to see Quinn. The kid was eating a fried chicken leg while watching some kind of TV show on his phone. No one was in the Gas & Go. When the door chimed, Sammi lifted his head and then went back to the phone. He had a black ball cap on with a flat crown, a cheap white T-shirt, and a gold chain dangling around his neck.

"Sammi," Quinn said.

The kid didn't answer.

Quinn slid a high school portrait of Milly Jones onto the counter. Sammi glanced at it and went back to watching his phone, announcers talking about a skateboarding competition.

"Know her?"

"Blackjack doesn't have a hundred people who live here," Sammi said. "What do you think?"

"You went to school with her?"

"Yes."

"And she bought her gas here?"

"Where else is she going to get gas?" Sammi said. "I knew Milly. And I know someone set her on fire."

"You know who?"

Sammi turned off the phone. He was seated on a stool on an elevated platform and Quinn had to look up at him as he talked. Sammi shook his head. "Naw, man," he said. "And if I did, I'd keep my mouth shut. I don't want to get into all this mess."

"You're in it," Quinn said. "I heard she was gassing up here right before she got killed."

Sammi shrugged. Quinn wanted to take the crooked ball cap off his head and whack him across the nose. He wanted the boy to sit up straight, shave that stylized beard, and pay attention. Instead, Quinn stayed silent, waiting for him to talk. Lillie taught him that, only push the folks you wanted to trip up. Like the Born Losers, she played that one just as she intended. She wanted them riled and nervous.

"Yeah," he said. "She bought gas. And then she left. You think I killed her or something? Shit, man. C'mon."

"Why would you say that?"

"Because you came back here again," he said. "This time, you are wearing a star. You people get off on hustling people like me? You hate me because you think I'm like people you used to shoot over in Iraq."

"I thought you didn't know who I was?"

"You told me you weren't the law," he

said. "You lied to me. You trying to play my ass?"

"I wasn't the other day," Quinn said. "But I changed my mind about some things."

"Because of Milly Jones?"

"Did you talk to her?"

"Sure," he said. "I talked to her pretty much every day. She'd come in for a ham biscuit and a Diet Coke."

"What about last night?"

"She bought a pack of cigarettes."

"And gas?"

"I think."

"You don't know?"

"OK, yeah," Sammi said. "She bought gas. This is a gas station. That's why we call it the Gas & Go. You buy gas and then you go on down the road."

Back in the Shitbox, they used to bring gifts — food, money — anything to help get people talking. The better the villagers liked you, the more they were willing to stay out of your way or tell you where the Taliban boys stored their cache. But Sammi was more Memphis than he was Kandahar. He wore that loose, cool, *Fuck the police* attitude Quinn saw mostly with teens in the projects. Or the *What you looking at?* rednecks who thought the world was against them.

"Did you talk to her?"

"Sure."

"What did she say?"

"A pack of Marlboro Lights," Sammi said, grinning. "Oh, and she thanked me when I gave her change."

Quinn smiled. "You didn't really know her."

"I liked Milly," Sammi said. "She was my friend. I'm sorry she's dead. But I don't know who killed her. She didn't tell me that someone was chasing her or something. She was just being cool, joking around and stuff. She said she was going on a trip."

"Where?"

"That's all I know."

"When did the Born Losers show?"

"Who?"

"You didn't notice the biker gang rolling up to the Gas & Go?" Quinn said. "Those machines make a lot of noise."

Sammi just stared at Quinn with big dead eyes. He'd shut all the way down. "No way."

"We know they were here," Quinn said.

"How's that?"

"Because the guy who runs them told me," Quinn said. "What happened?"

"Nothing," Sammi said. "They have a right to come here."

"Did they talk to Milly?"

"I don't fucking know," Sammi said. "Shit. I was inside here."

Quinn looked behind the boy to see a small TV monitor that clicked to different spots around the gas station: the pumps, the parking slots, the cooler, a wide shot of the aisles, and then back where Quinn was standing. A poster on the wall showed a trio of fit boys jumping off a yacht into blue water filled with bikini-clad women. It read EXPLORATION HAS ITS PERKS. LIKE DISCOVERING LOCAL FLAVOR. "I need your video from that night."

"Don't you need some paper for that?" Sammi said. "From a judge?"

"You want me to go get one?" Quinn asked. "Considering the situation, I don't think that'll be much trouble."

"They won't like it," Sammi said. "They'll blame me."

"Run back that video, Sammi," Quinn said. "All of it."

"I don't like you," he said.

"That's OK," Quinn said. "Get in line."

"My father says your uncle was just as bad. He said your uncle used to make him pay to do business because he was an immigrant."

Sammi stood up and opened up the counter, letting Quinn step up onto the platform, as he opened up a cabinet and fiddled with the surveillance equipment. "Go ahead," Sammi said. "I'm always happy to be this county's punching bag."

"Tibbehah County is in the house," K Bo said. "Damn. I smelled country as soon as you motherfuckers walked in the door."

"Where Short Box at?" Nito said, Ordeen hanging back, looking out the window at Elvis Presley Boulevard. Hand-painted sign on the plate glass reading in backward letters WING MACHINE.

"He cooking," K Bo said. "Y'all want some wings?"

"Yeah, sure," Nito said. "How 'bout you, Ordeen?"

"I like 'em spicy," Ordeen said, nodding. He was hungry as hell. Hadn't had nothing to eat since late last night, before they found out Milly was dead. After that, his whole mouth tasted like metal, insides felt like they were rotting out like he'd drank some Drāno.

"Spicy is what we do," K Bo said. "We got this shit called Bitch in Heat. You sure you country boys can handle that shit?"

Nito looked to Ordeen. Ordeen nodded and pulled down his hat over his weave. "Shit, yeah."

K Bo disappeared back into the kitchen, yelling at his brother to fire up the wings. And Ordeen and Nito found a booth by the plate-glass window, the wing shop down a mile or two from Graceland. The brothers ran the shop, a car detailing business, and all the other shit from that location. One-stop shopping: get your fill, your car tight, and some drugs all at the same place. Although Ordeen had never gotten drugs right here. He was pretty damn sure they kept things way on down the food chain so they didn't get hassled. A plaque on the wall said the Wing Machine had been a runner-up as *Favorite Hot Wings in Memphis.* Ordeen wondering why those boys didn't make best. They sure as hell did everything Top Fucking Dog since Craig Houston lost his damn head.

K Bo, or it might have been the twin Short Box, walked back out of the kitchen. He had on a black V-neck T-shirt, long black satin running pants, and the goddamnedest white running shoes he'd ever seen. They looked like they'd just been popped fresh out of the box. K Bo slid in besides Nito and said, "That shit'll be right out. Don't y'all pussy out on me now. Better eat 'em up."

"Mmm-hmm," Nito said. "Yeah."

"OK," K Bo said. "What's going on? When you called up last night, I thought you was high or something. I couldn't make out what the hell you talking about."

"I got excited," Nito said. Ordeen hadn't heard a word about no phone call. But Nito had geeked the fuck out last night, talking about power and protection. He kept on talking about how folks would be trying to jack his ass for things he hadn't done.

"What y'all need?"

"You still like my car?"

"Hell, yeah," K Bo said. "That's how me and you got to talking. What year is it?"

" 'Seventy-two," Nito said. "Belong to my granddaddy. When he got that lung cancer, it sat up on blocks. I had to work two years cleaning out toilet stalls to get her fixed. That paint made special. Call it Galactic blue. Like something not from this world. Twenty-inch rims."

"Yeah, I see 'em."

"Sound system rock your ass," Nito said. "You want me to punch it up?"

"Naw, man," K Bo said, sliding back into the booth, getting comfortable. Talking that deal, while Ordeen was thinking, Nito done lost his fucking mind. He loved that ride. And if he sold that bitch, how the hell were they getting back to Jericho? Hitchhiking?

"What you thinking?"

"Some cash," Nito said. "Some trade. What you got?"

"I got some spares out by the shop," K Bo said. "Man. You damn near made my day. Selling me that Here Kitty Kitty. I always said if that car don't get me pussy, nothing will."

"Guaranteed."

Ordeen couldn't stand it anymore and kicked Nito under the table, trying to pass along that *What the fuck you doing?* look. "C'mon, man," Ordeen said. "You and me need to talk."

K Bo wasn't no dummy and saw Ordeen was trying to fuck up the trade. He grinned at both of them. "Wings come out in a second," he said. "Wait till I tell Short Box. He shooting a new video next week for a new boy he producing. That car could be the showpiece."

"Oh, yeah."

"Nito," Ordeen said.

"A'ight."

Nito followed Ordeen out of the shop out in the parking lot of the strip mall. Two big tourist buses passed by, making a lot of noise and stirring up that road grit. Ordeen just stood there looking at Nito, not saying nothing, not having to say nothing.

"I need some money."

"That's it?"

"Yeah," Nito said. "Ain't your car, man. Belong to me."

"What's this have to do with Milly?"

"You trippin', bitch," Nito said, shaking his head and leaving his ass out in the lot. "Come on. Short Box comin' out with them wings. I don't want them to cool down or think we bitching out."

"Shit," Ordeen said. "How we getting home?"

Nito was already gone, walking back into the Wing Machine, door closing behind him.

17

Fannie was back in Jericho, running Vienna's bar at noon, judging some new talent onstage, pouring some beer, and waiting for Lyle and his boys to show up. Lyle didn't use a cell phone or email. If you wanted Lyle, you had to catch him face-to-face, the only way he'd do business. Which worked most of the time except for when Fannie really needed to talk to his crazy ass and find out just what the fuck was going on. Jericho and the Rebel looked just like Barnum & Bailey had come to town, jamming up the Square and loading down the diner with reporters and their crews. Their head cook, a huge black guy named Midnight Man, said he'd never slung so much chicken-fried steak in his whole damn life.

Nearing one p.m., Lyle busted open the door, laughing and jawing with three of his boys: Turkey, Q-Tip, and R.C. All of them had that stiff-legged walk, like they'd rode all over north Mississippi without taking a piss. Fannie knew the main goal for men in the motorcycle club was not to work. "Live to Ride" wasn't bullshit to them, it was part of their crazy-ass religion. They weren't criminals for the sake of being criminals or to get rich. They were criminals so folks would leave them the fuck alone.

"Beer," Lyle said. "And a shot of that Bulleit rye."

"We need to talk," Fannie said.

"Why?" Lyle said, grinning like he'd drank a half bottle already. "You finally gonna take me up on some fun over at the Golden Cherry? A real long ride? I can promise you, ma'am, you sure won't regret it."

Fannie just stared and his silly-ass grinning stopped. She leaned into the bar, forearms across the antique wood, and whispered, "Outside. Leave your boys here."

She poured him a beer and a shot. He knocked back both, wiped his face with the back of his hand, and walked with her out of the darkness into white-hot summer sun. Heat waves shimmered off the truck stop asphalt. He pulled on a pair of sunglasses and lit up a cigarette, straddling his Harley. The blue tank airbrushed with an arrow shooting down a one-way street.

"What happened?" Fannie said.

"I don't know," Lyle said. "We headed up into Tennessee. Found a good place to get barbecue and then we rode to a new titty bar in Memphis. Half-priced drinks. Girls were OK. We were thinking about riding on over to Nashville, but we ran out of money. Rode back this morning before dawn. Trying to sleep it off, but folks keep bothering us."

"The girl," she said. "The girl, Lyle. How'd you leave it with her?"

"Listen, don't talk to me like I'm nothin'," Lyle said, blowing smoke from his nose. "I did what you said. We took care of business before we rode. No reason to be jumping all over my ass. I was just kidding about the lay. I know what you think of me and the boys."

Fannie cocked a hip, snatched the cigarette from his hand, and took a long pull. God damn, how she hated this nasty stretch of highway. Nothing but eighteen-wheelers and cars zipping by, Jericho a place where you got fueled up and fed and moved on down the road. If Fannie had any luck at all, this county would be her personal rest stop on the way to a lot better things.

Lyle waited, staring at her profile, as she handed him back his cigarette. He had pulled his hair into a black ponytail and wore a fitted black tee with jeans and big black boots. A chain reached from his belt to his empty wallet. On his forearm was a bright red-and-blue tattoo of Woody Woodpecker pecking like hell into a hardwood tree, flattening his beak.

"You don't know," Fannie said.

"Know what?"

"The girl's dead."

"Oh, yeah?" he asked. "I heard something like that."

" 'Something like that'?" Fannie said. "Holy shit, Lyle. What the hell did y'all do? I saw it on the news down in Biloxi and sped all the way back here thinking we might get raided. Won't take long for the law to know she worked here. They'll bust us wide-open. How did it happen?"

"Hold up," Lyle said. "Hold up. Jesus Christ. Law came to the motel this morning and asked me the same shit. We didn't do nothing."

"I don't believe you," Fannie said. "Either you or one of your monkeys got into some rough shit. Did you try and burn her alive so she'd just shut her mouth? Did someone rape that girl? 'Cause if one of you raped that little girl, I'm going to slice off your balls and toss them into the barbecue pit."

"Fuck, Fannie," Lyle said. "Calm down.

Would you listen to me? Calm down. Jesus. I didn't know she was dead because she wasn't dead when we seen her. We did like you said. We scared her and took off. We been riding, drinking, and playing all night long."

"Where'd you see the girl?" Fannie said.

"Up in that little shit village," he said. "Up in the sticks. Blackjack. That's where she lives. We found her up at a gas station and I told her, toe-to-toe, she needed to think on what she'd done and bring that cash back to you and apologize. I told her she'd messed up bad, but you were a forgiving woman if she stepped up and handed over what you were owed."

"And that was all?" Fannie said, turning her head a bit. "All that happened between you two?"

"Hell, yes, that was it," Lyle said, scratching the back of his unshaven neck. "We caught a little shit from that foreigner who ran the station. But he backed the hell off when he saw our patches. He spoke English just as plain as a white man. I said, 'Inside, Ayatollah, or we'll drag your ass for a hundred miles.' You know, 'cause he was Mideastern and shit. It was funny."

Lyle's cigarette had grown down to a hot nub and he tossed it down on the hot asphalt. Two big-ass tractor trailers hauling for a coffin company in Batesville rolled into the lot at the same time. Over at the Rebel, Midnight Man was cooking up a whole hog on the outdoor pit and the woodsmoke and pork smell drifted over the parking lot. The smoke and that burning smell made her think of the girl and the problems that would surely follow. God damn, if Lyle was lying.

"You think I'm stupid?" Lyle said.

"If I don't answer that question, will you be offended?"

"You told me to talk to that girl," he said. "That's what I did. Hell, I didn't even think it was that much money. What? A couple thousand bucks? Why would I kill a person over a couple thousand? Ain't even my money."

"Did any of the Losers touch her?"

"Fannie," Lyle said. "Christ. I was there. I was the only one doing the talking. I had six boys riding with me. They laughed and looked mean. I said my piece and left. Cool?"

"What'd the girl do?"

"She didn't do nothing," Lyle said. "She just nodded. When we rode off, I thought we had some kind of understanding. I figured she got straight with you."

"Would one of your boys have rode back?" Fannie said. "To get mean or fresh with the girl?"

"You know what?" he said. "You been watching too many goddamn stupid biker movies. You know, where the Hells Angels roll into town and the first thing they do is start busting up the place and raping white women. Shit, Fannie. How long we been knowing each other? I will cheat at cards, hijack trucks, bust some heads, and kill on the occasion for respect or money, but we got a damn code here."

"Like when y'all hung that black soldier from a tall tree?"

"Jesus Christ," he said. "That was back in '77. I was still in diapers."

"But your old man."

"I ain't him," he said. "And that's all there is."

Fannie reached down and nervously fingered the ruby heart pendant on her neck, zipping it back and forth on the silver chain. She hadn't been outside more than two minutes but could already feel the sweat against her silk top, under her arms and wide across her back. It wouldn't surprise her a damn bit to see the local law and the state people rolling up to the Rebel and Vienna's and shut everything down until

239

they got answers. They'd be looking straight at her.

"That sand nigger who ran the gas station could make trouble," Lyle said, lighting up a new cigarette. "He ran outside dog-cussing us and I told him to shut the hell up, it's his people that were intent on blowing up the world. I said that if this country had any sense at all, they'd send him and his people packing. Am I right? Or what?"

Fannie nodded but wasn't really listening. She counted out eight news crews, in from all over the state and up from Memphis. They'd be inside, eating, but she'd give them maybe two or three hours before they'd be camped outside Vienna's, asking questions of the customers and the girls. All she needed was some knuckleheads to start some kind of titty bar vigil with candles and flowers like some kind of pussy-throwing Princess Di.

"This was a friend of the girl?"

"I guess."

"And he looked foreign?" she said. "Like from the Middle East?"

"He was some kind of camel jockey," Lyle said. "You know how it is. They all look the same. Most of the gas stations in north Mississippi are run by those fucking people. They take money from good, hardworking

Americans and send it back to al-Qaeda. You know I'm tellin' the truth."

"You know, Lyle," Fannie said. "I think a lot of people just might believe that."

"Believe what?" Lyle said.

Quinn returned to the Big Black River Bridge, where folks had already started a vigil underneath. In the final daylight, a bright, burning orange over the river and the rolling hills, the dark space looked like some kind of cave, flickering with Mexican prayer candles and piled with bunches of flowers still wrapped in cellophane. Quinn watched an old woman and a little girl walking out from under the bridge, empty-handed, both of them crying. The water flowed slow on by, normally filled with johnboats and fishermen. Now a dozen cameras were set up on the bank, eyes on techs and deputies, who kept most of the landing secure even though the Kia was long gone.

Quinn wanted to come back. See if Kenny or Reggie had found anything, maybe spoken to someone who'd come down to the scene. He stood at the edge of the Big Black, the water turning a nice coppery glow, swarms of gnats skipping over the surface and gathering under trees in shadows. As a teenager, Quinn fished here a lot and never seemed to catch a thing but a few cold beers.

"It's almost pretty."

Quinn turned to find Ophelia Bundren at his side. She had on jeans and an embroidered peasant top instead of the grim black funeral wear. Her white sunglasses were pushed up high on her head and her dark eyes didn't meet Quinn's. She just watched the river and heaved with a lot of sadness.

"They bring Milly back tonight," Ophelia said. "I'll be there. Main autopsy will be performed by two folks from Jackson. I can't say I'm looking forward to it. We pretty much know what killed her."

"Anything y'all learn will help."

"You believe that?" Ophelia said. "Her skin got burned 'way. Nearly all her clothes. Any bet of finding something was in that car that got burned up, too. How about the foot search?"

Quinn shook his head. "Two miles and expanding," he said. "Whoever did this set things down at the landing and drove off."

"Tires?"

"Nope." Quinn shook his head. "Caddy knew her. Or met the girl. She was in some kind of trouble, got kicked out of her dad's house. Had been disowned by her mother. Caddy helped her get on her feet out at The

River and figured she'd come back."

"Did she tell Caddy anything?"

"Nothing I can talk about," Quinn said. "But something that might help."

"Closemouthed Quinn," Ophelia said. "Keep all your secrets to yourself."

"Right until a steak knife comes whizzing past my ear."

"This isn't the place," Ophelia said. "Damn you. I just wanted to come out here, lay some flowers, and get ready for tonight."

"I'm sorry," he said.

"For me having to dissect the girl or for what you did?"

"All of it," Quinn said. "I wasn't thinking too clear."

"And you are now?"

Quinn looked to Ophelia, her brown eyes finally on his face, studying his sincerity, and then breaking away. "I never met this girl or knew her family," she said. "But, holy shit, this is a horror among horrors. I try to not focus on Old Testament stuff. But, God, I hope there's some revenge out there somewhere. I don't know if there's another way to make it right."

"You can't make shit like this right," Quinn said. "This is some kind of real sickness."

"I know what her family is going through,"

Ophelia said. "This shit will destroy you."

"I know."

"I think about what Adelaide went through every morning I wake up," she said. "There wasn't much of her left, either."

"I figured this might bring up your sister."

"She was the same age," Ophelia said. "It was the first thing my mom said to me today. This girl is same as Adelaide. Please help her. And so there's that on me."

"I'll do my best," Quinn said. "I promise."

"How about you do better than that?" Ophelia said.

Quinn reviewed the surveillance tape at the sheriff's office that night, Lillie still up in Memphis with the girl's family, and typed out the very little he knew. The video didn't show much — six bikers at the edge of the pumps, leaning on their handlebars, in silent conversation with Milly Jones. The interaction lasted less than ninety seconds and didn't seem to be threatening. At least, on video. The men stayed on their bikes while Milly pumped gas, hand cocked on hip. Sammi came out at one point and that's where you saw a little conflict and finger-pointing. The men rode off, Milly hung up the nozzle and headed off into the night. And an hour and a half later, she was dead.

He played it over and over, maybe twenty times, using the computer in the sheriff's office. Nobody knew where she'd been for those ninety minutes.

At 2100, Jason Colson knocked on the slightly open door and brought in a sack of fried chicken from Varner's and some sides. He had on his Stuntmen Unlimited hat, red-and-white ringer tee, and bell-bottom jeans with pointed-toe boots. "Didn't figure you'd be coming home tonight," he said. "I couldn't remember if you liked slaw or beans, so I went ahead and got both."

Quinn nodded to the old wooden chair across from the desk. Jason set down the greasy sacks and two bottles of Coke, sat, and propped his boots at the edge of the desk. "Unless you'd rather have coffee?"

"Already drank two pots today," Quinn said. "I could run up to Memphis and back again."

"Get something in your stomach," Jason said. "I've been watching TV most of the day. I saw that girl's daddy hold that press conference at the MED. About tore my guts out to watch what that family went through. You met him? Talk to those folks yet?"

"Lillie has," Quinn said. "The girl's father is the town fuckup. Used to be the septic man, but hasn't worked in years. Said he has post-traumatic stress after his old boss was hung on a cross by a white supremacist."

Quinn headed out to the small kitchen and returned with some plastic silverware and paper plates. He helped himself to a breast, a wing, and a few scoops of slaw and beans. Jason followed his lead and they ate for a long while in silence. Kenny came into the office, said hello, and said he was headed home. His eyes half-closed, fat face drawn. He'd been on duty since six the night before.

"Anything new?" Jason said.

"Not really," Quinn said. "No more than you heard from the reporters."

"Damn. Sure are a lot of them out there," Jason said, craning his head to look out the office window. "I had to park way down the road. Don't know how y'all expect to conduct an investigation."

"For the most part, they've been respectful," Quinn said. "We've set times for updates, press conferences. Lillie taught me working with the press is a two-way street. Sometimes, they turn up something you need to know."

"With all that technology, y'all will find that bastard right quick," Jason said. "I watch all those *CSI* TV shows. I saw all of 'em working down by the river."

"Yeah," Quinn said. "Sure, Dad."

"You can't do something like that to another human being without someone seeing something or talking," Jason said. "This isn't something any decent person could keep to themselves. Everyone's talking about that girl, Milly Jones. I saw the Sheriffs' Association has offered a ten-thousand-dollar reward."

"It's twenty thousand now," Quinn said. "After the story ran on CNN."

Quinn noticed the nervousness, the nodding, the overall customary catching-up between them, waiting for Jason to go ahead and say what was on his mind. Quinn had learned to appreciate his father, but he knew damn well Jason didn't come over just to deliver a fried chicken dinner. Quinn spotted a few crime scene photos on the desk, scooped them up, and dropped them in the right-hand drawer of the desk. Nobody should have to look at what that girl went through unless they were paid to do it.

"I've been thinking," Jason said.

"She walked nearly a quarter mile like that," Quinn said. "I don't know how she did it."

"I don't need much of your time," Jason said, stroking the long gray goatee. "But I know this thing is going to keep you away from the farm. I'm sorry but this just can't wait."

"She kept on trying to talk," Quinn said, leaning back in the sheriff's chair, spotting more hot lights shining in the jail parking lot from TV reporters doing stand-ups. "Rumor has it she told EMTs who did this to her. But that's not true."

Cleotha waddled into the office and set a stack of pink callback slips on Lillie's desk, smiling at Quinn and nodding to Jason. She closed the door with a tight click. Quinn leaned back into his seat.

"I'm ready to do business," Jason said. "It doesn't have to be tonight. Or even tomorrow. But I need you to get in touch with Johnny Stagg."

Quinn dropped his head into his hands, nodding. "I'm not leaving here until we get some kind of direction," he said. "Know where we're headed with the girl. Wait. Just what are you asking me about?"

"Land," Jason said. "The two hundred acres."

"Oh, that'll wait," Quinn said. "You think Johnny Stagg wants to do me any favors?"

"Longer we wait, the more Stagg will see the daylight from his prison time," Jason said. "He'll start thinking about working this county again and he'll want to hold on to every damn inch he's got."

"Let's talk after we make some arrests," Quinn said. "You think I can leave here? Or start making some kind of real estate plans right now?"

"I know," Jason said. "I know. But I figured no time was going to be right. If it ain't that girl, it's something else going south in this county. Tibbehah County is a damn revolving door of bad shit. It's been that way since the white man bought it from the Choctaws. I just need you to make a connection and you can step away. I'll do the rest."

"You want to talk to Johnny Stagg yourself?"

Jason nodded, Quinn shaking his head. Cleotha appeared at the door, cracking it open, and saying she had Lillie on line 2. "And she don't sound none too happy."

Quinn held up a finger, looked to his dad, and said, "I can't stop you from doing your own business. But if you expect me to call on Stagg hat in hand, it's not going to happen."

"Appreciate your directness, son," Jason said, standing, and winked at his son. "I never would want to make you trouble. But

if you and me are square on this, well, all
right then."

18

Ordeen Davis hadn't been home from Memphis an hour when Coach Mills called his cell and said he sure needed to talk to his ass. Ordeen tried to find Nito since Nito had that new ride, trading the Nova in Memphis for an '89 Chevy Impala and some cash, but Nito didn't pick up. Ordeen couldn't figure out what the coach wanted besides maybe giving him a come-to-Jesus talk or maybe tell him about some shit job he found. Stocking shelves at the Walmart or working out of a warehouse in South Tupelo where they needed strong backs.

Ordeen got his sister to drop him at Tibbehah Stadium, his momma preaching at the church late. Sign outside saying IF YOU WOULD SHUT UP, YOU COULD HEAR GOD'S VOICE. The lights turned on for practice still shining over the empty bleachers and green field. No one in the whole place as Ordeen walked onto the grass and down toward the facility where they lifted weights and did drills in the winter. He damn near lived there when he'd been in school. Coach told him if he worked hard, did everything he said, and lived right, he'd make it out of town. Ordeen followed that plan, but Coach didn't say shit about him being two inches too short and three-tenths of a second too damn slow.

Bud Mills sat in the dark practice facility on an old orange plastic chair. He was smoking a cigarette in the shadow, dead center on the Astroturf, marked off for twenty yards of fake field. Blocking dummies scattered across the bright green. Coach had on nothing but red coaching shorts, high white socks, and cleats. He had flabby old titties and a white tuft of hair between 'em.

"Ordeen," Mills said. "Come on in. Just finished up watching game film. You know, we got Holly Springs next week. Bunch of thugs. We don't watch out, they're gonna stomp our ass. Remember two seasons ago they came in here with all that finger-pointing and dancing bullshit. We got to shut their asses down real quick."

"Yes, sir."

"C'mon," Coach said, standing up slow with his bad back and bad knees, reaching for another school chair. "Something's been on my mind since you got picked up. I want to make sure we get straight on all that."

"What's that, Coach?"

"I'm worried about you hanging to ole Ranito," Coach said. "He's been acting real strange. I don't need to ask you who really owned that gun. Or those pills. I tried to let him know I was pulling for him. I told him he was more of a man than that. But I can't make him change. He's got to do that for himself."

"Yes, sir."

In the half-light of the still, silent building where there'd been so much goddamn noise and sweat, he looked at the rounded shape of Coach Bud Mills. He reminded Ordeen of a smooth-ass metal statue or something that had been weathered away for a million years. All the angles softened, belly and neck, until he was just a blob of flesh with eyes and a hole for a mouth. He plugged the mouth with the cigarette and asked how his momma and them had been doing.

"She good."

"Your momma's a fine lady," Coach said. "Always has been. And you're a fine boy. Let me ask you something. Hadn't Nito been acting real strange to you?"

"I'd rather not say."

"The other day, did he tell you what me and him talked about?"

"No, sir."

"You sure?"

"Yes, sir," Ordeen said. "I figured you just trying to look out for your boys now we out in the real world. Same like you said, Coach. Real world is a tough, messed-up place. You said it took heart and mental toughness if you wanted to find your way through."

Coach Mills nodded along with what Ordeen was saying, Ordeen dishing out a little bullshit just so Mills could get on to why he'd called him out to the practice field. *Don't hang with Nito. Don't do drugs.* Yeah, he got all that shit.

"Did you know that girl who got herself killed?"

Ordeen nodded. "Milly," he said. "Yeah, I knew her."

"I want this to be between us, son," Coach Mills said. "But do you know if her and Nito were going steady together?"

"No, sir," Ordeen said. "She wadn't ever with Nito. She couldn't stand his ass."

Coach took a long-as-hell drag on that cigarette and let it out slow and easy, a big gray cloud blooming around his fat head. "That make Nito mad?" Coach said. "Wanting a little cheerleader like that and her turning him down?"

Ordeen shook his head, trying to read Coach's face but just getting the soft chin and shadows, one clear blue eye. "Wait," he said. "You think he did something?"

"I don't know," Coach said. "But if I were you, I would keep far, far away from that boy. He's gonna get you kilt. I love you and your momma too damn much to see that happen. Y'all are some fine folks."

By 0800 the next morning, Quinn and Lillie sat in Linda Carlton's living room with her surviving daughter, Amber, talking over a plate of cookies and two Styrofoam cups of purple Kool-Aid. Must have been twenty or thirty folks in the small ranch house in the Blackjack community, lots of cakes, cookies, and cold cuts spread out from the kitchen to the dining room, neighbors knowing grieving people needed to eat. People spoke in hushed voices. At least two pastors had stopped by, praying with Linda and Amber, saying they hoped Milly found some peace. Quinn knew both ministers, one being his own from Calvary Methodist back in Jericho.

"I hadn't slept in two days," Linda said. "And I don't want to. Every time I close my eyelids, I see Milly's face. Not as she had been, but like she looked at the hospital."

"We're kinda fuzzy on a few things, ma'am," Lillie said. "We can't make out the last hour and half of where she'd been and might've gone."

"Well, we saw her at about five," Linda said, looking to Amber. "Right?"

Amber bit her lower lip and nodded.

Linda Carlton was a small, frail woman, in a pink sweat suit with no shoes. She looked pale and washed-out without any makeup, smoker lines around her mouth. Amber was fifteen, a stout girl in an XXL Tinker Bell sweatshirt and bright pink shorts. The front door kept on opening and closing, more food and more flowers pouring in. More tears and prayers. Every so often, someone would duck their head in the doorway and then disappear. Both Quinn and Lillie still in uniform.

"She wanted to grab a few things she'd left," Linda said. "I hadn't changed her bedroom a bit since she moved out. She took all her clothes but left all her trophies, stuffed animals, picture books, and things."

"What'd she take?" Lillie said.

Linda shrugged. "All I saw was a few picture books and that dumb pink bear she got from my ex-husband. I don't know why she loved that thing so damn much. Wash got it down at Gulf Shores, Alabama, while he was on a nice long drunk."

Lillie looked to Amber and Amber shook her head.

"Did Milly say where she was going?" Quinn said.

"Nope," Linda said. "But she did tell me she loved me. Almost like she knew what was gonna happen. We all hadn't really seen eye to eye for the last few years. I told her she was wasting her life sticking around Jericho. She needed to take her talents and move somewhere new. When she left, she gave me a big hug, whispering that I'd been right and she was getting on with her life."

On a large white wall hung three separate silhouettes of a boy and two girls. Around the frames were countless more pictures of little Milly, stocky Amber, and a young, muscular teenage boy. The kid had a wide, prominent smile and cheeks scarred with acne. In several photos, he wore a football uniform. Amber noticed Quinn staring and he smiled at the girl.

"You don't expect your babies to go before you," Linda said. "I lost two. That's too much for one woman."

Amber buried her face in her hands and hunched her back. Linda shook her head, getting choked-up, and clutching a wadded-up Kleenex to her nose.

"After I hugged Milly, all I could think to say was, 'Well, bye then,' " Linda said. "*Just like that.* Kind of like *You done came for your junk and now get out of here.* What the hell was I thinking to talk to her like that? No wonder she moved out and moved in with Wash."

"Was she close with Wash?" Quinn asked, looking toward the teen.

"No, sir," Amber said. "Milly hated him."

"It was more about the drinking than anything," Linda said. "When he started to drink, we'd get the hell out of the way. Hell, you know Wash Jones. His reputation in this town."

Quinn nodded, turning to Lillie, letting her take back over.

"Did Milly get personal bills at this address?" Lillie asked. "Cell phone or credit card statements?"

"Some," Linda said. "But I think that was part of what she picked up. I can look around the house."

"How about names of her closest friends?" Lillie said. "Who she stayed in contact with?"

Linda and Amber both said the name Nikki at the same time. Apparently, Milly and Nikki had been best friends since third grade and damn-near inseparable. "She's got a baby boy now," Linda said. "Cute baby named Jon-Jon. Don't know anything about his daddy except he's white."

"I know Milly was working at the Dollar Store and had just quit over in Tupelo at the Build-A-Bear," Lillie said. "Had she found any more work in town?"

Linda swallowed and shook her head. Quinn saw her reach out and grab Amber's knee and the fat little girl's face go blank.

Quinn waited, Lillie knowing damn well where Milly Jones had been making some off-the-books cash. She absolutely could not wait to get over to Vienna's with a warrant and go through security tapes and conduct interviews with any creep who came in contact with the girl. But Lillie said she had to be patient, build that case minute by minute. They needed to show a progression of details, everything heading on back to Vienna's, eliminating family and boyfriends.

"So this was all around five?" Lillie asked.

Both Linda and Amber nodded. Amber wiping her eyes.

"And you didn't see what she took?" Lillie asked.

"She got that old picture of her and Brandon," Linda said. "I saw the frame in the box as she was leavin'. And that bear. Wash's drunk-ass bear."

"Brandon was our brother," Amber said. "He died in a hunting accident."

The words *hunting accident* made Linda turn even a brighter shade of white and sent that Kleenex back to her nose. She breathed it in and closed her eyes.

"You mind telling us what happened?" Lillie said.

Linda spoke fast and hard, "Boy was cleaning his gun," she said. "Don't listen to any other mess about that. He had a hell of a lot to live for. He had just gotten his own truck, had him a sweet little girlfriend. A great athlete. Can y'all excuse me for a minute? I feel like if I don't lay down, I'll pass out."

Quinn and Lillie stood. Amber helped her mother to the bedroom and then returned to the big, flowered couch. She sat back down and smiled at Lillie and Quinn, crying down her big ruddy cheeks, pulling her chubby knees up into her sweatshirt.

"Any idea where your sister headed?" Lillie asked.

"No, ma'am," Amber said. "I didn't ask. And I don't think Milly would've told me."

"You know where she was working?" Quinn said.

"Yes, sir."

"And you think that's what got her killed?" Lillie asked.

Amber buried her face in her hands and nodded a few times, snuffling a bunch. She wiped her nose across the sleeve of her Tinker Bell sweatshirt and said, "Don't y'all?"

19

Jason Colson met Bentley at noon at a Waffle House down in Starkville. "No offense," Jason said. "But if we're gonna be doing a little business, best that folks don't see us together."

"I understand," Bentley had said. "Appreciate you thinking about us."

Jason got there early, spending thirty minutes in his old Chevy and then thirty minutes inside drinking coffee in a back booth before Bentley showed. He had on khakis and a white golf shirt, looking as if maybe Jason had caught him on the ninth hole. "Y'all got some real trouble in Jericho," Bentley said. "That burning girl is all over the news."

"No one wants to talk about much else," Jason said. "My son's gone back to work for the sheriff's office and I had to slide through all those reporters and investigators just to get a word in edgewise."

"Is he on board with us?"

"I don't know if he's on board with the whole idea of it," Jason said. "Buying up all that land and some more property. But he said he wouldn't stop me if I wanted to go ahead and get the ball rolling with Stagg."

"That's terrific," Bentley said, giving a little crooked smile. "Really great. But there may be a little trouble with that."

Jason added a little cream and a lot of sugar to his coffee, stirring with a sanitized spoon. The waitress came over and set down Bentley's large sweet tea. The boy shook the glass, getting it nice and cold, and took a long swallow.

"Mr. Stagg says he'll only deal with one Colson," Bentley said. "That being Quinn. I got the feeling some hard feelings were left between them and he'd like your son to show a little respect."

" 'Hard feelings'?" Jason said. "Shit, yeah, there were some hard feelings. Quinn helped put Johnny Stagg in federal prison and stripped away that whole redneck *Game of Thrones* he'd started. I'd call it a lot more than hard feelings. Quinn tore that play-house down to the studs."

"It does seem like Mr. Stagg has respect for Quinn," Bentley said. "Mr. Stagg, at heart, is a true Southern conservative who respects our veterans. That means something if we want him to sign off on the deal."

"So you talked with Stagg direct?"

"Yes, sir," Bentley said. "I sure did. I didn't know that Stagg had only owned the land for four years. The way y'all were talking, I thought it was the old home place or something."

"Johnny Stagg's people never had a home place," Jason said. "They crawled out of a shithole like some kind of swamp creatures from a B movie. Stagg's daddy ran a manure truck between New Albany and Jericho. Didn't pass a pile of shit he didn't stop to pick up."

"Ha," Bentley said. "You're kidding, right?"

"Just how much did your daddy tell you about Johnny Stagg?" Jason said.

The waitress coming back again, smiling at both of them, but, being closer in age to Bentley, smiled a bit more at the boy. She was wondering if they'd decided on lunch and they had. Not much to figure out at the Waffle House. Bentley wanted that patty melt with no onions and Jason was about ready for breakfast, as he'd yet to eat since fried chicken last night with Quinn. Hash browns, scattered and smothered. Two eggs, runny as hell.

"When I was coming up, Stagg was a joke," Jason said. "A lackey for the old supervisors who'd stripped the guts out of the county, skimming off road projects, clear-cutting timber. I'm not exactly sure, but I think Stagg worked as some kind of orderly at the old folks' home. The devil can be charming. And he charmed a lot of dying people out of their property while draining the shit and piss from their bedpans. Him and his daddy were true artistes when working with human excrement."

"That's how he built the Rebel."

"The Rebel was already something when he bought it," Jason said. "But it's fair to say he built it up. Brought in the Booby Trap, started making connections on all those side projects. Did a lot hand-in-hand with ole Larry Cobb, who's also now in prison. Pretty much ran the good, honest bootleggers like the Colson family out of business."

"Y'all were really serious bootleggers?"

"Damn straight," Jason said. "My daddy made the most gorgeous stuff you ever smelled in your life. He'd hide it up under floorboards of our house, each bottle clear and pretty, swaddled in cotton so it didn't shake when you walked over it."

Bentley drank some sweet tea and seemed

to be thinking long and hard on something. The Waffle House was set off from the highway, sitting smack-dab in the middle of what used to be a planting field. A half mile away there was a Tractor Supply, and down a ways along the railroad tracks sat a wide-open space advertising spots in a development to rent or own.

"My daddy thinks it's good to have some friends in Jericho," Bentley said. "With all this mess with this girl, I don't think Fannie Hathcock is going to last long. Just saw on the news that the girl was dancing at her titty bar. No one minds a whore dead in the alley, but if she's walking the street, people will complain."

"Did your daddy say that?"

"Yes, sir."

"Sounds like your old man."

"Everyone says he sure is a piece of work," Bentley said, long brown hair falling over his left eye, pushing it away to see. "If you can make this deal with Stagg, it would be nice to know we still got some good friends in Jericho. I heard your son might even run for office."

"Oh," Jason said. "He's not running. He's just taking on a little work before he heads back overseas. He's trying to sort out a complicated personal relationship."

"More than anything, Mr. Stagg wants to know his interests are being stoked," Bentley said. "He does you a favor by releasing that hundred acres and maybe you do him a favor on down the line. And so it goes."

"Your daddy and him are buds?" Jason said.

"They are," Bentley said. "For a real long time."

The waitress set down the two platters and ripped the check from her book. Jason had never seen anyone as quick as Bentley when it came to snatching it right up. "Oh, no, sir," he said. "This one is on us."

Lillie parked out on the county road and followed the gravel drive down a curved path to four trailers packed side by side. The trailers were older models, faded greens and a mustard yellow from back in the 1970s. No one had bothered to build steps, only laid some concrete blocks at the front doors. The dirt mess of a yard littered with old plastic toys, rusted car parts, and discarded furniture. Just in case you didn't know, these folks wanted you to understand they just didn't give two shits.

The door opened before she could knock and a teenage girl made her way down the steps. She wore a strapless white dress, no shoes, and held a toddler in her arms.

"Are you Nikki Rowland?"

"Yes, ma'am," she said. The girl had a hoarse voice, looking tired and beaten. She had bloodshot eyes and her chin shook when she spoke.

Lillie put her hands on her hips, trying to look like she'd yet to notice she was standing in someone's personal junkyard. The sun was directly overhead and hot as hell. "Need to ask you few things."

"Yes, ma'am," Nikki said, taking in a long breath. "I'd invite you in, but things are kind of a mess."

"I have a child, too," Lillie said. "I understand how things can get."

"All this," Nikki said. "This is all temporary. My folks own these trailers. They're letting me stay here until I go back to work."

"What do you do?" Lillie said, squinting toward Nikki in the hot white sun. Cicadas up and running as it was high past noon.

"I work in the food service industry."

"OK."

"Well," Nikki said, walking closer to Lillie, smiling. "I roller-skate and serve burgers and shakes at the Sonic."

"Need to talk to you about Milly."

"I was waiting for you," Nikki said. "Amber Jones just called and said you'd be heading this way. I've been crying so damn much, I think my insides have emptied out. I smoked a little weed to calm down my nerves. Hope you won't judge me on that."

"No, ma'am."

"She was my best friend."

"That's what I heard."

"Ain't no one deserves what she got," Nikki said. "I don't know if I can make it through this. If it weren't for my boy, I think I'd just crawl into a hole and die. You see what they did to her? God. I don't know if it's worse up close or just to imagine it."

"It was pretty bad up close," Lillie said.

Nikki was a pretty little girl, with apple cheeks, dark skin and eyes, and that two-tone black-and-blonde hair girls wore these days. The tops of her shoulders were sunburned and freckled. She looked like a girl who took care of herself and needed to grab her baby and run far, far from this place. She snuffled a little bit, big ole tears running down her cheeks until she wiped them away with a fist. Her bloodshot eyes refocused on Lillie.

"When did you see her last?"

"At the ball game."

"She came to the football game?"

"Yes, ma'am," Nikki said, the little boy crawling high up into his mother's arms but turning back for a few curious glances to Lillie. "We always went to the games. We agreed to support the squad even if we weren't on it no more. We both cheered for the Wildcats."

"Nikki, I need to know every single thing Milly told you Friday night," Lillie said. "Both big and small. Even if you think it's not important, I need to know. She was your best friend and you might be the best thing we've got."

Nikki nodded, the little boy even more intrigued by Lillie now, reaching out, touching Lillie's face and then turning back, quick and shy. Flirting.

"She was only there the first half," Nikki said. "We mainly watched the squad, talked about what they were doing right and doing wrong. Some of the girls really half-assing what they were supposed to do. Sometime in the second quarter, Milly told me she was leaving Jericho for good."

"Why?"

"I don't know," Nikki said. "She couldn't make money in town. Had busted up with the love of her life."

"Who was that?"

"Joshua Pitts."

Lillie nodded, she knew about Joshua. He was up next, but Lillie didn't expect much as they'd been apart for more than a year. Most of the time, he'd been living in Nashville. The kid had never had so much as a speeding ticket. But there'd be countless emails to go through, phone calls to check on.

"She'd had it out with her daddy," Nikki said. "Hold on. Hold on. *Hush. Hush.* Jon-Jon. Come on. Let go of Momma's hair."

"He tossed her out?"

"Yes, ma'am," Nikki said. "She'd been living in a car. I think she got some help at the hippie church out on Jericho Road."

"The River."

"Yes, ma'am," Nikki said. "That place. You might want to check with them? I think she was out there a couple days. I offered for her to stay here with me, but she said she had some things to do. She needed to get some things straight before she left town."

"Like what?"

"I don't know."

"Come on, Nikki," Lillie said, softly and with great patience. "I could really use something to go on."

The little boy had a good wad of the girl's hair, pulling it and stuffing it into his mouth. Nikki set him down and the toddler began to walk on shaky legs around the various sharp metal car parts and busted bottles. Lillie smiled at Nikki, picked up the child, and told her how much she loved kids and that her own daughter, Rose, was about to celebrate her fourth birthday.

"I love that little boy more than I love myself, but I sure wasn't ready."

"Never are," Lillie said.

"Milly had to take a job dancing to make ends meet."

Lillie nodded, bouncing the child up and down in her arms. He had on nothing but diapers and small red tennis shoes, chocolate stains around his mouth and down his fat belly.

"She'd only been at it a week when she decided to leave town," Nikki said. "I think she made enough money to take her to wherever she wanted to go."

"And where was that?"

"She didn't want to tell me," Nikki said. "She said she'd call me when she got settled. I figured it was somewhere down in Florida. Or on the coast. Milly loved the beach."

"What'd you think about her dancing at Vienna's?"

"I didn't look down at her or nothing, if that's what you're asking," Nikki said. "I make eight dollars an hour plus tips. Milly said she was making over a thousand dollars a night."

"Maybe I should start working the pole."

"You don't mean that," Nikki said, smiling a little. "You're somebody. You're the damn sheriff, Miss Virgil."

The cicadas boiled up loud and wide across the evenly planted pine trees. Lillie reached into her pocket for a handkerchief and began to wipe the boy's face. She just couldn't help it. The boy was small but had a lot of weight, heavy in her arms.

"You came and talked to our class once," Nikki said. "When we were freshman. You told the girls that the world wasn't a boys' club."

"I said that?"

"You sure did."

"Hmm."

Nikki took back her baby and held him close. "I just wish me and Milly had listened up better."

"When's the last time she and her boyfriend spoke?"

"A year," Nikki said. "That's a waste. Joshua's one of the sweetest people I ever met."

"How about Wash Jones?" Lillie said. "How mad was her daddy?"

"Mad as hell," Nikki said. "Called her a whore and threw her things out in the yard.

He's a sick man. I wish she hadn't gone back there. But she didn't have a heck of lot of choices."

Lillie nodded. "What do you think happened?"

"That girl bragged to me she had plenty of money," Nikki said. "I offered to let her borrow sixty dollars and she turned it down."

"All from dancing?"

"I never set foot in that place by the highway," Nikki said. "But I think Milly took something that didn't belong to her."

"Did she seem like she was in a hurry?"

"Oh, yes, ma'am," she said. "She was headed somewheres."

"She say anything else?"

The girl looked like she had something right in her mouth but was holding it with clamped jaws. Her eyes darted away from Lillie and she simply shook her head. "I loved Milly," she said. "We were sisters."

"Nothing else?"

"About Milly?" Nikki said. "No, ma'am."

"You think on it, Nikki," Lillie said. "And you call me. OK?"

The child reached out and grabbed the gold star on Lillie's chest, trying to pull it away, until Nikki stopped him. "Sheriff," Nikki said, clutching the boy's tiny hand.

"Wow. Damn, that's cool. I'd love to see a woman get the man who did this."

Lillie put on her aviator sunglasses and nodded, pretty damn sure now it wasn't a man who did it at all.

Wash Jones flushed the commode, stood by the bathroom sink, and started to run some cool water from the spigot. He waited a good minute before things got cold enough, flushing that hot stuff from the pipes, before he could lean down and splash his face. Reaching into the cabinet, he grabbed hold of a pill bottle and downed a couple trusted white ones with a handful of water. The water ran clean but smelled a little like sulfur, since their well didn't go down as deep as he'd like. You go any deeper and it'd cost you a few more thousand.

He'd thought about putting on his Sunday suit and had dressed in all that heavy gray wool but found it too hot for August and a little too high-dollar for what he needed to do. Instead, he picked out the same clothes he'd wear on a work interview and set them on his bed. He had a good pair of brown Carhartt pants, a thick blue T-shirt with a square pocket, and a pair of Georgia boots, the lowers made of rubber in case he had to do any septic work. Wash steadied his hands on each side of the sink and looked at his saggy face, seeing one spot he missed while shaving and taking another swipe with the razor.

As he waited for the pills to get going, he smoked a cigarette and pulled on his pants.

He was going to wear a brand-new ball cap proclaiming *Christ Is King* but then at the last minute switched it out for the one he'd just gotten in the mail from the NRA. If any of them sonsabitches was watching, he wanted them to know he was packing.

Wash's chest was slick with sweat, with heat, with worry, as he turned on a table fan set on the dresser to get himself dry. He put on some of that Axe Bodyspray, tugged on his T-shirt, and set his pack of smokes in the pocket. The NRA hat was a good touch. He wondered if he might wear a gun on his hip, too, although they'd taken away his open-carry permit after he tried to make a citizen's arrest of that woman at the Tupelo mall for shoplifting.

"Wash?" Charlotte said from the family room. The trailer was a neat little single-wide, carrying sounds through it like an empty coffee can.

"Huh?"

"You about ready?" Charlotte said. "Everyone's waiting."

"Yes, god damn it," Wash said, pulling on his work boots, using a soggy towel to clean off the dirt. "I'm comin'. Shit."

He sat on the bed for a minute. The mattress had grown real soft in the center where the dog slept. He put his face into his hands, feeling the weight of it start to pressurize and fill inside him. The damn grief of it all came spurting on up in a blubbering mass. He sat there crying alone for a couple minutes until he could feel those pills kicking in and everything softened a bit. He didn't even see Charlotte filling up the doorway, tears in her eyes now, the shit spreading from person to person like a flu, as she looked in on him.

"Wash," she said. "Oh, Lord."

"I said, I'm comin'."

He hefted off the bed, the center of the trailer dark as Hades, blinds rolled down, nothing but the TV giving off a glow. *Dr. fucking Phil.* All that commotion buzzed around the trailer, and Wash felt a sickness in his chest as he tried to pass by Charlotte, the fat woman clutching him and hugging him close like she was his momma or something.

"All right. All right. Hell. Let's go."

"You want me with you?"

"That's why I done told you to put on

makeup and a nice dress."

"You think I look OK?"

"Sure," Wash said, not even seeing what she'd put on. It was a dress of some sort. "Why wouldn't you?"

When she didn't answer, he saw she'd slipped into a big ole flowered number, bright blue and yellow. Wash wanted to tell her she looked like a g.d. circus tent, but everything with Milly had taken the dang piss and vinegar right out of him.

"She loved you," Charlotte said. "You know that, right?"

"No," Wash said. "She didn't. And it ain't till now that I understood why."

"Why?"

"Her momma set me up," he said. "Wanted me to be the one who ruined their life and I didn't say no better. But now I can make things right. I'm gonna find who did this. I'm gonna get out there and walk every inch of this county till we get some answers. I'm gonna be somebody. I'm gonna be Milly's daddy."

Charlotte stood by the thin aluminum doorway, feeling the heat come through cracks and all that talk and craziness echo off the metal siding. She looked to Wash, straightened the NRA hat on his head, and kissed him on the cheek. The door opened and right fast he saw the metal stand had been set up in his front yard. Dozens and dozens of reporters from all over the dang place had come to hear what Wash Jones had to say.

It was about g.d. time.

Wash stepped up, wiped something from his right eye, and opened his mouth.

20

"What's this?" Fannie said.

"It's a warrant," Lillie Virgil said. "I think we spelled your middle name right. Belle. With an *e*?"

"I know what it is," Fannie said. "I just don't know why you're here."

"You had a young woman in your employ named Milly Jones," Lillie said. "You might have turned on a radio or TV in the last twenty-four hours and heard someone set the girl on fire. She was eighteen, a cute little blonde, and someone's kid."

"All you had to do is ask," Fannie said. "We don't need all this."

All this meaning Lillie, Quinn, Kenny, Reggie Caruthers, Art, and Dave shutting down Happy Hour at Vienna's Place. Art and Dave watched the back door, the pulsing dance music gone silent, with Quinn, Reggie, and Kenny by the front. Lots of truckers made their way to the exit, Quinn checking their IDs, asking them questions, and making a list. The two girls who had been working the pole up front and the five girls in back who were getting up close and personal now gathered to sit on the main stage. They'd all slipped back into their bikinis and lingerie, wearing high heel plastic slippers that would break a regular woman's neck.

Fannie wasn't pleased, her pale white skin turning a bright red from her collarbone up to her face. She had on tan slacks and a black lacy top open at the throat, showing off a sizable ruby on her neck. Her hair was a deep red and she had thick black eyebrows. She wore a great deal of makeup, with bright red lips and wide cat eyes. Her perfume was expensive and cut through all the smoke and sweat in Vienna's. Her large chest heaved, sucking on a long brown cigarette. She ashed it and turned back to Lillie. "What do you wish to know?"

"I wish to know a lot of things," Lillie said, nodding at Quinn. Quinn nodded back, letting that nervous logger from Eupora through the front door to make his prayer meeting. "How about we start with her work schedule, any video you have of Milly coming and going, girls who shared her shift, and any special customers who might have enjoyed her talents."

"Our customers prefer privacy."

"Shame we had to meet head-on like this, Miss Hathcock," Lillie said. "I've been doing a lot of reading about all the adventures you've had. You sure are a true and authentic American success story."

"I'm not ashamed of how I got what I got," Fannie said. "But if you harass my customers, you'll find yourself being served with your own papers."

"We have witnesses who saw Lyle and his scooter riders harassing Milly Jones not ninety minutes before she was killed."

"And what's that have to do with me?"

"Everyone knows that you and the Born Losers cast the same shadow."

"That's a lie," Fannie said. "Those boys are customers and nothing more. I've known Lyle for years, but I am not his employer or his friend. You need to get your facts straight before running off to some judge, trying to make things look good for all these cameras."

"The Losers left town this morning," Lillie said. "We want to talk with them."

"I bet."

"What's that supposed to mean?"

Fannie smiled big, lifted her cigar from the bar top, and took a long pull. "Lyle said you were wild about him. Said you busted into the Golden Cherry and gave him some hell. He said this was the second time y'all met and, each time, you keep on getting flirty."

"Bullshit," Lillie said. "I wouldn't spit on someone so nasty."

"I see it," Fannie said, smoke floating in front of her face. "No need hiding it from me. Women love the feel of all that horsepower between their legs. Sometimes, it's the only thing that works."

"Get up," Lillie said. "Let's go on up to your office and start digging."

Fannie cocked her head, strange and coy, lifting the long hair off her neck and pulling it to the side. She played a bit with the silver necklace around her neck, the pendant dipping down between her low-cut blouse and lacy black bra. Fannie noticed her staring and smiled even wider. "Down here, we sell whiskey and pussy," Fannie said. "Up there, I'll make a call to my lawyer."

"Fine by me," Lillie said. "My assistant sheriff will make sure no one leaves this shithole until I'm satisfied."

"Take a look around," Fannie said. "Might see something you fancy. I don't make judgments on just what works for a woman. You'd be surprised how many ladies come here to get their fix."

"Work schedule, security tapes, and customer names," Lillie said. "This is a homicide investigation. We can run it here. Or we can run it at the sheriff's office. Might be a while before you open up again. For some country bumpkins, we can be thorough as hell. Not to mention it might be a pain having all those camera crews parked out front."

"You are a true piece of work, Sheriff," Fannie said, scooting her butt off the barstool and brushing a shoulder past the taller Lillie, bumping her a bit. Smoke spewed from the corner of her red mouth. "Lots of pretty girls around here," she said. "And bad boys."

"This won't end well between us," Lillie said.

Fannie smiled. "I know."

They came for him at twilight.

Sammi was counting down the Gas & Go drawer in back, Miss Williams working the register after making up the barbecue and sides, when he heard the approaching growl of the motorcycles. He knew they'd come back but didn't figure it would be so soon after the girl got killed. He hoped they'd have enough sense to ride far away from

Tibbehah County until everything got settled. But, like he'd told Quinn Colson, being Middle Eastern in north Mississippi made him an easy target. Somehow, they knew he spoke with the law. And whether it was Nito Reece or a gang of sweaty, stinky half apes, they wouldn't rest until he was in the ground.

Sammi wasn't his father. He didn't smile and laugh when they made fun of his people or joked that he just might be a terrorist. He'd spent most of his life in this county, and had done everything possible to blend in, wear the clothes, talk the talk, never wanting to be different. But he looked different, sounded different, ate different food, and prayed from a different book than most.

He jammed the day's count into a bank bag and zipped it closed. He punched up the combination on the safe, slid the money inside, and pulled out a .357 Magnum. He tucked the gun into his sagging blue jeans and let his Memphis Redbirds tee hang down low. He pulled the ball cap down in his eyes, walked hard out of the back room and through the store — Miss Williams asking him about needing some more hot sauce — and headed out into the hot, fading light.

The bikers rode in circles around the Gas & Go, gunning their engines, lurching up close to him, one riding so close, the handle-bar gored him in the ribs and knocked him to the asphalt.

The leader of the group rolled up fast, setting his front tire between Sammi's open legs and revving his motor. He had on wraparound sunglasses and no shirt, leaning into the handlebars. His black hair set into twin braids like he was Willie Nelson or something. "You kill that girl for Allah?" he asked, sort of whispering it.

"What?"

"I said you killed that girl for Allah."

Sammi's heart was up in his throat, his mouth dry, but he was aware enough to lift his right hand up under his long shirt. He felt his way under the material like it was a poncho, getting a good grip on the gun, waiting for Lyle to move that tire an inch.

"This is America," Lyle said. "We don't like you burning up white girls. We can't have no goddamn jihad down south. Some of my brothers got killed over there in Iraq. Your people setting up bombs in the ground, scattering their asses all around the desert."

Sammi swallowed and said, "I'm Syrian, you idiot."

"Syria, Iraq — what's it matter?" he said. "You all think alike. Y'all won't rest until you have every dumb son of a bitch sitting on a little carpet and praying five times a day. Let me tell you something. I only pray on Sunday. And sometimes not even then. What you did to that girl ain't even human."

"Did you know her?"

"What?"

"What's her name?" Sammi said. "Say her name."

Several of the bikers had crawled off their Harleys and stood over Sammi on the ground. Two of them held big sticks, another had a long length of chain. They were sunburned and smelled like that cattle truck that stopped by every morning for a tank of diesel. Some of them called him a sand nigger and a goddamn Arab. All of them saying *Arab* like it was two words.

"She was my friend," Sammi said. "Don't bring this here."

"Hey now," Lyle said. "Hey now. We ain't gonna hurt you. We're just gonna take you for a little ride until you confess that you lit that girl up like a candle."

Some of the bikers made *la-la-la-la-la* sounds as if they understood what the hell *ululation* meant. His left elbow dug into the ground, high right hand drawing the gun from his sweaty waistband, as Lyle revved his motor and scooted forward and then back. Forward and then back.

One of the men stooped down and tried to wrap his ankles together with a chain.

Sammi drew the .357 and aimed it dead center at Lyle's head. "Get the hell out of here."

"Shoot me," Lyle said, laughing. "Please shoot me. You do and it won't be like the girl. Won't be any of that dark meat to be found."

Sammi thumbed back the hammer, the trigger smooth and tight under his finger. He imagined what it'd be like to just let it go, see the man's ugly face explode into mess, watch him fall to the ground, and maybe take out a few more, before they got to him and dragged him on the back roads until he didn't have any skin left. That's what they all wanted. And hated. All that skin different than their own.

"Go ahead. Sam the Sham won't shoot," Lyle said, his face turning from a grin into a hard look with a lot of yellowed teeth. "Chain him up."

"Motherfuckers," Sammi said. "Mother-fuckers."

They pulled his gun from him his hand, knocked him in the head, and that's when the stomping started. The boots flew down on his head and into his ribs, over and over,

Sammi trying to cover up with his forearms, as he felt his feet being bound and the motorcycle lurching forward. The bikers making that high ululation sound like a group of excited women.

Fannie watched from high in the roost as the deputies walked out of Vienna's with four laptops, five trash bags filled with receipts, and at least two willing customers who wanted to make statements and help out that nice girl. Mingo couldn't understand how they'd just busted in, shut her down for nearly two hours, and walked away with her personal property.

"They can have it," Fannie said. "That woman got off on it."

"But your personal records?" Mingo said. "Stuff from your desk and in the safe?"

"Honey, you think I keep my personal records on the premises?" she asked. "Only a wet-eared fool would try that. I don't use the business phone and I don't email. You want to talk business, you tell me private. Don't forget what I'm telling you."

"Yes, ma'am."

"They tried to burn me on the Rez and they'll try to burn my ass up here."

She let the day shift go, the night girls, her A-team, coming through the front door, wanting to know just what the hell was going on. Fannie told them to go ahead and get pulled into those G-strings and cowboy boots. Nobody had shut down a damn thing. It's business as usual along Highway 45.

"Besides," Fannie said. "I got that woman's number."

"How's that?" Mingo asked.

"You ever seen a woman be so damn prissy with the fucking help?" she said. "Telling the girls to cover themselves up before they'd sit down and talk. Not looking them in the eye."

"So what?"

"That woman has a walk like John Wayne."

"Thought you said she was sweet on Lyle."

"I was just pulling her chain until I found there was a real chain to pull," Fannie said, ashing her cigarette. "Won't be long till I own her."

"Appreciate y'all inviting me here tonight," Coach Bud Mills said. "I won't ever pass up a chance to eat fried catfish and talk about the Lord."

The grayheads at the VFW all nodded along with what he said, most of them wanting to skip over the Jesus talk. Get right on to talking about next Friday night and what kind of plan he had for Holly Springs. Some of them were worried Tibbehah County might be a little intimidated like last year. He assured everyone that wouldn't happen again.

The VFW was a square cinder-block building a quarter mile west of downtown on Jericho Road. A big mural had been painted along the side of the building showing maps of Europe, Vietnam, and Iraq. A mobile sign outside flashed TONITE. COACH MILLS APPRECIATION. GO WILDCATS!

"What I appreciate most about this town is that we are old-fashioned," Mills said. "And I don't mind being called that one bit. We support our people, our churches, and our football team. To me, athletics has always been a way to serve the Lord. Some of them kids who come to me are like acorns spread out on the forest floor. They don't have a chance to grow being shadowed by family problems, drugs. Rap music and all that mess. But you take an acorn and plant it out into an open field, make sure it's got water and light, you see what happens. Happened with Dexter Thompson. Happened with Wesley Ruth before he made some bad personal choices. I have been fortunate enough to have coached eighteen college players, most of 'em going D-1.

Three of ours have gone onto the pros. I don't have to tell you a thing about a Pookie Woods or Rayshawn Pennywell. The Lord gave them talent. But they needed some more light."

Mills reached for a glass of sweet tea on the lectern. Thirty or so folks — men and women — sat at long folding tables in the banquet hall, picking at their catfish bones and munching on hushpuppies. Even though the theme of the evening was Christ and football, some of the old vets had filled their ceramic mugs with a little brown water. And although Mills didn't drink himself, except maybe a cold beer in the summer, he wasn't offended.

"I have loved working with y'all's children," he said. "I don't know how many more seasons I'll be here. But molding the future of young men through the blood, sweat, and tears has made this town a tougher place. I don't think I need to tell any of the men here about mental toughness. Y'all served your country. You went through boot camp. But most of our young people today don't take that opportunity. They'll never know how to toughen their hide to this world. They leave high school with high-mindedness of what they want to accomplish but no game plan to make it happen."

Coach reached for the sweet tea, took a long pull, and wiped his mouth with the back of his hand. He'd been on the coaching field all afternoon and he could still feel the sun on his skin, the white bristles along his jaw. He looked across the faces of folks he'd known the twenty-odd years he'd been in Tibbehah County and smiled. These were his people. They'd go to hell and back to support him and the team.

"Before we get down to a second helping of this wonderful catfish, I do want us to pray a moment for little Milly Jones. She cheered for our team. A hell of an athlete. I never saw a girl who could fly so high. She was a true angel among us. I knew her brother, a sweet young man who didn't possess the talent but had a heart bigger than most. I can't imagine what that family is going through right now. But when something like that happens in Jericho, it hurts us all and just tears the guts out of this place."

Coach Mills removed his ball cap, wiped his dry eyes, and spoke for a solid two minutes about the little blonde angel they'd been lucky enough to know.

21

Boom Kimbrough walked straight into the sheriff's office meeting room, pointed to Lillie with his prosthetic hand, and said, "Y'all got some serious shit going on up in Blackjack."

Quinn and Lillie had emptied out the receipts from Vienna's the night Milly Jones died onto the table. They'd gone through nearly one entire trash bag by the time Boom arrived, coffee mugs and a full ashtray in the center of the conference table. They'd written a possible time line on a grease board, lined up phone calls she'd made that week, and noted all the witnesses yet to be interviewed. Lillie stood up, hands on her hips. "Yeah?"

"I got Sammi Khouraki's ass out in my truck," Boom said. "He's been busted-up bad but doesn't want to go to the hospital. I was towing a county truck back to the barn when I saw a bunch of folks stopped to help at the gas station. He wouldn't tell me what happened, but a man told me he'd seen the Born Losers scooting around the store waving an American flag. One of them had a sign that said NO JIHAD IN JERICHO."

"Catchy," Lillie said.

"I'm taking him to the hospital," Boom said. "I don't give a shit what he wants. Y'all come on with me and talk some sense to him?"

Quinn walked outside into the hot early evening with Lillie and Boom. Boom opened the door to his big-ass tow truck and Quinn leaned into the passenger side. Sammi looked rough. He was bare-chested, with one eye completely shut. The skin over his stomach and arms was bright red and bloody. Deep red welts covered both of his wrists.

"How you been, Sam?" Quinn said.

"Better."

"Don't suppose you want to tell us what happened?" Lillie said.

"Would you believe I tripped and fell while stocking the candy aisle?"

Sammi grinned a bit. It looked like he'd lost a tooth on his wild ride with the Losers. He wheezed as he spoke, sounding like he might have some busted ribs.

"We'll talk more at the hospital," Quinn

said. "Boom?"

Boom nodded and scooted into the truck and behind the wheel. Sammi kept on saying he just wanted to go home and that he didn't need to see a doctor, the whole time gritting his teeth and wincing. "I got shit to do," he said. "This is nothing."

"Who's minding the store?" Lillie asked.

"Miss Williams," Sammi said. "She's got the night shift. I was shutting down."

"Go on, Boom," Lillie said. "Or we can call you an ambulance."

"No," Sammi said. "I just want to get cleaned up and get a ride home. I'm getting the hell out of here."

"Where?"

"The goddamn state of Mississippi," Sammi said. "What the hell do you think? Y'all can have it."

"How about you tell us what happened so we can round up those turds," Lillie said. "Stand up, Sammi. Don't let those fuckers run you off."

"I'm fine," he said, reaching for the door handle, fumbling to find it. "I'm fine. I don't want any more trouble. Shit. I got enough problems as is."

"Why'd they come for you?" Quinn said, standing by the open driver's-side door, looking over Boom to talk. "First Nito and now the Losers? You're making friends real fast up there."

Sammi focused his good eye on Quinn, holding on to the dash with his hands as if the truck was still in motion. "They say I killed Milly," he said. "They think I'm some kind of terrorist and I killed in the name of Islam."

Quinn turned to Lillie, Lillie shaking her head. "I'd like to go on record as saying that's the dumbest shit I've ever heard in my life."

"They're riding all around the store now," Sammi said. "They told me if I came back, they'd kill me. That one — Lyle, Wrong Way, or whoever the hell he is — said he was liberating everything my family owns."

"That's your store," Lillie said. "Your family's owned it for years."

"How about you tell 'em that?" Sammi said, laughing and then scrunching his face in pain.

"Fine by me," Lillie said. "Ready to roll, Ranger?"

Quinn caught her eye and nodded. "Yes, ma'am."

They walked together across the asphalt, sun just going down late in the day, to Quinn's Ford F-250. He hit the sirens and the lights, feeling good to be driving that

Big Green Machine so fast again.

"What the fuck?" Nito said, rolling past the Gas & Go, spotting the freak show going on at sundown.

"I hate those dudes," Ordeen said. "You ever smell 'em? Smell like farts and gasoline."

"What they doing up here?"

"Putting on a goddamn show," Ordeen said. "You see them cameras?"

"Where?"

"Right across the road, drive on past," Ordeen said. "Damn, man. I don't want to be on no TV."

A mess of those bikers were zipping up and down Blackjack Road, making circles around the convenience store, spinning out, pumping their fists, flags tied to the back of their bikes. Some of the flags were American, but there were a couple of those rebel flags, too. Ordeen wasn't too cool with stopping off for a cold six-pack with those boys waving the Stars and Bars. What the fuck were they up to?

A couple of big-tittied mommas in tight T-shirts and short-shorts were holding signs, raising them up high over their heads, with their wide hips cocked. Two of the girls had on bikini tops. Ordeen couldn't see the words on the signs till they were right up on them. JUSTICE FOR MILLY.

"Oh, shit," Nito said.

"Someone blaming Sammi," Ordeen said. "That's plain messed-up."

Nito drove his new ride low and slow, sinking down in the driver's seat, while he passed those girls and bearded dudes leaning against their bright chrome bikes. Ordeen looked straight ahead, seeing the long black ribbon of blacktop leading back to Jericho. The long damn heat of the day was wearing off, wind drying the sweat off his face.

"Folks sayin' this the last place they saw that girl alive."

"Probably 'cause she gettin' gas," Ordeen said. "Milly ain't never had enough money for a full tank. She was here damn-near every day. Damn, this is messed-up."

"Maybe."

"What you talking *maybe* for?" Ordeen said. "You got something wrong in your head for Sammi? First you bust his lip and now you believe he's a killer. That boy ain't no killer."

"He ain't made like you and me."

"How we made?"

"We straight-up dirty South," Nito said. "I don't mess with people who eat camels and shit."

"You known Sammi long as you known me," Ordeen said. "He ain't even ever seen no camel except at the Memphis Zoo. C'mon, man. What's getting to you?"

"That girl," Nito said. "That girl change everything. Fucked my mind up. Making everybody crazy as hell. Everybody pointing fingers at each other."

"Why you call her 'that girl' like you don't know Milly Jones?" Ordeen said. "Man, you been acting strange since y'all dropped me the other night. What'd y'all get into?"

"She gave it up," Nito said. "And then she died. It's just messing with my head, is all."

"Coach asked me to come see him last night," Ordeen said. "He know you ain't acting right. He says you gonna get us both sent to prison, you don't straighten up."

Nito didn't react, just rode south on that blacktop, windows down, a warm summer breeze washing through the car. He kept two of his right-hand fingers on the wheel, reaching over the visor to find the rest of that blunt he stuck up there. With his left hand, he cracked on a Bic and fired the roach up.

"He thinks you crazy as a shithouse rat," Ordeen said. "Told me that I needed to stay away from you."

"Come on, Ordeen," Nito said, a plume of smoke coming from his mouth. "Coach really say that?"

"Yeah," Ordeen said. "I told him you weren't like that. I said you and me been best friends most our lives."

"Fucking Coach," Nito said. "Ole Coach. That's one tricky ole man."

"What you mean?"

"He playing with your mind, Ordeen," Nito said. "Can't you see that? Games. Man love to play them games."

"Why he want to split us, then?"

"Guess he got his reasons," Nito said. "Shit, man. How about you just ask his old ass? You his boy now. Y'all loving on each other. He ain't got no more use for me."

A big-ass green truck with flashing lights passed them, headed toward Blackjack. Two patrol cars sped close behind.

"Oh, shit," Ordeen said.

"Johnny Law."

Nito slowed and turned into a short gravel drive by a trailer and then started to back up.

"What the hell you doing?" Ordeen said.

"Goin' back," he said. "Don't you want to see the show? This shit's just getting fun."

"Yeah?" Ordeen said. "OK. But how about you put out that blunt before I get my ass put back in jail?"

Lillie Virgil opened the truck door before Quinn even stopped. As he braked, she hopped out onto the asphalt and walked past the gas pumps, hefting her twelve-gauge tactical Winchester in both hands. Quinn reached for a nearly identical gun in the rack behind him and followed her toward the entrance of the Gas & Go. A few bikers zipped past her along the county road, cutting back after they were blocked by Reggie Caruthers in front of his cruiser. He hit the buzzer, light bar flashing, as Art and Dave blocked off the north end of the road, boxing in the bikers.

"Ladies," Lillie said to the women gathered at the roadside.

"We got a right to be here just like anybody else," said a blonde with enormous breasts, T-shirt tied up high under the pair. "If y'all would do your job, we wouldn't have to be out here."

"What's your job, sweetie?" Lillie said. "Besides grinding men's peckers down at Fannie's place."

"You don't know where I work," the woman said, blowing a bubble that popped quick. "Or a damn thing about me."

"Maybe next time don't pick the shirt that

says 'Vienna's,' " Lillie said. "It looks a little stretched-out."

Quinn shook his head, watching four bikers circling back to the Gas & Go, racking in a round to the twelve-gauge, feeling for his Beretta at his hip, thinking that within a few more meters he could knock them both off their bikes and send them scattering. He had on sunglasses, and his hat was pulled down low in his eyes. He steadied his breathing, holding the Winchester, watching the entire road from north to south, seeing them all caught, spotting only one way out — a back road that would lead them to an old cemetery — but knowing if they headed that way, they'd be even worse off. They'd have to leave their bikes and run. He knew they'd never leave their bikes. Boys like that loved their bikes more than their mommas.

"How much is Fannie paying y'all?" Quinn asked.

"She's not paying us," the girl said, chomping on some gum. "That dead girl was one of us."

"What was her name?" Lillie said.

"I know her name," the girl said.

"Say it."

"Like I said, I got a right to stand here and get folks' attention," she said. "This is a protest."

"Can't argue with stupid," Lillie said. "Oh, good. Here comes the brains."

More scooters rode up, the sun going down, huge and orange, to the west, setting over a big open field filled with weeds and rusted-out appliances. One of the riders was a stout-bodied guy with a shaved head and a goatee. The other biker looked young and a little scared and had some tattoo work on his face and a T-shirt that said FUCK SHIT UP. The bald guy wore a big shit-eating grin on his face, lifting the sunglasses from his eyes on top of his sweating bald head.

"Shut off that fucking bike and get off with your hands held high," Lillie said, moving toward him fast and with a hell of a lot of force.

"Oh, shit," the man said. "What the hell? Shit."

"Now," Quinn said, moving right by Lille's side.

"For assault and attempted murder," Lillie said, lifting her shotgun, barrel pointed straight at the bald guy. Quinn kept his shotgun straight at the other man, even uglier than the first. The one with the shaved head gunned the motor of the Harley, cocking a hand to his ear. "What'd you say? Can't hear you, sir."

Quinn walked over to the bald guy, Lillie

now watching the other, and reached for his ear, twisting it and pulling him from the seat of the bike to his feet. The bike teetered, nearly crashing to the ground, the man having to straddle it hard to keep his balance while he raised his hands. Quinn turned the key and shut it down and pulled the kid off the bike. More bikes growled on up as they forced the two bikers down on the ground, Lillie cuffing them while Quinn pulled two more off their scooters. The other deputies left the roadblocks and raced up in their patrol cars, slamming on the brakes and cornering the Born Losers in the Gas & Go lot.

Two more were left. Quinn recognized one as Wrong Way from the Golden Cherry. He parked his bike, set down his kickstand, and walked on over with a big smile on his face. "What's the problem, Officer?"

"Hands high," Quinn said. "On the ground."

"For what?" he said.

"Now, shithead," Quinn said. "On the ground."

"Not for you," he said. "Not for anybody. I respect few and take shit from none."

Quinn walked toward him fast and with great tactical precision. The man just grinned some more and shook his head as if he'd been victim of some crazy wrongdoing. He scratched at his beard. He wore twin braids on the side of his head, his face sunburned and wrinkled, giving him a craggy, leather look. Quinn watched his hands set on the handlebars.

"What we have here is a failure to communicate," Lyle said. Some of his boys snickered.

"How about I blast your ass off that scooter?" Lillie said. "Would that help?"

"Damn, woman," he said. "You sure are a pistol. We're all just trying to help. Guess a man's personal rights don't mean dick when you got the cooze as the sheriff."

"I think ole Wrong Way would like to pick buckshot out of his asshole for the next year," Quinn said.

Lyle shrugged, still smiling, dropping to his knees, hands held high. "Damn, when you put it that way . . ."

Art and Dave forced the four others off their bikes, none of them saying a word now as Lyle lay facedown on the hot asphalt. The girls screamed at the deputies, calling them a bunch of dickless turds. Art and Dave didn't seem to take offense as they forced the men's hands behind their backs and cuffed them. Six down on the ground. Lyle still laughing and yelling. "A real fucking failure to communicate," he said. "What's the world coming to when a god-damn Arab can set a white girl on fire?"

"Shut up," Lillie said. "Colson, how about you call dispatch for a little help in transport?"

"What about our bikes?" Lyle asked.

"Wrong Way, don't worry your pretty little head about that," Lillie said. "We'll show your personal property the same love and care you showed Mr. Khouraki."

"You put one scratch on my bike . . ." Wrong Way said.

Quinn got on one knee to see the man's face more clearly. He sure hoped he didn't have to transport this one in the Big Green Machine. It would take a bucket of Febreze to get rid of the stink. "And you'll do what?"

Wrong Way spit on Quinn's boot. It was about all he had left in him.

22

Nearly two weeks after his son had the run-in with those bikers, Jason Colson rolled up to the federal prison at Maxwell Air Force Base in Montgomery, Alabama, for a sit-down with none other than Johnny T. Stagg. Most folks said that Stagg didn't have a middle name, only used the *T.* to look halfway respectable, everyone knowing the Johnny was just Johnny, never Jonathan. Jason never asked him about the *T.* or really much of anything since Stagg had risen in power in Tibbehah, from dogcatcher to head county supervisor, about the same time Jason had found regular work out in Hollywood. Stagg took over the old choke-and-puke by the highway, Jason recalling it had been an Exxon station for a while, with real breathing tigers in cages to draw in the tourists headed down 45. PLEASE DON'T FLICK YOUR CIGARETTE BUTTS ON THE ANIMALS, the old sign read.

"Your buddies wouldn't take no for an answer," Stagg said, not long after they had the usual back-and-forth about who they knew, where they'd been, and exactly how were things inside a minimum security prison. "I already lost too much, as it is. But I prayed on it and, well, I figured talking can't hurt."

"Oh, yes, sir," Jason said. "I only wanted to see if you were open to the idea." He was a little surprised to hear Stagg talk about prayer as he knew all the stories about Stagg running girls, drugs, and elections with a heavy hand since he'd been back. Maybe all the caddying, bush pruning, and healthy outdoor recreating in the federal pen had made Stagg think on things.

"I don't know quite what to make of it," Stagg said. "I'd been thinking about putting a little house out there after I leave this place. Might even retire. Figured Quinn wouldn't mind having me a neighbor. *Ha, ha.* Since I'd served my time and made things right."

Stagg's skin had grown even more red and weathered since Jason saw him last, his classic 1950s pompadour barbered down to a more businesslike cut. But he still had the skeletal craggy face, the big veneers, and the hooked nose. He wore a prison-issue green T-shirt, green pants, and black sneakers. "But you'll have to remind me, Mr. Colson," Stagg said. "I own a bunch of land. How many acres is this parcel again?"

"Two hundred and fifty."

"Uh-huh," Stagg said, grinning a bit. "You plan on sticking around Jericho? Need a place to settle? Maybe put up a log cabin?"

"Something like that." Jason reached down next to the chair and brought out a small box of peppermints he'd bought at a Walgreens over the state line. Folks said Stagg favored keeping a fresh mint going, as his breath was like hot air escaped from inside a dead mule.

"Appreciate that, sir," Stagg said. "Well, I guess it's not much of a secret that me and your boy never saw eye to eye."

"Heard it was more than that," Jason said. "Y'all pretty much despised each other."

Stagg shrugged, "I think Quinn had a hard time adjusting to Jericho after being in the service," he said. "Lots of things had changed. Places he knew as a kid had closed up. Most of the business had moved off the Square and out to the highway. That Amsden girl he'd been seeing had married another man. Although I heard they're sweet on each other again. After war, the real world just seems kind of off-kilter.

Remember how it was for boys after Vietnam?"

"You bet," Jason said. "I had a buddy who told me he got spit on not twenty-four hours after stepping off the plane."

"I think your boy was respected," Stagg said. "But he had a habit of blaming other folks for his troubles. Mad at the world. He was still in the service when he came after me, blamed me for your brother-in-law Hamp Beckett dying. You and I both know that wadn't anyone's fault but Hamp's."

Jason nodded. He'd heard a lot of theories, many that implicated Stagg. But you didn't act like a hard-on coming hat in hand. A man gritted his teeth and tried his best to see that deal through. "Sure."

"Just how much are you willing to pay?"

"Land is stripped," he said. "And what's left is a real mess."

Stagg grinned with tombstone teeth big enough to pop the cap from a beer bottle. He folded his hands on the picnic table and nodded and nodded. "Cleared," he said. "And ready for development."

"You expect much development up there around Fate?" Jason said, smiling back. "Only business up there is a scratch-and-dent grocery and a deer processor."

Stagg's grin didn't wave, only stared at Jason, waiting for him to get on with it, tell him a price, as that was the only thing that got a man like Stagg's attention.

Jason said, "Fifteen hundred an acre."

"Oh, hell."

"That's twice what it's worth," Jason said. "I appreciate your predicament. But as I told our friends, I'm not here to bargain. Only to make an offer. If that's not acceptable, it's your land and you can do with it what you want."

Stagg scratched under his nose with the back of his forefinger. A prisoner on a riding lawn mower passed by the patio, kicking up a plume of dirt and grass as he passed, drowning out the business talk for several moments. Stagg wore a different expression now, less cocky and more thoughtful. "What's Quinn doing?" he said. "Now that he's not the sheriff."

"Overseas work," he said. "He trains Afghanis how to be cops."

"Signs and wonders."

"But he's back now, working a little bit for Lillie Virgil."

"That woman gets elected sheriff and every boy and man better check his cojones at the county line," Stagg said. "You think Mississippi is ready for a woman running the show? One who knows how to use a big

312

gun and shoot?"

"Lillie's a fine woman," Jason said. "I've known her since she was a little girl. Quinn says she's twice the lawman, or lawperson, or whatever you're supposed to say, than him. He said he didn't know much about detective work, investigations, details, and all that when he came home. She was the one who trained him."

"Don't I know it," Stagg said. "They did a lot of training out at the Rebel, trying to toss my pecker into that churning meat grinder."

Jason looked around at the prison grounds. Lots of manicured bushes, small islands of roses, and neatly trimmed maples and magnolias. It looked more like a celebrity rehab center, as Jason had visited plenty of those, than a federal prison. "Doesn't look so bad, Mr. Stagg," Jason said. "Definitely isn't Parchman."

"I wouldn't wish Parchman on anyone," he said. "Except maybe a couple folks. But I'm reading the Bible every day, attending prayer meetings, trying to let go of all that kind of stuff. I read in *Time* magazine that anger can contribute to heart disease and the cancer."

"I once dated a woman out in Los Angeles who could tell how much hate a person held on to by the color of their aura," Jason said.

"Los Angeles," he said. "*Whew.* I got to visit there someday. They still got the Brown Derby?"

"Burned down about twenty years ago."

"Fifteen hundred?" Stagg said.

"Yes, sir."

"I don't want to be ugly here, but in the grand scheme that's not a whole lot of money," he said. "By my standards."

"You might consider it had been in Quinn's family for more than a century."

"Are you buying that land?" Stagg said. "Or is Quinn?"

Jason took a breath, smiled, and waited. The lawn mower passed again, chipped bits of leaves and grass flying up onto the patio. Both men having to wait until the machine headed out toward the parking lot, trimming a narrow path along a sidewalk. Damn, it was hot as hell out here. Late August, but still pushing a hundred degrees. Stagg seemed to thrive in it.

"Mr. Colson, let's lay it all out on this table," Stagg said. "I don't really give two shits about some logged-out crap hole in Fate. That land's been worth holding on to just to piss off your son."

"Pretty much what I figured," Jason said, pushing himself up from the table. His bad knee giving him hell. "Sorry to have wasted your time."

"But," Stagg said, waiting, drawing it out. He held up the flat of his hand. "I do have an interest in a fifty-acre parcel not too far from what used to be my truck stop."

"OK."

"Got some high-minded owners who would never sell to me," he said. "And if someone starts making phone calls from Jackson, they might get real ambitious. Nervous and all."

"Sorry," Jason said. "I'm not following you, Mr. Stagg."

"I see that land you want to be worth about the same as this fifty acres," Stagg said, cracking a mint with his back teeth. "I got no problems in swapping deeds with you."

"You thinking about getting back in business soon?" Jason said.

Stagg swallowed, hot wind scattering his dry white hair. He pressed the hair down to his head and winked. "Sir, I always heard you got all the charisma in the family," he said. "And now I know it."

Lillie had done a week's shopping at the Piggly Wiggly, cart loaded down, with her daughter Rose, now four, riding high in the kid's seat. Lillie had come straight from her shift, wearing her uniform, gun on hip, making her rounds, aisle to aisle, making sure she got the Cheez-Its and Capri Suns for Rose's lunch box, hell to pay if she didn't. She was loading it all into the back of her Cherokee when she saw Wash Jones standing by the front door of the grocery. A group of women from the Baptist church were having a bake sale, the proceeds to help Milly Jones's family in their time of need.

Wash saw Lillie and Lillie saw Wash. He walked across the lot in big strides, shaking a few hands and saluting people from across the way. Wash, who'd gone from Town Loser to Town Hero in two whole weeks, gaining a lot of purpose and confidence as the man who'd sired the murdered kid. A long way from apprentice to the county's septic tank king.

"Howdy, Wash," Lillie said.

"Been trying to call you, Lillie," he said. "Internet's heating up. Did you know our Facebook page now has more than ten thousand followers? Ten thousand! We got folks from up in Ohio trying to make sense of this. All over the dang twitterverse."

"Good for them."

"I'm just saying, folks are starting to wonder."

"Wonder what?" Lillie said, lifting Rose from the cart and helping her climb up into the car. The dark-eyed, dark-skinned little girl smiling up at Momma as she scrambled into her car seat and tugged at the straps. Rose had gone from Guatemala to a foster hell and into a loving Mississippi home in her few short years.

"Hmm," Wash Jones. "I recall Milly at that age. She sure was a hellcat."

"We're doing all we can," Lillie said. "This is the first time I've spent time with my child since the night it happened. Babysitter said we'd run out of every bit of food."

"I don't fault you, Miss Virgil," Wash said. "I just need something to tell folks. I don't want people pointing fingers at you. Wondering just what's happening. Two weeks. A murder like that? Folks start to wonder who is doing what."

Lillie helped Rose strap in, then leaned inside and started the car to get the air-conditioning going. She turned to Wash and crossed her arms over her chest. Wash, dressed in brown overalls and a stained white T-shirt, smiled back at her, eager, wanting to know the latest facts for him to parcel out to his people, folks online who called him "courageous" and a man with "intestinal fortitude."

"We still don't have autopsy results yet," Lillie said. "Given the circumstances. Well, it's tougher than most."

"What about the crime scene?" Wash said. "Did y'all find some clues? You know, like a cigarette butt with some DNA? Tire tracks? Some of that dang thermo-imaging?"

"No, sir."

"But you did bag some evidence, find some fingerprints?"

"Your daughter's vehicle was incinerated."

"Lord God."

"We're doing our best," Lillie said. "We have some leads."

"Who?"

"I don't want to point fingers until we have someone solid," Lillie said. "Right now, it's all hypothetical."

"Huh?"

"We're throwing darts and see where they land."

"She was my baby," Wash said, scratching his whiskered chin. "Baby love. My lovey."

"I better get going."

"You know we got Greta Van Susteren flying in from Atlanta tonight?" Wash said. "She's that hatchet-faced broad from the OJ show on ole CNN. I figured we'd get her a Mex meal down at the El Dorado. Ain't much, but they got tequila."

"I promise to keep you posted."

Wash walked close up to the Cherokee, peering into the glass at Rose, waving to the little girl. Rose, being a smart little tyke, looked embarrassed and glanced away like she didn't see him. Wash did a little impromptu dance, shifting his sizable weight from side to side, foot to foot.

"Hard not having a daddy."

"Should be any day for those autopsy results."

"You got a boyfriend or something?" Wash said. "Some kind of man for the child to get to know?"

Lillie bit her damn tongue so hard that she thought it might just bleed. She tried to think about what the man had gone through, his daughter walking a back highway while completely on fire. A teenager walking while on fire. Her windpipe damnnear cauterized.

"Aren't y'all glad you could wipe me from the books?" Wash Jones said. "I mean, damn. I guess it pays to be a Walmart customer, that video showing me and Charlotte buying that thirty-inch Sony at the exact moment. I think about that. What if our TV hadn't gone out? Charlotte wanting to watch *Dancing with the Stars*. I mean, y'all might've still thought I could have

319

done it. Leaving things like that with Milly. But, Miss Virgil, I want you to know I never had that kind of hate in my heart. Whoever did this wanted to send a message. It's like what they call on those cop shows a real Message Killin'."

"We have some leads," Lillie said. "We have suspects. I wish I could tell you more."

Wash swallowed, took a few steps forward, and scratched his hairy neck. "Y'all are looking at that redheaded bitch at the Rebel. Ain't you?"

"We have some leads."

"That's a goddang den of iniquity down there," he said. "But who am I? I didn't do nothin'. Might have just gone ahead and sold my sweet girl to some white slavers. They used her ass up and then burned her. Why? Why would that woman burn my girl?"

"We're making inquiries."

"You ask me and I'd look at those damn Born Losers people," Wash said. "Folks say that them and Fannie Hathcock are thick as thieves. I'd raid that damn place and put that bitch in jail till she done repent."

"Good to see you, Mr. Jones," Lillie said. "Sorry for your loss."

"Get that bitch," he said. "Y'all go get that fucking bitch."

Lillie opened the Jeep door and Rose called out, wanting to know who that weird man was talking to Mommy. Wash Jones took two more steps forward, his heated breath hell on earth.

"You didn't think I could do that to my Milly," Wash Jones said. "Did you?"

Anna Lee had been painting when Quinn came over, getting the old Victorian ready to sell, since eight bedrooms and six baths was a little too much house for a single woman and a three-year-old girl. She'd been in love with the house since they were kids, Quinn always calling it the old spook house, the place reminding him a great deal of the mansion on the *Addams Family*.

"My mom has Shelby in Tupelo for the day," Anna Lee said, wiping the flecked paint from her eyelashes. "They were going to the Buffalo Park to see the zebras and then have lunch at the mall. Any excuse for Momma to leave Jericho."

"What's your excuse?" Quinn said. "Three days in Memphis is a record."

"Getting Shelby settled," she said. "You know Luke got her a spot at Hutchison?"

"And who's paying for that condo in Germantown?"

"It's best for everybody," Anna Lee said.

"We've agreed to rotate custody every week. Shelby gets to live in the same place. When he's there, I'll be back in Jericho. It'll really keep any ugliness away from her and away from us."

Anna Lee had opened all the windows and the back door of the house, the smell of paint fumes still pretty strong from the old master bedroom she'd shared with Luke. It was hot without the AC and she wore a pair of small cutoff jeans and an old *Dukes of Hazzard* T-shirt. She'd cut off the sleeves and hemline, showing off her coppery skin and tiny blonde hairs along her arms and stomach.

"I haven't slept in a while," Quinn said. "Hard to think straight."

"Y'all got anything new?" she said, walking up to him, placing her long arms around his neck. Her skin smelled of sunshine and sweat.

"You know, the bikers bonded out."

"But you still think they did it?" she said. "Or were at least involved?"

"With their history in this town?" Quinn said. "You bet."

"But they're younger," she said. "Not the ones your dad used to run with."

"Couple old-timers left," Quinn said. "I think they drink more than make trouble.

And, to be exact, Jason never rode with the Losers as much as he was coerced."

"His Peter Fonda phase?"

"Yeah," he said. "Something like that."

Quinn kissed Anna Lee hard and long on the mouth. She was a strong kisser and dug her long nails into the back on his neck. She let go after a long moment, paintbrush dripping mineral spirits on the floor, and walked off to shut the back door. Without a word, she passed Quinn as she stripped off her T-shirt and tossed it on the landing, walking upstairs to one of the many bedrooms.

Quinn followed.

It was rough and sweaty for a long while until they both lay on top of the pressed white sheets, cooling off, a fan spinning overhead while they caught their breath. She lay her head on Quinn's chest, the strawberry blonde hair now loose from the bun and splayed across him.

"Tomorrow," she said. "After I finish up the master and hand over the keys to the realtor, it will be my week in Memphis. OK?"

Quinn didn't answer. He took a long deep breath, watching the ceiling fan spin, rocking and squeaking off balance.

"I knew what you'd say," Anna Lee said.

"You'd offer us the farm, maybe even moving in with your momma for a while, if it didn't look right to people. But that's too hard. Doesn't make a hell of a lot of sense. And Hutchison is a great school for Shelby. Tibbehah County isn't the best place to get an education."

Anna Lee's arm crossed over his stomach, Quinn listening while he smoothed down the golden hairs and felt her breathing against him. She had lots of tiny freckles across her back and shoulders.

"It's not forever."

"But Luke's paying?" Quinn said.

"He offered," she said. "And I wasn't in a spot to turn him down."

"I don't like it."

"You do what you can for your kids," Anna Lee said. "Someday that'll make sense to you."

Quinn carefully pulled away her arm, stretched his legs, and got up from the bed. He found his pants, belt still through the loops, and his pair of cowboy boots. Anna Lee was silent, reaching for the covers, pulling them over her naked body.

Quinn slipped into his jeans, and boots, walked to the dresser for his gun and his badge. He left without saying another word.

23

"Pull off right over there," Coach Mills said.

"Where?" Nito asked.

Coach Mills, not feeling comfortable in the passenger seat, pointed to a dirt road off the main highway that led up to a muddy pond and an old barn falling in on itself. Nito turned, dust kicking up behind them, hard sunlight crisscrossing through tree branches growing wild and untouched. Nito pulled into the little space by the barn and parked, the hot engine making ticking sounds. It was nearly one, cicadas making so much damn noise it was hard for a man to think. Coach Mills wiped his sweaty face and wondered why the hell did he have to look out for every damn soul in Tibbehah County.

He'd already taken off fourth and fifth period to get all this shit straight. He'd have to be back by three, get to a meeting with the assistants, and then on the field for warm-up and stretch by three-thirty. He had three days to prep for Holly Springs. He didn't come home with a goddamn V and the season just might be shot. You had to get your mind right, focus on what was important.

"OK," Nito said. "Ain't no one gonna see us now. We straight? What's up?"

"Ordeen's worried someone may have seen you riding around with that Jones girl."

"So what?"

"The police are gonna try and fry your ass for that," he said. "They're looking for someone — anyone — and Nito boy, you ain't exactly chamber of commerce president these days."

"I didn't do nothin'," Nito said. "I was ballin' the bitch. But, hell. So what? Since when's that illegal?"

"Just don't look good, son."

Nito leaned back in his driver's seat, this car a lot plainer and less flashy than the blue one Coach always saw him drive. This one just a plain old high-polished white with standard wire wheels and bad tires.

"I just got one of you boys out of trouble and don't want to see you getting mixed up in this shit," Coach said. "This ain't something I can just make disappear like I do for my other boys."

"You and Ordeen sure getting tight," Nito said, grinning with those silly-ass gold teeth, a big gold cross hanging on his neck encrusted with fake diamonds. "You done tole Ordeen that I was some kind of mental defect. Crazy as Kanye."

"Boy." Coach stared at him, tilting his head. "What the fuck you talking about?"

"Nothin', man," Nito said. "Shit."

Coach Mills felt a little tic under his eye, trying to keep it all together with all Nito's too-familiar talk, calling him 'man,' back-talking, and not doing what he said to do. Maybe that's why Nito never made it as a starter. Coach had been trying to get his mind straight all week, keep focused on the task at hand, the damn game this weekend, and not worry about distractions. It was just like Vince Lombardi said: "Fatigue makes cowards of us all." He just wished he could help Nito make the right moves. Coach had been mentoring the boy since he was nine years old.

"You remember how I took care of you and your momma?" Coach said.

"Yeah."

"You say, 'Yes, Coach.' "

"Yes, Coach."

"Y'all didn't have two sticks to rub to-gether," Coach said. "Who bought you groceries? Got your momma out from working that life down at the Golden Cherry? Got you into that football camp at Ole Miss when you weren't even ten?"

"Coach Bud Mills." Nito lolled his head on the headrest and looked right in his eye. "Jericho's Citizen of the Fucking Year."

Coach snorted, folding his arms over his big belly, ketchup stains from lunch dripped all over the blue golf shirt. "What we discuss between us is personal," he said. "Remember that. Make jokes, but what we say is between us."

Nito grinned. "Just like the old days."

"What the hell's that mean?"

"Don't try and play me, Bud," Nito said. "I'm not that cute little boy no more. I'm a grown-ass man."

The cicadas went wild again and Coach felt a coldness spread across his back and up his neck. He knew that feeling, his damn mind messing with him, working on that distraction like it was a piece of meat in his teeth, that fatigue that could make him start making mistakes, keep his mind off the game. The will to win was nothing, it was the will to prep that won the damn game. Distractions. Lazy-ass kids who didn't have any appreciation or respect. They didn't know what it's like to be a man, the pressures and tension that can build up in you like a gosh-dang Hawaiian volcano.

"You just keep yourself out of trouble, Nito," Coach said. "Maybe go on up to Memphis for a while. Leave town till everything gets right. I only want the best for you, son."

Nito leaned forward, cranking the car, taking a few times before the engine turned over. "Ain't no making this right, man."

"Just take me back to my car," Coach said. "And don't you ever 'Hey, man' me again. I'm Coach Mills, not some damn black you jive around with down in the Ditch."

"Yes, sir, Coach."

"Did anybody at all see you with that girl?" Coach said. " 'Cause I don't want to see your black ass end up in jail like Ordeen. Folks would try to make something of it, like they did with that Arab boy."

"Naw, man." Nito reversed the Impala, hit the dirt road, and knocked it into drive, kicking up lots of dust. Shafts of light and darkness scattering across his deep-black face. "Only Milly knew we knock boots. Unless she bragged how good she got it."

"Better be damn sure," Coach said. "Wild talk can kill a man faster than a bullet."

"Did you really have to drag him behind

329

y'all's bikes?" Fannie said.

"You said you wanted a show," Lyle said. "So, what the hell. You got a fucking show."

"I wanted a distraction," Fannie said. "A little protest of scooters. I guess I can't complain. It worked for a while. The damn vultures stayed camped out at the Gas & Go for a week and left us alone. But now they know where the girl worked. And some damn idiot at the sheriff's office told the *Commercial Appeal* that I was absolutely a person of interest. I can't get a helluva lot of horny truckers to walk past those live cameras to see some nice young snatch."

"What's the world coming to, Fannie?"

It was midday, hot as hell outside but cold and dark in Vienna's. Two girls in bras and panties sat on the stage checking their cell phones. Fannie looked up from behind the bar and snapped her fingers. "Dance," she said. "Get up there and shake your asses."

"Ain't no one here," said a white girl with purple hair. She popped her gum.

"Do I look like I give a shit?" Fannie said, shaking her head. The music from the unseen DJ filling up the big, barnlike room. The girls dropped their phones and started to circle the poles as Fannie leaned forward into the bar and Lyle. "You know what happened to that Muslim boy? Sammi?"

"Don't know," he said. "Don't care. I still think he's guilty as hell. How does it look that Sam the Sham was the last one to see that girl alive? You know, this country is filled with terrorist cells just waiting for the damn Ayatollah-Assahola or whoever to start jabbering on about Allah's Will. Am I right?"

"Just how far did you get in school, Lyle?"

"Fuck you, Fannie," Lyle said. "How about we just don't talk about this mess and you pass me a cold beer? I've been riding all day and the inside of my mouth tastes like a dirty cat box."

Fannie reached into the long cooler and brought out a cold Budweiser, cracking the top and laying it down. Without him even asking, she poured him a shot of Jack on the side. "If I were you, I'd just get on my bike and keep on riding," she said. "This shit show can't last forever."

"That's what I should do," he said. "But how often do I ever do what I should?"

"They don't want you anyway," Fannie said. "That bull dyke sheriff won't sleep until they get me before a grand jury making me seem like a goddamn Jezebel Lizzie Borden. You know, she wants her entire case to lead back to me. You should've seen the way she looked at me when she busted down the door to Vienna's. The top of her lip was slick with sweat, she was so damn excited, heated up with the idea."

"All I know is that I never touched that little girl," Lyle said. "How about you?"

Fannie reached for her gold butane lighter and fired up the three burners, turning that cigarillo around in the flame. "Does that really seem like my style?"

"This coming from a woman who keeps a steel hammer in her purse," Lyle said. "Christ Almighty."

Every day Nikki woke up, she prayed that it had all been some kind of rotten dream, some kind of bad liquor or fever from eating the fish tacos at the El Dorado. But, instead, she'd walk the trailer half-asleep, fetching Jon-Jon his bottle and turning on the news to find Milly Jones just about everywhere. There wasn't an hour went by that some news crew didn't come knocking on her door, wanting to know the inside story of Milly, their friendship, and who might have set her best friend in the world on fire like that. Nikki would refuse to talk and try and close the door, but, damn, if they didn't get tricky, push that microphone in her face, realizing they'd been taping her the whole time. They'd say they only wanted to know the real Milly, make their viewers understand the tragedy that had taken place in Mississippi. They even had a graphic for it. TRAGEDY IN MISSISSIPPI on Fox News, the morning news blonde downright giddy when a new piece of the puzzle slipped out: *Bikers Rally Against Muslim Suspect, Strip Club Owner a Person of Interest, Dead Girl's Father Speaks.* It went on from that, day to day.

Milly had it right. Run, run, run until your car didn't have no more gas.

She's been so damn struck by the horror of what happened that it took her a week to go through the mess Milly had given her. Most of it didn't make a damn bit of sense. A lot of her journal pages seemed like something out of a ninety-nine-cent romance novel, names changed to protect the guilty. She'd written the thing like a movie of the week: *Young Cheerleader Hits the Skids, Young Brother Takes His Own Life,* both growing up in a *House Filled with Violence.* But what got her was the continual mention of a man Milly just called The Devil. The Devil had entered Brandon's life. The Devil forced his hand on that twelve-gauge that day, making sure that he left the earth with the shame he felt. But who was The Devil? What had scared Milly so damn much that she wouldn't tell her best friend? Nikki had tried and tried to get that old phone, the one Milly said was Brandon's, to work. But if she found out what Milly had known, what the hell would she do with it? Nikki didn't care to be doused in gasoline and left to walk some lonely old road.

So day to day, she'd stayed in the dark house with her baby. It was cool out from all that heat. At night, she'd go to the Piggly Wiggly and get some groceries. Sometimes, her momma would stop by, her face showing shame for the filth her daughter was living in, begging her to come on back home and take her sister's room. She said these trailers weren't meant for any decent white person to live in. Damn, she was sick of it.

After she tucked Jon-Jon back in for his nap, she returned to the chair by the television. Wash Jones himself on CNN standing at the foot of the bridge close to where Milly had been set on fire. He wore one of those T-shirts she'd seen around town. A high school picture of Milly with photoshopped angel wings and the dates of her birth and death. "I just want to thank everyone for the kindness and love they shown our family. And I want to thank the sheriff's office here for all the hard work they've done on Milly's case. But it's been two weeks now since my daughter got set aflame and I don't believe we're any closer to getting justice than the night she died. I beg that if anyone knows anything to please speak out. My daughter can't rest until we get out the truth."

Nikki shut off the television, sitting in silence, the hum of the AC unit buzzing under a cracked window. Everything was so dark. The room a strewn mess of baby clothes and bags from Sonic, open cartons of Chinese from Panda Express. Nikki didn't know the last time she'd taken a shower, wearing the same cheerleading camp tee from two days before.

She had to get up.

She had to do something.

The slam of a car door startled her. She heard footsteps crunch on the gravel outside, and the loud knocking started her heart racing. The baby started to cry. *God damn it.* When the hell would these people leave her alone?

She peered through the blinds into the white-hot light and saw the face of Nito Reece. Nito tilted his head, knocking harder, smiling with his big gold teeth. "What's up, Nikki girl?" he asked. "You gonna let me in or what?"

■ ■ ■ ■

"You can stay here as long as you like," Caddy said, letting Sammi into one of the minicabins behind the barn. "There are fresh towels in the bath. You can wash what you like in the machines right next door. We have a breakfast in the barn every morning. Help yourself to what you need in the commissary."

"What's that?" Sammi said.

"Big metal building where we keep the pantry."

The boy looked terrible. One of his eyes had swollen shut, there were bandages over both arms and deep cuts and scrapes across his neck and face. When he spoke, there was a slight wheezing sound from the two broken ribs. Those bastards had really worked him over.

"This is a church?" Sammi said.

"Of a kind."

"You people aren't going to try and make me a Christian," Sammi asked. "Are you? I go to mosque every week in Oxford."

"Nope," Caddy said. "That's not what we do. We're not those people."

"What people?"

"People who make judgments," Caddy

said. "The man who founded The River wanted it open to everyone. We had a Buddhist family from Vietnam stay here for the last six months. They arrived Buddhists and they left Buddhists. Although they really did seem to like some of the old-time gospel music. It was a real kick to hear them sing 'Blessed Assurance' with those accents."

Sammi followed her into the one-room cabin, a small bathroom in the rear. A bed, a dresser, an old school desk, and a bookshelf loaded down with Christian books and paperback novels. She'd also stocked the shelf with books from C. S. Lewis, Thich Nhat Hanh, Zane Grey, and Eudora Welty. Sammi laid a gym bag down and took a seat on the edge of the bed. "I'm not a villain," he said. "A bad guy."

"I know."

"People have been calling me a terrorist my whole life," Sammi said. "We moved to Mississippi when I was six. But I was born outside Detroit, in Dearborn. I sort of remember what it was like there. Lots of Muslims, families getting together without people looking at us funny. I was happy. Everything seemed a lot brighter up there. More trees. More love. I guess coming down here after nine/eleven wasn't the best idea. My father had a brother who worked down in Gulfport. He set him up with a few stores, and here I am."

"Don't judge this town on those bikers," Caddy said. "They're not even from here."

"It's not the bikers," Sammi said. "Even before all this, people looked at me funny. They laughed at me in school, calling me Jihad Johnny and all that shit. They once evacuated the high school after I got into a fight with another kid. The kid told the principal I planned to blow up the lunchroom."

"What'd your parents say?"

"You know my father?"

"I've met him," Caddy said.

"Well, it's always the same thing," Sammi said, trying to push himself off the bed but getting met with some pain. He gritted his teeth. "He always said we were lucky to be here. Anytime there was something bad in Syria on the news, he'd have us watch it. He'd talk about how we lived in a better place and to ignore the bad stuff. He told us to never talk religion or politics with y'all. He said work hard in school, do your best to become a doctor, engineer, or something. But look at me. I barely got a degree. I'll be selling live bait and Moon Pies until I'm an old man. I guess it's made me hard. I don't care how much folks try and hurt me."

"I know what you mean," Caddy said. "This is a place to rest up, heal, get a new life plan. Think of this place like a base camp. You stay here until you're strong enough to either go back to work or do something new."

"My father wants me back at the store today."

Caddy nodded. "You just got out of the hospital," she said. "Give yourself some time."

"What if they come back?" Sammi said. "What if those men ride up here on those fucking Harleys and try to start trouble with you?"

"They've been here before," she said. "And I asked them to leave."

Sammi smiled, Caddy seeing he'd busted a couple of teeth. "You asked them?"

"Nicely," Caddy said. "And I pointed my uncle's old twelve-gauge at the ugliest one."

"They're all ugly."

"True."

"The Quran commands me to stand out firmly for justice," he said. "Even if that means going against yourself, your parents, or kin."

"The Bible likes justice, too," Caddy said. "How you go about it just depends on what volume you read."

"If those men killed Milly, I want them to die for it," Sammi said. "I think about her every minute. I could have helped her."

"How?" Caddy said. "Even Satan disguises himself as an angel of light."

"Tell me exactly what he said," Quinn said.

"He asked me if Milly had been talking about him," Nikki said. "I told him no and he called me a liar."

"He threatened you."

"Not exactly," Nikki said. "He went around it. My son had woken up when he drove up. I opened the door and told him I was busy, but when I walked back to the crib, he was right behind me. He kept on telling me babies freaked him out because they were so delicate. Jesus God. My blood just ran cold."

"Did Milly talk about Nito?"

"Only that he was a complete unhinged freak," Nikki said. "She told me he was always asking her out, saying that since she'd gone black with Joshua, there was no going back. But Nito wasn't Joshua. Joshua was a good-looking, smart guy. Nito Reece is nasty. He's a damn drug dealer and a thug."

"I can bring him in," Quinn said. "Talk to him."

"Please, please don't use my name," Nikki said. "God. I have a baby. Do I look like I have a whole lot of options around here?"

Quinn stood with the girl in what could only be politely described as a shithole. The baby was back inside with his grandmother, Quinn standing sure-footed in the dirt yard smoking a Drew Estates Maduro he'd started that morning. Nikki sat down on a toppled old refrigerator. A stained mattress lay nearby, along with a bunch of Coke cans tossed around the yard. A hot wind blew through the trees, a dog barking from down the road.

The dog got the attention of Hondo, who poked his head from the passenger side of Quinn's truck and sniffed at the air. Quinn wrote his cell on the back of an old business card and handed it to the girl.

"Nito Reece gets within a mile of you, you call me."

"He's crazy, you know?"

"Yep."

"But I don't see him killing Milly," Nikki said. "I think what happened has just made everyone crazy. And if you're crazy to start, that ball can really start rolling."

"I've heard a lot about Nito," Quinn said. "But this is the first I've heard about him knowing Milly Jones."

"What if he knows me and you talked?"

"I don't think it'll be me who'll pull him in," Quinn said. "The sheriff's better with people skills."

"Lillie Virgil?" Nikki said, sort of laughing. "Are you kidding me?"

24

"Can a man get a fuckin' Mountain Dew around here?" Nito Reece said. "I mean, shit."

"We're full-service, Ranito," Lillie said. "We have some extra barbecue from the Fillin' Station in the fridge. Would you like me to heat that up, too?"

"Fillin' Station?" Nito said. "Yeah, well. All right. Got any sides?"

"Beans and slaw," Lillie said. "Maybe some white bread."

"White bread," Nito said, laughing. "Shit. OK."

Nito sat at a small table in a small, square cinder-block room at the sheriff's office. The walls had been painted a light blue, Lillie being told it would soothe the suspect into talking. In her years of being a cop, she never found that to be true. Usually when you force a human being into a small, crowded space, they grow more defensive.

She got Nito the Mountain Dew and asked Mary Alice to heat up the barbecue. God knows, they had enough food, piles being brought in by concerned folks around Tibbehah who wanted them to keep up their strength, go ahead and hurry up and make that arrest.

"I know what's going on here," Nito said. "Y'all trying to get me to roll over on Ordeen for that bullshit charge during that illegal stop. But that shit ain't happenin'. All I can say is, that wasn't his dope or his gun. Someone setting his ass up."

"The thought never crossed my mind," Lillie said. "Wasn't he arrested driving your car? I guess he felt comfortable to take his stuff and hide it in your glove box."

"Damn," Nito said. "Shit."

"You're a convicted drug dealer," Lillie said. "You've been in twice already. I hear you do business with the Bohannan Twins in Memphis. So how about we all talk straight? I need your help."

"Y'all straight trippin'," Nito said, rubbing his pink tongue over his gold teeth. Hands folded in front of him like a good church boy.

"How long did you and Milly Jones date?" Lillie asked.

"No," Nito said, standing up. "Hell, no. I

thought you ask me to come in here and talk about my boy, help y'all get straight in your mind he didn't do nothin'. Now you asking me about that dead white girl. Shit. You set my ass up."

"Folks up in Blackjack saw y'all riding around together," Lillie said. "That electric-blue car of yours is pretty hard to miss."

"I don't have that car no more," Nito said. "I sold it. If someone said they saw me and Milly riding around in that Nova I had, then they lying out their damn assholes."

Mary Alice knocked, poked her head into the interview room, and asked if they still wanted a plate. Lillie nodded and Mary Alice came in smiling, steam coming off the barbecue, and sat it in front of Nito. Service with a smile.

"We gonna be here for a while?" Nito said. " 'Cause I got shit to do."

"Depends on you, Nito," Lillie said. "Sit down. Are you going to help us out? I don't want to have to look into who really owned the gun Ordeen had on him. You know it was stolen from a fella in Clarksdale? You go over to the Delta much?"

"OK, so I knew Milly Jones," Nito said, sitting down. "Everybody know each other in Blackjack. We got a population of two hundred folks. Girl like to party. She like those bad boys."

"Were you intimate?" Lillie asked.

"You mean, were we fucking?" Nito said, unlatching his hands, leaning back, stretching his arms up over his head.

"Yeah," Lillie said. "Were you fucking?"

Nito leaned back into his seat, massaging his chest, feeling cool and comfortable to be back on familiar ground. He grinned, saying it, bragging about it, without opening his mouth. "Few times," he said. "Didn't mean nothing."

"Where were you the night she got killed?"

"Damn, that was like three weeks ago," Nito said. "I drank some beers, smoked a blunt, and went to the football game. If you hadn't noticed, ain't a lot more to do in Jericho, Mississippi. You want me to find some folks who saw me at that game?"

"Yep," Lillie said. "We would. How about after the game?"

"Motherfucker," Nito said. "Why'd y'all get on my ass? 'Cause I'm the closest black man? I want me a damn lawyer."

"That's cool," Lillie said. "And we can hold you until they show up. Might be sometime tomorrow afternoon."

"Y'all ain't the good guys," Nito said. "Never have been. The old sheriff was the one who killed my daddy. No one even asked shit about it. You think you doing right 'cause you got the gun and the badge? But you ain't nothing but straight thug just like me. Only difference is, you got the law behind you."

"Yeah?" Lillie said. "Pretty big difference."

"OK," Nito said. "So I smoked it up, went to the game, watched Tibbehah almost get their ass kicked, and then I went home, watched some shit on TV, and fell asleep."

"Who was at your house?" Lillie asked.

"My momma," Nito said. "You want to talk to her, too?"

"Yeah, I would," Lillie said. "What were y'all watching?"

"Shit."

"Can you be a little more specific?"

"I don't know," he said. "It was late. I like to watch them home improvement shows. You know, where they get a real shit show and then within a day they make it look like a palace down on the beach."

"You're into that?" Lillie said.

"Sure," Nito said. "Also watch those infomercials for sex products. Those two ladies who talk about selling those big black things. You like that stuff?"

Lillie sat down across from him, leaning forward a bit, elbows resting on the old scuffed table. "Ever hear Milly talk about

Fannie Hathcock?"

"That bitch owns the truck stop."

"Yeah," Lillie said. "That same bitch."

"Maybe," Nito said. "You think she might've killed her?"

"What'd you hear?"

"I don't know," Nito said, mouth lit up with all that gold. "*Hmm.* What's that worth to me?"

"Will you go on record?"

"Girl might've taken some shit didn't belong to her," Nito said. "Damn, she was scared of that bitch. Said that woman wanted to kill her ass."

"I'm cooking T-bones," Jason Colson said. "How about you stop by? Ain't that far, just a short walk through the cornfield."

"I know the way," Quinn said. "Need to catch up on some sleep."

"Man's got to eat."

"I can't."

"I'm watching Little Jason tonight," his father said. "He saw your truck drive up."

Quinn blew out his breath. "OK, Granddad."

Quinn hung his uniform shirt in an old armoire, set his Beretta in the gun safe, and picked up a fresh bottle of whiskey he'd been saving for a long time. The whiskey

348

was for him. Jason wasn't drinking this week. Or so he said.

As he walked from the old farmhouse, he could see the colorful Christmas lights strung from two four-by-fours, crisscrossed back to Jason's trailer. The cherry-red Firebird now off the blocks, sanded down and painted with a flat-gray primer. He'd put wheels and tires back on the car, too.

"Is she running yet?" Quinn said.

"Close," Jason said, standing under the lights, flipping steaks on a Weber grill. "Boom picked up the engine last week. He's got it out at his place. He's seeing what he can do. But we may have to go all in and get a new one. Transmission, too."

"How's the body?"

Jason grinned. " 'Bout like mine," he said. "Lots of miles and wear, but still road-ready. You want a baked potato? Got a few in the oven. Little Jason loves a baked potato. Doesn't care for red meat. You know that boy told me he was a vegetarian? Just like that. When I was his age, I didn't even know what that word meant."

Quinn nodded. Jason covered up the grill, funneling the smoke, as Little Jason bounded out of the trailer, where he'd been watching cartoons. He wrapped Quinn's waist in a big hug. Quinn had been gone a

349

long time and when he'd gotten home he'd barely seen his nephew. They'd been through a lot. Jason was his fishing buddy. He'd just gotten him a bow-and-arrow set that he'd pass along whenever Caddy approved it.

"Nice night," Jason said. "No moon at all. That's when I think I love coming back here best. I can turn off all the lights, sit back, and just look at all those damn stars. You could never do that in Los Angeles. In L.A., you had to head on out to Joshua Tree to make sense of the world."

Quinn nodded. He slit open the top of the bourbon bottle and poured out a little in a coffee mug. The coffee mug was emblazed with the symbol for the 75th Regiment, a lightning bolt through a shield of a sun and star.

Little Jason found an old metal porch chair and pulled it closer to the grill to watch all the action. He admitted the steaks smelled good but still didn't want one.

"Doesn't even eat hamburgers."

"Except when Grandmomma's meat loaf gets forced on him."

Jason shook his head. "You really think that qualifies as a meat product?"

Quinn straightened his legs out in front of him, crossing his boots at the ankle. He thought about lighting up the rest of his cigar but figured it could wait until after dinner. Something was on Jason's mind and there was no use rushing things until he was ready to talk.

"Can you at least take the night off?" Jason said.

"Lillie interviewed a subject this afternoon," Quinn said. "We had a meeting and agreed to come back to the SO at 0600 unless something comes up."

"Y'all got something?"

"Lillie thinks so."

"And you?"

"Not really sure what we got," Quinn said. "Folks around here are pretty good at pointing fingers at each other."

Jason nodded, stroking the gray goatee. "Don't I know it." He had on a Gram Parsons T-shirt, once telling Quinn it had been personally given to him by an original member of the Flying Burrito Brothers who was from Meridian. He lifted up the top of the Weber, poked at the steaks, and asked Quinn to go inside and get him a plate.

"They got the *WWE* on tonight," Jason said. "Who's that guy again?"

"The Beast," Little Jason said. "They said it was the first time he's wrestled in twelve years. That's longer than I've been alive."

"What's he look like?" Quinn said.

"I can promise he ain't pretty," Jason said, grinning.

"It's Roman Reigns and Dean Ambrose in a Triple Threat match," Little Jason said. "Someone's gonna have their dang ass handed to them."

"Jason?" Quinn said.

"Yes, sir."

"Watch your mouth and go grab us a plate," Quinn said. "Looks like your granddaddy is about ready."

Jason lifted his eyes from the fire, forking the meat off the center of the grill to let it cool and rest before they ate.

"OK," Jason said, soon as they heard the screen door thwack closed after Little Jason. "I got us a deal. But I need some help."

"Hold up," Quinn said, raising the flat of his hand. "Did you talk to Stagg?"

"Drove all the way over to Montgomery, Alabama," Jason said. "Stopped off at the Hank Williams museum before I drove back. Got you a bumper sticker in my truck."

"Son of a bitch."

"Stagg looks like a damn accountant," Jason said. "They cut off most of his hair. He said he's been mainly doing yard work, pruning bushes and things like that."

"Has he found the Lord yet?"

"Says he's working on it," Jason said. "Goes to Bible study regular."

Little Jason brought out the plate and bounded back into the trailer for some tofu hot dogs.

"Well," Quinn said. "What's he want?"

"That part's a little tricky," Jason said. "How about we talk after we eat?"

Quinn just stared at his father as he stabbed the bloody meat and placed the steaks on the plate. Jason swallowed, nodded, and handed Quinn what he'd just cooked up.

"Even with the investors, we'll need you to put up the farm for collateral."

"No way."

"Now, hold on."

"You think Jean will go for that?" Quinn said. "She'd disown me."

"I know leaving here was wrong," Jason said. "But what in the world does that woman still have against me? You turned out all right."

25

Ordeen met Nito down at Shooter's on the Square later that night. Shooter's pool hall was in the basement of the old Jericho Five & Dime that had been defunct for about a thousand years. Nito was in the back corner of the pool hall, practicing by himself on the only one of the ten tables being used and smoking a long-as-hell cigarette. Nito didn't move when he saw Ordeen, just took it slow and easy and knocked in two solids, back-to-back, into a corner pocket. "Whew," Nito said. "You see that shit?"

"Yeah, I saw it," Ordeen said. "What's up, man? I got to work tomorrow."

"Work?" Nito asked. "Since when?"

"County work," Ordeen said. "Cutting trees and shit. Coach set it up."

"Go, Coach, go."

"Why you down on Coach?"

Nito chalked the cue, circled the table for the next shot. "Hmm," Nito said. "Maybe 'cause that fat white motherfucker trying to cornhole us both."

"How you figure?" Ordeen said, hands in the pockets of his shorts, Tibbehah Wildcats T-shirt crisp and laundered, with his braids pulled back into a ponytail. "I said the man just got me a job. He got me out of some real trouble. What else you want from him?"

"Oh, yeah?" Nito said. "You think he's doin' for you 'cause he's the coach? Mr. Fellowship of Christian Athletes and all that."

"I do," Ordeen said. "I think he just might be."

Nito leaned into the table, set that shot, running the cue between his two knuckles, and popped it hard and fast, damn reverb shot off the wall and into the side pocket. Ordeen recognized when his buddy was jacked-up and Nito was jacked-up as hell, running the table, talking shit. He was on something and Ordeen didn't want no part. Back toward the door, old man Shooter was cleaning beer bottles off a few tables even though serving beer was illegal at a pool hall. It was the law, but no one really made a big deal of it. They used to have a town cop, a marshal, or something that did that sort of thing, but he was dirty and got shot.

"How long you known Coach Mills?" Nito asked.

"Junior high," Ordeen said. "He used to come watch the young boys play. Said he was keeping his eye on me and that made me feel real good."

Nito held the cue in his hand like a staff, reaching down below the table for a pint of flavored vodka in a paper bag. Ordeen smelled his breath from across the table.

"Keep an eye on you," Nito said. "That sound like ole Bud."

"Man, what are you talking about?"

"I know'd Bud since I was eight years old," Nito said. "He knew my momma. Found out she had some kids and he started trying to preach to us, teach us football and shit. One Christmas, he bought me a whole damn Ole Miss uniform. I'm talking shoulder pads, helmets, and cleats. Wasn't no Walmart special. I'm talking just like the team play in."

"So what's your problem?"

"Coach running me down to you," Nito said. "And running you down to me. He thinks we both mixed up in this Milly Jones business."

"That's bullshit."

"You tellin' me?" Nito said. "He told me that folks are already talking about seeing

356

you and me riding around with Milly Jones. How's that look, sweet little white girl riding around in my damn pussymobile with two black thugs. They gonna hang our ass high."

"Coach would never do that," Ordeen said, feeling his heart race, hands gone cold. "He look out for us. He's just telling us to watch our backs."

"Let me ask you something, Ordeen," Nito said. "Are you sure those charges been dropped?"

"Yeah."

"How you know?"

" 'Cause Coach told me."

Nito shook his head, took another swallow of that flavored vodka, under that low light. Ole black-ass Shooter playing some Chitlin' Circuit soul from an old stereo. Music Ordeen's grandmomma liked but his pastor momma hated. Denise La Salle. "Trapped by a Thing Called Love."

"Coach told me a lot of things when I was little boy," Nito said. "He used to make me feel real special riding in his truck, going to the games. I got to stand on the sidelines, help him pick up the jerseys and shit, do the wash. I wasn't ten years old and I felt like I was already a Wildcat, on the team."

"Coach is a good man."

Nito swallowed, looking like he was in some pain, red-eyed and swaying a bit. He shook his head, crooking his finger at Ordeen.

"What?"

Nito leaned into the table and whispered something up to Ordeen, dead-faced and serious as hell. But when he was done with it all, he doubled over and started laughing so hard, he squirted that vodka from his nose.

"You sick, man."

"I'm sick?" Nito said. "You got that shit twisted. And a man like that sure as hell want to be a hero to everybody else. You know, he might sell us out, talk about what we done. What he knows. Lead them bloodhounds right to our ass."

"I didn't do nothin' to Milly Jones."

"Since when does the truth matter?"

"You drunk," Ordeen said.

"Well, you high," Nito said.

"What?"

Nito lifted up his sagging T-shirt and showed a bright silver automatic stuck down between his drawers and his jeans. "About time we take Coach Bud outta the game."

"Now I know you crazy."

"I need some help," Nito said. "Can't do

what needs doing without someone on my team."

"Ain't gonna be me."

Nito shrugged, leaning down to take another shot, this one sending the cue ball banking hard off the wall and landing in the pocket. "Figured you might say that."

"So we straight?"

Nito shook his head. The front door to Shooter's opened and an ugly white boy walked into the pool hall wearing a gray hoodie. He waved to them both, pulling the hoodie from his bald head, a bunch of scratches and bruises showing on his face, and smiled with rotted teeth. Ordeen knew the white boy but never liked him.

"D. J. Norwood?" Ordeen said. "You lost it. You gone."

"I do what I got to do to get by," Nito said. "It's either me or Coach. If you don't believe it, get the fuck out of here."

Ordeen raised his hands high in surrender, turned his back, and walked from Shooter's, brushing past Norwood on the way out. Norwood muttering to himself. "Pussy," he said.

"Why's it wrong to teach a boy to shoot?" Jason asked.

"Wasn't that it's wrong, it's that you

didn't ask permission from his momma," Quinn said.

"Why do I have to ask permission about my own grandson?"

They were speeding north, headed back from Jericho, where they'd dropped off Little Jason with Jean after supper. Quinn behind the wheel of the Big Green Machine, Jason in the passenger seat. He and Jean had it out in the driveway when she found out Little Jason had been shooting guns with his grandfather again. Jason had pointed to Quinn, wanting to place him in the middle of their problems, and said, "Well, he did. Worked out all right for him. They gave him some damn medals."

"We all want Jason to stay a boy," Quinn said. "He'll be a man soon enough. Don't need to rush it."

"A boy isn't a boy unless he can fish, hunt, and kick some ass," Jason said, laughing. "Right? You would have never made it out in those woods if your Uncle Hamp hadn't taught you. Well, Hamp is dead. You're busy as hell. It falls on me."

"Do you want to know what happened in the woods?" Quinn said, reaching for his cigar. "It wasn't some kind of coming-of-age ceremony when Daddy wipes deer blood across your face. It was damn instant manhood for me. We lost our childhoods. I don't wish that shit on anybody."

"I am sorry for being gone," Jason said. "I left for a good reason, but I didn't come home out of selfishness. I was living from movie set to movie set. It's a damn nomad life I'd been leading since Mr. Needham hired me. I thought it was normal. I guess I turned gypsy."

"Caddy was raped in those woods, Jason. She was eight years old."

Jason didn't say anything, the hot wind racing through the cracked windows, dashboard lit up in a soft blue light. Quinn sped up along Highway 9, passing a few cars, clicking on the brights during the long black stretch. Good, he'd finally said it. It was out of him.

"Who did it?" Jason said, all the laughter and easygoing bullshit gone.

"I poached some deer in a state park," Quinn said. "The warden got some kind of crazy hard-on for me, wanted me to go to a reform school or something, wouldn't leave me or Momma alone, so I left."

"What's that got to do with Caddy?"

"I ran for the woods," Quinn said. "That being the only place where I felt safe, in control, and Caddy followed. She wouldn't leave me. She was scared I'd get shot. I was only ten."

"And this man, the game warden, he touched Caddy."

Quinn ashed his cigar. "Did more than touch."

"Good Lord Almighty," Jason said. "Glad I wasn't there. I would've killed him."

"You didn't need to," Quinn said. "I did."

Quinn turned off on his country road, slowing the car, the big moon high above the wide-open pasture and the acres of land Johnny Stagg had clear-cut. The radio played a classic country station out of Tupelo, the volume so low that Quinn could barely make out one of his favorites. Waylon. "I've Always Been Crazy."

"What they do to you?"

"Nothing," Quinn said. "Uncle Hamp took care of everything. Got rid of the body, wrote a missing person report on the bastard, and that was about all of it."

"And you came out of the woods a local hero," Jason said. " 'Country Boy Can Survive.' "

"I never wanted to go in that place," Quinn said. "And I didn't want to come out so damn different."

"Holy Christ."

"How about we just give Little Jason a break," Quinn said. "Boy likes wrestling.

Just keep on telling him that it's real."

Jason was quiet until they hit the circular drive in front of the old farmhouse, lit up like a gold candle inside, shining down in a bright slant along the green hill.

"Can I tell Caddy I'm sorry?" Jason said.

"No, sir," Quinn said. "That's not your place to say."

26

"You got some real trouble," Boom said.

"Don't I know it," Lillie said. "But can you be a little more specific? If you hadn't noticed, I've got a leading role in this American Shit Show."

"Coach Mills," Boom said. "He's scared as hell. Says Nito Reece wants to kill him."

Lillie dropped the sack of biscuits on the table inside the County Barn. She sat down on the backseat sofa and grabbed one for herself. The sun wasn't up yet and she'd already given a press conference, gone back to the crime scene, met with Milly's mom, who was convinced Milly was an undercover informant, and gone into Jericho to Varner's for the biscuits.

"But he won't have him arrested."

"Nope," Boom said. "He told me all of this confidential."

"Of course he did," Lillie said. "So why are you telling me, Boom?"

"I love that man," Boom said. "But me and you don't ever keep secrets. You know, I played all four years for him. Coached linebackers for five. I'd do anything he asked."

"Lots of folks feel that way," Lillie said. "You want sausage or ham?"

"Whichever you don't want."

"What's Nito's problem with Mills?"

"Coach says Nito been borrowing money from him for a long time," Boom said. "Not much. But it's added up. This time, he said no and Nito showed him a gun. But here's the thing. Coach believes Nito might have something to do with Milly Jones getting killed."

Lillie added some sugar and cream to her coffee. She looked up at Boom, leaning against her Jeep Cherokee, Boom wanting her to turn it in and get something more modern. "That does interest me."

"He a suspect."

"You bet," she said. "Even if he's pointing the finger at someone else."

"What you got on him?"

"Quinn heard he was rolling with the Jones girl right before she died," she said. "Problem is, our witness is scared to death. When you light someone up like a candle, not a whole lot of folks raising their hands to help out. And, besides, Nito commands some respect in Blackjack. You think Mills can help?"

"I want to keep Coach's name out of this thing," Boom said. "He's got a lot on his mind. He wants to do the right thing. But, you're right, this thing has become a real shit show. Coach's name means too much in this town to be drug through it."

"No offense, Boom, but someone lit a little girl on fire," Lillie said. "I don't really give two shits who's inconvenienced by me asking some questions. Here. Get your biscuit."

Boom walked over, reached for it with his metal-clamped hand, and unwrapped it with his real fingers. He ate for a bit, leaning against Lillie's truck, dressed in camo pants and a short-sleeved Carhartt shirt. Boom always looked like he was ready to go hunting, even if it was off-season.

"Coach Mills doesn't mind working with you," he said. "He wants to help. But you tie his name to Nito Reece, start saying the man was giving money to a convicted drug dealer, and he'd lose a lot more than his job."

"What's bigger than his job?" Lillie said, leaning back, propping her boots on a coffee table made with plywood and concrete blocks.

"His reputation," Boom said. "Bud Mills been here more than twenty years. If he didn't give so damn much for this county, he might be the head coach in the SEC somewhere. He believes in the high school system, mentoring kids. I'll tell you, he did it for me. If it hadn't been for him, I might be in jail right now."

"You and Quinn both," Lillie said. "Not many kids get a second chance after stealing a fire truck."

Boom smiled. "I got no idea what you're talking about, Sheriff."

"Talk to Mills," Lillie said. "Tell him I can meet with him confidentially. He has anything on Nito Reece and I need to know it."

"I kind of liked the beard," Ophelia Bundren said. "And the longer hair. Didn't figure it would last."

"It felt sloppy."

"How'd you begin your day?" she asked.

"Five-mile run."

"Of course you did," Ophelia said. "Always got something chasing you, Quinn Colson."

They'd met right off the Square at the Fillin' Station diner, Quinn taking the back booth, the spot where he'd often done business as sheriff. He'd been there for three cups of coffee before Ophelia showed, carrying in a file of the final autopsy report of Milly Jones. Ophelia was dressed down that morning — light blue V-neck tee, slim-fitting khaki pants, and a thick brown belt with a heavy clasp. She carried a navy blazer over her arm, but it was too hot outside and too hot in the Fillin' Station with the grill heated up. She'd wear it back at Bundren's Funeral Home, where it was always a cool sixty degrees, colder in the refrigerator.

Quinn looked through the file, lifting his eyes every few minutes to make sure no reporters were coming through the door. Most of them were still camped out at the sheriff's office or down at the Rebel Truck Stop. National news really loved the Rebel, with its big neon Confederate flag sign just made for TV.

"What am I looking for?"

Mary brought a cup of coffee for Ophelia. Ophelia thanked her and said she'd already had breakfast. She lifted the cup to her red lips and took a long sip, dark eyes still filled with apprehension about getting too friendly with Quinn again.

"Someone bashed her head in," Ophelia

said. "We didn't know that."

"With what?"

"I'm a coroner, not a psychic, Quinn," she said. "Blunt force trauma, as we like to say. But given the size of the indention in the skull, I'd say something like the back end of a pistol or a pipe."

"It caved in her skull."

"You bet."

"How the hell could she even move after that?" Quinn said. "Damn, that's rough."

"OK," she said. "That's why I wanted to meet with you and Lillie and share a few ideas of my own."

"Lillie will be along," Quinn said. "Her Jeep broke down."

"Why won't she just get a new vehicle?"

"If you hadn't noticed, Lillie is a little stubborn," Quinn said. "She won't go to the supervisors with hat in hand."

"I'd call that just thickheaded," Ophelia said. "She's the sheriff."

"For now."

"OK," Ophelia said, reaching for the photos and reports in front of Quinn. "Did you get the idea?"

"Those pictures were pretty exact."

"You bet," Ophelia said. "But you're on the right track. How could the girl be conscious after a blow like that?"

Quinn nodded and drank some coffee. A couple walked into the front door, bell jingling overhead, but it was just Mr. and Mrs. Jenkins who ran the drugstore. He waved to them and they waved back, taking the first booth near the door, as was customary. Mary arrived with a pot of coffee and cups, talking about another hot one outside.

"I believe the killer thought she was dead," Ophelia said. "She'd have been out cold, maybe even with a slowed heartbeat. The fire may not have been torture but a way to dispose of the body, and any evidence."

"Changes things from a revenge killing."

"I wouldn't say it was accidental," Ophelia said. "With that kind of blow. That kind of cracked skull. It's damn murder. But the method and motive changes a bit."

Quinn raised his cup to her.

"Wasn't all me," Ophelia said. "Hard to tell, at first. But the state people confirmed my thinking."

"Now we just need to find a lead pipe with her DNA on it," Quinn said.

"And a suspect."

"We have a few of those," Quinn said. "Ruled a few out."

"Wash Jones?"

"Wash Jones can barely change his underwear, let alone set his daughter on fire,"

Quinn said. "He's a mean drunk. But he's not evil."

"Miss Hathcock?"

"Among others," Quinn said.

"You know much about that woman?"

"I don't know much about women at all."

"Ancient history."

"Y'all doing OK?" Quinn said. "Your momma handling all this? I know it all seems pretty familiar to you."

"I don't know," Ophelia said. "At least Milly Jones had a body we could examine. My sister had been run over so many times, you could barely tell she'd been human."

"I'm sorry."

Ophelia nodded, looking fresh-scrubbed and pretty that morning. High cheekbones and dark eyes, tight red mouth that held back most of what she might want to say. Ophelia had always kept things close, tight, to herself. He'd only ever seen her explode twice. Once, when Jamey Dixon came home from prison, saying he didn't have anything to do with her sister's death. Next, when Quinn told her he didn't really see a future between them. She'd wanted to kill Dixon, and she'd thrown a steak knife right at Quinn, finding a solid place in a nearby wooden wall.

"I haven't ever said it," Ophelia said. "But

371

I do hope you find happiness with Anna Lee. Y'all have always loved each other."

"Yeah?" Quinn said. "That would be nice."

Ophelia tilted her head and studied Quinn's face. The front door opened again, bell jingling. Lillie Virgil walked in, looking to each of them, smirking. She slid into the booth beside Ophelia. "What the hell did I miss?"

"What's in it for me?" D. J. Norwood asked Nito.

It was a solid question, as Nito wanted him to join in on a felony against a man he didn't have no trouble with. Nito didn't speak, just passed the blunt they'd been smoking, roaming those back highways of Tibbehah on a hot Friday. Hotter than two rats fucking in a wool sock.

"You know what I'm saying?" Norwood asked.

"He's got money and shit," Nito said. "We can clean him out before we give him the beatdown. Jack his ass and then take him back to his place. Do it sometime early tomorrow, before the football game."

"You don't care about what he's got," Norwood said. " 'Cause you got some personal thing going on."

"Yeah," Nito said, taking back the joint, blowing smoke into the Caprice Classic. "I want to close his fucking mouth before I end up in prison."

"I played for him in ninth grade," Norwood said. "The fat man look at me and said, 'Boy, you even worse than your two brothers.' Which is bullshit 'cause Larry was a hell of a strong safety, crazy as hell, until he got on the meth. And that shit just cleaned out his brain like Drāno. Motherfucker started talking to a tree like it was our grandmother."

"You can have his credit cards, ATM, and shit," Nito said. "I don't want none of it. We cool on that?"

"Yeah?" Norwood said, slunk down low in the seat, wearing gas station shades and a sleeveless black CAT T-shirt. "I am flat-ass broke."

"He's got a big-ass TV for watching SEC games and shit," Nito said. "All yours, man."

"Maybe I could sell it," he said. "I don't know. What else?"

"Man has guns," Nito said. "A shit ton of guns. Has a whole fucking room filled with them."

"I do love guns."

"Yeah?" Nito said. "Well, OK then."

"But if we do it, we got to do it smart. How you plan on getting to him without anyone seeing us?"

"I got some things to say to the man that he don't want no one hearing," Nito said. "Figure I might get him to meet us out on the Trace, him thinking we's alone, and then you pop out of the car and stick a gun up his ass."

He passed back the joint to Norwood. " 'Up his ass'?" Norwood said. "Just what'd that bastard do to you?"

"He's running his mouth how I kilt Milly Jones."

Norwood started to gag on the weed smoke, coughing a bunch, leaning forward into the floorboard so he could get a breath in. "You didn't, right? 'Cause I ain't getting into that shit. Sure, I'll do this with you — jack him and scare that old man. But if you killed Milly, I don't want no part of that. I'm still looking at time for stealing that old woman's Kawasaki. That was just a misunderstanding. She's got the damn Alzheimer's, can't remember letting me borrow it. And then that stupid-ass woman sheriff knocked me in the head. You believe that? I been talking to a lawyer up in Memphis who said I might have a case to sue. I got to see a doctor in Tupelo for a CAT scan 'cause my lawyer wants to know if it done something to my cognitive ability."

"Coach killed Milly," Nito said. He blurted it out just like that, like he was talking a fact about Ole Miss football or deer hunting. Coach Bud Mills killed the cheerleader.

"Bullshit," Norwood said.

Nito shook his head, reached down in the floorboard for that flavored vodka they both liked, and took a long pull. His black face slick and dark as night. "Wants to pin it on my ass."

"How's he gonna do that?" Norwood said.

"Man's gonna tell the law about what happened to my Nova," Nito said, handing over the vodka. "They run a black light over my backseat and it'll light up like a fucking Christmas tree."

"Son of a bitch," he said.

"You gonna help?" Nito said. "Or what?"

Norwood thought about it, scratching the scuff on his chin. "I better wear some kind of mask. He knows me. Like a ski mask. Or something I got for Halloween."

"Whatever you want," Nito said.

"You should, too."

"Nope," Nito said. "I want him to see me plain as day."

"You ain't gonna kill him or something

375

crazy?" Norwood said, laughing. "Come on. You ain't the law around here."

"Oh, no?" Nito didn't laugh.

"Well, hell," D. J. Norwood said. "He got a TV, guns, and shit?"

"Yes, sir."

"I guess it does seem like the right thing to do."

27

"I don't think she's coming back," Quinn said.

"You don't know that," Caddy said.

"She's living in Luke's condo every other week," Quinn said. "She's put Shelby in Hutchison. Says she can't get a good education down here."

"You blame her?" Caddy said.

"Nope."

"But you think she's getting back close with Luke?"

"I don't know, sis," Quinn said. "But she's doing her best to put a little distance between us."

They sat side by side on the porch swing outside the farm watching Little Jason run and play with Hondo. Hondo was a big fan of sticks. The sun was going down, the bare spots on the hill hard-packed and baked in it.

"You know, women are like cats," Caddy

said. "You try and pick 'em up too fast and they'll jump out of your arms and run away."

"Or scratch your eyes out."

"You just better step back, let her figure out what needs figuring," Caddy said. "You know how I feel about Anna Lee. But, damn, you gotta give the woman a little time to adjust to you being back. And to the divorce. All of it."

"You and Lillie never liked her," Quinn said. "Even before I left. Y'all always thought she'd ruin me."

"Not ruin," Caddy said. "Just change. We just kind of like you the way you are."

"Anna Lee wanted me to go to Oxford this weekend," Quinn said. "She said she'd like me to meet some of her friends in the Grove. I told her I couldn't leave. Not with everything happening. How would that look? Me out drinking while there's a murder investigation going on?"

"Don't you see?" Caddy said. "Jesus Christ, Quinn Colson. The Grove? Do you even own a pair of khaki pants?"

"I got camo."

"Yep," she said. "That's you. Camo and denim."

"What about Ophelia?" she said. "Momma said you and her been seen together, having breakfast at the Fillin' Station yesterday. That's something, right? You rethinking all that?"

"Yeah," he said. "We had an intimate breakfast over some crime scene photos of Milly Jones. She broke down the manner of death, blow by blow. Her last walk."

"Ophelia," she said. "Damn, she's dark. But get a drink in her and she's fun as hell. Cute, too."

Quinn pushed the swing a bit more with the toe of his boot. The late-summer light had turned a burnt orange over the oaks and pines, a haziness coming from the shadows of the deep woods. Gnats swarming down by the creek. They kept on rocking back and forth, as they had since Quinn could recall.

"Daddy got the old Firebird running again," Quinn said. "Boom put in a new engine. Old one had rusted to shit."

"He still say that was the car they used to jump the bridge in *Hooper*?"

"He said it was one they used when they burned down that factory town in the last scene," he said. "The big apocalyptic finish before Burt and Jan Michael Vincent had to make the jump in the rocket car."

Caddy shook her head, patted his knee. "You know, it never happened."

"What?"

"The jump," Caddy said. "It was impossible. They used a damn model car to make it look like it flew. You can't fly a damn Firebird over a river. It's bullshit. Classic Jason Colson bullshit."

Quinn didn't know what to say. The story had become as much a part of the legend of Jason Colson as the time he'd jumped a dozen Pintos on a Harley-Davidson. That one was true — they still had the newspaper photo hanging by the toilet in the Fillin' Station diner.

"Doesn't bother you that he's now got a fast car?" Caddy said.

"He's too old to race."

"Not too old to jump behind the wheel and blow town."

"Nope," Quinn said. "He's got too much at stake. He's putting some kind of deal together that will help him buy up Stagg's land."

"Holy Christ," Caddy said, putting down her foot, stopping the rocking. Little Jason and Hondo tired from the running and fetching, both laying on their backs in the grass, hugging. "You helped him?"

"Maybe."

"What'd you do?"

"You got to trust him sometime."

380

"What'd you do?"

"It's my farm," Quinn said. "Uncle Hamp left it to me."

"Holy hell," Caddy said. "I won't tell Momma. But, damn, if there won't be a shitstorm headed this way."

Quinn didn't move from the swing, shifting it back and forth on the jingling chains, the ceiling overhead painted the color of the sky. "She's not coming back," Quinn said.

"And lying to yourself about Daddy won't help."

"Give him a chance?"

Caddy shook her head, pushing open the screen door to grab her purse and keys, door thwacking shut behind her. "Just when I thought this old place couldn't get bigger and lonelier."

"What is it?"

"Nothing," Caddy said. "Shit, I can't breathe."

"Lady, you can't bring a damn baby in here," said the Indian-looking boy working the front door at Vienna's.

"Says who?" asked Nikki, tired, worn-out, and looking for some answers. She balanced Jon-Jon on her hip and wiped the sweat off her face with her forearm. "I don't see any signs."

"This is a titty bar," the Indian said. "Not a place for titty babies. You want to work, you need to come back by yourself. Miss Hathcock wouldn't appreciate you showing up with an infant. There's second-hand smoke and alcohol on the premises. Not to mention the nudity."

"My boy probably dreams about titties flying about," Nikki said. "Why don't you call down Miss Hathcock and let her know Milly Jones's best friend wants to have words with her."

The Indian's face changed a bit, softened a little, him rubbing his temples like he was thinking on it. He picked up the house phone from behind the counter, turned his back, and started to talk. It was hard to hear from where Nikki stood, between the front door and the double doors leading into the lounge. A blackboard in the hallway promised *2-for-1 Lap Dances Noon till 6.*

"Nope," the Indian said. "Like I said, no babies in the club."

"OK," Nikki said, dropping her head, turning and making like she was headed out. She turned back to look over her shoulder, Jon-Jon seeming to enjoy the bass sound of the music, and saw the Indian making change for a gray-headed man in a blue coveralls. Without a lot of fuss, she walked back the other way to the twin doors and busted into the club, barely hearing the Indian telling her to stop. The club was dark, with lots of flashing lights and neon, naked girls splayed out on the stages, zipping around the pole, the first bit of an old song she and Milly had loved — "Can't Be Tamed."

Nikki spotted the curved staircase and went for it, trying to be a good mother in the strip joint by covering her baby's delicate ears, pulling him close in, as she twisted and turned up to the roost and headed straight for the door to Miss Hathcock's office. The woman stood as Nikki entered, the Indian yelling behind her to stop and Miss Hathcock holding up the flat of her hand to him, or her, or both.

"She just ran in," the Indian said. "I tried to tell her."

"That's all right, Mingo," Hathcock said. "I've got it."

"Miss Hathcock, my name is Nikki Rowland," she said. "I am nineteen years old, a high school graduate, a good mother, and a member of the First Baptist Church. I don't care to get naked or shimmy around on your poles. I'm looking for answers about my best friend in the world, Milly Jones."

Miss Hathcock lifted her chin, checking

her out from head to toe. "A shame," she said. "I had two girls quit on me this morning. You look like you'd do fine. But you'd have to lose the kid. You ever hear of OSHA?"

"I said, I came for some gosh-dang answers about Milly."

Hathcock sat down, a cigarillo burning in an ashtray on her glass-topped desk. She stubbed it out and waved away the smoke. The music nearly shut out high in the office, just the muffled bass and sweet voice of Miley Cyrus. "And why do you want to talk to me?"

"Because Milly came here for work," Nikki said. "And because I was told you wanted her roughed up pretty good."

Hathcock gave a funny little laugh, sounding fake as hell. "Who told you that?"

"I can't say."

"And why's that?"

" 'Cause I'd rather not be set on fire," she said.

"You really think I'd kill a girl for sneaking out a few twenties in her snatch?" Miss Hathcock said. "Good Lord, girl. I did that, I might as well dig a cemetery out back."

"You wanted her roughed up," she said. "Right? I heard she left this place with nearly two thousand dollars that wasn't hers."

Miss Hathcock leaned back in her chair and smoothed her red hair. Nikki started to cry. It had been a long two weeks, not much sleep, only thing that had gotten her out of bed every day was Jon-Jon screaming for her. Funny what you'll do when someone else needs you.

"Who told you about the money?"

"Milly."

"No, she didn't," Hathcock said. "Who was it?"

"I'd rather not say," Nikki said. "God, it's hot up here. You mind if I sit down?

Miss Hathcock nodded her to a chair. She sure was a put-together woman, with the black silk shirt, the gold rings, huge diamond earrings, and ruby red heart pendant.

"I don't care if you smoke," Nikki said. "My mother smokes like a damn chimney. Figure the boy's got to get used to the mess sometime."

"Someone lied to you," Miss Hathcock said. "I knew exactly what your friend did and I was mad as hell. But had I had something to do with it, I'd have gotten my money back. As it is, it's a total loss. I'm down a dancer and a few thousand bucks. What's a girl to do?"

"She was sweet," Nikki said. "Spunky as hell."

"Like I told that policewoman," she said, "I wish I could help. This is all bad for business."

"Holy hell," Nikki said. "My friend is dead. How could you just say it's bad for business?"

"You sure you don't want a job?" Fannie said, reaching into her purse and pulling out a tin of little cigars. She plucked one in her mouth, making sure to fumigate the place to get rid of Nikki and Jon-Jon. "You look like a size zero, but with a nice rack."

"I'm breastfeeding, and I'm a size zero 'cause I haven't gotten much to eat lately," Nikki said.

Fannie lit up with a small gold lighter and waved away the smoke. "Drop the kid with Granny," she said. "Floor's open."

"I'd rather suck the devil's peter on the Fourth of July."

"I guess that's a no." Fannie shrugged. "Oh, well. Condolences on your friend."

"What's the worst of it?" Deputy Reggie Caruthers asked. "Trying to enforce the law around here?"

Lillie was behind the wheel of the Cherokee, taking Reggie on some tours of the Tibbehah back roads that he didn't even know existed. From up around Carthage and Fate, down through Blackjack and onto the southernmost roads of Sugar Ditch. "I guess having to know how your friends turned out," Lillie said. "It was easier when I was in Memphis. They weren't my people. But when you got to go see Josie Swain at her produce stand and see a black eye and a purple bruise covering half her face, it's hard to take."

"She got trouble with her husband?"

"They're not married," Lillie said. "But they have trouble. Main trouble is, her making excuses for his sorry ass. Josie and I were thick as thieves back in high school. She was on our basketball team with your cousin, TaNiya. She was short, but a great rebounder. Tough as hell. All grit and elbows. You see what's happened to her, ten years plus in, and it makes you want to puke."

"Why didn't you stay in Memphis?"

"My momma got sick."

"And then what?"

"And then she died, Quinn came back, and life marched on."

"You and Quinn?" Reggie said. "What y'all got goin' on?"

"Are you kidding?"

"If you stayed, he must've meant something more than being the sheriff," Reggie said. "Y'all work real well together."

Lillie turned off 9W to a little dirt road that went by the old Providence cemetery, the town of Providence being the original settlement of Tibbehah when it was bought up from the Choctaw. After the Civil War, Confederates hid up in its hills, refusing to give in, taking shots, raiding the Yankees until they'd been brought in or were dead. Folks who live there now still clinging to old ideals, same ways. The SUV kicked up dust and grit, passing a man-made gulley filled with old AC units, tires, and deer parts. Folks not having respect for the land or themselves. But god damn you to hell if you let them know there was another way.

"Quinn's a good friend," Lillie said.

"You ever think there might be more?"

"Damn, Reggie," Lillie said. "That's getting a little personal, isn't it?"

"I see how it is," Reggie said, grinning, showing off his dimples. "Y'all joke back and forth, talk to each other in that code of yours. It's like when you work, you got some kind of telepathy going."

"He's a pro."

"Mmm-hmm."

"Besides, haven't you heard?" Lillie said.

"I'm a woman-crazed dyke, spending my free hours at lesbian clubs down in New Orleans, picking up chicks."

"When you're not enforcing the law and taking care of Rose?"

"Yeah," Lillie said. "In that in-between time."

Reggie was quiet for a while, taking in the dirt roads and deer paths Lillie showed him, the scattering of trailers and cabins, hard-scrabble and rusted, up in the hills. He was a quick study, never asking the same question twice. Reggie had also proven good with people, making friends, making connections with the town folks and the county people, knowing that respect went both ways.

"Well," Reggie said, letting down his window. "If you and Quinn hook up, I guess y'all might mess up what works."

"He's not going to stay."

"You don't think so?"

"If you had a choice," Lillie said, "what the hell would you do?"

"I have a choice," Reggie said. "So do you. We all got a chance to leave Tibbehah. But we love it because it's home. Right? We want to make it better for all our people."

"Even if it does come with a big old side dish of corruption and bullshit."

"Even then."

"You're a smart man, Reggie Caruthers," Lillie said. "I'd like to keep you around."

"Just try and recall that on my six-month eval."

Lillie laughed just about the time the radio crackled on from dispatch, Cleotha wanting Lillie to call in to Boom Kimbrough on her cell. She picked up the mic and gave her a 10-4, steering out of the dusty dry-dirt hills and down back to the flat land where she could get a decent cell signal again.

"What'd you ever do about Josie Swain?"

"Tried to talk to her," Lillie said. "Make some sense of things. I go to her vegetable stand every week, pretend I need tomatoes and greens, which I can buy in town."

"Y'all still friends?"

Lillie nodded, hitting Boom's number on her speed dial, tires hitting asphalt again, looking straight at the Swain Farms hand-painted sign for *Tomato, Corn & Peppers. Homegrown. Fresh & Safe.* "What's up?" she asked.

Boom said, "Coach Mills is gone."

"He finally have a heart attack?"

"Wife's out looking for him," Boom said. "Didn't show at the pep rally or the pre-game. They got Pontotoc rolling into town in one hour. Won't answer his phone, nobody can find his truck."

"Shit."

"You thinking what I'm thinking?"

"Goddamn Nito Reece," Lillie said, spinning the wheel into a hard U-turn and heading south to Jericho.

28

Yeah, he killed the bitch.

But, god damn, she made him do it. She'd called him up right after that first home game and said, "Coach Mills, I need to square away something with you right here and now."

The familiar way she'd spoke to him in that quiet country twang of hers made his blood boil and his heart about jump out of his dang chest. He'd drove straight down to the old Big Black River to hear what the hell she knew and just what she'd been scheming. There had been so much confusion and downright lies coming from that road trash family of hers that you never knew what to expect. He rolled on down the hill in his new Dodge and saw her standing there by that little white Tic Tac of a car, arms crossed over her flat chest as if he was the one who needed a talking to.

And the damn threats, outright lies,

fantasy, and filth that flew out of her mouth was enough to make a Christian man want to vomit. Little Milly Jones, nothing but a hot-bed cheerleader, told him that if he didn't want to step forward and be a man, that she'd do it for him. The threat on the manhood had about done it. He tried to calm her, put a hand on her shoulder, her shaking him off until he tried to talk some sense. Girl wouldn't listen until he got a few licks in with that damn tire iron from his GMC. Didn't mean to kill her. Just make her think straight. But her head wasn't made for toughness and just kind of broke apart, her landing in a crumpled heap down by the boat landing. All that filth and lies she'd been spewing replaced by the sound of crickets and frogs. Quiet and peace.

Animals making an obscene bit of noise while he tried to think, figure out just what he needed to do. This little girl didn't mean nothing when it came to the town, the county, the tradition of all he'd done. Damn her soul. Damn her to hell.

That's when he called up his old trusted standby to help him shift things 'round a bit. Nito would know what to do.

"And now you fucked me," Nito said. Right here and now, standing direct in front of him, off the Natchez Trace by a little lookout over the Indian Mounds, little rounded heaps of dirt that had weathered wars, disease, and a whole lot of dancing around the ole fire. Lots more than what he'd been through. Coach would get through this. Bud Mills didn't get knocked down without getting his ass right back up.

"What do you mean, I fucked you?"

"You fucked me then," Nito said. "You fucking me now."

"Has everyone in this whole goddamn town gone crazy?" Coach said. "I thought you had me out here 'cause we needed to talk private. You ain't no better than that little ole girl, wanting to ambush me and talk a lot of trash."

"I ain't a kid."

"No," Bud Mills said, spitting some Skoal into the dirt. "You ain't. You're a dang grown-ass man. So how about you hitch up your britches and let's move on. If you ain't heard, I got a game to coach tonight."

"You remember what you used to tell me?"

"Aw, hell," Coach said. "I gotta git."

"You told me you were toughening me up, doing things men do to help with that pressure," Nito said. "I didn't understand it. I tried to tell my momma and she wouldn't listen. Said I was a liar."

"Come on now."

"I was eight years old," he said. "And I'm still dealing with your sickness. I ain't your boy no more. What we done to Milly ain't right."

"I got no idea what you're saying, boy," he said. "All I know is, I bought y'all's groceries and kept your momma from being a dang receptacle for truckers at twenty bucks a throw."

That's when Nito hit him, hard and fast, across his mouth, knocking that dip from his lip and starting it bleeding. "Come on now, Nito," he said, trying to laugh it off. "Don't tell me you didn't like it. You talk and then everyone will know'd what you did then. And now."

"All I remember is, your fat ass weighing on me," he said. "I couldn't breathe, your hands all over me, pulling off my pants."

"That's enough."

"Damn right, it is," Nito said. "Telling Sheriff Virgil that I killed Milly Jones, saying what happened to my Nova up in Memphis. What the fuck you thinking? She sweated my ass long and hard for that."

"You put that little girl in your fucking car, Nito," Coach said. "Use your head. Use your fucking head. That's why you never could make it. You couldn't read a dang

English book or a defense. All your teachers said you was a damn mental deficient."

Nito struck him again. And, this time, Coach had enough, gripping a good bit of Nito's black tank top, taking some of them rapper's gold chains in the mix, and standing up toe-to-toe, man-to-man. "I didn't kill her," Coach said. "Whose idea was it to burn up the car and pour that gasoline down her throat?"

"You stuck yourself in my mouth," Nito said, screaming. "You done it to me. You done things like that forever. I ain't your friend. I ain't your boy."

Coach pulled him closer, wanting to bite a big old plug from his black cheek, knock those gold teeth from his mouth. He'd taken the girl out. He sure couldn't be stopped by a worthless black ass like ole Nito Reece. And, god damn, he was crying. Crying, for shit's sake.

"Let me tell you something," Coach Mills said. "And I want you to listen up and listen good. I am Bud Mills. I am somebody. You? You're worthless. You're nothing. Ain't nothing can be done about breeding. You ain't nothing but a fucking mongrel dog eating roadkill stuck to the highway."

And then came the hard thwack, metal on meat and bone, and Coach Bud Mills falling sideways, flat to the ground. He couldn't see right, but he could hear voices sounding almost like they'd come to him underwater. He'd been hit like that only one time before, when he'd been a sophomore at North Alabama, blindsided on a kickoff. A long, ragged wheeze came out of his mouth like a punctured football.

"Shoot," a country-ass peckerwood voice said. "I was about tired of hearing that fat SOB talking. You get his legs and I'll get his arms. We can lock him in the trunk till we clean his place out."

"You hear that?" Nito said. "What that fucker said to me?"

"No," the peckerwood said, rough hands feeling around in his coaching shorts, sound of jangling keys being taken from him. "Why? He saying something about all them guns and that jumbo TV?"

"You don't need to be harassing me like that," Ordeen said. "I'm just trying to watch the damn game."

Quinn and Boom had walked the stadium until they saw Ordeen Davis sitting up in the top row with a few other North Side Boys, smoking cigarettes and drinking moonshine out of a Gatorade bottle. They called him out and walked him down from the bleachers into the half darkness of the stands by a little concession booth. The game had already rolled over into the second quarter, with one of Coach Mills's assistants taking over, folks saying Coach had come down with the flu. After the National Anthem, the stadium announcer had asked everyone to please pray for a quick recovery for their beloved Coach Bud.

"Take the damn moonshine," Ordeen said. "You really gonna bust my ass for that bullshit?"

"Where's Nito?" Quinn said.

"How should I know?" Ordeen said.

"He tell you about having trouble with Coach Mills?" Boom said.

"And who the hell are you?" Ordeen said, looking Boom up and down, eyes lingering on the missing arm.

"I'm fucking Boom Kimbrough, is who," Boom said. "And your black ass better pray that your boy doesn't touch Coach."

"Y'all crazy."

"When'd you see Nito last?" Quinn asked.

"Shit, man," he said. "I don't know. It's been a few days."

Boom stepped in, placing his one sizable hand on Ordeen's shoulder. Ordeen having to lift his chin to look up into Boom's unsmiling face. The Tibbehah marching band launched into "Seven Nation Army," a favorite of Quinn's when he'd been overseas with the Regiment. He'd had his old iPod loaded down with a lot of White Stripes, Reigning Sound, and Tyler Keith. Always good stuff before running and gunning.

"Hold on," Quinn said. "Ordeen's a reasonable man. He's got sense. And, besides, nobody wants to see Coach hurt."

"Hurt Coach?" Ordeen said. "Man, I don't even know what y'all talking about. You got problems with Nito, go see Nito and leave me the hell alone. I just heard the Coach got the shits. Me and Nito don't have nothing to do with that mess."

"Where's Nito?" Boom said. "Where do we find him?"

"Come on," Ordeen said. "I'm missing the game. Tibbehah's already up by a touchdown. Damn, if they ain't playing better without old coach calling the plays."

"Did Nito tell you he'd been with the Jones girl?" Quinn asked.

"Oh, I see," Ordeen said. "That's what this shit's about. Coach done point his finger at Nito and now you think Nito wants some revenge? Y'all really reaching for it. Making everything a goddamn mess for that white girl. Why you give a shit about that white girl, Mr. Kimbrough?"

"Coach is gone," Boom said. "Nobody's seen him. Last time I talked to him, he was scared Nito might kill him. Said Nito had been asking for money and threatening his ass."

"That's some bullshit," Ordeen said. "Nito don't need to ask no one for money."

"Business that good?" Quinn said.

Ordeen looked back and forth to Quinn and Boom. He tilted his head and scratched at his neck under the long braids. "Can I go?" Ordeen said.

"Where's he hang, man?" Boom asked.

Ordeen shrugged. "He either at the pool hall or the house."

"We checked both," Quinn said.

"Then I can't help y'all," Ordeen said.

"You need to find him," Quinn said. "You can do it on the outside or with us bringing you in. Doesn't make much difference to me."

Ordeen tried to look tough, hands in his pockets, flat-crowned ball cap high on his head. "I see him, I'll tell him you been asking around."

"Nope," Quinn said. "You see him and you'll let us know where to find him. Or I'll consider you an accomplice."

Ordeen shook his head as the band's horn

section heated up, drums pounding a steady pulse. *Let's go. Let's go. Let's go.* Feet hammering on the aluminum stands, making it seem like there was an earthquake in Tibbehah County. "You gonna give me back my Gatorade or what?"

Quinn handed him back the moonshine, the stuff smelling like kerosene when he'd unscrewed the top. "Knock yourself out."

Quinn and Boom stood there as Ordeen turned his back and walked back toward the bleachers. Someone scored a touchdown for the Wildcats and the fans went crazy, yelling and clapping, the announcer letting everyone know the home team was now up by thirteen points.

"Seem that long ago?" Boom asked.

"Nope."

"Yeah?" Boom said. "Now who's lying?"

"You know he got a new car?" said the girl, Shartesia Cousins. "Nito sold off that blue Nova he had. The one with those big rims? Can you believe that? He once told me he loved that car more than a woman. Said it smelled so goddamn nice."

"Y'all still together?" Lillie asked.

"Sometimes," the girl said. "Sometimes, we just drive around and shit. He got a baby with some girl down in Eupora. Why don't you ask her?"

"Because we know you," Reggie Caruthers said. "Figured you might have seen him."

They found Shartesia down at the gas station in Sugar Ditch, hanging out with the boys who played spades on a Friday night. They ran a regular game under a prefab carport with a sign that read *Only $599 Installed!* Someone had made the effort to fill it up with a couple old church pews, some old easy chairs, and a long folding table. Now it was a nightclub of sorts on summer nights. A few folks scattering when the law drove up, Lillie not caring less.

"I don't want to see him," Shartesia said, sitting on a weathered picnic table outside the carport. "That boy crazy."

"Crazy how?"

"I only deal with his ass when he's smoking weed," she said. "Chills his ass out. He got someone kind of mental problems. Always believe someone out to get him."

"He ever say anything to you about Coach Mills?"

Shartesia shook her head. "Nah," she said. "I know he played football for Coach. They friends and shit."

"You know where he might be?" Reggie said.

"He love to go down to the pool hall," she

said. "He do his business there. Or at that gas station up in Blackjack. You know the Gas & Go?"

"Been both of those places," Lillie said. "No one's seen him."

"Where'd y'all go if you just hanging out?" Reggie said. "Drinking, partying a bit."

"We at his momma's place when she at work," she said. "Ride around a lot in his car. Smoke it up."

"What about when y'all tired of riding?" Reggie said.

Shartesia caught his eye and smiled at him, a sly kind of devilish look. Reggie had a way with the ladies. Even a tough one like Shartesia Cousins, hard as hell at twenty-five, two kids with two different fathers, and an older brother who'd run the drugs in Tibbehah before Nito Reece. The brother now in lockdown at Parchman for a twenty-year stretch.

"He like to shoot rats."

Lillie looked over at Reggie, Reggie nodding to Shartesia to tell him all she knew. She leaned forward on the picnic table, glancing down at her smartphone and back up at him. "I don't smoke no more," she said. "But when me and Nito got to smoking, he like to drink and shoot them rats. Sometimes, we fooled around a little there.

403

But I didn't like it. Nasty as hell, lots of broken glass and all that."

"Where's that, Shartesia?" Lillie asked.

"That old factory by the train station," she said. "Y'all know what I'm talking about?"

"The cotton compress?" Lillie said.

She shrugged. "I don't know what it is," she said. "Place been closed down long as I been here. It's the place you go when you don't want folks seeing what you up to."

D. J. Norwood decided to bring his brother, Larry, along since Larry had a little meth, a fresh bottle of Aristocrat vodka, and that pressure washer they needed. But, damn, if ole Nito was pissed, wanting to know just what fucked up his brain so much that he'd bring his dumb-ass brother with him. Norwood put up his hands, trying to calm his black ass down, saying only Larry knew how to get the thing started. It was an older engine and needed a little sweet talk and a lot of Gumout in the carburetor. "Besides, Larry ain't gonna just leave it," he said. "This damn piece of equipment keeps him employed."

"I'm a part-time painter," Larry said, showing off his brown and rotted teeth. "And a full-time pussy hound."

"He better stand outside," Nito said. "Keep watch and shit while we do our work."

They stood by their vehicles behind the old cotton compress, headlights on high beam, while Larry backed the washer down off his truck. "I don't even think this place has a roof no more," he said. "Heard it done blowed off in the tornado."

"We just trying to get some shit clean," Nito said. "Figure no one will mind if we make a bunch of racket out here."

"Our daddy used to work here," Larry said. "Ain't that right, Norwood? Machine man. He could fix damn-near anything before the strokes."

Larry called him Norwood, like everyone else, even though they both shared the same last name. Larry had on a Teenage Mutant Ninja Turtles T-shirt with the sleeves cut out. On second glance, Norwood was pretty sure the bastard had stolen it from his drawer. Norwood didn't have on a shirt, just cutoff blue jeans and some shower shoes. Son of a bitch, Larry, stealing his clean shirt from the Walmart.

"You change the intensity with the nozzles," Larry said. "See right there?"

"What's the highest one?" Nito said.

"Red," he said. "Red will take the dang

paint off. You start off with maybe green, just to test her out, and see how it works. But you better be careful and wear some gloves and boots. That water can near cut the whale out of you."

"What'd you do with that vodka?" Norwood asked.

"It's in the truck," Larry said. "Why? You want a hit?"

"Hell, yes," Norwood said. "Maybe burn some shit, too."

"I know'd you didn't bring me along just for my washer," Larry said, grinning with those brown rotted teeth. "How about you, Nito? You like to party?"

"Damn right," he said, walking around to the open window of the Caprice Classic and turning up the radio. Yo Gotti, "Down In The DM," talking that dirty talk to women on that Snapchat, asking them to show all their goodies.

"Damn, Norwood," Larry said, unscrewing the top of the vodka. "I like black people, but I can't stand to hear no nigger music."

"Oh, yeah?" Nito said, taking the bottle from his hand and knocking back a good bit. "Y'all peckerwoods ain't happy unless someone's crying in their beer or fucking their best friend's momma."

"How you gonna run the water?" Larry asked. "I got about two hundred I can pump from my truck. You reckon that'll be enough?"

"I guess it's got to be," he said. "Don't see no spigots 'round here." Nito leaned against the car and felt the heavy hands slapping at the trunk, Coach yelling like hell for someone to let him the hell out. The old fat man beating that trunk so hard, the whole body of the Caprice Classic shook. Nito grinned with excitement.

"Dang," Larry said. "I'd rather be shot than listen to that rap shit. Sounds like a man bein' tortured."

29

Quinn drove up on Lillie and Reggie Caruthers, who'd parked down the road from the old cotton compress, near the vacant train station north of town. With his truck windows open, he could hear the band playing a half mile away at Tibbehah Stadium and see the bright lights shining all the way from Jericho. Kenny followed Quinn in his cruiser, parked, and met them at Lillie's Jeep, the deputy moving with a slight limp after getting shot last year.

"Game's tied," Kenny said. "Twenty-one, twenty-one. Don't know if they're gonna pull it or not. Defense is weak as hell."

"What got y'all here?" Quinn asked.

"Nito's ex-girlfriend told us he came here some," Lillie said. "When we checked it out we spotted a red-and-white Sierra Classic parked out back. The truck had water lines running from a portable tank into the building. Heard some music and a motor running from inside. Truck's registered to one of the Norwood brothers."

"Sounds like a dang keg party," Kenny said. "Those Norwoods like to drink and fuck shit up."

"We think Nito's with them," Lillie said. "And I believe they got Coach Mills with them."

"Why the hell would Nito Reece be running with the dang Norwoods?" Kenny asked.

"They go way back," Reggie said. "And do a lot of business. Only color those boys care about is that green."

"If Nito's got him, you really think that man's still alive?" Lillie said.

"Any word from Coach's wife?" Quinn said.

"Yeah," Lillie said. "After he walked off from the high school, she went home to find their house had been robbed. Someone took a couple TVs, some pistols and shotguns, and raided their deep freeze of two quarts of butter pecan ice cream and six Red Baron pepperoni pizzas."

"What'd I tell you?" Kenny said. "A party. We used to raise hell in that place. Everyone used to meet up there after the law ran us off cruising the Square. Damn, I hated the police back then, always messing up the fun."

Reggie grinned and showed them all a little sketch on a yellow legal pad he'd been working on, diagramming out the guts of the old building. Quinn, Lillie, and Kenny watched as he marked off what he recalled from playing hide-and-seek there as a kid. "I don't think that place has changed much in twenty years," Reggie said. "Offices up high on a platform, looking down on where the machines had been. Only closed-off spaces I know of."

The diagram showed a wide-open, empty floor plan, lots of room to cross with absolutely no cover or concealment.

"How do you get to the second floor?" Quinn asked.

"There's a staircase," Reggie said.

"Open or closed-in?" Quinn asked.

"It's open," Reggie said. "Maybe twenty steps up one way and then curves back around to the top."

"Y'all stay here," Quinn said. "I'll do a quick walk-around. See what we're dealing with."

"I'm coming with you," Lillie said.

"Up to you, Sheriff," Quinn said. "But I can do it quicker alone."

"OK, Gary Cooper," Lillie said. "But be

quiet and please don't fuck it up for every-one."

"Yeah?" Quinn asked, smiling. "Love you, too."

Lillie looked down at the diagram's fluttering pages and then met Reggie's eyes from across the Jeep's hood. Her face colored a bit, Reggie grinning at her as Quinn turned away, confused, and walked toward the road, the far-off sound of the crowd roaring and the band starting up. Tibbehah must've pulled ahead.

They'd stripped his ass naked and tied him to a school chair with duct tape. The chair had a big old hole through the plastic and the coach could feel every time a warm breeze ran through the cracks in the roof. At first, he thought he could talk his way out of this, always knowing how to work over Nito Reece, until they wheeled in that fucking pressure washer and set it on high. And then all bets were off. Nito and that dumb-ass kid, D. J. Norwood, shooting it around the small room, playing with it, zapping at Coach's bare feet while someone played some loud-as-hell rap music down the steps from where they came.

"What do you want, Nito?" Coach said. "Money? I'll give you money."

"Nope."

"Then what is it?" Coach said. "What the fuck do you want, boy?"

"The truth," Nito said. "I want the truth, Coach. Every time you open your mouth, a damn lie comes out."

"That's bullshit and you know it."

Nito walked up on him fast and raised that water gun, shooting fast and hard at his nut sack like it was dead center on a dartboard. A red-hot, mean pain shot through Coach's whole body and he yelled every profane word he knew until he backtracked to prayers with tears in his eyes. "Lord God Almighty," he said. "Help me, Lord."

"Jesus ain't on the premises, motherfucker," Nito said, pacing the room with a .45 stuck in his waistband. "I want you to tell folks what you done. I want you to take back what you told the law about my car. I want my name clear. I want you to tell them you the one who killed Milly Jones."

"She was alive, Nito," Coach said. "I just shook her around a bit. Tried to knock some sense into her. You the one who poured gasoline into her mouth."

"You damn knocked her brains out with that tire iron," Nito said, blasting him across the chest and over his big round stomach, feeling like a needle poking right through his organs, his skin tearing away. "You tole me to fix it. You're gonna tell the sheriff what you done to her and then you gonna tell them what you did to me and all those other boys."

"Drugs," Coach said, shaking his head sadly, feeling tears running down his face. "Kills our community."

As soon as the words left his mouth, he knew he shouldn't have said it, damn Nito shooting another direct hit right on his low-hanging sack and trying to knock 'em out of the ballpark and on over to China. The second hit was even worse than the first, the nerve endings good and heated up, ready and willing to receive that pain. He started cussing some more, using words he'd vowed to erase from his vocabulary last Easter, and then going back to ask Jesus to save him.

As soon as he stopped screaming, he turned his head to the white boy, Norwood. "Help me," he said. "This nigger's gone crazy."

The skinny, bucktoothed shitheel just shrugged, took a long pull of some clear liquor in a pint bottle, and turned to Nito as the man in charge. "I had a cousin who said Coach Mills liked to stay a long time in the shower, licking his lips, and rubbing himself. Said he nearly tripped over himself running when them freshman boys got off practice. Couldn't wait to get to the locker room."

"That's a lie," Coach said, screaming. "A black lie."

Nito shook his head sadly, "You just don't get it, Coach," he said. "We got your number."

"Then leave me the hell alone."

"Damn," Nito said. "I don't know if I can do it anymore."

"Now you're talking some sense. Me and you are in this together. And we're gonna get out of it together. OK? We good on that, boy?"

Nito lowered the spray gun and shook his head at his white buddy, Norwood. "I can't be having all the fun. You try it, man. Coach leans a little to the right, you got to shoot right at the curve of his little thingamajig."

Norwood, with his caved-in, skinny chest tattooed with some kind of Indian nonsense, stepped right on up, took the gun, and scored him a direct hit, laughing, the damn jungle music and the roaring pressure washer drowning out all Coach's screams for help. Coach screamed and screamed, all the noise echoing and drowned out in the big concrete hole.

"Hold on. Hold on," Norwood said, giddy. "Let me go get Larry. This is more fun than busting balloons at a county fair."

Quinn walked the perimeter of the old building, still sweating on a dark, humid night. The sliver of a moon above had a heat haze around it. He wiped his face with the sleeve of his uniform shirt and made his way close to the concrete-block wall, edging through privet bush and weeds, broken glass and trash. The walls vibrated with loud rap music and the chugging sound of a small work engine. The engine buzzed from up on the second floor, but from what he'd seen on the layout, he'd have to enter the building to know everything that was going on. As he moved around the north side of the building, he spotted the old red-and-white GMC Sierra that Lillie and Reggie had seen. A water hose ran from a tank in the back of the truck bed up the stairs to the offices. Quinn moved close to the wall, through the shadows, but saw no one near the truck. Toward the east wall, the road sloped upward, and as he moved away from the building, the more he saw into the gaping hole of the roof.

Quinn kept walking up the hill toward the

train tracks, where he looked down into the building and saw bright headlights on in a sedan, shaking with the music, but with no one around it. No one was up on the landing to the offices.

He used his cell to call Lillie, telling her what he'd found. The way the old cotton compress had been torn apart by the storm made him think of Kabul, of a forgotten textile building, half-blasted to shit, torn strands of material buffeting around in busted-out windows. They'd tracked three insurgents through a graveyard of Soviet tanks and into the ruined building. Two men and a woman, the woman walking toward Quinn's team with a detonator in her hand. So much yelling and screaming, the woman refusing to back down, headed straight for them. Looking back once to get a strong nod from her husband before she pressed the button, taking a couple of Quinn's soldiers with her. *Jesus.* He hoped Nito had less conviction.

Quinn moved clockwise around the building a second time, hearing but still not seeing anyone, the sounds of a party but without the guests. At the south side of the building, a big bay door had been ripped away and Quinn used his right knee to press himself up onto the landing, catching a quick glimpse inside the old factory. He was closer to the sedan but stayed well in the shadows and away from the bright shining lights of the car. As Reggie had drawn, most of the building had its guts ripped away, leaving a wide-open floor under the torn roof and an east wall for offices that had looked down on the workers. Water poured over the lip of the second-floor landing, dripping down in a heavy sheet, splashing down in a black pool below.

Quinn took a quick shot of the interior with his cell phone, glancing up at the hose trailing up the staircase. He got close enough to the sedan to note the make and model matched Nito Reece's new ride. He stayed in the darkness by a far wall for ten minutes, waiting for more faces to appear. Instead, he barely made out the screams coming from one of the open doorways on the second floor.

He made his way back out and then ran down the road to Lillie, Kenny, and Reggie, telling them it looked like Nito had someone up that landing and was working him over. He had a good sweat going as he met up with them.

"Coach?"

"Don't know," Quinn said. "Pretty sure they're not running a Sunday service up there. Someone is getting a good workover."

"How many?"

"Two vehicles," Quinn said. "Someone was screaming. But no one entered or left that one room. I stayed as long as I could."

"I don't give a shit," Kenny said. "If they got Coach, let's go get him. Last thing we need is some kind of Waco situation."

"What do you say, Sheriff?" Quinn asked.

"Can't be more than three or four of them," Lillie said. "I say enter with caution and assess the situation."

"We get closer than me and the only assessing you'll be doing is when to pull the trigger."

Lillie met Quinn's eye, took in a deep breath, and nodded. She had on her sheriff's office hat with the gold star, the brim pulled so low, she had to lift her chin to get a good look at things. "I'll head up on that roof," Lillie said. "You take Kenny and Reggie with you. That's what you're thinking, right?"

"Your call, but I'd feel better with our best shooter watching my damn six."

Quinn glanced up the hill, beyond the cotton compress, to the abandoned brick train station. "Nice big hole and enough light to work," he said, nodding behind him. "You think you can get up there?"

"Just watch me."

"Where'd your damn brother go?" Nito said.

"He wanted to smoke," he said. "It's Friday night and he's been painting all week. What do you care if he wants to get fucked up?"

"Who's watching the road?" Nito said.

"Hell," Norwood said. "I damn near forgot about that. Aw, fuck it."

"And this pressure ain't worth shit," Nito said. "How much water we got left?"

"How much you need?"

"Enough to stick this wand straight up Coach's ass until he bust apart."

"Hey now," Norwood said. "I didn't sign on for no shit like that. I ain't gonna get involved in any homicide of our own Jericho, Mississippi, legend."

"He's a piece of shit, is what he is," Nito said. "Come on. Come on. Go fix that shit so we can shut it down and get the fuck out of here."

"Don't kill Coach."

"Why you want to save that white man?" Nito said. "Don't be a pussy, Norwood. You want to work with Nito Reece, you need to buck up and be a goddamn man."

"That sounds like Coach talking."

"Fix that shit," Nito said. "Get me some damn water here. And Norwood?"

"Yeah?"

"Make sure you bring back that vodka and whatever y'all smoking," he said. "That shit sure do hit the spot."

After Lillie called Quinn from the train station roof and said she was in place and had overwatch, he told Kenny and Reggie to turn off their cells, their police radios, and anything that made any noise. Lillie said she'd seen D. J. Norwood leave the third doorway from the landing, walk out on the balcony, and piss far and wide into the old factory. As far as she could tell, all the activity was happening in that one room.

"A dang herd of elephants could bust into that place and they wouldn't notice," Kenny said.

"We move just as I've shown you, Kenny," Quinn said. "Reggie, you're the last man through the door. I'll hit the far left corner, Kenny heads to the far right. We keep moving from corner to corner until we know it's all clear. We used to practice this at the shoot house with Ike McCaslin. Ike's a good man, but I bet you're a hell of a lot faster."

"About twenty years younger," Reggie said.

Quinn drew it out twice on Reggie's legal pad and then they walked through the way it should work. "Let's hit that room hard and fast."

"And don't shoot Coach Mills," Kenny said. "That might really piss him off."

"We can be surgical," Quinn said. "We have at least two bad guys, D. J. Norwood and Nito Reece. But we can't be sure there aren't more."

"Those Norwoods are some mean sonsabitches," Kenny said. "Two of 'em put a friend of mine in the hospital for spilling their beer down at the Southern Star. That damn redneck shithead mentality you're dealing with."

"You see a gun," Quinn said. "Shut 'em down."

"Yes, sir," Kenny said.

"Guess you did this kind of thing a few times?" Reggie asked. "Over in Iraq and all."

"A few."

"My unit didn't do much close combat," he said. "What's it like?"

"Dirty and messy," Quinn said.

"Yeah?" Reggie said. "That all?"

"And almost never what you expect."

"Dance, motherfucker," Nito said, hitting

Coach's little fat toes. "Dance, you fat bastard."

"Larry said he's running out of water," Norwood said.

"How much do we got left?"

"Don't know," Norwood said. "Larry said he's too goddamn high to make a fucking important judgment like that."

"OK, Coach," Nito said, hitting that lighter below the crystal pipe. "It's drill time. I want you to get on all fours and open wide."

Coach was sitting on his ass, covering himself with closed legs, shivering, although it hadn't dropped below ninety all damn day. He just kept shaking his head, pretty much realizing that he wasn't about to get out of this place alive. 'Course Nito never saw that kind of concern on his face when he'd bashed in Milly Jones's head, only when they set that car on fire and that dead girl come to life, walking out the open passenger door and headed for the road. He and Coach jumped in their vehicles and got the hell out of there.

"You're going to have to kill me," Coach said. "I won't be violated."

"Bend over, Coach Bud," Nito said, taking in the hit, letting it out real slow. "Take it like a man."

"Why?" Coach said. "What are you gonna do to me?"

"Time you learn to get some of that intestinal fortitude you always talking about."

Quinn was right. Lillie had a nice viewpoint on the train station roof, watching as Quinn and the other two deputies filed into building from an old loading dock. Nearly half of the roof had been ripped off by the tornado two years ago, letting some moonlight shine in, the entry to the staircase illuminated by the headlights of Nito's Caprice Classic. She was no expert on this stuff, but she was pretty sure he was now playing Yo Gotti, featuring Boosie Badazz and Blac Youngsta. "The Good Die Young." Lillie had gotten hooked on Hot 107 in Memphis, hard music to stop liking. *I see the hate on their face. Praying for better days.*

That Memphis sound always brought her back to Orange Mound, not two weeks on the job, when she saw too much blood spilled on an outdoor basketball court from two teenagers fighting over bullshit territory and kid pride with insults and Glocks. She had to call on the sixteen-year-old's momma, the woman in shock but handling it, saying, "I always knew it would end like this."

Quinn led the way, as Quinn always did, across the big empty floor, around the support beams and over the toppled chairs, desks, and spilled paint buckets. Kenny headed up the open staircase next, followed by Reggie. Reggie moving pretty damn good for a rookie, falling right in with Quinn's Army drill. Quinn rotated up onto the next landing. Everyone trained muzzles to his own corner, moving fast but careful. Or, as Quinn said, don't be in a damn hurry to get yourself shot.

It was hot, humid as hell, and Lillie wiped away the sweat from her right eye, finding the landing again, watching Quinn move down the row of open doors, passing the two empty ones and going right for the third. Quinn lined up, looked in the direction of Lillie, and bolted inside. Kenny followed and she saw the room light up and heard two shotgun blasts. And then silence. Reggie lingered at the door, shining a Maglite over a Glock. Lillie felt that familiar surge of adrenaline, waiting for Reggie to turn around and give a thumbs-up or all-clear sign. He seemed to be talking to someone, Lillie again wiping the sweat from her eyes. She was pretty sure they had them.

What a fucking mess.

When she returned to the scope, a quick dark shape charged from the second open doorway, running toward Reggie Caruthers, who had his back turned. Another Norwood brother.

The man was yelling something and lifted a pistol from the back of his pants.

Lillie took a deep breath and squeezed that trigger, her Winchester bucking in her hands. A fucking mess, she thought, the man falling and her cell ringing.

It was Quinn.

30

"How's Lillie?" Anna Lee asked. "Dealing with the shooting and all that crap that came next."

"She should have never gone on national TV," Quinn said. "I should have talked her out of it."

"You really think she would have listened?"

"I guess not," Quinn said. "I don't blame her for going off on the host, that blonde woman dissecting every move for the last two weeks, saying that Coach Mills was the true hero, standing up to Nito, and second-guessing that Lillie put his life in danger by what we did."

"What's wrong with blondes?" Anna Lee said, hefting up another box in her arms, turning to walk out from the old Victorian and pack up the truck. The house was nearly cleared out, everything Anna Lee owned either in storage or headed up to

Memphis. Anna Lee let Quinn know the commute was getting too tough on Shelby and too tough on her. But, son of a bitch, he'd miss seeing her walk. Anna Lee Amsden moved like a cat.

"Well, Lillie didn't do herself any favors by asking the woman if she got her journalism degree in a Crackerjack box."

"At least she didn't say fuck," Anna Lee said. "Could have been worse."

"If you watch it back slow," Quinn said, "you can hear her say it when she rips out her earpiece. She calls the woman 'a fucking dumb bitch.' But you got to really turn up the TV to hear it."

"Sheriff Virgil?"

"Yep."

"Can you follow me up in your truck?" Anna Lee said, hefting the box into what little room was left in the U-Haul.

"Luke will be there?"

"I can tell him you're coming," Anna Lee said. "Nobody wants drama in front of Shelby. You can stay the night, help me get settled in, and head back tomorrow. I'll even buy you sweet potato pancakes at the Arcade."

"I promised to take the night shift for Lillie," Quinn said. "She's worn out. Hadn't spent hardly any time with Rose since all this began. I think all of us need a little downtime, hope things go back to normal."

"I really hope you'll consider staying stateside," Anna Lee said. "Memphis is only ninety miles away. Last time, you were over there for six months."

"They did promise to get me home for Christmas."

"Nothing to change your mind?"

"No," he said. "Not now."

Anna Lee nodded. They headed back inside together, the house emptying bit by bit, the echoes more pronounced as they walked and talked with nothing to cushion the sound. Quinn moved out a couple antique chairs and latched them to a railing inside the truck, making sure they didn't jostle too much.

"But Lillie will need your help."

Quinn took off his ball cap, wiped his brow, and pulled it back in his eyes. The sun was setting along the hill above town, looking into Jericho and the oaks surrounding the Square. He shook his head.

"Lillie doesn't need me," Quinn said. "Everyone in town supports the decisions she made to go into that building. Hell, Nito Reece was trying to kill Coach Mills. He was doing worse than waterboarding him up there, taking out some serious rage."

"You ever find out why?"

"He thought Coach was turning on him," Quinn said. "Something broke in his brain. He killed the Jones girl and went to the next person who wronged him. Mills had gone to Lillie and said Nito had gone nuts, on drugs, getting violent with him. Mills was the one who told us Nito sold off that vehicle to a couple bad dudes in Memphis."

"Y'all got the car?"

Quinn nodded.

"You going to that big celebration for Coach tonight?" Anna Lee said. "The mayor's going to give him some kind of award and a lot of his former players are going to speak. I'm sure Boom will be there."

"I'll be working traffic," Quinn said. "After the presentation, they got some kind of gospel bluegrass group out of Tupelo playing. You know, barbecue, fireworks, the whole damn deal."

"You don't like him?"

Quinn shook his head.

"Why?"

"I'm sorry for what the man went through," Quinn said. "But I never had respect for him the way Boom did."

"You never liked authority."

"Until the Army beat that outta me."

"But that was different."

"Sure," Quinn said. "Respect is a whole 'nother deal. Mills wore all his bullshit on his sleeve and I never bought it. He always came off phony to me."

They finished emptying out the house, Quinn unhooking the TV, stereo, CD player, pulling the last few framed prints and photos off the wall. Most of them of Shelby, a few shots of Anna Lee and Luke vacationing down in Costa Rica or someplace. Quinn studied one shot for one moment, Luke's hand around Anna Lee's bare waist, pulling her close and kissing her with closed eyes.

"He wants you back," Quinn said.

"Why do you say that?"

"Because this — us — doesn't feel the same," he said. "You put your hand up between us when you kiss me."

"There's a lot to take in."

Quinn nodded.

"This move," she said. "Let me get settled. I just need a little time."

Quinn lifted up the loading platform and slammed it inside the bottom of the truck. He reached up, grabbed the strap to the door, and pulled it closed with a sharp snap of the latch.

"It's not over," she said.

"I guess it never will be."

She lifted up on her toes and kissed him, her mouth stiff and hard, before she turned away and got into the truck. Quinn turned. But, this time, he didn't watch her go.

"You can't just say shit like that," Fannie Hathcock said, fanning out a match at Vienna's bar. "I may not know about being in the public eye, but you can't call some woman a stupid bitch on national TV."

"It's kind of funny," Lyle said, scratching at his scraggly beard. "If you think about it. I didn't hear the whole thing. Some people say she called her an old witch."

"Nope," Fannie said, taking a long puff of the cigarillo, spiking the ash, and cupping her chin with her hand. "She straight out said the woman was a dumb bitch. Which was true, but nothing good will come of it. Damn, I can't wait to see that girl unravel."

"Why do you hate that woman so much?" Lyle said, thumping his chest with his fist to stifle a burp. "I mean, she treated me fair. Even got a trusty to bring me some water when I was in the hooch."

"She ain't after you."

"You think she's got a hard-on for you?"

"In matter of speaking," Fannie said, puffing on the cigarillo. "Or not."

"Can I have another shot and a Bud?"

Lyle reached into the cooler for a tallboy, poured out the Jack in a tall shot, and turned to the television over the bottles and blazing neon beer signs. She turned her back to Lyle as she watched, casual today in a flowy black silk top and slim black cigarette pants. As she smoked, a little ash scattered on her freckled chest and ruby pendant and she brushed it away with the tips of her fingers, shaking her head at the coverage still in Jericho.

"Least those cameras and shit ain't here," Lyle said.

The ticker below the reporter read MISSISSIPPI TOWN CELEBRATES HERO AMONG US. The woman was someone different, not the one who the sheriff called a dumb bitch. She stood in the middle of the Jericho town square, having a little heart-to-heart with Bud Mills about his near-death experience and exposing a killer. Coach did his best to look modest, wearing a gold T-shirt that read WINNERS FOR JESUS and a Tibbehah High ball cap. He thanked God a lot, his wife, and all his players and assistants. He said the will to survive and something he'd read in a book called *Shout it from the Housetops* by Reverend Pat Robertson gave him strength in a time of need.

"I tried to minister to the boy some," Coach Mills said. "Make him understand there was another way. He didn't have to keep on hurting people. What he did to Miss Milly Jones was a downright abomination."

The woman on TV nodded at the coach. "Can you talk a little about what Mr. Reece did to you?"

"He tried to get rough," Coach said. "But I fought that boy, tooth and nail. I can promise you, he never broke me. That's when the Reverend Robertson's words came to me."

"The sheriff mentioned something about the use of a pressure washer," the reporter said. "Can you tell us about that?"

Coach shook his head, wiping away a tear. "I don't want to focus on the negative," he said. "I just want to pray for the boy's family, friends, and his former teammates. There's little doubt drugs and alcohol got their hooks into him."

Fannie reached over, snatched up the remote, and turned off the television. "That sanctimonious son of a bitch."

Lyle bit the shot glass and tossed his head backward to drain it. He set it back down with his mouth and smiled at his talent. "You know him?"

Fannie nodded.

"A friend of the working girls?"

Fannie shook her head. "Knew him a while back," she said. "He had a specific kind of taste back then. And it had nothing to do with ministering to the youth."

"Damn, that Jack stings," he said. "Can I have another to take off the burn? I got to ride down to Natchez tonight."

"If that dumb hick sheriff had shown me an ounce of respect, I could have helped her out," Fannie said, stubbing out the smoke. "But I'll let her just keep talking and grinning and missing the point of the whole goddamn story."

Lillie had brought dinner home, a couple take-out plates from Pap's Place, a restaurant that celebrated Elvis, fried catfish, and Jesus in somewhat equal portions. Rose loved the fried catfish filets, fries, and peach cobbler for dessert. For a little Mexican girl, she had grand Southern taste.

They ate together in the kitchen, Lillie feeling good to have the night off. She thought about making an appearance at the appreciation night for Coach Mills on the Square. Rose would love the music and fireworks. But she didn't really feel like walking around and kissing asses tonight, there'd be enough time before November to make sure all that was in hand. The way Bud Mills had been talking to reporters, he'd make sure to thank the sheriff's office for saving his skin. He was also appreciative no one had mentioned him being sodomized by a water hose.

The night had turned unseasonably cool and she opened up the front porch to her bungalow, leaving the screen door shut while she did the dishes. Rose had settled into the living room, in the same house where Lillie had grown up, to watch a show called *Adventure Time,* about a bubblegum princess, an elastic dog, and heroes who could be made of root beer.

She'd turned on the radio, listening to a classic country station playing "Dead Flowers" by Townes Van Zandt, trying to think on things other than what Nito Reece had done to Milly Jones. And feeling good he was dead, that maybe for a short while evil didn't walk among them and that Tibbehah County could be an idyllic community. A countrified *Pleasantville,* if she worked hard enough.

Lillie rinsed off a china plate, dried it with a dish towel, and set it in a rack. She helped herself to a big glass of wine and walked out onto her modest porch, Townes now singing "I'll Be Here in the Morning."

Lillie closed her eyes, resting, nearly falling asleep, until she heard a car pull into her driveway. Nikki Rowland headed down her walkway, past the tall red canna lilies her mother had planted decades ago and a small garden of purple verbena and bright orange lantana.

"I didn't want to just bust up in your house, but I needed to talk."

Lillie told her it was fine, pointing to an old metal porch chair, where the girl took a seat. She had on small khaki shorts and a black T-shirt. Her dark hair had been highlighted in some kind of purple wash and she wore a little nose ring in her nostril.

"I wanted to give you something."

Lillie nodded and asked if she'd like something to drink. She had some white wine and lots of sweet tea. Nikki shook her head, opening up the top of a shoe box on her lap.

"Milly give this to me the night she died."

Lillie's mouth felt dry and she swallowed, reaching for the wine. Nikki showed Lillie an old blue Samsung phone and three small journals wrapped in rubber hair bands. From inside the house, she could hear Rose's laughter.

"I couldn't make sense of it," Nikki said. "And I was afraid if I handed it over, Nito might come for me. He had threatened Jon-Jon."

"What's on it?"

"Most I can tell is that Milly was writing some kind of inspirational book," she said. "There's a lot about her brother. Well, it's made up, so the character who is like her, it's that character's brother. The phone, I don't know. That was most important to her, but I couldn't get it to work. It has a passcode on it. It's a few years old and takes an old kind of charger that I couldn't find."

"Her phone got burned to a crisp," Lillie said. "Maybe she used two?"

"This isn't hers," Nikki said. "It was Brandon's. She's kept this phone ever since he died."

Lillie nodded, checking out the outdated cell.

"She was a good girl," Nikki said. "What's been written about her being fast, a town tramp and all that, is just a bunch of trash. She took that job with Fannie Hathcock because she had to. I can tell you one thing, it never broke her. Milly was my bright light. I think about her every minute, send her texts, thinking that one day I'll hear back or maybe she'll know she was loved."

"I'm so sorry."

"I'm not a coward," Nikki said. "But I got

my son to worry about."

"I understand."

"If I'd known he would do that to Milly, I'd have given up my own life."

Lillie nodded. Nikki began to cry and Lillie patted her shoulder, before going inside to pour her some ice tea. When she came back, Nikki was backing out of the driveway.

The shoe box filled with Milly Jones's most valuable possessions was sitting on the old metal chair.

31

They found Wash Jones four days later at the local Chevy dealership, doing a live interview on a right-wing talk radio show about the decline of morals in America, a recent loss by Ole Miss, and the tragic and untimely death of his eldest daughter. He sat at a card table in the middle of the two talk show hosts, headphones on, still wearing the image of Milly's angel on the front of his T-shirt. The owner of the dealership stood nearby, showing a Hispanic couple the insides of a metallic orange Silverado 2500.

"Almost like he's enjoying himself," Lillie said.

" 'Almost'?" Quinn said.

At a station break, Wash shook the hands of the radio hosts and limped his way over to Quinn and Lillie. He wore a Tibbehah County Wildcats ball cap and a big smile. His face shone with sweat, big belly stretching the material of his T-shirt. "Missed you the other night, Sheriff," he said to Lillie. "Heck of a night. I 'bout broke down when the band played 'Angel from Montgomery.' I hugged Coach Bud and thanked him for all he did to get Milly's killer to justice. Want to thank you, too, Miss Virgil. I don't think I could have gone living with her killer being out there, unknown to us all."

Lillie smiled and nodded.

"You mind if I ask which one of you shot up that black son of a bitch?" he said, grinning. " 'Cause I'd sure like to shake your hand."

"Mr. Jones," Lillie said. "We've just gotten some new information about what Milly might've been doing that night. And we're hoping you might help us understand."

"So you won't tell me?" Wash said. "I heard it was one shot. A dang killshot right through the brain. Listen, y'all want a hot dog or something? Dealership has free hot dogs and balloons for the kids. Also might let you take a test-drive, Quinn. Get you out of that old Ford you been driving."

"I'm loyal," Quinn said. "Thanks."

Wash followed them back to Lillie's Cherokee, parked near the service department. The man hadn't shaved in a few days, his weak chin bristling with white hairs. He sniffed, rubbing a finger under his nose, and stood splayfooted for some more news about Milly he might be able to share with some cable news hosts. He'd fast become a late-night favorite, commenting on everything from gun rights to his personal hopeful in the presidential election. Online, there had been a movement of Wash Jones for President in deference to his straight talk and outrageous sayings.

"Did your son ever tell you he'd been molested?" Lillie asked. Lillie never being one for small talk.

"What?" Wash asked, looking even more dumbfounded than if he'd been slapped across his ruddy face. "What's Brandon got to do with nothing?"

"We believe Milly wanted to expose his rapist."

"Where did y'all get that trash?" he asked. "Dang. He wasn't more than sixteen when he died. He wasn't raped no more than me."

"Your ex-wife said he'd confided in her," Quinn said.

"And your daughter," Lillie said. "She said y'all took him to get counseling in Tupelo right before he killed himself."

"My boy didn't kill himself," Wash said. "Holy moly. Everybody knows that boy got injured while chasing a twelve-point buck.

How's this helping? How's this supposed to do a goddang thing but throw muck at my family? I spent most of my life as a hard-working American knee-deep in shit, but this sure do take the cake."

A portly woman wearing a MILLY JONES IS MY GUARDIAN ANGEL shirt walked up to Wash and without a word gave him a long, deep hug, saying she'd be praying for him. He patted her back and smiled, saying he sure did appreciate her support and that she could find out more tonight on *Nancy Grace* at eight Central.

"Milly had Brandon's old cell phone," Quinn said. "We unlocked it this week and found hundreds of texts between Brandon and an older man. Brandon wanted to tell the truth to everyone, but the man threatened his life and the safety of your whole family."

"Trash," Wash said. "Nothing but trash. I don't want to hear a word of it. Do you know what I've been going through, a first-class trip through the depths of hell? Brandon has been gone a long while. We healed up on that. Do y'all think the Jones family hasn't suffered enough?"

Lillie put her hands on her hips, looking to the carnival set up in front of the showroom window, kids playing around in a jump house, a clown making balloon animals, and the owner of the dealership handing out sacks of popcorn and free hot dogs. The air smelled of a county fair.

"Before high school, Brandon was a manager for the football team," Lillie said. "He helped out with the equipment, chasing down footballs, running water out to the players."

"You bet," Wash said. "Done that for two years. Coach Bud respected him so much, he took him on road trips. You know how many young kids wish they had an opportunity like that? Made him feel part of the team."

Quinn looked to Lillie. Lillie said, "How'd he get to and from the games?"

"On the dang bus," he said. "Sometimes, he rode with Coach. Just what are y'all getting at?"

Lillie's radio on her hip started to squawk with Kenny working an accident scene over on County Road 221. She turned down the radio, tilted her head, eyes against the sun, and said, "This isn't for public consumption," she said. "Especially for *Nancy Grace* tonight. But those text messages were coming from Coach Mills."

"That's a lie."

"Afraid not." Lillie shook her head. Quinn

stood ready if Wash Jones wanted to show his true self right there at the Chevy dealership among the sales folks, kids, and clowns. But Wash just hung back, mouth wide-open, breathing in and out, eyes unfocused and fuzzy, trying to make sense of just exactly had been said.

"Coach Mills is a hero," Wash said. "Without him, y'all would have never splattered Nito Reece's black ass all over that damn cotton compress."

Quinn shook his head. "Milly wanted him exposed," he said. "The last call she made was to Bud Mills, thirty minutes before that trucker found her on fire."

"A lie," he said. "Y'all are lying. Ole Job never had to suffer words and horrors like this."

"We're bringing in the coach for raping Brandon and other boys," Lillie said. "If you know something, now's the time. This man may be responsible for the deaths of both of your children."

"Y'all have an agenda of filth," he said. "And I ain't going to that fuckin' circus."

He spit on the ground, eyed Lillie and Quinn up and down, and shook his stupid head sadly and theatrically. "You don't want Nito to be the one."

"Come again?" Lillie said.

"Y'all just can't stand that some poor ole nigger boy murdered an angel of this world," he said. "You got to tear us all down, make us no better than the blacks, to work on whatever weak tea liberal-ass agenda you got."

"It's not just Brandon," Lillie said. "There's a long list. Milly's the hero. She's the only one with guts to stand up to him."

Wash shook his head. "Get the hell out of here," he said. "And, god damn, you ain't the nephew to Hamp Beckett. That man is doing somersaults in his grave right now, hearing 'The World Turned Upside Down.'"

"I expect you're right, Mr. Jones," he said. "Uncle Hamp kept a file on Bud Mills, thick as two phone books. Years of young boys like Brandon. Last night, I found it in the mess I inherited and we've been calling up victims all day. I wouldn't have known where to look if it hadn't been for Milly."

"Good Lord Almighty," Wash said.

"Thank the Lord, the apple fell damn far from the tree," Lillie said. "You're right. Milly was a special woman."

"What the hell do you want?" Ordeen Davis asked. "You want to try and fuck with me some more?"

"Everywhere I go today," Quinn said, "I make friends."

"Y'all wanted Nito and you got him," Ordeen said. "I wasn't about to help with that bullshit. You had it in your mind to kill his ass and that's what you did."

Quinn didn't have an answer, as he had killed Nito. He'd rushed right into that small box of a room, seeing Nito Reece grinning ear to ear while running a pressure wash gun up the rectum of three-time Mississippi Coach of the Year Bud Mills. D. J. Norwood raised a .32 pistol at Quinn and Quinn blasted a hole through Norwood with his twelve-gauge, turning to Nito as he pulled a gun from his jeans. But Wash Jones had been wrong. Quinn had shot Nito not once, but twice.

Ordeen stood with a soapy sponge in hand, a bucket full of suds, and a garden hose running down his driveway. Nito Reece's electric-blue Nova, sporting twenty-inch spinning silver rims, was parked out in front of Ordeen's mother's brick ranch house a few miles outside town. Same tag reading HERE KITTY KITTY.

"We think Nito might have had some help killing Milly Jones."

Ordeen tossed the sponge in the bucket, walked over to the spigot, and turned off the water, suds and bubbles raining down off the slick blue hood and shiny silver rims. He crossed his arms over his chest and nodded. "Son of a bitch," he said. "I wondered how long till y'all were going to start bird-dogging my ass on this."

"I'm not looking at you, Ordeen," Quinn said. "You have my word. I just need to know what Nito told you about Milly Jones."

"Nito said y'all was trying to set him up," he said. "And that Coach Mills helping y'all out. Telling a bunch of lies."

"You might be right."

"Oh, yeah?" Ordeen said. "Y'all found his Nova up in Memphis and checked out every damn inch. You know, it's clean as hell."

"He sold it to folks who run a detail shop."

"I paid them cash for this car," Ordeen said. "They didn't want it no more. I'm gonna drive it out of respect for Nito. I'm putting his name on the back window. He's a damn victim in this thing just like Milly Jones."

"Nito may have been coerced," Quinn said. "But he helped."

"Bullshit, man," Ordeen said. "You try to play some head games with me? Everybody loves Coach's ass for bringing in the law to string up my boy. Y'all were too happy to kill some black folks. But I ain't playin' that. I don't have nothing to do with nothing."

"We just arrested Coach Mills," Quinn said.

"Bullshit."

"He's been molesting kids for a long time," Quinn said. "Milly Jones was going to out him for what he'd done to her brother."

The words struck Ordeen, standing there, nodding and listening, in his white wife-beater shirt and low-hanging jean shorts. His braided hair looking wild and unkempt as a lion's mane. All of sudden, he started to shake his head and burst out laughing. He wasn't faking it, laughing so hard he dropped his hands to his knees like he'd just finished up a long series of wind sprints. "Like I said," Ordeen said, "bull-fucking-shit. Ain't nobody can take down Bud Mills. He's bigger than any law or politician in Jericho."

"Did Nito ever tell you about him and Coach?"

"He told me enough."

"I mean, when he was a kid," Quinn said. "Did he ever talk about being with Coach while his momma was out working late, getting arrested for drugs and hooking? I found an old report from my uncle that said his mother believed Nito had been molested. But nobody took her seriously."

"I ain't getting into this mess," Ordeen said. "I'm done. I'm done with all this shit. I don't trust you."

"Why not?"

"Because you the same as everybody else," he said. "Your uncle kilt Nito's father and you kilt Nito. And now you ain't gonna rest till I'm dead, too."

"No," Quinn said. "I need you to stand up."

" 'Stand up'?" Ordeen said, laughing again. "Bullshit, man. Bullshit."

"Bud Mills raped children," Quinn said. "He raped Nito and he raped Milly Jones's little brother and probably a hell of a lot more boys. I think you heard something from Nito after he got pulled into this mess. I think you need to quit hangdogging it and feeling sorry for yourself and stand up and act like a man."

"Just like Coach," Ordeen said. "You sound just like Coach."

"Why would you want to stick with him?" Quinn asked. "After what he did to Nito? Why don't you go ahead and let everyone keep believing Coach Bud Mills shined the light on the black drug dealer who raped and murdered an angel?"

"Fuck you, man."

"Listen up, man," Quinn said. "I never liked Mills. He was a bully and a walking freak show. But I need you to stand up. What we got isn't strong enough."

"What you got?"

"An old phone and the word of a dead kid."

Ordeen walked back over to the spigot and turned on the water, rinsing off his dead friend's ride, taking slow, special care on the hood and windows, sluicing with soapy water. He kept shaking his head, muttering to himself. "Ain't gonna happen."

"Why's that?"

"You send Coach Mills to prison and then folks around here gonna have to start looking at themselves. Since when has that shit ever happened? Even a goddamn tornado and the hand of God on this county couldn't rattle that cage."

"Help us out, Ordeen," Quinn said. "Putting a *Fly High* sticker on that old Nova won't do shit for Nito."

Ordeen stared at him for a long while. Then he nodded.

Jason Colson met Bentley at a cigar lounge down in Jackson after the kid stopped returning his phone calls and emails. Bentley swore nothing was a-matter, he'd been doing a lot of work for his father and for a Washington lobbyist who'd given him an internship straight out of Ole Miss. Jason walked into the smoke-filled room lined with brown leather couches, easy chairs, and framed prints of women with big jugs in seductive poses with cigars between their teeth, thinking this was going to be it. He could finally seal the damn deal and hustle on back to Jericho to get on the bulldozer, clear the lands, and plan on that big beautiful barn that would sit on top of that stark, naked hill.

The kid offered him some twenty-three-year-old Pappy Van Winkle that had been a personal gift from the governor. But Jason refused, telling him that it had been a while since he drank but he had no trouble being around it. "I ain't no Seventh-day Adventist," Jason said, clutching an accordion binder under his arm, pearl Stetson down in his eyes. "I just have too many miles on my liver and don't have the time nor inclination for it to expire."

"Glad you came down," Bentley said. "I was just remembering all those crazy stories you used to tell me. I finally got around to watching *Sharky's Machine*. I loved it. Was that really you that fell out of that hotel in

Atlanta?"

"It was actually my friend Dar Robinson," Jason said. "He fell two hundred and twenty feet, although the actual fall wasn't used in the film. They only showed the first part of the gag, Dar falling backward out of the window with the glass breaking. Last I checked, it still held the record for the longest free fall in a movie. Dar was a pistol. Ended up getting killed when he drove a dirt bike off the side of a cliff. Before that, he never had so much as a broken bone."

"Well, it was impressive as hell," Bentley said. "You stuntmen are a different breed."

"Appreciate that, Bentley," Jason said. "And I think you know how I feel about you and your dad. Y'all looked out for me for a long while. I was kind of a mess when I got back to Mississippi."

Bentley smiled, a puff of smoke over his face, looking much like the sun going behind a cloud and then returning much paler than before. He tipped the ash of his cigar, Jason thinking about all the times he'd seen Quinn do the same thing. But the big cigar looked odd in the kid's hands, the smoke too large for his little fingers, almost like something that Emmett Kelly would have plucked in the side of his mouth as a joke.

"I tried to call you, Mr. Colson," he said. "I guess you didn't get my messages."

"No, sir," Jason said, holding that smile so long his mouth hurt.

"I tried and tried, but I couldn't get that arrangement figured out," he said. "I even talked to my daddy, but he said it would be a hell of a risk for some stripped-out land."

And it seemed for a moment that time just kind of stuck right there in the leather-padded room with all that fine wooden furniture and happy big-titted women. It was much like that time in a gag where you're free-falling or jumping your motorcycle over some cars when you could hear the wind in your ears but nothing else, everything working 'round and 'round in slow motion, until you stuck that landing or tumbled with bones sticking from your arms or legs.

"Y'all had promised."

Bentley shook his head, waving away the smoke. "I promised to try," he said. "You're a good friend of the family. I never even got up on a horse before I met you. Daddy said you did a hell of a job keeping his barn in top shape. Feeding and shoeing our horses."

"Appreciate that."

"I'm sure you got a lot of options," Bentley said. "Did you think to try a bank in

Jericho? They might have something more to work with since y'all are close by. Maybe you can put up that ole relic from *Hooper* on eBay? I bet some crazy movie fan would empty his pockets for that. How far did that car jump?"

Jason dropped the smile. He took off his Stetson and waved away the smoke, standing and looking down at Bentley comfortable in the back room, a nice bottle of whiskey sitting within arm's reach. The kid, just a little bit high, had both of his palms set loose on the armrests.

"I didn't make the jump," Jason said.

"What do you mean?"

"I mean, it was in the movie," Jason said. "But it never jumped that river. No car could ever do that. It was just movie magic. The prop boys made a model of it. It wasn't any more real than a spaceship in dang Star Wars."

"But you said," Bentley said, still smiling but now looking a little superior.

"It was a just a funny story for a kid," Jason said. "You're too old to be believing that kind of crap. I ain't Santa Claus."

"Oh, yeah?" he said. "Sure then."

"I better get goin'."

"Well, good luck, Mr. Colson."

"As my daddy used to say, 'Wish in one

hand and shit in another,' " Jason said. "Go and see which one gets filled first."

Bentley slapped his knee and laughed, walking Jason Colson to the door, before turning back to his buddies in the lounge.

32

"Can we make it fast, Reverend?" Lillie asked. "It's not the best time for some fellowship."

"Came to talk to you about Coach Mills," Reverend Zeke Traylor said. "I am horrified and shocked about these things being said about him in the press. He's been a member of my church for more than twenty years. My wife and I just discussed the matter over breakfast at the Huddle House. We both just knew our sheriff was out to keep a fair and balanced look at the situation."

Lillie had been up all night with Mills, the coach still in their custody with bail being set by the judge in the morning. He'd spent hour upon hour denying allegations about Brandon Jones, Nito Reece, and the three other boys — now men — who'd stepped forward when they heard the charges against him. He was nervous, sweating, muttering to himself, when they talked. He kept on referring to himself in the third person, telling her and Quinn that Coach would never do such a thing. Coach is a man among men. *Christ Almighty.*

"If you want to be a character witness," Lillie said, "save it for the trial."

"Little lady," Reverend Traylor said, face beaming with a high wattage of enthusiasm and contempt, "I think you're a mite confused about what exactly went on here."

Traylor wore a dark blue suit, light blue shirt, and a bright gold tie. He had a big smile on his sagging old face, white hair coiffed and sprayed down, gold-frame glasses glinting in the office light. He smiled and nodded, waiting for Lillie to respond.

Lillie didn't say a damn word.

"Who of us hasn't stumbled a bit in our walk with God?" Reverend Traylor said. "Coach Mills admitted to me he's been tempted by the devil and the pleasures of the flesh. The Bible tells us the devil comes to steal, kill, and destroy. But it's Jesus who gives us the life everlasting."

"Amen," Lillie said, resting her elbows on her desk. "You got a point to all this? Or is it just time to pass the collection plate?"

"You are a true pistol, Lillie Virgil," Reverend Traylor said. "Not much different than your daddy. I went to high school with him and he was a straight-out wild man. Did I tell you about the time he got arrested for drag racing on Main Street? I'm just saying, we all slip a little."

"You want to tell me something I don't know about Bud Mills?" Lillie said. "Because I got about a dozen phone calls I need to return from more victims stepping forward. Coach left a big river of shit in his wake coming long before Milly Jones was set on fire."

"What's Milly Jones have to do with Coach?"

"Stay tuned and you'll find out, Pastor."

Reverend Traylor smoothed down his gold tie and smiled as if comforting a small child who had a minimal understanding of the way the world worked. He nodded, took a deep breath, and said, "This may seem old-fashioned and corny to you, Miss Virgil, but, through the power of prayer, Coach sought forgiveness this morning. I think what all he's been through, the beatings and the violence at the hands of that Reece boy he tried to help, will only strengthen his walk with the Lord. He always had a prayerful heart, and you must believe that he removed himself from any temptation he'd had in the past."

"You're asking me to have faith?" Lillie said.

"Yes, ma'am."

"I'm not a preacher," Lillie said. "I'm the law. I work with evidence and facts."

"Surely you don't believe what these children and their parents have said?" Reverend Traylor said. "They're trying to tear down a good man who was trying to show some Christian fatherly love."

"By fondling scared young children?" Lillie said. "Where in the Bible does it talk about showering with kids? Touching them in twisted ways?"

"A lot of what Coach did was misinterpreted."

"Even if a sliver of it's true, he'll be in jail for a long while," Lillie said. "I'm glad to listen to what you have to say, but I don't appreciate you coming into my office and telling me to go easy on Coach because he took ten minutes to pray with you this morning."

"We don't need to drudge up all this ugliness when Coach has gotten straight with God."

"I tell you what," Lillie said. "You get Jesus to come down here and write ole Bud a hall pass for whipping it out when the mood struck him and I'll do just that. But let me tell you something, Reverend Tray-lor, I'm taking this growing list of victims serious as hell. I'm not in the forgiveness business."

"You do understand what kind of families we're talking about?" Reverend Traylor said, giving a knowing smile. "These aren't the dang Rockefellers of Jericho. These boys you mention come from broken homes, from alcoholics and drug addicts. I think a fair amount of them would want to stand in line just to see if there was some kind of lawsuit money in it for them."

"You said Coach had gotten straight with God?"

"Yes, ma'am."

"Then if he'd done nothing wrong, what did he have to get straight?"

"Coach admits he made some bad choices, getting too personal with those boys," he said. "Boys will be boys. They all like to wrestle, tussle, and play. Nothing more than that. And maybe he showered with them. That's what you do after football practice. He was teaching them you work hard, sweat, keep yourself clean."

Lillie leaned back in her chair. "The methods he employed for cleanliness are ones I hadn't heard outside of a barnyard."

Reverend Traylor shook his head. His

glowing smile of the *Good News for Modern Man* soured a good bit, leaving him looking like he's just sucked on a lemon. "Most people around here support Coach," he said. "They don't believe what these trashy people are saying."

"Spoken like a true man of God," Lillie said. "I read enough of the Bible to know that my Jesus would think you were a true phony asshole."

"You sure are a pistol," Reverend Traylor said, standing. "I guess an alternative lifestyle can lead to many unorthodox views."

"Oh," Lillie said. "Milly Jones's sister told me that Milly had come to you a few days before she got lit up for not getting with the program. Do you want to tell me what y'all talked about?"

"No, ma'am," he said. "I sure don't. Little Milly was an angel in this world and all you're doing is casting a dark shadow over all her bright light. I don't think folks around here want to hear that garbage. And they'll be thinking long and hard on it this year."

"Good to see you, Reverend," Lillie said. "I'll make sure you get one of my election signs for your front yard."

"Two have recanted their stories," Lillie said.

"Which ones?" Quinn asked.

"Judd Aron and Tommy Cain."

"Son of a bitch."

"Damn straight," Lillie said. "The Good Reverend has been making the rounds. Aron's and Cain's families are longtime First Baptist. Traylor spooked them."

"How can we be so sure?"

"Because the son of a bitch came calling on me this morning, wanting me to find love and forgiveness in my heart."

Quinn about spit out his coffee. Instead, he set down the thick mug and shook his head. Lillie had just rolled up to the farm, coming down off her shift and turning the night back over to Quinn. Between both of them, they'd interviewed two dozen witnesses who'd noted some highly inappropriate behavior by beloved Coach Mills. But Aron and Cain had been their best bet. Both boys, now in their twenties, had fit the profile — coming from broken homes, working for Coach as ball boys, and being a part of Coach's summer mentoring program. Coach took them hunting and fishing, spending time in cabins at the Tishomingo State Park. Both boys had been in his uncle's old files, their mothers coming to him for advice and help they never received.'

"What do the boys say now?"

"They say their memories may have been clouded," she said. "And that it was a long time ago. They absolutely don't want to testify."

"When's Coach get arraigned?" Quinn said.

"Tomorrow morning," Lillie said. "DA won't be pleased with what we've got now."

"But we still have one possible witness, Brandon Jones's cell phone, and Ordeen Davis?"

"Wouldn't take much of a lawyer to get two of those tossed out."

"How about Coach Mills pleading out?"

"You want us to make a deal with that bastard?" Lillie said. "Besides, the fucker still says he didn't do anything wrong. He said he's a good ole Christian role model for those boys, wanting to teach 'em all how to be big strong men."

"Maybe I can reason with him."

Lillie slipped her hands into her pant pockets and rolled her shoulders. The sky above had turned a bright orange and black, long swirling clouds strewn over the pasture and over Jason Colson's trailer. Quinn had heard him earlier, still tinkering with the Trans Am. Occasionally yelling, "God damn it. Son of a bitch," when the engine wouldn't turn over.

"I need you to do me a favor."

Quinn nodded.

"I need you to talk to Ophelia," Lillie said. "You know her brother played for Coach? Cash was part of that mentoring bullshit ten years ago."

"He doesn't fit the profile," Quinn said. "You don't get more respectable than the Bundrens. They have money, everyone in town knows them. I don't see him needing Coach's approval or affection."

"Except for when his sister Adelaide died," Lillie said. "I heard Coach really took it to heart to make sure that boy got out from under a tent of grieving to be out among the living."

"The devil comes in all forms."

"And we're looking at a short, potbellied one who I seriously believe doesn't think he did a damn thing wrong," Lillie said. "Remember how he'd drop in little stories about tickle fights and going skinny-dipping, like the good old days. He's trying to seed a grain of truth in any story that might come up."

"I'll talk to Ophelia."

Lillie pressed her backside on the edge of the railing, folding her arms over her chest.

Since Quinn had been away last year, Lillie had gotten in some serious shape, running five miles a day, taking on a CrossFit program down in the old bakery, climbing ropes, doing pull-ups, push-ups, and weights. She reminded him a lot of some of the female officers he knew in the Army, not only running with the boys but making sure she ran a hell of a lot better. She looked muscled and tanned, freckles across her nose and across her chest where the top of her uniform was unbuttoned.

Quinn wanted to tell her she looked good but was afraid she might punch him in the nose.

"Anything going on with you two?" she asked.

"Nope."

"But you and Anna Lee?" Lillie said. "Saw her house is up for sale."

"She's up in Memphis," Quinn said. "Says she's doing everything for Shelby getting a better education. She's sorting through things with Luke. It's over."

"With him?"

"With me."

"I'm sorry, Quinn."

Quinn shrugged as Hondo came trotting down the hills from the curving dirt road. He carried a partially decomposed deer skull in his mouth, damn proud of the find. He dropped it on the porch at Quinn's and Lillie's feet. He was panting from the run and the heat.

"I don't want you to ask about Ophelia's brother if there's something between y'all."

"I don't mind talking to her about Coach," Quinn said. "She said something to me once about her mother never trusting him. Always believed there was something more to the story."

"More folks have to step up," Lillie said. "He's been here more than twenty years. All of Hamp's old reports are fair game. No statute of limitations on rape."

Quinn was already dressed for work, in a crisp sheriff's shirt with patches, starched blue jeans, and shined boots. He wore his Beretta on his hip, as standard, and he'd just cut his hair regulation earlier that day. Hondo stood close, shaking the dust from his mottled gray-and-black coat.

"I wish you'd stick around," Lillie said. "Till we get this all figured out."

The sun had started to turn gold across the pasture and spilled up onto the porch, casting Lillie in strange half-light, the sun turning her eyes a deeper shade of green, almost making them glow. She smiled at

Quinn, eyes wandering out to the field and back.

The front door to the farmhouse was open, buffeting a gust of wind past them, through the house and shooting out the back. The back screen door rattled briefly.

"Before you leave again," Lillie said. "We need to talk."

Quinn stood straighter. He reached for his mug of coffee and took a sip.

"Some things might be a mess," she said. "But some things are a lot clearer."

"Lillie," Quinn said. "Hold on."

"You need to hear this," she said. "I've been wanting to talk to you for a long time. But there was always Anna Lee. And then that crazy-ass woman with the ATF, and then Ophelia Bundren, and then back to Anna Lee. If I don't say this now, we might not get another chance. I don't know where you're headed. Damn, Quinn, you've been home almost five years now."

Quinn stepped up to Lillie and reached out and held both of her hands. She closed her eyes, Quinn leaning forward and kissing her long and hard on top of the head. Her head smelling of sweat and sunshine. They stayed there for a long while, with Hondo scratching at his jean leg. Not breaking apart until Lillie's radio started to make a racket. She pressed back, still holding his hands and watching his face.

"I need to be by myself for a while," Quinn said. "I haven't been alone enough in the last two years. That's why I made a hell of a bad mistake."

"Sex with a married woman?" Lillie said, smiling, lifting her hands from his. "I'd be glad to talk Reverend Traylor into forgiving your sorry ass."

"Appreciate that."

Lillie turned and called in to dispatch, walking from the farmhouse steps halfway across the yard and then turning back to Quinn. "That's strange," she said. "Fannie Hathcock called in to Mary Alice and said she wants to see me as soon as possible."

"You want me to come along?"

"Figure this is woman talk," Lillie said, grinning. "No testosterone allowed."

Outside Vienna's Place, a half-dozen bikers lounged by the front door, sitting on their Harleys, drinking and smoking, making low catcalls at Lillie as she walked past. She ignored them, fucking morons not worth her energy, stepping out of the fading sunlight and into the darkness of the titty bar. No one waited by the front booth, and, through the second door into the club, the wide-open space was vacant and silent. The brass poles stood empty. No one behind the bar. Lillie could hear the clomp of her own boots on the polished concrete floor as she headed back to the spiral staircase that led up to Fannie's office.

When Lillie was halfway across the floor, Fannie called out to her. Lillie looked up to see the woman leaning over the edge of the railing, staring down into the club. Fannie had on a bright white embroidered dress of some type, lots of material about the arms giving her the appearance of having wings. Her usually styled red hair had been pulled up into a neat bun.

"Thanks for coming, Sheriff."

"You called it," Lillie said.

"Heard you're having trouble keeping that son of a bitch locked up, after everything he's done."

"Don't see how it's any concern of yours."

Fannie gave a short little laugh, looking down, hands on the railing. Her ruby pendant rocking forward from her chest on its chain. "You know, I was just sitting here in my own club, minding my own business, and you came busting into my world for no good reason."

"One of your girls had been set on fire,"

Lillie said. "Folks saw the Born Losers with her."

"We got off to a bad start, I guess," Fannie said. "Despite what you may think of me, I don't plan on going anywhere for a long while. Stagg's gone and this is all mine. It can be hell or we can figure out a way to play nice."

"Next time you want to be philosophical, how about you just call me on the phone?" Lillie asked. "Dispatch told me that you had an emergency and wanted to talk direct."

"What I got to say isn't for public consumption."

Lillie wanted to get home, put her feet up, and rest up before the arraignment tomorrow. Somehow, she and Quinn would have to find some more boys who couldn't be mind-fucked by Reverend Zeke. "Fine by me," Lillie said, her voice echoing through the dark club. "But can you get to the point? My neck's starting to hurt, having to stare up at you."

"People have always hated me because I'm direct."

"I got no problem with that."

"They don't like a tough bitch in charge," Fannie said. "They think I have no place running a business like this. What I hate are the type of pious mealymouthed shit-for-

470

brains we keep in this state. I know what I am. I don't need anyone to tell me. You may hate this, Lillie Virgil, but you and me are cut from the same cloth."

"I doubt it," Lillie said. "Your cloth is too expensive, for my taste."

"Y'all are screwed because no one in this backwoods county will stand up and call out Bud Mills for the degenerate piece of shit he is."

"That's about the tall and short of it."

"People are walking away from you faster than Milly Jones walking that back road."

Lillie craned her neck forward and then back again to loosen the muscles, hands on hips, and waiting for Fannie Hathcock to get to the goddamn point. Instead, the bitch took out the little cigarillo case and fired one up, blowing smoke into the fans and office light behind her.

"I have some friends down in New Orleans who've been watching that son of a bitch for a long time," Fannie said. "They might be able to help you nail down some times, places, maybe some surveillance video of him on vacation with the kiddos."

"New Orleans?"

"We deal in flesh. But this kind of shit makes you want to puke."

"He brought the boys over state lines?"

Fannie blew out a stream of smoke, scattering in the overhead fans. "Shame," she said. "Feds just might have to take this flaming pile of shit off your doorstep and make up a good old-fashioned federal case."

"You mind if I ask why you're doing this?"

Fannie shrugged. "It's a long, sad story," she said. "And I don't think either one of us is the crying type. How about we just call it a truce?"

"OK," Lillie said. "Works for me. You'll be in touch?"

Fannie nodded and Lillie gave the madam a two-finger salute. She walked out of the smoke and darkness into the daylight.

33

"I'm such a lucky girl," Ophelia Bundren said. "First cool morning of the fall and I get to spend it working the crematorium."

"At least you kept warm," Quinn said.

"Two bodies," she said. "Miss Ashland and Bobby Hartwick."

"Bobby Hartwick died?"

"Saturday," she said. "Heart attack. He was about to turn fifty-five. He was out changing the oil in his truck and just keeled over. What they call the widow-maker. Although Bobby had been divorced for a while. He sure loved the ladies. His brother said he did a lot of Internet dating with women in Russia."

Quinn sat in the quiet coolness of the sanctuary at Bundren Funeral Home. The wood-paneled walls, green shag carpet, and little raised stage with lectern hadn't changed in decades. Artificial light shone warm and yellow from the back of a fake stained-glass window.

"I heard Hartwick was thinking of running for mayor."

"Not anymore," Ophelia said. "Shitty job. Might be better off this way."

"You don't mean that."

"Would you want to be sheriff again?"

Quinn didn't answer. He leaned forward in his folding chair, elbows on his thighs, thinking about it. He and Ophelia seeing a lot of each other over the last month and a half. And since Anna Lee had left, she'd called only twice. There was a lot of talk about separation, deep thinking on their relationship, and, in the end, what would be best for Shelby. Both of them knew the answer to that, Anna Lee more guilt-ridden than ever.

"Lillie's screwed," Ophelia said.

"Looks that way," Quinn said. "But she has to see this through. Especially after Cash stepped forward. What your brother did was stand-up. I respect the hell out of him. Couldn't have been easy talking about seeing Coach in that shower with Brandon Jones when Brandon wasn't even ten. What he said made the case."

"But you can't get him on Milly?"

"Doubt we ever will," Quinn said. "Best we can do is make a tight case on all the

474

molestations. I think once people understand he's not shaking loose of this thing, more victims will step forward. He's been preying on kids a long time."

"But you believe he — or he and Nito Reece both — killed Milly Jones?"

"Yes, ma'am."

"Whoever cracked her skull used something hard and nasty," Ophelia said. "Did y'all ever find anything like a tire iron or a hammer at Mills's house to test?"

"We did, but nothing with blood or DNA," he said. "Whatever he used was probably flung far and wide into Choctaw Lake."

"Y'all call out the town monster and folks go after the messenger."

"Lillie's got thick skin."

"It's going to cost her the election," Ophelia said. "Have you seen all the crazy stuff online supporting Coach and calling Lillie all sorts of horrible names? They can't imagine a legend like Bud Mills could be such a sick son of a bitch."

"We didn't find a murder weapon," Quinn said. "But we found a shit ton of kiddie porn on his computer. He also kept stacks and stacks of photo albums of his victims. He kept a collection of nude photos of kids. Stuff that would turn a normal person's stomach inside out."

"Don't men like Mills always get raped in prison?" Ophelia said, smiling.

"I'm sure ole Coach will have his dance card punched a few times."

"Good-hearted Bobby Hartwick gets burned up into ash and scattered down at the beach somewhere while we still have to stick around and make room for Bud Mills."

"Can I buy you dinner?"

Ophelia grinned. "Fine by me," she said. "But I'd skip the steakhouse."

"Those knives too tempting to toss at me?"

"Just don't give me a reason."

Quinn nodded and they walked out into the cool October evening, dead leaves scattering about in little dust devils in the empty parking lot.

It was mid-October when Lillie had arranged a handoff with the Feds for Bud Mills, where he'd now be facing charges for not only child molestation but taking children across state lines for those purposes. Lillie had gotten her hands on some surveillance video from a casino hotel elevator in New Orleans. Fannie Hathcock, god damn her black heart, good to her word.

Reggie brought out Mills from the jail,

checked the cuffs behind him, and settled him into the back of Lillie's Jeep. Reggie took the shotgun seat and Lillie got behind the wheel, wearing her sheriff's ball cap and aviator glasses. She was chewing gum, trying to get out a little nervous energy, glad to get this turd out of Tibbehah but not looking forward to the shit show she'd be passing on the way out of town. According to Kenny, hundreds of die-hard football fans had lined the commercial road out to Highway 45, holding banners and homemade signs in support of a hometown hero.

Kenny seemed embarrassed to say, "A lot of them weren't very complimentary of you, Lillie. Real stupid shit out there. Just keep your eyes on the road."

Lillie started the Jeep and headed north, turning right at the Square, the circus already beginning with dozens of people in their black-and-gold clothes, trucks honking their horns, old fat men in moth-eaten lettermen jackets with their fists raised high. Lillie glanced into the rearview to see a little smile on Mills's thin, purplish lips.

Passing the old Hollywood Video, the Dollar Store, and the new Walmart, a crowd had gathered on both sides of the street. Signs reading WE LOVE YOU COACH, WILDCAT PRIDE, GOD KNOWS THE TRUTH, and

TIBBEHAH NEEDS A REAL SHERIFF. There were also a few with the words *bull dyke,* but spelling it *dike* with an *i,* Reggie commenting that he had no idea how incredibly stupid folks can be.

"Stay with the the sheriff's office and you'll find it out pretty quick."

"I'm sorry, Lillie," Reggie said. "Son of a bitch. This whole damn town's gone batshit crazy."

" 'Cause they know what's right," Coach Mills said from the backseat.

Lillie lifted her eyes again to the rearview, not saying a word.

"You better start looking for work back in Memphis 'cause you're about to be run out of town on a rail."

"You ever think about her?" Lillie said.

"Who?" Coach asked.

"Milly Jones," Lillie said. "I think about her every time I'm at the Big Black Bridge, seeing that path of road she had to walk while completely on fire."

"You can't blame me for every damn crime."

"She called you out," Lillie said. "Had you meet her at that bridge. And even with the flames burning off her flesh and gasoline burning her throat, she kept on moving ahead. That's what I call tough. Your whole life is the definition of a coward."

"I can't hear you," Coach said. "What are you trying to say, Miss Virgil?"

Lillie hit the accelerator away from the crowds, passing the Rebel Truck Stop, Vienna's Place, and turning, thank God, onto Highway 45 up to Tupelo and then to Oxford. "I'm saying it's an hour to Oxford and we'd both appreciate it if you'd just shut your fucking mouth."

"You can't win," Mills said, laughing.

"As soon as I hand you over to the Feds and fumigate my truck, I already have."

Two weeks after Mills was sent to Oxford, Lillie asked Quinn to run for sheriff. The last thing Tibbehah County needed was a situation like they had with Rusty Wise, only with dumber and more corrupt candidates. One of the men who'd put his name on the ballot was running on an anti-Mexican platform. Tibbehah had a population of about fifty Hispanics. Another man wanted to put Christ back into politics, saying that, as sheriff, he'd damn well enforce the Ten Commandments.

Quinn agreed to run since it seemed the only person who held him responsible for Mills being arrested was Boom. Boom hadn't spoken to Quinn or Lillie since the arrest. Mad or embarrassed, Quinn didn't know.

Two weeks before the election, after attending a fish fry at the Kiwanis Club and campaign fundraiser at the VFW hall, Quinn headed back to the farm. Ophelia had promised to stop by after some unexpected work came into the funeral home. He promised he'd keep the porch light on and the bourbon uncorked.

He parked up on the Indian Mound near the farmhouse and walked around to the side porch by the kitchen to let in Hondo and pour out his supper. As he'd grown so accustomed to the red, blue, and green Christmas lights shining bright from his dad's trailer, the dark cornfield surprised him. It wasn't even nine o'clock yet and Jason Colson hadn't turned in early a day in his life.

They'd spoke earlier that day, Jason saying he nearly had everything all lined up for the bank meeting in the morning. Tomorrow, they'd be partners in the farm expansion and, by spring, they could get busy cleaning up the mess Johnny Stagg's greed had left behind.

After Hondo ate, Quinn poured out a little Blanton's in a coffee mug and snatched a Liga Privada from his humidor. He slipped into his uncle's old suede ranch coat, finding his familiar Zippo in the pocket, and headed down his dad's place, a little worried something had happened. His father hadn't been sick, besides some old stunt injuries, and figured he was maybe having some issue with the electric company as Jason was often late on the bill.

He knocked several times without an answer. The door was unlocked and Quinn walked inside the trailer to find some of the furniture missing and all of his dad's clothes, picture frames, movie posters, and other Hollywood mementos gone. Quinn went back outside to the little grouping by a small fire pit, where he'd spent many nights with his dad catching up, trading stories about Afghanistan and his days in Hollywood.

Quinn lit up the cigar, a brisk cold wind crossing the empty field from the west. Four concrete blocks sat empty, the grass underneath yellowed and slick with oil.

The cherry-red Firebird had finally hit the road. "Son of a bitch," Quinn said to himself.

Quinn sat down in an old metal chair by the fire pit and smoked half the cigar. Hondo lay at his feet until it was time to walk back home.

■ ■ ■ ■

Ordeen knew the Twins had come down
from Memphis to work out an arrangement
with Miss Fannie. Ever since Nito got
killed, the good-looking redheaded lady had
showed him a lot of respect, comping him
for drinks at the club, lap dances, and picking his brain about the Bohannans. But he'd
told her straight off that he didn't want to
get involved in any drug shit. Ordeen said
he was going straight, out of the life, but he
appreciated all the hospitality.

It wasn't until she said she needed a little
help since those nasty motorcycle creeps
had gone to Florida for the winter that he
finally agreed and met her at some kind of
old airport deep in the county, hidden by
thousands of acres of scraggy pine trees.
Damn near had to drive four miles down a
nothing road till it came up on you, big and
cleared and all lit up. Five old military-style
buildings lined up beside a couple of
eighteen-wheelers chugging diesel fumes
out in the cold. Ordeen had on his black
parka with the fur hood over his braids,
breath clouding from his mouth.

Miss Hathcock was talking to one of the
Twins, Ordeen pretty sure it was Short Box,

when he came up on them. Short Box gave him a big hug and told him how much he appreciated the hookup and all that. He told Ordeen that they were gonna be doing lots of business next year.

And Ordeen said, "Oh, yeah? OK."

He glanced over at Miss Hathcock, who looked damn fine in a long black coat over a sparkly black dress with a V-neck so deep, you could see the woman wasn't wearing no bra, and tall stiletto black boots. This woman had some class. Standing there, hand on her hip, giving some mean Memphis thugs direction with the burning tip of a little brown cigar. But, damn, if he got back into the life, he'd break his momma's heart. He had to walk up to her and tell her again, "I ain't messing with no drugs. I been down that road and ain't going back."

Without a word, wind whipping around all that red hair, Ordeen getting a good whiff of her sweet gardenia perfume, she walked straight over to the truck and jacked open the cargo door. Ordeen stepped up and swung it open, expecting to see a mess of boxes but instead seeing a bunch of eyes staring back.

The light coming from the truck behind them, shining into half the space, showing up twenty or so young brown girls, sitting on the truck floor, squinting into the light. Some rested their heads on backpacks, others held paper plates of food and bottles of water.

Damn, Ordeen had a thousand questions but couldn't make the words to speak.

Fannie walked up close on him, tall as hell in those stiletto boots, handing him a key. "You can drive a stick," she said, grinning. "Can't you?"

ABOUT THE AUTHOR

Ace Atkins is the author of nineteen books, including six Quinn Colson novels, the first two of which, *The Ranger* and *The Lost Ones*, were nominated for the Edgar Award for Best Novel (he also has a third Edgar nomination for his short story "Last Fair Deal Gone Down"). In addition, he is the author of four *New York Times*–bestselling novels in the continuation of Robert B. Parker's Spenser series. Before turning to fiction, Atkins was a correspondent for *The St. Petersburg Times*, a crime reporter for *The Tampa Tribune*, and, in college, played defensive end for the undefeated Auburn University football team (for which he was featured on the cover of *Sports Illustrated*). He lives in Oxford, Mississippi.